MYTH

A No

"Alice, do you see this ___ ___ ___ ___. It's the storm," I said. I glanced up again at the boiling clouds. "It's trying to force its way into the starting grid."

"Like it's alive," she said.

Great green spheres tumbled within the gathering cloud, jerking and whirling as if caught in the frenetic grip of madmen on speed. Some of the spheres splintered, revealing blobs of quivering yellow black sludge, like melted wax, or another part of my mind screamed, like putrefying flesh. The sludge ran together and massed towards the starting grid, as if attempting to form some hideous monstrosity, probing at the edges of our sanctuary. Before each new terrible form could congeal, it fell back before beginning anew to grow into something even more appalling, like sentient waves of chaos lapping at the foundations of reality...

Emerald lightning stabbed from the nearest thunderhead, leaping across the threshold, breaking my fascination with the green globes and what they disgorged. The bolt transfixed Sanders, straight through his forehead. Like a fishing line of laser light, the tendril pulled the man upright. Sanders' eyes and mouth snapped open. His irises flamed the same green as the lightning falling all around us.

THE STRANGE

BRUCE R CORDELL

MYTH OF THE MAKER

A NOVEL OF THE STRANGE

ANGRY
ROBOT

ANGRY ROBOT
An imprint of Watkins Media Ltd

20 Fletcher Gate
Nottingham
NG1 2FZ
UK

angryrobotbooks.com
twitter.com/angryrobotbooks
Meet your maker

An Angry Robot paperback original 2017
1

A catalogue record for this book is available from the British Library.

ISBN 978 0 85766 649 9
EBook ISBN 978 0 85766 651 2

Set in Meridien and Desdemona by Epub Services.
Printed and bound in the UK by 4edge Ltd.

For Torah Cottrill, without whose encouragement and inspiration there would be no Strange. And for JD Sparks, who still puts up his defenses in a recursion seeded by the joys and exploits of all the Hong Kong Cavaliers.

"The Fermi paradox is the apparent contradiction between high estimates of the probability of the existence of extraterrestrial civilization and humanity's lack of contact with, or evidence for, such civilizations [...]. Hence Fermi's question, 'Where is everybody?'"

Definition of FERMI PARADOX, Wikipedia.org

"Fermi's question, 'Where is everybody?' shows how amazingly stupid humans are. Who are we, to imagine we have even the faintest chance of understanding where everybody is?"

TORAH COTTRILL

"The universe is not only stranger than we imagine, it is stranger than we can imagine."

JBS HALDANE

1: RECURSION
Carter Morrison

The disaster that nearly wiped out the planet began in our VR lab on Tuesday morning. Earth survived, if you're reading this. But if someone else gets too clever with math like the six of us did, the same thing could happen all over again. And there's almost nothing anyone can do to stop it.

I'm really sorry about that, by the way.

Retrofitted computers loomed on tables along one wall of the lab. Screen-savers coiled jagged fractal designs across the monitors. Cable bundles held down with duct tape connected the whirring machines to the five lounge chairs we called our "VR rigs." I was wearing my favorite purple hoodie with the University of Washington logo stenciled on the front. It wasn't too warm because we kept the lab cool on account of all the computer equipment. Losing that hoodie still makes me sad.

Early for once, Jason Cole walked in with a couple of pizza boxes. Jason's confident posture managed to convey the physicality of someone much older than his actual age of twenty-seven. His black hair was thinning a bit at the crown, and his brown eyes looked out over an impressive beard that he was inordinately proud of.

The delicious smell of roasted peperoni and baked cheese

had me salivating even before Jason flipped the first box open. A familiar red hut symbol was printed on the grease-stained cardboard lid.

"What, no Pagliacci's?" I asked, reaching for a slice.

Jason laughed. "They don't deliver. You'll eat this and like it." Jason and I went way back. We met as roommates in our sophomore year of college, and got each other through computer science degrees, then our Masters, and even pursued doctorates in the field until we quit academia to found our own indie game studio. Three years after that, our game company went bust.

"At least you remembered the red pepper," I conceded. The white packet tore open and I scattered hot flakes over my slice, folded it Brooklyn-style, and gulped it down. It was warm, but not so hot I burned my mouth. In other words, it was perfect.

"So. What do you think; is today the day?" asked Jason, reaching for more.

"Could be. Everyone's got to catch a break sooner or later." Our experiments had been beset with problems. Problems that we'd solved one by one, of course. Because that's what you do, unless you decide just not to get out of bed in the morning.

"Hey, Carter, leave some for us!" called a woman with red hair worn in a long braid down her back. She hurried over, followed by a man in loose chinos and a white polo perpetually stained with coffee. She was Melissa – Mel, as everyone called her – Perkins; and he, Michael Bradley.

"Did you get any with pineapple?" Mel asked.

Jason guffawed. "Why would I ruin a perfectly good pizza with fruit?"

"Variety is the spice of life, Jason," she replied with a hint of exasperation in her voice. "Have you ever even tried it?"

"As if. What about you, Bradley. You like pineapple?"

Bradley only shrugged and chewed. His mind was obviously still on the power issue he'd been tasked to solve.

Like Jason and me, Mel and Bradley were fellow survivors of my failed game studio. We'd gone down in flames after *Ardeyn, Land of the Curse* – our online roleplaying game – failed to move out of beta. My coding skills, which were impressive, if I do say so myself, hadn't been enough to get us the wider attention we needed for a successful crowdfunding campaign. Frankly, the whole episode had been a fucking disaster.

Dead in the water, we'd had no funds, no jobs, and no prospects. Made all the worse by the fact we'd done it to ourselves. As a group, Jason, Mel, Bradley, and I had left the promise of academic research, however poorly paid, to follow our dreams of making games. Dreams that'd led nowhere. *Ardeyn, Land of the Curse* had turned out to be a curse in truth. Thinking about it still made my stomach hurt.

Then a hero rode in. Our old academic adviser Peter Sanders got in touch, wondering if we could help him out. He asked us to return to research at the university, even if only for a few months.

We're not idiots. We said yes.

Sanders put the whole undergraduate team back together using grant money he'd somehow pried from the University of Washington science committee. Our job was to figure out how to exploit the astonishing results in Sanders' latest paper, "Infinite Processing Through Quantum Recursion." With his breakthrough as our blueprint, we fashioned the superposition chip. We thought we'd discovered free, unlimited processing power.

We were wrong.

Jason and I moved aside from the pizza so Mel and Bradley could graze from the open boxes.

"How's the power integration coming?" Jason asked Bradley.

Bradley's mouth was full of pizza so he just nodded. Besides electronics,

Bradley's claim to fame was prodigious coffee consumption. If anyone drank more coffee in a single day than him, well, they'd probably be dead.

"It's done," Mel answered for Bradley. "We're ready for a simultaneous connection in the enhanced environment." She wiped her hands on a napkin, and then went for another piece. Mel had been a graphics modeler in the game studio. She fulfilled the same role here, helping to put together the starting grid and other enhanced environments.

"This is going to be radical," Jason said, looking at the VR rigs. "All of us, connecting at once."

We all knew he was lying, just a little. Jason had a touch of claustrophobia, which he pretended didn't exist. He was both excited and nervous about putting on the goggles again. To hide his trepidation, he usually resorted to impatience. He said, "I can't believe it's taken us four months just to get to this point. You're sure we've solved the power spike issue?"

It was Mel's turn to shrug. She looked at Bradley.

Bradley assumed the pained expression of someone wrongfully accused and said, "Hey!"

Our last attempt to coordinate a multi-POV session in the starting grid resulted in a couple of burnt-out motherboards. All the extra uninterruptible power supplies under the monitors were Bradley's solution.

"I'd be more worried about whether Carter came through on de-bugging the code," called Alice Lee, who was fiddling with a chip-set on an empty table she called her workbench. Alice's brown skin was shiny with sweat, and she wore her black hair pulled back under a kerchief decorated with pink unicorns. Alice hadn't been part of the game studio, but I didn't hold that against her. She'd been working with Sanders as a graduate student, before his grant money materialized and he expanded the team with the rest of us.

"Don't worry," I told Alice and everyone with exaggerated bravado. "I've got you covered." The number of hours I'd spent tweaking the code utilizing the superposition chip had been exhausting, but everyone knew it. I didn't have to toot my own horn... too much.

"Right," said Alice, but she smiled. She was probably a better coder than I was, but Sanders had her working on hardware, and me on software, because *she* was definitely better at circuit design than anyone on this continent.

"No pizza for you?" Jason asked Alice.

Alice shook her head and went back to fiddling.

Neither she nor Sanders liked pizza. That didn't stop Jason from buying it whenever it was his turn to get food for the group. Jason was a lot of things, many of them good, but sometimes he came off as a bit of a jerk. Especially when it came to pizza. He couldn't understand how anyone could say no to pepperoni.

Peter Sanders, the sixth member of the team and our fearless leader, appeared in the doorway, briefcase in hand and white hair managing to look messy despite its shortness. When he saw the pizza boxes, the corners of his mouth turned down a tiny bit. Most people wouldn't notice, but I've known Sanders for many years.

"Jason," I muttered, "next time you draw lunch duty, just tell me and I'll get food for everyone."

"Suits me," he said without the least trace of shame. "You can be the hero next time and get sushi."

Yeah, sometimes Jason could really work your last nerve.

On the other hand, he'd been the one who'd helped me put together the game studio, then stood by longest when everything went south. He was loyal, just not especially empathetic.

Sanders set his briefcase aside and loosened his tie. "I got your message," he said to Mel. "Are we still a go?"

Mel gave him the thumbs up. "We're ready to rock and roll, Peter."

He nodded, and then looked at the floor without meeting anyone's eyes directly. We didn't take it personally.

Only someone as brilliant as Sanders could've written his quantum recursion paper. I mean, I'm pretty smart, don't get me wrong. Everyone says so. But next to Sanders, I'm like a drooling child. Already, single-POV immersions in the starting grid were startling in their clarity and response time. To create an artificial experience for five people at once would require a hundred times the processing power. The superposition chip promised to give us that. All because of him.

When the pizza was gone and everyone who had to go returned from the toilet, we took our places in the VR rigs. It took a few minutes to buckle in and put on the equipment. Bradley started music playing over the lab speakers, which had become something of a tradition when we tested. This time, the Beatles serenaded us about strawberry fields and how nothing was real.

"Ready?" said Sanders when the buckling and muttering subsided. His voice was muffled.

Everyone but Bradley was strapped in. I glanced around, as far as I could in the rig's embrace. The belt around my waist pulled a little too tight, so I loosened it with my gloved hand. The rig included a seat-belt added for safety, and a foot plate for haptic transfer. Jason, Sanders, and Alice had their goggles down. Mel and I were the only remaining hold-outs. I gave her a wink. "Wouldn't you prefer a nice game of chess?" I asked, modulating my voice to sound artificial, like a computer's.

Mel laughed. "You're such a nerd."

"That's why you love me, Mel."

"You wish."

"What?" said Jason, his voice smothered by his rig. "Are you two-timing me, Carter? You told me that I was the one you dreamed about at night!" The forced lightness in his voice was hardly noticeable. He was dealing with his issue with enclosed spaces pretty well this time.

"You're both delusional," Mel said. "No one loves Carter more than Carter. Everyone knows that!"

We all laughed, because it was probably true. Except for the times when imposter syndrome intruded and made me wonder what the hell I was doing.

"Hey," interrupted Bradley from behind the monitors, "Give it a break. Time for hardware check."

"Mr Bradley is correct," said Sanders. "I've got a seminar in three hours."

Alice said, her voice similarly muted, "You guys can clown around in the VR. Unless we crash the starting grid again."

"Sorry, Alice," I said. "I know you can't wait to see how deep the rabbit hole goes."

Her goggles prevented me from seeing her eyes roll at the old joke, but Mel laughed, which was almost as good.

Bradley appeared in my field of view and pantomimed lowering goggles. "C'mon, Carter. Stop delaying. If this doesn't work, it's not the end of the world. We'll try something else."

He knew me too well. If this didn't work, we'd have little to show the science committee when it came time to ask for a grant renewal to continue developing the superposition chip. My ego couldn't take another failure.

Pulling the box-shaped device down over my eyes wasn't easy because I was already wearing the haptic gloves. The hardware was partly scavenged from early-adopter VR sets that had recently hit the market, and partly of Alice's design. We weren't testing gloves and goggles today, though; we wanted to see how the recursive VR chip handled more than a single point of view simultaneously. What seemed unbelievably realistic to just one person might prove a grainy, jerky, nausea-inducing obviously artificial environment when two, three, or as we'd decided to test today, five sightseers entered the same virtual starting grid.

The goggles showed an expanse of blank LED gray, bright, but not enough to blind me. When the simulation went live, the goggles would display the same scene to each of my eyes, slightly offset to give the illusion of depth. The superposition chip's ability to "find" extra processing power never failed to impress. What would've otherwise been a pixelated tutorial region swiped from a popular resource mining game would instead be rendered with life-like clarity. Trees, grass, water, and the sky above would look real.

Even the blocky crafting table would be sleek and elegant, because I'd tweaked the code to turn the blank slab into a terminal resembling the navigation console from the second Star Trek movie. It granted control over the simulation from "inside" the starting grid.

"Begin check," Sanders said. We verbally ran through several tests to make sure all the equipment was working. Haptic gloves and boots, the hydraulic lifts in the chairs, the audio, and the all-important goggles. After dealing with a tiny glitch with Mel's headphones, Bradley announced it was time.

"Ready!" I said, amidst a hail of assents from the others.

Boiling fog flooded my field of view. It unaccountably smelled like the sea.

"What the hell?" I muttered. Damn it. My goggles were borked. I should've been seeing the starting grid, the VR environment we'd programed. Not all this... static.

Through the mist, indistinct forms lumbered. I stepped forward–

And fell into an abyss with sides as sheer as scissor blades. A phantom weight jerked me down. An equation cut a labyrinthine pattern across my skin, drawing blood. Before I could recognize it or cry out, it transformed, becoming an infinite series, spiraling away from me like a burned-out galaxy. Beneath the spirals, the bottom of the abyss resolved as the surface of a frozen ocean instants before I smashed through its crystalline face. Ice water embraced me, swallowing my screams in a zero-degree sea, holding me in a cocoon of cold–

And stepped into the starting grid, right next to the terminal.

Peter Sanders appeared. Then Jason, Mel, and finally Alice.

Alice scrubbed at her eyes. Sanders toppled, hit his head on the edge of the terminal as he went down, and began to twitch. Jason yelled, "Bradley, shut the fucking simulation down! Something's wrong!"

Mel only pointed.

Mind still frozen, I looked in the direction she indicated, past the faux-brick wall that enclosed the starting grid.

Beyond it was Chaos.

Did I scream? Cry? I don't know for sure. The endless, shuddering expanse was deeper than any real sky, and it absorbed my gaze. Within its infinite wheeling eternity, a hunger stirred. My heart raced and my breath was coming in short gasps. Everything I knew was wrong.

Voice trembling, Jason said, "I can't get my goggles off."

"What?" I ripped my gaze from the strangeness, and saw Jason patting at his face.

"I can't even feel my goggles. The immersion was never this good, even after we upgraded the haptics."

Our VR rigs were designed to make users forget they were actually sitting in a lab, but Jason was right. Normally the sensation of the goggles snugged to my face was ever present. Pushing them off my head to see the lab, even with my hands swaddled in force-feedback gloves, should've been as simple as thinking about it. But I couldn't. It was as if I wasn't in the lab at all anymore.

The fear that kindled when I'd glanced beyond the

starting grid's borders threatened to make my heart burst. So I clamped down on it. Running in circles wouldn't solve a software malfunction, or whatever this was. Only logic could fence out panic. Aloud I said, "How about you, Mel? Can you take off your goggles, or your gloves?"

Mel's eyes were big as she shook her head. Sanders didn't respond at all, but at least he'd stopped twitching. Of course, he wasn't really hurt, because we were just in a simulation...

Alice was already at the terminal, hands flickering over one of the keyboards. She glanced up and ordered, "Take a look at this."

"Bradley!" I shouted at the empty air. "End the simulation. Emergency! Damn it, I mean it, this isn't funny. We're having real issues in here!"

Bradley had apparently stepped out of the lab, leaving us strapped into our VR rigs, untended. That was fucking irresponsible of him.

When I joined Alice at the console, only gibberish danced across the screens. I keyed for a status update. Reams of data rolled past. I let it auto-scroll, hoping I'd see something, anything, to anchor me. Just more gibberish. Except...

Except it wasn't. My gift for pattern recognition engaged. Pressing a key, I slowed the data dump to manual scrolling. I saw the hint of an underlying order. I typed more commands to the system. My queries brought up new rafts of data. It all pointed at something that was, simply put, unbelievable.

"Are you seeing this?" I said to Alice.

"Yeah. Some kind of hardware crash. I can't seem to stop it cycling. None of this makes any sense."

"It does if you, um... shift your paradigm. See, right here? The superposition of our qbit processing chip became entangled with an entirely new regime." I spoke calmly instead of shouting. Or screeching. A detached part of me was proud of my self-control.

"That's what it's *supposed* to do," she said uncertainly.

"Not to this degree. We've been squeezing a lot of extra cycles out of your hardware, sure, but this is beyond anything we could've ever imagined. It's like we've tapped into a preexisting network, one that seems... limitless. I don't think our starting grid is being hosted on our lab server anymore. We're someplace else."

"That's impossible," Alice said. "Stop being a jerk."

"Look," I said, and typed a new command, my hands shaking. "We still have a link to the original server, but it's outside this environment. The starting grid was downloaded from there. And..."

"And what?"

A splinter of an idea pulled me from my daze. I said, "We can use this console to arbitrarily change the rules inside this virtual reality environment."

"Well, sure. We can spawn more trees, torches, or crawlers to our heart's content. We can change the color of the sky. That's how we programmed the terminal. But what good does *that* do us when we can't get our goggles off?"

"It means we're not trapped here," I said.

"Huh?" she said. Then, "Oh, because you're saying we'd be *trapped* in the simulation otherwise. Shut up. I don't think you're funny."

"I'm not trying to be."

Alice hunched her shoulders and scowled at me.

"Unless you're having better luck getting out of your rig–"

"You're wrong. There's no way we can be trapped in a VR. It makes no goddamned sense."

"OK." She wasn't wrong, it didn't make any goddamned sense. That didn't change the fact that I couldn't figure out how to get out of the simulation."

"But you *are* right about one thing," Alice muttered, transfixing me with a glare as if this was all my fault.

"Which is?"

"We need to fix this."

I nodded. Alice and I bent to the console.

Elite athletes talk about being "in the zone," that magical place where mind and body work in perfect synch and movements seem to flow without conscious effort. Coders experience the same thing, when time becomes meaningless as fingers deliberately strike the keys, problems slowly resolve, and solutions eventually emerge. I fell into that flow as I delved into the strange substrate beyond the starting grid. My fingers hit the keys with more authority, harder and sharper.

"Carter, you were right about something else," said Alice at one point. "The system hosting this simulation is impossibly large."

"Yeah," I mumbled. We were looking at the same data. Words failed. *Nothing* was big enough to contain the network. Nothing, unless it lay in the quantum foam that lapped past the edges of the universe itself. Maybe the dark energy that underpinned reality was the shadow cast by this network, or maybe dark energy *was* the network, living in the wavelets of virtual particles and curled magnetic fields. Compared to the wind-tossed white-caps of our visible universe, dark energy constituted the unending depths beneath, vast and alien.

And we'd plunged in like fools. What if the quantum states of our minds had transferred, interpolated by a system whose resources dwarfed galaxies? It was sort of like being trapped in our own avatars.

Something caught my attention. Among all the other wonders hinted at, the data streaming from the console suggested that if we requested it, the dark energy network would print a version of us at some arbitrarily defined location. Print, as in recreate a full, three-dimensional version of a living person, without the need for a physical printer to do so other than the network itself.

"What do you make of this?" I asked Alice.

"What?"

Not wanting to prejudice her, I just pointed out the relevant sections.

She squinted, scratched her head, and frowned. It was amazing, the fidelity of the experience. This didn't seem like VR; it seemed real. A simulation so true to life that it might as well have been reality–

"This code seems to suggest the network is designed for travelers," Alice said, interrupting my thoughts. "Travelers who upload scans, then print out new instances of themselves elsewhere... in the universe?"

"That's what I was thinking."

"But everything's scrambled. Like there was some sort of major crash, and the system only came back part of the way."

Shivers of awe ran down my spine. This was cosmic. This dark energy network we'd stumbled into – was it designed to create doorways, by printing travelers at the destination they desired in the world or normal matter? If so, by whom? Where had they gone, and what'd happened to create such chaos in the system? Maybe the answers to those questions were linked.

Someone – Jason, I realized – grabbed my shoulders and spun me away from the console.

"Hey!" I said. "I was right in the middle of..."

A storm had rolled in while Alice and I had been lost in the data. Clouds piled higher than worlds threatened to tumble across the borders of the starting grid. Green lightning danced in their depths. Pretty. Eerie, too, but...

I bent back to the console. Data scrolling on a side screen revealed new, ancillary code, something that we hadn't written and something that hadn't been present before now. It was so complex that I couldn't begin to scroll through it all. And it was active. New threads lit up the screen by the hundreds. Something was actively trying to crash the program describing our virtual space and overwrite it with billions more lines. When I tried to analyze it, all I got was noise. Encrypted, of course. Unlike our starting grid.

"Alice, do you see this?" I pointed at the screen.

She glanced over, and frowned. "What the–?"

"It's the storm," I said. I glanced up again at the boiling clouds. "It's trying to force its way into the starting grid."

"Like it's alive," she said.

"Oh, fuck." The grid hadn't been built with security in mind.

Great green spheres tumbled within the gathering cloud, jerking and whirling as if caught in the frenetic grip of madmen on speed. Some of the spheres splintered, revealing blobs of quivering yellow black sludge, like melted wax, or another part of my mind screamed, like putrefying flesh. The sludge ran together and massed towards the starting grid, as if attempting to form some hideous monstrosity, probing at the edges of our sanctuary. Before each new terrible form could congeal, it fell back before beginning anew to grow into something even more appalling, like sentient waves of chaos lapping at the foundations of reality...

Emerald lightning stabbed from the nearest thunderhead, leaping across the threshold, breaking my fascination with the green globes and what they disgorged. The bolt transfixed Sanders, straight through his forehead. Like a fishing line of laser light, the tendril pulled the man upright. Sanders' eyes and mouth snapped open. His irises flamed the same green as the lightning falling all around us.

"Motherfucker!" I shouted.

Sanders convulsed, bent over, and heaved. Nothing came up. He wiped his mouth, then looked up at all of us. His eyes were still green. He opened his mouth, as if to speak, but all that came out was strange noises, like he'd forgotten how to talk, or even use his tongue.

When he staggered and almost fell, Mel grabbed him. "Peter! What happened? Are you all right?" I wanted to tell Mel to get away from him, because he was obviously not all right. But I couldn't make my mouth form the words.

Sanders began to shake like a leaf in Mel's grip, then just as suddenly stopped. His emerald eyes fastened on to her, and he tried to speak again. His voice was the sound of fabric tearing. He said, "Let. Us. In."

"What?" Mel said.

"Maybe don't touch him," Jason said, his voice tight. I nodded agreement.

Mel released Sanders. The man swayed like a marine plant, but didn't go over. In a strangely boneless gesture, he pointed up at the clouds. Behind them, the hint of vast creatures swam. My eyes threatened to cross, because what they saw were things like starfish crossed with industrial equipment, if starfish were the size of entire city neighborhoods.

"Holy shit!" I yelled. That clinched it. Those cloud things were after us. They were actively trying to enter the starting grid. And–

"Carter," said Alice, her voice oddly composed, given that Sanders seemed to be possessed, and creatures straight out of Lovecraft swelled in ever greater density at the edge of our Earth-like domain. Her firmness helped me control my rising panic. I glanced at the screen she indicated. More data splayed, hinting at new secrets of existence... but I was too rattled to make any sense of it.

"What am I looking at?"

"This represents our connection back to the lab," she explained. "However we got injected into this network, a connection remains. We could use it to get back, if we had time to decode what's going on. But, *look*!" Her finger jabbed. "Our connections are compromised! They're corrupted.

Whatever those things out there are, they've already tapped into us. Sanders is worst, but we're all affected. I think they're going to use us – our bodies back in the lab – to route traffic back to our origin. Out of this network and back to Earth."

Sanders groaned again, blinked, and repeated himself, maybe in warning, "Let. Us. In."

Insanity. It was unbelievable. All of it was like a bad dream that I desperately wanted to wake up from and laugh about.

And yet, there we were. *You need to get your shit together, Carter. You need a plan.* The analytical part of my brain clamped down on the panic, the part that wanted me to look stare out at the cloud-swaddled green spheres and completely lose my shit.

Alice's explanation got me part of the way to understanding. But an intuition whose source I'm still not certain about got me the rest of the way there. I somehow *knew* Alice was right. It was obvious. Sanders, Mel, Alice, Jason, and I would serve as a physical point of connection out of the dark energy network into the world of normal matter. We'd be a beachhead for vast creatures that'd had been swimming in this dark energy network for who knows how many millions or billions of years.

"They've done this before," Sanders muttered, sounding more like himself, thank God. "They've done it millions of times. Billions. They never stop. They reach out forever, consuming…"

"Done what?" yelled Jason, his voice a strangled entreaty. I've never seen him more scared.

Sanders coughed, staggered, blinked some more. Finally he managed to speak, "Eaten any world that connected to their network. They're like… carnivores that eat planets."

The term came to me. "They're *planetovores*," I named them. Then I caught Sanders' horrific implication. "This is why we've found no evidence for intelligent life elsewhere in the universe. They were all eaten when they discovered this fucking network."

Sanders nodded, green liquid dribbling from the corner of his mouth. He said, "I can feel them in my mind. They're excited. Hungry. Unstoppable."

And here we were, responsible for opening the door to Earth for them. It was the end of the fucking world, and we were to blame.

Unless I did something unthinkable.

Jason jostled me as he made room for himself at the console. His wild eyes scanned the screens. He said, "Carter, get us out of here. If you can't, we're all going to end up like Sanders!"

"I'm trying," I panted, pointing at the data. "But it's not that simple. See? Earth and this new network are connected; they weren't before. We're the link. *Us*. If we don't sever the connection…"

Jason's hands went to the controls. He started typing, and I saw immediately what he was doing. He'd always been a quick study. He was going to pull all of us straight back out of the system, despite the corruption.

"Jason, stop!" I grabbed his shoulder. "We're compromised! *All* of us, not just Sanders."

"See?" I yelled, gesturing to include everyone. "We can't just disengage. We have to–"

Jason shrugged out of my grasp, muttering, "That's not going to happen to me."

"It has already!"

He ignored me. Of course he did. I knew what he was like. He wasn't going to listen. And if Jason finished his desperate attempt to jack all of us out, the planetovores would come along, using the "printing" technology to manifest themselves in reality. They'd overwrite their new environment. To them, regular matter, including our minds and bodies, were probably just another operating system to be cracked and exploited.

Stopping that from happening was the only thing that mattered.

I put my hand on Jason's sternum, then shoved him away from the console as hard as I could. Unprepared, he fell and rolled, yelling "What the hell?"

"It's got to be me," I said as I called up new menus on the console.

"Saving yourself, is that it? You selfish prick, Carter!" Jason went for me again, but Alice and Mel got in the way, even though they weren't quite sure what I was doing. Sanders did, but he was too far gone. But maybe I could save him, Earth, and all of us from a similar fate. Or, at least save Earth...

The next moments were vague. Maybe the same corruption that was in Sanders whispered knowledge into my mind, or maybe I'm just that good. Either way, I was able to commandeer the virtual particle printing array inherent in the network; its *raison d'être*. If we recalled our conciousnesses, as Jason had just tried, we'd cement the creatures' connection to Earth. They might even be already back there, using our bodies for themselves, like demons possess people in religious stories. So I had to get out a *different* way. By using the printing function embedded in the dark energy network to print a *new* instance of myself without using the compromised link to my old body. In effect, there'd be two of me at once.

There wasn't time to get everything exactly right. Clothing, for instance, wasn't going to make the trip back. So I queued up the commands to print myself as close as I could to where my original body was strapped into a VR rig dreaming, but somewhere I could appear without drawing undue attention.

The command executed, and I was funneled up the link, out of the network, and back onto the university campus, a freshly printed dark energy traveler.

Leaving everyone else behind.

2: DISCONNECTION
Carter Morrison

Falling in the men's shower knocked the wind out of me. Of course, five seconds ago my lungs hadn't existed, at least not here. When I printed back onto the university campus, I'd somehow managed to appear two feet higher than the floor, then fallen straight down on my back. Idiot!

My chest heaved and my heart thundered. Sucking molasses through a straw would've been easier. The floor was cold and gritty on my skin. My fingers curled spasmodically. Ineffectually. Is this what panic felt like?

A scrap of breath hissed between my teeth. Then another. Finally the fist in my chest unclenched, and I gulped in lungful after lungful of air. I was going to live a while longer. A chance to get older, but probably not any wiser.

"You all right?"

I realized I was laying naked on floor of the showers in the university athletic center. The guy inquiring about my health was two stalls down, his hands poised in mid-shampoo.

Trying to speak, I coughed instead. I settled for nodding.

"You sure?" he said. "Looked like you were having some kind of fit."

"Slipped and fell," I finally forced out. "Knocked the wind out of me, is all." I patted my chest.

27

"OK, good," he said, obviously relieved he wouldn't have to administer CPR to a nude stranger.

Staggering out of the showers, I snagged a towel from a stack near the door and dried off. Which gave me a chance to look around for something to wear. I'd never stolen clothing before, but as I'd hoped, a locker room was a great place for that kind of petty larceny. No one noticed as I pilfered an unattended locker, so I avoided difficult questions.

In borrowed blue jeans, a gray T-shirt, and Converse sneakers, I exited the athletic center. Hopefully they didn't belong to the helpful guy from the shower. The shoes pinched and the pants were too loose, but it was lucky they fit as well as they did. My plan, such as it was, didn't immediately fizzle for lack of a belt.

Running past the biology building onto Colorado Street, I headed toward the engineering building, which housed the VR lab. To be safe, I'd tried to print back at a distance from the VR lab so Bradley wouldn't see a duplicate me appear out of nowhere and freak out. Was that what I was – a duplicate? I felt like *me*. Not like a copy...

Probably better to worry about my philosophy of existence later, if there was a later, I told myself. Finally bursting into the engineering building, chest heaving and mind spinning, I raced for the VR lab.

A man in a coffee-stained white polo stood outside the lab entrance, a mug in one hand and a red metal toolbox dangling from the other. Michael Bradley.

Bradley squinted at me. I rubbed one temple, wondering how to explain myself. Bradley had been monitoring us when we went into the VR simulation. Which, according to the wall clock, was less than thirty minutes ago. It seemed much longer...

"Carter?" Bradley said. "What're you doing out here?"

"Hey," I replied. "Um, call of nature."

"Mmm hmm," he grunted, nodding slightly. "You had too much coffee." He sipped from his own mug.

I nodded as if agreeing. "What about you?" I asked. "Why aren't you in the lab?"

I'd printed back at a location outside the VR chamber because I hadn't wanted anyone to witness my arrival. If I'd known Bradley wasn't monitoring us, I could've saved myself a lot of time.

"Server sent up a couple of faults," Bradley said. "I had to replace some fuses, if you can believe it." He rattled his toolbox. "Electrical fluctuations, I guess. But the extra power supplies smoothed everything out."

"The test environment couldn't handle all variables," I said, remembering the shuddering expanse that opened beyond our virtual starting grid, strange beyond all reckoning. We thought we'd reached into some sort of perfect mathematical abstraction promising as many cycles as we'd ever need for truly lifelike VR. Instead, we'd pinged a network so primeval that it predated the solar system. A network crawling with hungry things eager to reach the orbits and atoms of our natural universe.

Bradley snorted. "Variables? Shouldn't make any difference. Probably the idiots over in aerospace are using some unapproved CAD extension."

I shrugged as if unconcerned. "Sure." I wiped sweat from my upper lip. "You better finish with those fuses. I'll hook myself back in." *Please*, I thought, *turn around and head back to the server room. Don't make me–*

"Naw. I'm done."

Shit. "Oh, good," I said, my voice faint. Shit, shit! How was I going to deal with Bradley? How, really, was I going to deal with everyone? I hadn't given the next part of my plan much thought. It was too horrible, going far beyond what I'd already done. Yet there I was.

I opened the door and gestured for Bradley to precede me. He walked through and set the toolbox on the shelf inside the entrance. I followed him in and, without thinking about what I might use it for, quietly lifted the toolbox. It was cold and heavy in my hands. Bradley didn't notice.

The Beatles lilted from the room speakers, singing about a girl who came to stay. No one plugged into the VR could hear it, thanks to sound-canceling headphones.

The five lounge chairs – each sprouting a garden of wires, LED status lights, oversized gloves, and blocky goggles – were exactly as I'd left them. One seat held Jason. I let my gaze slide off him. The other four seats held Sanders, Mel, Alice, and... me.

Bradley hummed along to the song as he checked his monitors. Then he froze.

"Carter, what the fuck?" He was staring at my original, still snugged into the rig.

I swung, bringing the toolbox crashing down on Bradley's head. He crumpled without a word.

"Shit," I whispered, then swallowed. I tried not to think about what I had to do next. About whether I'd just heard the sound of crunching bone.

Stepping past Bradley's lolling form, I approached Jason. He looked relaxed, as if asleep.

Jason and I had been inseparable for years. The memory of the hundreds of times we'd made midnight runs for fast food after late coding sessions overwhelmed me. More times than not, I was short on cash. Jason always picked up my tab.

Maybe I should reconsider. Maybe I was wrong. Maybe–

Stop it, I told myself. *You have to be sure. You can fall apart later.* So I emptied the toolbox on the floor at Jason's feet. He didn't so much as quiver at the metallic racket. I rooted through the pile and finally selected a long screwdriver and a mallet.

I had to sever the connection between the flesh in front of me and the things that lived in the dark energy network that had absorbed Jason's soul. Things had gone way too pear-shaped to simply remove his goggles and unplug him from the rig. Quantum entanglement meant that contamination had already occurred. I'd seen it happen.

Goggles hid his eyes, and I was glad.

The screwdriver stung my hand each time I brought the mallet down on the butt, driving the fucking thing into Jason's head. An unplanned scream ripped my throat raw. The speakers lamented about trying to leave a girl. What was Lennon trying to tell me?

Damn it, focus! You're only doing what's logical, I told myself. Jason's body was already compromised, and his mind – perhaps even his soul, if such a thing existed – was elsewhere. He'd made the transition and was still, in some sense, alive down in the substrate. Unless what I'd done to ensure that I was the one standing in the lab with the mallet and screwdriver, not Jason, had sealed everyone's fate. Everyone's but mine.

Bending over, I threw up on the carpet.

You don't have time for this, I told myself. *Stop it.*

I stumbled to the next rig, concentrating on anything other than what I was doing.

Were my friends still safe on the other side, or was I really murdering them? My plan required the former to be true, for the sake of my sanity.

Everyone got the same brutal attention. Sanders, Alice, even Mel. I told myself they *were* all still alive on the starting grid. I wasn't actually killing them – the planetovores would do that.

Part of me was sure I was a coward and a liar, and I retched twice more before I got to the fifth and final rig, but only dry heaves. Nothing was left to come up.

One more time. Don't think about it, that he's got the *exact same* L-shaped scar as you from a boating accident fifteen years ago, that–

The original Carter Morrison twitched in his chair then fumbled off his goggles. I met my own gaze. Something was wrong with his eyes: fractals bloomed there in the green of old phosphor computer monitors. I screamed.

He howled wordlessly along with me.

My original struggled in his – *its* – traps, but remained snared in the buckles.

I whacked it with my mallet, over and over. What was in my original body wasn't me. It was something from the primeval matrix, something that had sniffed fresh data and was hungry for more. Here on Earth, it had discovered a whole new world of information encoded in molecules and atoms, optical fibers and nerve impulses. The things that lived in the dark energy network were predators of a whole new class: planetovores.

I stopped hitting it with my mallet when its strangled wail ceased and the green in its eyes guttered out.

Someone was still screaming. When I covered my mouth, the sound stopped. "Carter," I whispered to myself, "Now's no time to lose it."

I nodded. "Right," I replied. "You're a smart man, Carter." A couple of giggles escaped me before I clenched my teeth together so hard my molars clicked.

A soulful voice over the speakers encouraged me not to carry the world upon my shoulders. That it's a fool who–

When I smashed the mallet into the CD player, blissful silence followed.

Things remained to be done, even though blood was stiffening my clothes and making my fingers tacky. Lurching to the computer interface, I narrowly escaped stepping in my own vomit.

My hands left red smears on the computer keys as I checked

the backup server in the basement that hosted all our work.

Calling up a command line, I scheduled a complete data wipe at the blinking cursor prompt. The wipe included all the remote backups describing our work. Just as important, I triggered a failsafe in Sanders' experimental chip. In half an hour, all the qbits composing the chip's heart would fall out of superposition, rendering the thing into so much useless silicon.

No one else would be able to recreate our experiment. That was important. Assuming my plan worked. Shutting down all the servers would be like pulling up anchor, I hoped. Once the servers were offline, nothing else in that strange network we breached could use the same hack I'd used to print myself back to Earth. Maybe.

Actually–

What if there was another way to pass between Earth and the dark energy network, one that didn't require a quantum chip like the one we'd used? The unexpected intuition tickled my brain, hinting at a way different than how I'd returned. A way to translate instead of extruding a duplicate physical instance, a way to make the shift without worrying about air for lungs, clothing, specific location–

No. That wasn't possible. Leaning like a drunk on the computer terminal, I barely held myself upright as new doubts tried to break my conviction. With no open connection, reaching between the real universe and a network hosted in dark energy wavelets would be extraordinarily difficult. *Please, let that be true.* Otherwise, I'd just killed the bodies of my friends for no reason.

Oh, shit...

Was the Earth still fucked?

The planetovores knew about Earth. They'd continue to swarm around the naked grid we'd stupidly created. The grid was like an open wound gushing blood into shark-infested water. The wound needed to be sealed off, like slapping a cap onto an undersea oil gusher.

Was there something else I could do?

Maybe. I sucked in a long breath, and had an idea. A brilliant, wonderful, half- baked, and undoubtedly insane way to further protect the world from the primordial network. I didn't have something perfectly suited for what I imagined, but I *did* have a fat chunk of functioning code and twenty-five minutes before the servers were wiped and the chip fried.

Why not give it a shot?

Typing furiously at the main computer, I opened a link to *Ardeyn, Land of the Curse*. Although it never fully launched, a limited beta version of the failed game remained active across a handful of fan sites. The beta code was unwieldy, bloated, and more than a bit buggy. But maybe – *maybe* – it would impose rules to a sector of the strange substrate. A substrate completely unformatted before we'd created our starting grid and created a direct connection between Earth and the network. Ardeyn would smother and block that connection, if imposed on the network, or at least encrypt it.

Please, let that be true.

I began transferring the code from the game directly into the server hosting the superposition chip. There wasn't time to disconnect the two thousand or so playtesters currently connected to Ardeyn. They probably wouldn't notice anything as the code base around them replicated down in the stratum.

"Stratum" had a sort of ring to it. Maybe that's what I should call the network? No, too geological. The network was far more... strange.

Only a minute remained on the wipe clock when the copy completed. It was either working, or it wasn't. The only way I could know was go look.

Which would be dangerously insane. But what about my friends' entangled minds, still down there? My mind was safely extricated. If I went back in, I'd risk losing myself all over again, but maybe I could save their souls. What would that mean for me? Looking at the corpse that shared my face, limp and slick with blood, made the decision easier. Here, I was already dead.

With shaking hands I stripped the VR equipment from Carter – from *me* – and loosened the straps holding the flaccid body upright. I shoved it out and took its place. The gloves and goggles were still warm.

Static boiled against my eyes and ears. It scratched my skin and tasted like metal.

I logged in. My consciousness was swept down the connection, plunging into unfolding fractal architectures. My eyes reflexively closed against the overwhelming complexity.

Then I stepped through to another place and pulled the door shut behind me. When I opened my eyes again, everything was different.

3: INVESTIGATION
Katherine Manners

Three years later.

The port scanner failed to turn up a single open connection. The email spoofing attack hadn't fooled anyone. And the packet sniffer was a complete bust because there just wasn't any data. Kate's usual techniques, plus a few of Raul's paranoid schemes, had been for nothing. BDR's servers were locked down.

So Kate resorted to social engineering. It was a cliché, but only because it worked. Success just required a bit of play-acting. Picking up the phone and pretending to be an angry supervisor threatening the job of a confused customer service rep had gotten her results before.

Not this time.

Banks Digital Realty wasn't large enough that she could pull off impersonating a nameless authority in HR. And as far as she could tell, there wasn't a remote connection available for off-site administration. Which made no fucking sense. What if the servers needed to be rebooted in the middle of the night? What if one of Seattle's notorious "snow" days turned the roads into parking lots and no one could get in?

Kate escalated. She donned a uniform, rented a cart,

and decorated it with a red watering can and a handful of houseplants. She pushed the cart into BDR's lobby minutes before closing. She flashed her lanyard (*PLANT CARE SERVICE*, it proclaimed in friendly green letters) to the security guy. A departing employee was kind enough to hold the elevator for her, which normally required a key card. Most people are instinctually helpful, even if it meant breaking security procedures. She smiled and thanked the nice man as the steel doors of the elevator closed.

She exited on the third floor and started rounds, confident as if she'd visited a dozen times before. Anyone watching the video feed saw her watering the plants. The servers she was looking for were on this floor, somewhere. Moving from planter to planter through the dimmed office built up the layout in her mind. She found the server room after about five minutes.

Even if the entrance hadn't been labeled, the sound of the fans would've given it away. White noise filled the hallway and thrummed through doors as she approached. The cooling system ensured that the machines didn't overheat. A computer serving web pages, rendering 3D images, and executing dozens of other applications generated heat like someone running a 5K in the Mojave Desert. Without someone to throw ice water every hundred feet, they'd go nowhere.

Kate knew servers. A computer science degree had landed her a position at Microsoft. She'd pen-tested systems and looked for exploits that needed closing. But the glory days of the company's stock options were past. She'd left after a few years and started her own online security consulting firm. On a lark, she'd also enrolled in an internet university's private investigation course. She learned about courts and the shortcomings of the legal system, civil and criminal case investigation, and most importantly, how to break into places.

Her actual business card, as opposed to the fake one on her lanyard, read:

KATHERINE J MANNERS, PI

SECURITY CONSULTING & PRIVATE INVESTIGATION

DISCREET, PROFESSIONAL, EXPERIENCED

FULL SERVICE, FREE CONSULTS

Most of Kate's caseload came from suspicious spouses. Talk about work that would turn even the most idealistic do-gooder into a cynic. But bills needed paying.

When a case came her way, she could usually scan a database remotely from a coffee shop using its free wifi, correlate the results with whatever she was trying to discover for her client, and call it a day.

But she enjoyed actual investigation, too, especially when she could dress for the part. Like the gown and high heels she'd worn to attend an ambassadorial ball. Of course, that time she'd been invited. Someone had to make sure the visiting ambassador from Kobe, Seattle's sister city, could get a video connection back to Japan for the "hands across the ocean" celebration. And they'd served sushi.

But tonight it was back to coveralls, "Comfort Fit" sneakers, and her plant watering cart. Her client, Michael Bradley, wanted her to locate evidence of malware infecting the BDR servers.

According to Bradley, the BDR servers were rotten with malicious exploits. But because BDR didn't want the bad PR, didn't care, or didn't have the resources to deal with the issue, they'd ignored Bradley's warnings. As a client whose web pages had been hacked over and over because of the hosting company's malfeasance, Bradley was already pissed off. He said he wanted more than just his money back for the six months he'd rented server space – he wanted BDR to admit it was culpable, or better yet, to get a judgment against the company.

Kate had worked with too many nontechnical managers with the same mindset as BDR when it came to news they didn't want to hear, and frankly, didn't really understand. Sometimes, people had to be hit over the head with a blunt object before they'd admit the sky actually was falling.

Tonight, Kate would find the evidence required to serve as that blunt object. Life was good.

She opened the thrumming doors.

Servers towered in the dim space beyond, at least four or five rows of them. The wail of the fans pummeled her but she decided not to stuff foam plugs in her ears. If the security guy left his desk in the lobby, she wanted a chance to hear him, even over the background whine.

Kate parked her plant cart along the wall in the hallway, then entered the server room. The computer that administered all the others, the one she hadn't been able to ping remotely, would be in here somewhere. She began walking the rows. Actually, unless the managers at BDR were total dicks, the administrator's computer would be in a side room with walls and a door to block out fan noise.

She found the control computer sat right out in the open, at the end of the third row of servers.

Total dicks, then. Good to know.

Kate sat. Her reflection – red hair and pale skin – frowned back at her until she called up the command line. She began acquainting herself with the workstation's login procedure.

The lights in the room flickered. She looked up, brows gathering. Then the fans cut out, and her hands fell from the keyboard. The lights dimmed further, and the fans stayed off. All the lights that'd been dancing on each server bank were gone. It was probably a coincidence, but...

Time to call it a night. If a brown-out had disabled BDR's

primary power, systems engineers would be crawling over the place in ten minutes to make certain the back-up power sources came online.

All the overhead fluorescents failed completely, leaving her blind in absolute darkness.

Kate waited a few seconds, but nope. Whatever had killed the lights had taken the "uninterruptible" backup batteries with them. And... what the hell? The red glow that should've illuminated the EXIT letters over the door was gone. Either she was facing the wrong way, or... Or she didn't know what. Exit signs that lost power were bad news however you sliced it.

Clattering erupted somewhere behind her. She jerked round. Brilliant light flashed on-off/on-off from around the farthest bank of servers.

Was it a server shorting out?

No, the power outage meant there wasn't enough juice for that kind of mayhem. Maybe she'd missed an engineer on night duty. If so, what were they doing over there, welding? Didn't seem likely.

Kate considered bolting. But, really? Any PI worth her gun would investigate. Fuck!

Speaking of which... Good. A quick pat reassured her that her Beretta 9mm remained in the holster strap beneath her coveralls. It wasn't illegal for her to carry a hidden handgun in Washington, so long as she carried her Concealed Pistol License, too. She'd got the gun used, but God she wished the owner hadn't felt compelled to tell her the gun's name was Malcolm. Who names a gun? That guy, apparently.

Raul didn't like that she carried it. He said it was more likely to get her shot; statistics proved it. Maybe. But Raul had passed on that gem long after she'd gotten used to wearing the thing. C'est la vie.

Kate padded closer to the sound and light. Though she was tempted to draw it, she left Malcolm... Damn it, now she was calling it by name! She left the gun in its holster.

An odor like burnt rubber curled her lip. She rounded a server and saw the light's source. Her mouth dropped open.

A twisting pillar was growing up from the floor. No, that wasn't it. The shape wasn't growing so much as it was being built, like something a 3D printer might produce, one layer at a time. These days she couldn't go a week without seeing at least one breathless tech story about how 3D printers were poised to change the economy, could print entire houses, and might one day be used to construct a moon base.

But printers were bulky, boxy, slow devices able to extrude something the size of a toy plushy after a couple of hours. Whatever was growing before her eyes was already four feet tall, and adding inches every second. And... where was the 3D printer itself? Nowhere.

As the final layers of the object slapped into place, she saw that the "something" was a "someone." A man with no clothing.

The flickering light died before she could see anything else. The burning tire smell was worse than ever, but without the strobing light, the room was pitch black again.

"Who are you?" Kate shouted into the black.

No answer.

Realizing that she was on the verge of hyperventilating, Kate concentrated on drawing deeper, calming breaths. No easy task. She had never liked the dark. She had a flashlight app on her phones, but she didn't really want to confirm whether or not a man had been assembled out of nothing, right before her eyes, in mere seconds.

Had she just suffered a stroke? Or was someone playing a trick to dupe the private investigator who didn't realize her cover was blown?

A groan emerged from the dark.

"Oh, shit," she said, flinching backward. Whether she was

having an aneurism, was the target of an elaborate anti-industrial espionage sting, or especially if a mute mandroid had beamed down to flash Earth women, it was time to go. Which meant she needed to see.

Her phone's LED blazed. A clear view of the way out beckoned... except she couldn't help herself. She swung the beam back.

The man wasn't a hallucination. But he was no longer standing. Instead, he slumped against the servers, head in one hand. When she held the beam on him, a hint of bones and organs showed through translucent skin. Shocked, she played the beam across him again. Yep, she could see his ribs, his lungs, his heart... and an enormous ring on one hand that wasn't the least bit transparent. Holy shit.

Kate wondered why she wasn't running away, maybe trailing a scream for effect. Really, was that such a bad idea?

But, she thought, what would the fictional heroines she admire most do in this situation? No, they wouldn't run. Dana Scully would do something stupid, of course. She would investigate.

The man lifted his head and fixed her with watery brown eyes. "Help," he said. His voice was strained, but human.

She realized the intruder wasn't a mandroid. He was just some poor slob who needed a hand, never mind what she'd thought she'd seen. A perfectly reasonable explanation, once she heard it, would clear everything up.

Relief and concern made her giddy as she went to him.

The same relief she felt was mirrored on his face, but... yuck. She could see the bones of his skull. "What the hell happened to you? What's your name?" He was obviously incredibly sick, though with what she couldn't guess.

"I'm a messenger," he said, his voice weak. "Call me Jason. But something's wrong!" His free hand caught hers. "Please help me?"

His skin was damp and soft. His grip was weak as a baby's. Kate didn't pull free. The stranger needed a good Samaritan. She said, "Don't worry, Jason. I'm calling 911. The hospital is a couple of blocks from here. An ambulance will be here in five minutes. You're going to be fine." Saying it didn't make it so, but it sounded reassuring.

"No, I can't go," Jason said, his voice weaker than before. "I have to talk to Liza. Her anchor isn't stable. Look at what happened to me. I'm to give her the Ring of Desire. But now that I'm here, I don't really want to die…"

"Die? Listen. You're sick, but you'll be all right," she said, though the more she played her light on him, the less she believed it. "You need medical help, right away."

"Won't do any good. Thanks for trying to help. I didn't expect kindness. It almost makes me wish–"

The man's words slurred into a coughing fit.

"Jason?"

"I'm sorry for my part in this. I didn't realize I had a choice, until I came here. The ring–" A fiercer coughing fit overcame him.

"What about it?"

Back to silence and darkness. Kate abandoned the call to 911 mid-dial. In the LED's light, she saw that he'd stopped moving.

"Jason!" she said. His hand somehow slipped out of hers. Kate reached to retrieve it, then froze.

The man liquefied all at once. Arms, torso, legs, and all the rest of Jason slumped like a wax candle in a frying pan, forming a circle of cloudy pink goo.

"I'm losing my fucking mind," she whispered. She was in an episode of the *X-Files* after all.

When the widening circle of liquid threatened to lap over the soles of her sneakers, Kate retreated a step. All that remained was the oversized ring she'd first seen Jason wearing. It hadn't melted.

Mind numb, she retrieved it with her free hand. Tiny inscribed designs, maybe words in a language she didn't know, spiraled around the band set with a massive transparent green stone so large that it had to be costume jewelry.

A small section under the ring was loose. When she wiggled it, the whole piece came away, revealing itself as a sleeve for a slender metallic square. The silver square was perfectly sized for insertion into nearly any computer she could name.

The ring and a USB flash drive nestled in her palm.

4: DUPLICATION
Jason Cole

The Lord of Megeddon had many names. To some, he was War. To others, Legion. To most, he was simply the Betrayer. But among himselves, he was Jason.

Homunculi peered at Jason from their stations on either side of the exit. Each was a copy, but their bright scarlet coloration denoted their status as inferior clones of the original.

Of him.

Jason said, "Open."

A mechanism chattered. The gate slabs parted. Jason and his lieutenant swept into a passage lit by violet flames, and up two further flights of charcoal-toned stairs.

The sound of slapping feet on the stairs behind made Jason look round.

A clone scampered up from the warrens they'd just quit, gabbling excitedly. Its green skin marked its low grade. Three reds charged after it, cursing, their carapace-like armor clacking.

Jason frowned at hearing his own obscenities in the mouths of reds. It was almost as upsetting as the clones' failure to shut the gate after he'd left. Because of their lapse, a runner was loose.

One red pursuer brandished a club. The club wielder and

his two sibling clones cornered their quarry on the landing below where Jason and his lieutenant watched. The green homunculus realized it was trapped, but made a break for freedom up the next flight anyway, hands clutching for its progenitor: Jason.

Jason stepped forward to meet the runner with an elbow. The impact literally smashed its face in, though Jason felt only a satisfying jolt. The homunculus gave a bubbly exhalation rather than a scream as it collapsed. Its left leg twitched a few times before it went still. As usual, he felt no remorse. In a way, his homunculi were even less real than everything else in Ardeyn, and he despised them even more than everyone and everything else because of it.

The red handlers who'd chased their charge up from the warrens, only to lose it at the last moment, stared at the Lord of Megeddon with wide, panicky eyes.

"Get out of here!" Jason yelled. "Before I recycle all of you!" Seeing his own reflected, albeit red-hued, features contorted in fear pissed Jason off. Lucky for them he was anticipating good news. Fresh rumors of progress in his Contact Foundry promised an end to Jason's imprisonment.

The clones snatched the limp body and hustled away.

Jason said, "Why is it the greens who always manage to get loose?"

"Because," replied his translucent-skinned lieutenant named Gamma, in a voice most people would find indistinguishable from Jason's own, "they're determined."

"How can they be determined?" Jason said. "They're hardly smarter than rabbits."

"Exactly," Gamma said. "Greens don't understand repercussions or grasp consequences. They act in the moment."

He knew that, of course. A clone without a trace of soulcode to govern it almost invariably came out of the vats with the wits of a beetle. But the power resident in Jason's "truename" was already stretched as thin as he dared expand it. Green and yellow grade clones got nothing from Jason except his likeness and a few reflexes. The higher-grades rated a share of the Betrayer's unique identifier number, his "soulcode." And they only got a bit. The only clones who received a nearly complete copy were his lieutenants. Which was why Jason manufactured lieutenants who were completely translucent, so no one would ever mistake an ersatz homunculus for the real deal. Ever *again*, he thought. That time himselves revolted had taught Jason a lot. Starting with how to begin from scratch with an entirely new batch of homunculi. The carapace-armor he still allowed his lieutenants was see-through. He didn't want them hiding anything from him.

Back when his Ring still functioned, Jason had been able to substantiate hundreds of instances with a thought, maybe even thousands, if given enough time. Before his Ring was broken and the Maker was betrayed and slain.

Jason touched the cracked metal circle he wore around his neck on a chain, and brought it to his lips, then gazed through it. Even damaged, the Ring of War contained a trace of its former power. Despite all his searching for alternate ways to tease out multiple simultaneously active instances of himself, the scrap of metal was the only thing that still allowed Jason to share his soulcode at all, even if just partial copies of it to a few hundred homunculi in Megeddon, enough to give a few of them a semblance of competence.

"You've been doing that a lot lately," said his lieutenant.

"Doing what?"

"Looking through your ring like it was a window to a better time. Do you miss your friends after all this time?"

"Piss off," said Jason. Of course, Gamma wasn't wrong. Gamma was partly *him*, after all. And despite everything, sometimes Jason missed Alice, Mel, Sanders, Bradley, even

Carter. He and Carter used to get root beer floats once a month. They'd both joked about how childish their tradition was, but Jason was sure Carter looked forward to it as much as him. That was long before everything went bad. Ancient history.

For a long time, he'd felt horrible that his move against Carter ruined his friendship with the others. Stripped of their Incarnations like he had been, Mel had slunk off and ended up taking over Hazurrium, vowing to never speak to him again. Everyone else had simply disappeared. He hadn't had the heart to go looking for them then, and by now, they were probably all dead. He hadn't kept tabs.

He dropped the Ring which flopped back onto its chest, its chain clinking. The trinket had once granted him the power of a god in Ardeyn. Back when the Maker had counted him a friend. As Ardeyn's aspect of War, Jason could become a literal army with a thought. His thoughts raced simultaneously in every instance, and his capacities were magnified to superhuman levels. It'd been mind-blowingly awesome. Probably.

Actually, it was difficult to recall with real clarity what being War had been *truly* like. Retaining even a tenth of the thoughts and plans and exultations that'd flashed through a thousand minds at once was impossible in his current limited state. Plus, separating what'd actually happened, and what'd been part of the extrapolated Age of Myth, was no easy task. Carter's injection of faux history had made everything possible in the Strange, given structure to chaos, and had been the difference between living and dying when they'd all accidentally come here.

But Jason still hated Carter Morrison. Or, as he'd later come to be called, Carter Strange, the Maker. It should've been him, not Carter, who'd become the god of Ardeyn. But as usual, Carter had to steal all the glory for himself. Then strand him here in a place where magic worked, wonders walked, and they had become like gods... except, it was all a lie. It had seemed real enough to fool everyone, even Jason, for a time. But he'd come to realize it was a prison. He couldn't return to Earth, and killing the Maker had only further limited his options instead of providing an escape route back to reality.

Though if Jason had it all to do over, even though it meant breaking his Ring again, he'd still kill Carter.

"We have an appointment," Gamma said, breaking Jason's reverie. "Stop obsessing. We're close. It's all still possible."

"Didn't I tell you to piss off?" But Jason fell into step beside his clear-skinned clone. There wasn't enough difference between himself and the seven lieutenants who shared most his soulcode for him to become *too* angry with any of them. Usually. In this case, the homunculus was right. If his latest scheme panned out, he'd surpass even what he'd been before. He'd claim for himself not only War's full power, but also the Maker's mantle and abilities, as it should've always been. Then he'd remake Ardeyn, out of spite, as a new recursion. It would be a whole new world, one where Jason called the shots. But returning to Earth was goal one.

They passed around the monstrous mouth of the Pit Reactor. Purple light glimmered in its torpid depths. It was supposed to have been a source of unlimited power. But for all its promise, the Pit Reactor remained a disappointment, good for providing extra light but not much else. Siphoning energy directly from the insane, infinite flux of the Strange was tricky. Jason and his homunculi consistently erred on the side of caution, rather than see Megeddon blasted out of existence by a flare of loose chaos. Maybe that was why the Pit consistently failed to deliver.

His other projects were more or less in the same lackluster state, except for a few standouts.

One foundry was devoted to scraping soulcode from slaves

purchased in Ardeyn, then repurposing the unique identifiers for Jason's lower-grade homunculi. Despite a few snags, his lieutenant Theta who oversaw the repurposing project claimed that the problems were nearly licked. Theta had been saying that for years. Jason was beginning to have his doubts about Theta.

In the next chamber, reds labored to understand and utilize a collection of items imbued with magical power gathered from around Ardeyn. Jason had claimed a couple for himself after his Ring failed, including his belt that granted him greatly increased strength for limited periods. The chamber also stored relics washed up from the depths of the Strange on Ardeyn's border. Those were mostly confined to a vault and rarely experimented with, because those who did the experimenting had a tendency to disintegrate.

And of course there was the Electronics Foundry. He'd added it only forty years ago. For decades, Jason had labored under the misapprehension that because magic worked in Ardeyn, regular science wouldn't. Thankfully, he'd been proved wrong. Sure, he hadn't been able to do anything he couldn't have accomplished back on Earth, and in most cases given his lack of tools and an industrial base, far less. But he'd had a few successes in the last couple of years. Jason had the unique advantage of being able to cheat using magic. He and his clones started with transistors, and worked their way up from there. It'd been grueling, but he'd achieved his goal: an operating system capable of storing and accessing vast amounts of data. Moreover, one with data pointing the way back to Ardeyn and the Strange, based on Peter Sanders's seminal research so long ago...

Jason walked past the Xenobiology Foundry where his ace-in-the-hole waited with the infinite patience of ice. The kray had helped him before. That aid had come at a price. The kray were not sentient in the same way humans were.

He'd only make a new deal with them as a last resort. The creatures were not of Ardeyn; they were of the Strange, and all too real for Jason's liking. They scared him.

Thankfully, the era of fear and quisling bargains was over. Earth had called! Someone was replicating Sanders's work, trying to wring more computer cycles out of quantum inflation. They didn't have what they needed to make a solid or even lasting connection to the Strange. But that's where Jason's carefully devised flash drive came in.

If everything worked as he'd devised, his dreams were on the cusp of–

His elation faltered. The two dozen massive crystal screens in the Contact Foundry, each manned by red homunculi on high catwalks, were dark, or showed only static. Eta, his lieutenant in charge of Contact, was fiddling at the open face of a massive piece of engineering. Eta called it the Baryonic Interferometer Transport Relay, or "BITER" for short.

"What's wrong?" he asked.

Eta looked up. "What's it look like?"

Jason balled his hands into fists. He took a deep breath. "Don't test me, clone."

Eta's eyes widened. Simultaneously, he heard a surprised breath from the other homunculi in the chamber.

Eta's expression flattened in a way familiar to Jason. His translucent lieutenants were most like himself. They *hated* to be called out as clones. It was their unspoken rule.

At that moment, Jason didn't give a rat's ass. But he didn't have time for theatrics. To smooth things over, he lied, "Listen, sorry about that. Mea culpa, all right? Just tell me what happened to our connection with Banks and Paldridge."

Eta fumed. Jason wondered if the homunculus was stupid enough to jeopardize everything himselves had been working for, over a slight. If so, Jason was ready to make an example.

"The entanglement remains," said Eta after swallowing his

anger. "We haven't lost the connection. Timescales remain conjoined."

"Thank the Maker for that. If we'd lost it..." Well, he didn't have to imagine that dismal hell. "And the status of the courier? And of the trove?" The trove was a repurposed Ring – the Ring of Desire – holding the flash drive. Apparently, War and Desire had had a thing, back in the Age of Myth, before Jason's time. His memory, or rather, War's memory, suggested that Desire had enjoyed an unhealthy influence over War. Or in other words, Desire had wrapped War around her little finger more than once. Which was why Jason was glad to consign the Ring of Desire to Earth. With Desire out of the picture in Ardeyn, he removed one more potential complication to his plans. Besides, Rings seemed to be about the only physical objects, besides his own copies, able to make the transition.

Eta shook his head. "We detected the printing event. As we suspected, uplink fidelity was barely sufficient to make the transfer. Even hardened to withstand it, the homunculi barely integrated."

"Did the courier make the handoff? Do Banks and Paldridge have what they need?"

"The courier lost cohesion after printing. He either spontaneously dissolved, or something took exception to his appearance. But" – Eta held up his hand, seeing Jason's imminent interruption – "I've confirmed that the trove made the transfer intact."

"Excellent," he replied, relief like a weight falling from his shoulders.

Even if Liza Banks and Paldridge did nothing with the courier's gift, Jason had hidden autorun code on the flash drive. It would automatically install itself if inserted into any USB port, and then begin uploading onto hundreds of torrent sites, as well as other sites computer geeks favored. Sooner or later, someone would find Jason's instructions on building a better computer, and implement them.

It shouldn't take long, either way. Banks was already moving in the right direction, half-assed as it was. Virtual-particle printing in the baryonic world required specified coordinates in space-time, and even more importantly, a connection made first from outside the network. All the computational power of the primeval dark energy network couldn't change that.

When what he'd coded on the trove was implemented into hardware running the proper software on Earth, a pure locational signal would stir the Strange. And like the planetovores who'd been attracted to their first intrusion, Jason would be waiting. He'd swarm up that link before the kray or anything else out of the dark energy network could do so. He would establish a new node of control, fling wide the doors to the Maker's Hall, and become the god of Ardeyn he should've been all along. Until he remade it something else. Or, he might just leave while the getting was good, and let Ardeyn rot. It was tempting.

"You're smiling," Gamma said, though the clone's face also wore a wolfish grin, as did Eta's. Jason laughed. They all laughed. It was all still possible, indeed.

"Soon, my brothers," he said, feeling magnanimous, "We'll be one again, a gestalt mind with limitless power. We'll be War!"

Most of himselves cheered. He wondered if some of them were worried he'd abandon them all and go to Earth. Probably. They were partly him, so they knew his secret urges, too.

Turning his back on the mastery the Maker's Hall would grant him, even if he *did* return to Earth, was going to be difficult. He knew himself. What if he could retain the power of War, or even of the Maker, on *Earth*? How crazy would that be? Here, it hardly mattered what he did among the kingdoms of make-believe. But back home, actual people would see. *Real* people. Frankly, he was surprised he hadn't fully committed to taking power in the universe of normal matter before. Sure, he'd considered it, wondering if he had the balls to try. Now that things seemed to be going his way, he was decided. He'd go for it. Why should he leave all his advantages gained in Ardeyn behind?

"And after we make Ardeyn ours, we'll have Earth for dessert!" Jason shouted. Louder cheering. He yelled, too, giving the V for victory sign–

"Don't you feel even a little bit guilty?" said Delta, the one clone who hadn't cheered. "Earth was our home."

Jason didn't want to ruin the moment, so he didn't kill Delta. Instead he said, "Look at it this way. It's going to happen, sooner or later, even if we do nothing. Eventually, someone else on Earth will rediscover the right energy domains, either with a quantum computing advance, or when the Large Hadron Collider achieves high enough energy. Every sentient species in the universe that doesn't kill itself some other way eventually trips the trap. It's destiny. At least *we* are human. The children of Earth should be the ones to reap the rewards of the Strange, not some emergent AI intelligence or alien parasite. Unlike what normally happens in this rat-eat-rat cosmos."

"Sounds as if you've been practicing that in a mirror."

Jason shook his head. "No. Well, yeah. But that doesn't make it untrue. I'm being proactive. For all its size, Ardeyn can't stand up to what lies beyond the Borderlands. We've been lucky so far, but luck doesn't last forever. The kray are bottom feeders compared to what else swims farther out. And the kray almost killed us all without half trying, even when the Maker and all the Incarnations were still kicking!"

Jason realized he was yelling. Damn it. The homunculus had put him on the defensive. He balled his hands into fists.

"You doth protest too much, methinks," said Delta.

"That's it," said Jason. He clapped the clone on the forehead. Delta didn't realize what he was doing before it was too late. Jason knew, because he could feel Delta's mind as it came apart, when the portion of their shared soulcode merged. The body dropped to the floor, moldering to dust in seconds.

Jason met the stares of the others. No further comments were offered.

The advantage of heading an organization made up of your own clones was knowing them so well. An occasional demonstration of where the balance of power lay was required for someone of his particular temperament. But, shit, now he was down a lieutenant. At least Delta had been assigned to the Pit Reactor, not one of the more critical Foundries.

All he had to do was wait and let the flash drive that'd been printed on Earth do its work. No need to accelerate the process by involving the kray, thankfully. Each additional piece of lore gained from his alien "friends" robbed Jason of more independence. And given that he was an Incarnation, one of the manifestations of the Seven Rules that kept Ardeyn safe, making deals with the kray probably weakened Ardeyn's defenses, too. But without the kray's initial aid, he would never have managed to kill the Maker in the first place, and more recently, learned how to build BITER.

He nodded to himself. The kray expected Jason to continue asking for help. They expected they would be the ones calling the shots eventually, not Jason. Not that the kray thought and planned in the way people did, but whatever.

A chime rang through the chamber. Jason didn't immediately realize where the sound originated, or its significance.

Surprise blossomed on Gamma's face. The clone pointed at Jason.

Jason looked down at his chest. His cracked Ring glowed

red like an ember kicked out of the fire. The noise of the tolling chime was dying away, but had obviously originated from the loop of metal.

"Oh, no," he whispered. Lines from an old Earth movie slithered into his brain: *When our joy is at its zenith, when all is most right with the world, the most unthinkable disasters descend upon us.*

Except it wasn't unthinkable. Unlikely, but there it was. That fucker Carter had hidden a sleeper somewhere in the cloud. A sleeper who was waking up.

In Ardeyn, or lost in the infinity past the Borderlands, or maybe even on Earth itself, Carter Morrison – also known as Carter Strange – was back.

5: RESURRECTION
Carter Morrison

A line burned across darkness. My eyes stung like I'd touched them with hot sauce still on my fingers. Blinking eased that sensation, but the bright splinter in the blackness remained. Craning my head around, I tried to make out where I was lying. The glow was just enough to illuminate the walls of a smallish room. The floor beneath me was stone-hard and cold. Cement, maybe? Felt like it. I was...

I was apparently having a nap in a self-storage unit. The light leaked in from under the single closed garage door. Why the hell was I sleeping in a storage unit? And, holy shit, where were my clothes? Had I been drinking?

A couple of plastic bins were stacked along the wall. A tarp-draped car filled most of the space. I could just make out a dark bulb in a fixture overhead. The smell of oil and dust filled my nose and throat, and I sneezed.

Pushing myself into a sitting position, something furry crushed under my left palm before I could snatch my hand back. *Ugh!* Dead mouse? I didn't want to know.

Waking up and not remembering where you are can be sort of pleasant, as long as it doesn't last for more than a few seconds. Which is why I felt the opposite of worry-free. The last thing I remembered was...

Nothing came. "Oh, crap." My voice was hoarse with disuse. Movies where people were slipped memory-wiping roofies – *those* I suddenly recalled. Had that happened? I didn't remember being at a party, but then again, I suppose I wouldn't.

My legs were like two dead stumps, I discovered, when I tried to stand. Luckily, the dusty tarp hiding the car was close enough to collapse on.

I waited a few seconds, then stamped experimentally, leaning on the car for support. Numbness gave way to a fire of pins and needles. I groaned, but continued my stamping, shuffling dance until I trusted myself enough to reach for the dangling cord.

The bulb washed the room in bleach-white light. Squinting, I checked out the two bins. The top one was labeled with black marker on masking tape with my name, Carter Morrison. It contained a full change of clothing, including underwear, shoes, a pullover, and navy blue pea coat. I didn't recognize any of the articles, but they were all my size. How considerate of my kidnappers. Though I didn't want to think about why they'd stripped me in the first place.

The other bin held a couple of protein bars, a bottle of water, key and a fob, and a cell phone. The cell was dead of course, but my oh-so-thoughtful abductors had dropped me in a storage unit with an outlet, charger already plugged in. I did what was apparently expected of me, and connected the phone.

While the mobile charged, I checked myself for stitches or incisions, in case I'd fallen afoul of organ thieves. Those stories were probably just urban legends, but when you find yourself undressed and clueless in a storage unit, you have to examine your assumptions.

No obvious signs of medical interventions, which relieved that particular anxiety. So I dressed. Eventually, the pieces would fall into place, one way or the other, I hoped. Until then, I needed to keep moving forward. It was that, or have a freakout. Maybe I'd save panic for later.

The sweater was fleece, and I zipped the collar up tight. It was cold in the tiny garage. I couldn't have been lying on the cement for long, or I would've frozen to death.

The shoes were brand new Doc Martens, my favorite. Which meant my kidnappers knew my tastes. I filed that away for later consideration as I slipped them over my feet. They'd take a little breaking in, but–

A poster was tacked to the closed garage door. Beneath an image of someone riding a winged fantasy beast across the stars was a message:

ARDEYN
Land of the Curse
Releases May 20th
Preorder your copy today!

Relief flowed through me like a cooling summer breeze. I remembered that poster! Oh yes. I nodded at the advertisement like the old friend it was. Jason, Mel, Bradley, and I spent three difficult years creating the code base for Ardeyn. Ordering the promotional posters had been putting the cart *way* before the horse. On the other hand, we'd purposely left the year off the release date, because we weren't complete idiots. Someone thought they were being funny by slapping the poster in here with me. I wonder who?

If the game had launched, things would've finally come together for me. For starters, I'd have been sipping lattes in a palatial bedroom looking out on a fabulous view of the Cascades, instead of waking up witless in a glorified garage.

But Ardeyn had run into corporate inertia. Funding shortfalls saw to the game's death before its debut, despite everything I could do.

At least, that was how I told the story to everyone else. To myself, I couldn't lie. Ultimately, it came down to my own knack for pulling failure out of the jaws of success. Ardeyn was one more debacle in a long string of fuck-ups. My ego had brought Ardeyn to the precipice – where I refused to give up the least iota of control of "my baby" to anyone else. And that was that.

Without jobs and a failed MMORPG on our resumes, it was easy for Peter Sanders to reel us back into the academic careers we'd abandoned for our game. In fact, it was Sanders's paper on recursion–

It all came back to me then. We'd been mapped onto an alien network, mapped so completely that our minds transferred. Maybe even our souls. Except I'd clawed my way back out of the system. I'd... severed the connections our left-behind bodies retained. The memory made my stomach taut and I gagged.

After murdering my friends, I'd dropped a copy of *Ardeyn, Land of the Curse* into the primordial network by imposing the rigid rules the game represented into the unformatted chaos. I'd hoped to hedge out the planetovores that'd already gotten Earth's scent. Maybe even sever the connection completely.

Then like a harebrained idiot, I'd tried to go back into that strange stratum and find my friends to see if I could save them.

After that, I recalled nothing. Had I found my friends or even reconnected? My mind was as empty of memory as a cloudless sky.

It was as if no time had passed at all. Until I woke up shivering on cement wondering about the state of my kidneys.

"Motherfucker," I muttered. I approached the Ardeyn release poster. One edge was peeled back. I lifted it, and saw a message I'd never seen before scrawled on the back:

Find Bradley. He'll tell you what you need to know.

The message was signed by me. The signature looked careful, like the way I sometimes did when I wanted my name to be at least halfway legible. But I knew, viscerally and completely, that *I* had not written that message, signed it, or for that matter, prepared this storage unit-bunker for myself as the presence of the poster implied. How I was so sure, I don't know, but I was certain about that, if nothing else.

But if not me, then who? And why?

The freakout I'd promised myself earlier clawed up the base of my spine. Fear of the unknown had always been my downfall. I was a planner. Goal-oriented, my high school counselor had said. My post-doctoral adviser had agreed, even when I left the PhD program code a game. But here was the Unknown with a capital U, staring me down in my own handwriting. How could I plan for something I couldn't even comprehend?

My hands, suddenly trembling and nerveless, let go of the poster. The edge settled back until it was flush with the wall once more.

6: PARANOIA
Katherine Manners

"Subs didn't have conning towers in World War II," said the woman at the table next to Kate's.

"Are you crazy?" replied a man sporting massive sunglasses. "I just watched a show on the History Channel. *Great Ships*. It was practically a–"

Kate adjusted her ear plugs to drown out the conversation. The same opinionated crew gathered every morning at Canyon Street Roasters. She didn't like sitting too close. They guffawed every time a watered-down dirty joke was offered, which interrupted her flow. The coffee bar staff didn't hassle her about spending a few hours a day on their Wi-Fi, but it wasn't the quietest of places.

Some days, the idea of renting a desk at one of those trendy shared office co-locations seemed like the way to go. Today especially; big-sunglasses guy was giving her the creeps.

No. She was just off-balance. Most of her clients were more comfortable meeting in a crowded cafe. Maybe because it provided anonymity, or because it made them less conscious that they were seeking the services of a private investigator in the first place. Meeting over coffee just seemed so normal.

More than anything, she craved normal after what had happened.

Kate rubbed her forehead. Trying to think of something other than two nights ago at BDR wasn't working. Why should it, when the world had shown her it was a far stranger place than she'd ever suspected? She'd found herself reeling like a drunk a few times, but sans the alcohol. Reality had crumbled before her. She kept seeing that man appearing a layer at a time, his desperate eyes, and finally, the pool he'd become.

Her phone chimed with the Los Lobos ringtone she'd selected for Raul. She snatched it, relieved at the interruption.

"Hello?" she said into the handset. "Raul, where the fuck are you? I've been here for twenty minutes."

"Katherine Janeway Manners?" came Raul's voice, his slight Mexican accent softening the consonants.

She sighed, and said, "I knew telling you my middle name was a mistake." Her parents had been fans of the Federation.

"What's the passphrase?" came Raul's voice again, now tinged with a trace of anxiety. Raul was a security researcher who sometimes did odd jobs on the side when he wasn't collecting bug bounties on enterprise-level software packages. Odd jobs such as working with her.

Kate suppressed a second sigh, instead reciting into the phone, "Tiny purple fishes."

"Ah. Thank you, Kate. You can never be too sure."

He always said that. "Yeah, right. I'm glad I can help out with your issues. I hate to think what your monthly psychiatrist bill must be. Where are you?"

A few seconds ticked by, then someone tapped her shoulder. She didn't spill her coffee, but only because the top was secured.

"Raul," she said, keeping her voice level, "I'd worry less about hidden enemies, and more about pissing off your friends. Some of them have guns."

Raul took the seat across from her, smirking. He set a cup

of tea on the table and slid his computer bag to the floor at his feet. "You don't need a gun," he said.

He'd said the same before. And as before, she pretended not to hear it. She replied, "Thanks for showing up."

"It's Sunday. Don't tell me you didn't expect me. So what have you got for me, *mi chula*?" He sipped his tea.

She wrestled her irritation into submission so her voice wouldn't be tight or rushed. Raul was sensitive to those sorts of things, and she didn't want to spook him. Nor did she want to give him any reason to suspect she was about to lie, if only by omission. For someone good with computers, Raul was surprisingly good at reading people.

"I'm on another case. Like the one you helped me out with last time."

Raul pursed his lips. "Another forged ID?"

"No. I've already infiltrated the target. What I need is for you to break the encryption on a flash drive and tell me what's on it."

"I might be able to help," said Raul. "Depends on how they implemented their crypto. See, if–"

She stopped him with a hand on his wrist. "Yeah, yeah. I just need you to take a look." Raul knew her background, but he couldn't help lecture her anyway. Probably one of the reasons they'd never hit it off was because she was afraid she'd eventually take his infuriating habit of explaining everything personally.

He furrowed his brow. "I assume you want the information for a client. Why not just give him the flash drive?"

She just looked at him, wondering how to explain what she'd found.

"Him, or her," Raul amended.

She grinned. "No. I mean, yeah, my client is male. But I can't get in touch. Not that Bradley probably has anything to do with the flash drive. He had me looking for exploits on a server, but, um… I found the flash drive instead."

"What's it to you, if your client doesn't want it?"

"Something weird happened, and the USB might help explain."

"You sound upset. Is everything all right?"

Shit. So much for your plan not to spook the paranoid. Plus she'd told Raul Bradley's name. Not professional.

Kate said, "I'm upset because there was a, um, a third party. And I have his flash drive." That explanation approached the truth.

Raul's brows furrowed. "A third party? You mean, like a foreign national? Or someone closer to home? CIA? Or NSA, maybe?"

"Definitely not local." She couldn't imagine anything more foreign than a melting man. "He said his name was Jason. I found him in the server room, hurt. He asked for my help. Then he died. It was… terrible."

"He died?" Raul's eyes widened and he unconsciously pushed back a few inches from the table.

Kate put a hand to her mouth. Damn it, she hadn't meant to admit that. She was more shaken then she'd realized. Now Raul would pack up and leave.

Except he didn't. Instead he said, "I'm sorry. It must have been awful."

He wasn't going to bolt, at least not immediately. Maybe she'd underestimated him.

He continued, "You'd never seen him before? And he had no ID?"

She said, "The only thing he had on him was this custom USB stick."

"Where did this go down?"

"BDR," said Kate. "Banks Digital Realty. It's a commercial server farm."

"Any police involvement?"

"No," Kate said, "But I have no idea what happened after I left."

Raul pulled his laptop from its bag and fired it up as if it was the most normal response in the world.

She grabbed his hand and squeezed. "Thank you, Raul."

A smile lit his face. He said, "I'm happy to help, *mi chula*. Now, then... I haven't heard of BDR, but let's see what the internets have to say. And can I see this mysterious drive?"

"What, you want to check it here?"

"Where else? I'm not going to pop an unidentified USB stick into a device connected to my home network. Public Wi-Fi is the only way to go. If the drive is loaded with malware, and tries to phone home when we plug it in, I don't want to be pinged by them."

Like good paranoids everywhere, she reflected, Raul referred to all the various government and corporate organizations he feared were after him as "them."

"Wait," Raul said, meeting her gaze with eyes wider than when she'd told him about the stranger dying. "You didn't plug it into your home network did you?"

"Raul, what kind of idiot do you take me for? Why do you think I called you?"

"Right, right. Sorry." His eyes returned to his screen, fingers tapping the keyboard.

"Banks Digital Realty," he read from the screen. "Twenty-four hour support, unlimited bandwidth, server hosting, and... other stuff. These guys offer everything." Raul settled back in his chair. "I hope whatever's encrypted on that drive is more interesting than this web site."

"Me too." She handed him the ring. "Be careful."

"Don't teach a dog to fetch, Kate," he said as he examined the large costume jewel on the ring, and after a little fiddling, exposed the USB end as she had. "Custom case, eh?"

"Yeah. Ever seen anything like it?"

He shrugged. "No. But some people are into mods. I've seen USB drives that look like dolls, cigarette lighters, car keys, and toys."

"I don't think it's a toy."

"Yeah. It's too dramatic," said Raul, "It looks more like a movie prop."

Kate sucked in a breath. Could it be? Had she crashed some sort of special effects demonstration? If so, maybe she hadn't actually seen a man melt. Except, there'd been no "Lights, Camera, Action!"

"This Jason," said Raul. "You never saw him before?"

She shook her head. Nor would she see him again, given what'd happened. She said, "Just tell me what I've got here."

Raul did something to his keyboard, and restarted his laptop. Then he plugged the business end of the ring into a port on the side.

"It's mounting," he noted.

Kate studied Raul's screen. She didn't recognize the diagnostics program he was running. Not a huge surprise. She knew a lot about computers, alternate operating systems, and was a fair coder in more than one programing language. But Raul was in a league all his own. A few years back, he'd won a cash prize at a hacker conference for being the first to find a critical bug in a popular laptop model. A year later, he won another prize for demonstrating how the leading browser could be "pwned" simply by directing it to a web page loaded with malware.

Making a living by publicly demonstrating how other peoples' top selling products were actually piles of dog shit was a great way to make enemies. Raul had received more than one anonymous threat. As their volume and vehemence grew, his peace of mind disintegrated. He'd finally gone into hiding, certain his name was on some secret NSA file or corporate hit list, targeted for elimination... or something.

Kate doubted that men in dark glasses would ever show up to haul Raul away.

Then again, after what she'd witnessed two nights ago, her confidence in the definition of "realistic" was shaken. Maybe she'd been wrong to doubt the man's convictions. Maybe he knew deeper truths about the way things worked that she needed to discover.

Raul tapped more keys. Data streamed across the screen.

They'd met before she'd left Microsoft at a tech conference. Raul might've had romantic intentions, but nothing ever came of it. After she'd started her own business, and Raul had "gone to ground," they'd kept in touch. She received an email with a coded phrase letting her know who it was every time he moved into new digs, which was at least twice a year.

"Anything?" she said. She could see the screen as well as Raul, but she must have been reading it wrong, because–

"Yes and no. There's a lot of data here. Terabytes, which is unheard of for such a small package."

"Whoa." She hadn't been reading the screen wrong. "How many terabytes?"

"That's another thing. I can't actually tell. The profiler is still estimating the drive size."

She studied the end protruding from Raul's computer. Plugged in, it looked out of place. Alien. She crossed her arms. "Are you sure it's safe?" she said.

"So far. It's still encrypted."

"Can you break it?"

"We'll see. I've started running dictionaries against it."

She cocked her head. "That could take a while. Have you tried 'monkey'?" Monkey was the most used password, statistics showed. People who chose it thought they were being clever. They weren't, just predictable.

"Of course," said Raul. He grinned, probably at the foolishness of noobs everywhere.

But his smile faded. After a few minutes he said, "This isn't working. If the password was easily guessable, we would've had something by now. Which means it's probably secure."

"I was afraid of that," said Kate. In time, any password could be cracked. But the more complex the password, the longer the search. Throw in an upper case letter or some punctuation, and most importantly, increase the encryption key's size, and even a massive cracking array making billions of guesses a second would take centuries. She summed it up, "Well, then we're probably screwed."

He shrugged. "Give me a little credit, *mi chula*. I've got more tricks up my sleeve."

Every so often, Kate wondered what *mi chula* meant. It was a pet name of course, but she hadn't given Raul the satisfaction of asking for its definition or checking the internet herself. Instead, she said, "Those tricks are why I called you."

"See that?" Raul pointed to one of the open windows on his screen. Data from captured traffic filled it.

She said, "I've seen a few of those terms, but I'm not sure what this means."

Raul tapped the flash drive, then raised his eyebrows expectantly, as if waiting for her to get the punch line.

"Wait," Kate said. "Is the flash drive doing that?"

"Yes. As soon as it mounted, it began requesting network access. I've blocked it."

"Who's it trying to call?" She thought of Jason, then imagined cold-war bunkers filled with flesh melting chemicals.

"I don't know," said Raul. "Yet. But if we let it try to make the connection, I may capture enough data to break the encryption."

"That sounds stupidly dangerous. Do you remember when I said the man I met died? It wasn't normal! I think he might've been murdered."

"I remember. I was worried that was exactly what you meant."

She sighed. "I haven't told you everything, Raul. And I don't intend to, for your own peace of mind. This little USB drive scares me."

"I can reformat it, wipe it clean. Then it won't be anyone's problem anymore. Want me to take it off your hands?"

Kate considered his offer. Part of her wanted to tell Raul to do it. Quickly, before she thought better of it.

"No. It's important, I just don't know why. As much as I'd rather just trash it and walk away, I need to know what's on it, where it came from, and why that man died."

"Then we have to accept some risk."

"Hearing *you* say that is sort of funny."

Raul chuckled, obviously appreciating her point. Kate liked a man who was able to laugh at his own foibles.

"The process won't have free rein. I'll keep it sandboxed. But it needs enough leeway so that the process believes it's actually making a connection."

Kate felt like she was on a rollercoaster cresting a steep rise, getting her first view of the screaming drop ahead.

"All right," she said. "Do it."

Raul tapped a key.

7: SOVEREIGN
Elandine, Queen of Hazurrium

Sword in hand, Elandine walked the borders of the Strange under a red sun. So close to the edge, the light seemed old and used up. Beneath her boots, the land was convulsed. Long ruts dragged scars down to the west as if made by the monstrous talons of a colossal Stranger unable to retain its grip on Ardeyn. The occasional cactus and thorny tree drooped, wilted with pestilence.

The splintered landscape was Ardeyn's boundary, where only the insane or suicidal trespassed. Beyond it drifted a sporadic scatter of free-floating skerries like barnacles on reality's border. And beyond them lay the Strange. She rarely glanced that way.

Elandine traveled a path parallel to the chaos that spurned all rules, not into it. The Strange would not try her strength, not today.

The Maker willing, it never would.

Her sword was potent enough – it held an enchantment for slaying, and had a secret name only she knew. *Rendswandir*. But *Rendswandir* was nothing compared to the chaos beyond the world. Not even her Ring, which outclassed her sword by no small margin, would avail her there. The Ring had seen better days, but it was still equal to most trials contained in Ardeyn.

It had another name once, when it was mighty. Now it was called Peace. Elandine had Peace from her mother, who'd got it from her mother before her, and so on all the way back. The Ring was a relic of the Founding. Without it, the queendom of Hazurrium would've crumbled ages ago, as opposed to merely sliding into senility over generations.

Perhaps it was finally happening, and the queendom would fall. After all, how else could she explain her sister Flora's death?

"Elandine?" said Navar.

The queen glanced around, blinking away nascent tears.

Navar's jackal-visage was fixed on a nearby cave, tall ears forward. Navar sat on a silver-maned Lorn Charger, the giant breed famously foaled in the easternmost fiefdom of Hazurrium. Navar's kind were sometimes feared for the exploits of her shadow-kin, the sark. Sark were qephilim who'd rebelled against the Seven Rules. But as the First Protector, Navar had shown herself to be a more loyal defender than any other, including even Elandine's own mother. The First Protector was also something of a friend.

Seeing she had Elandine's attention, Navar gestured to the right of their path. A cavern gaped there.

The queen glanced at the dripping cave mouth, partly hidden in the folds of earth and foliage, no more than a stone's throw away. She'd been paying too much attention to the regrets lined up inside her skull to notice the cavity.

Where there's a cave, there's almost certain a creature's lair. That wasn't one of the vaunted Seven Rules, but it might as well have been.

"You've got a keen eye, Protector," Elandine said.

"I'll call for your mount." The knight raised a hand to signal the courtiers and guards making up the queen's detail following behind. She said, "Let's move away from here."

"No," said Elandine. "We should search the cave.

Brandalun's trail led here."

Navar snorted. "Trust me, Your Majesty. Brandalun detests caves. I served as her Protector for twelve good years before you. She wouldn't enter a place like that."

Elandine recalled growing up in the vaulted halls of Citadel Hazurrium, and how her mother couldn't abide a dark room. Every chamber had at least four lamps for light, and most far more.

The queen loved her mother, but Brandalun had made a shambles of an already bad situation. She had ignored her duties too long, in favor of the increasingly single-minded pursuits contrived by what some claimed – in whispers – to be a doddering imagination.

After her mother's abdication, Elandine took the vows of rulership. She became the ruler of Hazurrium. She'd inherited a queendom under threat of an alliance of shadow qephilim, the kray, and the Betrayer. That eel-cuddling Betrayer was probably behind the whole thing. If Elandine the Young didn't prove more apt at her duties than Brandalun the Distracted, it would be under her watch that every human still alive in the refuge of Ardeyn would become extinct. The Seven Rules codified by the Maker would finally break, and the endless chaos outside the world would wash it all away.

Aloud she said, "Navar, you knew her before she entered her dotage. Who really knows her thoughts now, and if she still fears the dark?"

The First Protector's ears twitched, first one, then the other. Elandine had learned that meant uncertainty. But Navar said, "Brandalun would've headed away from that cave, past the edges of Ardeyn. More likely to find fragments of that blasted device she was always going on about. Begging your pardon, my queen."

Elandine said, "Unless a sirrush or dragon caught her and her traitorous guards napping, and pulled them all into its den against their will."

"All right, all right, I yield," said Navar. "But after we check the cave, we must return to Citadel Hazurrium. You made me promise to hold you to a deadline on this outing. And we've come close to missing it."

Elandine nodded impatiently. Ardeyn's previous ruler was nowhere to be found, having apparently undertaken a self-appointed quest to find the parts for a mystical mechanism, a mechanism she learned about via a "vision sent from the Maker." Elandine didn't believe it for a heartbeat. It was more likely Brandalun had simply been unable to face her youngest daughter Flora's demise. Either way, it wouldn't do the queendom any favors if Brandalun's inheritor was seen following in her mother's footsteps. Flora... She blinked away the thought before it could take root.

Elandine said, "Don't worry about the deadline. Look, see that skerry out there? The one with the attending red tumblers? I've been watching it, and I think that, once we clear the cave, we–"

"We'll miss Flora's interment," interrupted Navar.

Elandine froze. Then she shrugged.

"Is that what this is really about?" asked the qephilim. "I can understand why, you know I do. But others may see it differently. Besides, Flora would've–"

Elandine spun to face the First Protector. "Don't you dare tell me what Flora would want! Do you think I don't know? Do you think I don't care? It's not for you, or anyone, to judge me. Keep to your place, Protector, and all of us will be better for it."

Navar stiffened in her saddle, and her ebony ears laid back almost flat against her black-furred skull. The knight turned to regard the cave mouth again. She waited a moment and said, "As it pleases Your Majesty."

Which only made Elandine all the more furious. She yelled,

"It doesn't please me! My sister died, and all the royal power in Ardeyn can't change that!" After that, words deserted her entirely. Rather than sputter, Elandine just glared at the First Protector, half-hoping Navar would offer some additional fuel for her fury. Being angry felt better than being heartlorn.

Instead Navar called behind for the captain of the queen's detail and a contingent of four soldiers to search the cave. "Watch for crawlers," she instructed the captain.

Five soldiers shuffled into the cavity, one with a lantern, two with spell staves called rune ashurs, and two with glittering swords.

Elandine clasped her rage close. If she could keep that coal burning, images of Flora wouldn't swim up from the depths. Flora, who loved to write poetry. Flora, riding behind her through Melis Forest at dawn, a grin plastered across her face as they evaded the royal escort. Flora, who was the only one who could make Brandalun laugh with her awkward puns...

Flora, gasping in the healer's hall of Citadel Hazurrium, her pain so extreme that she shuddered almost constantly, so that she hardly knew Elandine. The numbing influence of greenwasp venom brought only momentary relief, and the royal soulmancer offered no hope. When Flora's end finally claimed her and she passed over, it was almost a relief, because her suffering was over.

Elandine was bereft and alone without her younger sister, and her emotional barriers were tumbled to ruin.

Flora died almost a month ago, and her spirit had descended into the Night Vault. But as was proper, on the thirty-third day following death of anyone in Hazurrium, the deceased's remains would be interred west of Citadel Hazurrium, in the great wall called Ur. A funeral celebration would follow. By any estimation, Elandine should be there. When someone was interred in Ur, the queen should be on hand to say a few words. If that someone was the queen's sister? Unthinkable that the queen should miss it, but that's exactly what Elandine had decided to do.

Whenever she let her guard down, she was ambushed by the singular memory of her sister's passing, literally in her arms in the brightly lit healing hall that smelled of candles and medicine. All Flora's limbs had loosened in a slow but unstoppable wave, before a stillness more silent than the deepest sleep settled over her. After that, Elandine had only tears. And recollections, moments that played over and over.

Time would heal her heart, she was assured by those stupid enough to brave her grief and rage. But after thirty-one days, the wound was just as raw. It was all she could do to not think about it, and focus on retrieving her mother instead. By the Maker, if Brandalun wasn't around to attend the internment, then neither would Elandine.

One of the soldiers assigned to explore the cave emerged. He sauntered up to Navar and said, "The cave holds the rotting corpse of a sirrush, dead for a month, maybe more. Nothing else."

"Dead?" said the First Protector. "Any sign of what killed it?"

The man shrugged.

Elandine frowned at the disrespect the soldier showed the First Protector. Plus, something tough enough to slay a sirrush should warrant something more than a shrug. She stepped up to the man, checked his insignia, then demanded, "Captain, answer the Protector's question. What killed the sirrush? Where's the rest of your detail?"

The captain's head swung her way, a bit jerkily. He said, "The others are becoming acquainted with their new shells. And yes, we found what killed the beast. It's with me now."

Pale stalks parted the man's hair, folding out from his head, questing like fingers.

"Kray!" shouted Navar.

The captain was gone; he'd been hollowed out and worn like a hat, just long enough to gestate a kray.

The kray-wearing captain vomited a colorless gout of webbing. Elandine evaded the twining strands. Anything cocooned in it was changed or entirely removed from Ardeyn. She came up on the kray's left and hacked off two emerging stalks with her blade, then dispatched the kray with a straight thrust before it completely emerged. Her relic breastplate, for all its sturdiness, was also wound with spells that made it almost as light as a simple shift.

The Maker is merciful, she thought, providing a distraction from thinking about funerals. Where there was one kray, more would follow–

Three more soldiers clambered from the cave, moving with suspicious awkwardness. Navar rode two down in a brutal display of horsemanship, but the third jumped away. The kray inside that last walking corpse was almost completely free, and when it stood up, it was on crablike legs instead of human feet. Two and half times as tall as its dead host, pincers with spinnerets at the tips aimed at the First Protector as she wheeled her mount.

Elandine raised the Ring called Peace and called on its only remaining function. She wasn't close enough to distinguish between Navar and the kray, so all were engulfed in a dim haze of tranquility that slowed thoughts, hearts, and even time.

Outside Ardeyn, the Ring had little power over the kray. But by entering the world, they bound themselves to Ardeyn's rules. So Peace snagged the Stranger as surely as if it was a native.

Elandine rushed to close the distance. She had just seconds to end the fight.

The kray jerked back to awareness. It swung the hollowed man that'd birthed it like a bludgeon. Elandine was knocked sprawling. Her head rattled against a boulder. She scrambled to regain her feet, but everything was spinning.

The thing advanced, holding the dead husk high, ready to strike again. Elandine gasped, "Motherless son of Lotan! Get away from me!"

A thunder of hooves heralded the remainder of her detail. Twenty-some soldiers strong, they rode the last kray down. Rune ashurs inscribed with potent-enough sigils were deadly against most Strangers, but halberds, swords, and hooves did just fine, too. What remained after the charge was only a mess.

"Your Majesty!" yelled Navar as she rode up, "Are you hurt?"

"No," Elandine said, and stood. "Truthfully, I haven't felt this fine in days." She wished more than four kray had emerged from the cave. But the fight seemed done.

Navar said, "Let's have the physician take a look, shall we?"

"In a moment," Elandine said. "After we make certain nothing else infests that hole."

"How in the Maker's name did they get across the border this time?"

The queen shrugged. "They have a knack for bending the Seven Rules. Or they paid, or tricked, someone into opening a door, however small."

Navar looked thoughtful. She said, "There's so many choices. One of the Betrayer's homunculi, a wandering devil, a saboteur from the Court of Sleep, or just some poor wanderer who strayed too close to the edge. The answer might be any of those, or just a surge out of the Strange."

Elandine frowned. The elation from the fight was fading, though not yet completely gone.

"In any event, this represents a serious intrusion, wouldn't you agree?" Elandine said.

The First Protector nodded. "Of course! The region could

be compromised. It would be foolhardy to ignore this. Not *all* of us need to return for the internment–"

"*None* of us will attend," Elandine interrupted. "Especially me." She raised the Ring of Peace so Navar couldn't miss it. Peace was their most potent weapon against Strangers. "In fact, once the physician has her say, I'll lead a sortie…" Her eyes focused fully on Peace.

Instead of its normal golden hue, the Ring was red as blood. It'd never done that before.

Then it chimed. Completely new behavior, too. The sound rolled across the landscape. The chain on which she normally wore it parted and slipped to the ground. Elandine nearly dropped it in surprise.

"Did you do that?" said Navar.

"No."

Elandine studied the Ring. Brandalun used to tell her stories about Peace. The Maker had given each Incarnation a mighty weapon in the form of a Ring, a sort of manifestation of their abilities. Elandine was descended from one of those Incarnations, if family histories could be believed. Elandine never had. The story had it that when the Maker was betrayed, the Rings lost most of their strength. The Incarnations became mortal, and the Age of Myth ended, ushering in the Age of Unrest.

Brandalun had sometimes wondered if the Rings would someday remember some of their ancient power, when – not if – the Maker returned. Peace was one of those Rings, though it started with a different name. When first forged, its power was more fell, and feared.

The Ring of Death, it had been named. Death had the power to slay whosoever the wielder chose, and raise back from death anyone the wielder touched.

Elandine said, "It's clear some measure of the Ring's old power has returned." Her plan crystallized in a moment. The queen slid the Ring onto her right index finger. It settled as comfortably as if she'd always worn it there instead of on a chain around her neck.

"Navar," she said, "I've changed my mind. We must leave the Borderlands. Thank the Maker, we're close to where we need to be."

"Your Majesty?"

"I aim to see my sister smile again."

8: RECONCILIATION
Carter Morrison

The phone from the plastic bin had an address and phone number for Michael Bradley. When I called my old friend, Bradley didn't pick up. I didn't leave a message.

An electronic fob with a Chevrolet logo meant my benefactor had probably left me with wheels. My benefactor. A funny concept, considering that he... was me. Right? The thing was, I certainly didn't remember arranging for this storage unit.

I wasted a minute trying to remember it anyway.

Then I opened the garage door a crack and peered outside. A normal Seattle day waited for me, complete with familiar skyscrapers on the skyline, clouds, and drizzle. No sirens, no columns of smoke, or any other sign of planetovores claiming another mote in the normal universe as their own. I breathed easier.

Surprised I hadn't already, I checked the date on the phone–

Three years. Three years had passed. Jesus.

For me, it seemed like only minutes. What happened in all that time? Especially in the dark energy network we'd touched, after I'd returned the second time? It was a blank, as if whatever had happened, had happened to somebody else.

The Ardeyn release poster came off the garage door with

a few gentle tugs, and I began to roll it up. Thinking better, I laid it on the floor to study it one more time. *Ardeyn, Land of the Cursed.*

In the fiction of the game, Citadel Hazurrium was a central bastion in a land cursed to be the literal prison for Lotan the "Reaper of Sins," our mythical "big bad." Qephilim – my word for angelic beings – of all sorts lived on, above, and beneath Ardeyn, including Lotan's celestial jailers, the qephilim who made up the Court of Sleep. The Court of Sleep in turn answered to demigods called the Incarnations of the Maker, who watched over Ardeyn from the Maker's Hall…

I shook my head.

The important thing was the poster, and my handwriting on it. Its presence implied, at minimum, that I'd come back here after trying to download into Ardeyn. Except, I didn't actually remember anything like that.

Had I fallen into some kind of hibernation, and only awakened now in the garage? But then why the poster? Why my handwriting?

No, the implication was that my frantic upload of Ardeyn to the network had worked. And that I'd gone there, even if I couldn't bring it to mind. And then, had I printed myself back to Earth a *second* time? Why? Maybe only an *instance* of me had printed back here, if that was possible. Maybe I was that instance. Jesus.

Regardless, the poster was a cryptic message from myself. It's how I would've done it. If some random stranger had entered, the poster's significance and short note would be completely opaque. It was a contingency "I" had set up as some sort of failsafe. I just wish I knew what I'd been thinking when I'd done so.

I called Bradley again. The same recorded voice picked up, "Hey, I can't come to the phone right now. You know what to do."

This time, I said after the beep: "Hey, Bradley, it's me. Sorry about the toolbox-to-the-head thing... Yeah. Hey, apparently you have some something for me? I don't remember what. Anyway, I'm heading over to your place."

A canary-yellow Camaro waited under the dusty tarp. I'd never been a sports car guy, but on the drive over to Bradley's, I realized that was maybe because I'd just never had the opportunity. Now wasn't the time to check out the car's ability to handle at top speed. But driving it put me, somehow, in a better mood.

Bradley still rented a tiny house in Queen Anne, a neighborhood northwest of downtown. It was a safe part of the city, but I didn't like seeing that his door was ajar. Since he still wasn't answering his phone, I crept in through the front door quiet as a cat.

Tumbled books, overturned furniture, and liberated pillow stuffing covered the front room. The scene fit my movie-bred expectations for the aftermath of a home invasion. Swallowing, I wondered what the hell I should do next.

Weapons hadn't been included in the garage stash, not even a tool box for bashing heads. Whoever'd created the mess in the front room carried, at minimum, a knife for slashing paintings and helpless cushions. Damn it, I hated being indecisive, but I was positive that I'd hate being stabbed even more. So I dithered.

But I didn't leave. Bradley might be inside. And whoever'd done a number on the furnishings was probably long gone. Only one way to find out...

"Bradley?" I yelled from the entryway. I examined the broken furniture in the next room for an improvised weapon.

When neither Bradley nor a guy in a ski-mask appeared, I screwed up my courage and darted into the living room. Snatching a rusted fireplace poker, I yelled, "I'm coming for you, you bastard!" hoping to rattle the ski-mask guy if he were actually still around.

After searching the whole house, it was apparent that the home invaders were gone. But I found Bradley out cold on his bed. His head was haphazardly wrapped in a towel, which was bloodstained. He was breathing, thank God.

Once I elevated his feet with a pillow, I applied ice from his freezer to the swelling on his scalp. He made small noises, but didn't wake.

Too bad the phone I'd found in the bin wasn't a smart phone, or I could've searched the internet for how to deal with an unconscious person. Instead I relied on memory. Let's see… I pinched his thumbnail to see if he responded to harmless pain. An EMT friend told me it was one way to see if someone was really unconscious.

"Ow!" Bradley moaned.

"Hey! Wake up!" I said. "How do you feel?"

"Oh, man," he said. His eyes opened, and he groaned. Then "I feel like shit. What's the…"

His bleary eyes finally focused on me. They widened. "You!"

I wanted to ask him what'd happened, who'd trashed his house and beat him up. But I realized he probably had a few questions of his own. "Yeah, Bradley, it's really me. Weird, huh? Believe it or not, I'm probably more surprised than you."

He tried sitting, but I kept gentle pressure on his chest. I said, "Slow down. You might have a concussion."

He settled back. "Might have? I definitely have one, because I'm talking to a hallucination."

"I'm real. I think. Anyway, I came over to see you, found your house tossed, and you like this."

"Yeah." Bradley sighed, and gingerly touched his head. He said, "You know, last time I woke up feeling like this, I eventually found out you were responsible."

He was talking about the red toolbox to the head. "Uh. About that–"

"The only good thing about being knocked unconscious in the VR lab was that I didn't have to see the bodies. I woke up in a hospital."

The floor seemed to drop beneath me. "Oh, Jesus, Bradley. I had to stop the..." What I wanted to say sounded insane.

"I know, Carter. You explained it."

That made no fucking sense. "Bradley, I don't remember that. I don't remember talking to you. My last memory is of returning to Ardeyn."

"What do you mean, you don't remember?" New anxiety colored his voice.

"I don't remember anything after that day in the lab. Last thing I remember is trying to connect to a version of Ardyen I'd installed over the starting grid. The next thing I remember is waking up about an hour or so ago, lying on a garage floor."

It was Bradley's turn to look confused. More confused, anyway. He said, "How come you're not all dressed up in your, um, superhero costume?"

The question came so completely out of left field that I just stared at him with my mouth open.

"You know," he continued, gesturing vaguely with one hand, "When you showed up last time, a few months after you bashed me on the head. Wearing that black armor made out of... magic runes? It was all freaky and shit. You said something about an inapposite gate being required to throw Ardeyn out of temporal synch with the dimension of normal matter, whatever that means... No?"

"'Inapposite'? I don't even know what that means. I think your concussion is talking," I said.

"Maybe," he agreed. "But if not, then I need to tell you a few things."

"I'm listening."

"Though I gotta warn you, you're not going to like the ending."

"I already don't like the beginning."

He chuckled, then coughed. I gave him some water.

"Hey," he said. "Think you can get me a cup of coffee? A pot's already brewed."

Finding a clean cup was harder than locating the coffee maker, but I finally brought him what he wanted, my anxiety mounting all the while. Had I found Jason, Mel, and the others on the other side after all? If so, why couldn't I remember any of it?

Bradley sipped gratefully, then said, "You were one of the bodies. In the lab. You were good and dead. I attended your funeral."

Why weren't there two bodies, I suddenly wondered? The original me I'd killed, and then the body of the newly printed me that reconnected back. Something must have changed after I'd downloaded Ardeyn into the primordial network. But Bradley was still talking, so I put it out of my head.

He continued, "Then you had the nerve to show up alive and kicking a few months later. Fuck if I didn't think I'd thrown a gasket. After I shat myself, you explained things. You said that you were the one that nearly staved my head in, and explained about the alien network that swallows worlds."

I furrowed my brow, trying to recall any of it, but couldn't. "I said that?"

"You really don't remember? You said that, *and* a whole lot more. About how you'd discovered why there was no evidence of other intelligent life in the universe, and how everyone else on Earth almost learned why, too."

I shuddered. "I don't remember telling you. But it's true, about dark energy – it's a trap. Use computers long enough to hit on the right superposition of qbits, and bam!" I smacked my palm.

"So I gathered."

"But I still don't remember anything else."

He eyed me carefully. "You look like a regular person again. Normal. Last time I saw you, it was more than just the clothes that were different. *You* were different. Fresh-faced, bigger-than-life, and you sort of came across like… I don't know how to describe it. Like you'd just stepped out of a movie, complete with make-up and special effects. It convinced me you'd really come back from the other side."

"Yeah…"

The memory of "printing" to Earth after the initial fiasco was more like a memory of a dream then something that'd actually happened. I hadn't been able to specify clothing, or even oxygen. I'd just asked the limitless processing power of the network to copy and translate "me" back to atomic scale, without understanding a billionth of what was actually happening. Thankfully, it was as if the entire network was designed to do exactly that. Sufficiently advanced technology, blah blah blah: magic. Yeah.

"So, what else did bigger-than-life me tell you?" I asked.

"That our game had installed on a dark energy, um, partition, with nearly-infinite fidelity. By doing so, it created a buffer of specified rules, capable of protecting the Earth from arbitrary attack by things that lived in that network. You called them planetovores. You were so fucking convincing. You made me believe. Of course, when a corpse shows up with a story of alternate realities and portal jumping, it lends credibility to the narrative."

"I remember uploading Ardeyn, mostly. I didn't know if it would work. Did I say how everyone else was?"

"You said the others weren't dead. That they were alive down in the network; Jason, Mel, Alice, and Sanders."

"Oh, thank God." Relief and astonishment made my hands shake. How that could be true, I could hardly imagine, but I desperately hoped Bradley was right.

He took another gulp of coffee, then, "All of you had assumed the roles of avatars in Ardeyn, you explained. Something from our old game, before we came to work with Sanders. Four of you merged with the four of the seven Incarnations. Jason was War, Alice was Silence, Mel was Death, and Sanders was Lore. You reserved the Maker, the creator, for yourself."

"Jesus on a stick," I muttered.

"Sort of. Except the Maker has no son, remember? When we made up Ardeyn's cosmology, we didn't want to replicate Christian theology, except for the especially interesting bits." He laughed, weakly.

I shook my head.

Neither of us said anything for a while. What was there to say?

Except... "Why am I here now, with no memory of being the Maker, or any of this shit?"

"You're asking me?" said Bradley.

"Of the two of us, you're apparently the only one who remembers the last three years."

"Yeah," he said, though he didn't sound so sure. "Maker-you told me to keep tabs on quantum computer research, VR, and look for anything that might lead to a repeat of what we did. Including experiments with particle colliders that reached energies of a specified level. If I saw anything like that, I was to interfere."

"Uh huh," I said doubtfully. "Am I here because you interfered with something?"

"Maybe so. I've been investigating a place called Banks Digital Realty."

"They were looking into quantum computing?" I asked. What was surprising was that more companies weren't doing the same, actually.

"Probably. But I must've somehow shown my hand. Three guys came by yesterday and beat the hell out of me. They wrecked my house for good measure. Probably thought they'd killed me. They didn't realize my skull is practiced in taking hard knocks." He gave me a significant look. Yeah, subtle.

"Who is this Banks?"

Bradley set his coffee down, picked it up again and sipped. "Liza Banks. A reformed con artist turned tech entrepreneur. For the last few months, I've been digging up everything I can about her. I must've slipped up, and she found out about me."

An image of the starting grid made me swallow. My voice tight, I said, "If Banks is messing around with the wrong kind of qbit, we need to–"

"I hired a private investigator to check out the server farm where she's tweaking her hardware. The PI might've found something."

"You told someone else this story, and he didn't have you committed?"

A smile, then, "*She* didn't have me committed. No, I didn't explain why I really put her on retainer. She thinks she's looking for exploits."

I chuckled. "Smart. All right, who's this investigator? We need to talk."

9: CONSULTATION
Katherine Manners

Kate's phone rang. Not recognizing the number, she sent the call to voice mail. If it was important, they'd leave a message.

She glanced at Raul. He was still hunched over his laptop, headphones clapped over his ears and eyes glued to his screen. He hadn't moved since he plugged in the drive three hours ago. She'd offered him a couple of suggestions, one of which he actually took, miracle of miracles.

So she waited, drinking coffee and surfing sites where security professionals discussed the latest hacks, exploits, and vulnerabilities. Unsurprisingly, sys admins were having the same issues they always had: stupidity and human culpability. As entertaining as that was, none of the forum threads had anything to do with spontaneously melting men. She sighed and closed her browser.

Maybe she should contact her client. Despite what she'd told Raul, she hadn't called Michael Bradley after the incident. She'd assumed that Jason and his strange USB stick had nothing to do with what her client wanted. But she'd been bitten by making assumptions before. Maybe Bradley knew something that might lead to a clue about Jason.

Her phone rang again. This time, the name on the display was Michael Bradley. The hair on her arms prickled.

She swallowed, accepted the call, and said, "Hello? Weirdly enough, I was just thinking about you. I have questions about the case."

A few seconds of silence met her greeting, then an unfamiliar voice said, "I doubt you were thinking about me, because I'm not Bradley. I'm a friend of his. Is this Katherine Manners?"

"This is Kate. Who're you? And where's Bradley?"

"Michael hit his head. He's under the weather. I'm calling on his behalf. I'm Carter Morrison. Call me Carter."

Kate's what-the-fuck radar buzzed, but she decided to see where the conversation went. "Heya, Mr Morrison. Nice to meet you. What can I help you with? I see you're using Bradley's phone to make this call."

The man chuckled. "You didn't answer when I called you on my phone, so I tried this one. I'm actually working with Bradley. How're things going with your Banks Digital Realty investigation?"

Having just faked her way into BDR, Kate was sensitive to anything that smelled like the same ploy. And this joker stank of it.

She said, "As I'm sure you appreciate, Mr Morrison, I can't discuss cases with every stranger who claims to be a friend of a client, even when that self-proclaimed friend dials in from a client's number."

"That makes sense," Carter said. The sound of muffled voices came over the connection. Then someone else spoke.

"Kate? This is Michael Bradley. Sorry, I should've told you before. Carter's working with me. In fact, he's the one who first identified the, uh, issues at BDR. Carter asked me to help out, and I hired you."

She imagined this Carter guy holding a gun on Bradley.

"Are you all right?"

Bradley replied, "Well enough. I have a whopper of a

headache though, and bright light hurts my eyes. I hit my head."

He didn't sound scared, just tired. She trusted her instinct to tell the difference, even over the phone. She said, "You hit your head?"

"Stupid household accident. I need to stay off my feet for a couple of days, in case I managed to concuss myself."

"Ouch," she helpfully offered.

Bradley said, "Anyhow, how's the investigation going? Did you find anything suspicious at BDR?"

Kate chewed her lip. What should she say? "Yeah, I found something. But it wasn't an exploit or an unpatched SQL database."

"What was it? Wait, Carter wants to talk."

"Ms Manners?" came Carter's voice again. "You still there?"

"Yeah," she said, and glanced at Raul. His posture was terrible, but he'd come by it through years of similar sitting. With his headphones cranking Chuck Wild, he hadn't even realized she was talking to someone on the phone.

"Bradley says you found something?"

"Yeah," she repeated, wondering how much to reveal. If she told the whole story, Carter would decide she was batshit crazy and hang up.

"What?" prompted Carter.

Kate said, "Nothing to do with servers. In fact, what I saw was a bit... *Twilight Zone*-ish."

She heard Carter draw breath, then, "Try me."

"Well, here's the thing. I met a man who wasn't there."

Silence, then, "Um, what?"

"OK, listen up, Mr Morrison – Carter. In BDR's server room, I saw someone appear out of nowhere. A man with no clothing. He was sick, said a bunch of stuff that made no sense, then he just... melted. What do you have to say about that?"

Excited voices tripping over each other crackled from her handset. Apparently Carter had put her on speaker. Finally Carter shushed Bradley and said, "This... the man... We should meet. There's no time, if people are printing across the boundary. Jesus. I need to get back into BDR, where you found this man. And–"

"Just tell me what the fuck is going on, Morrison."

"Liza Banks got a courier from the other side."

"Other side of what?"

Carter fell silent.

"Before he melted," Kate offered, "Jason said something about giving Liza a ring. Does that have anything to do with–"

"Jason? His name was Jason?" yelled Carter.

"Yeah, that was his name. But–"

Carter said, "Ms Manners, meet me at BDR. Bradley and I will double your pay. Something catastrophic is happening. It's gotta be stopped."

Her palms felt sweaty, but she resisted the urge to rub them on her jeans. "What, specifically, is happening? You're not making any sense."

"No time to explain over the phone. But if Banks got what she wanted from her visitor, her servers are more dangerous than nuclear warheads."

Kate's eyes fastened on the USB ring still protruding from Raul's laptop. "Banks didn't get the information Jason carried. I think I intercepted it."

A man wearing a dark pea coat loitered in the parking structure where Carter said he'd be, even though she was running late. Sometimes a woman needs a bathroom break. Kate parked five cars down.

He was alone. So was she. Raul remained at the coffee shop. Kate had departed so abruptly he'd become suspicious, especially after she reclaimed the flash drive ring. Raul's probably hadn't believed her lame story about having to walk her dog. She didn't have a dog. He probably knew that. She didn't enjoy lying to one of her few friends, but she didn't want to pull him in any more than she already had.

Besides, it was possible, despite Carter's assurance to the contrary, that she really had gone mad. Maybe Bradley had infected her, and Carter had infected Bradley... She didn't want to pass on the crazy to her friend, who was already a bit of an odd duck.

Kate grabbed her pack, left her vehicle, and walked across the garage to the man in the pea coat.

"Katherine Manners?" he said.

She extended a hand. "And you must be Carter Morrison. Call me Kate."

He gave her a quick smile and squeezed her hand. He said, "Do you have Jason's flash drive?"

He obviously wasn't one for small talk. Fine. She said, "Yes. It's yours, after you tell me what you meant by servers becoming nuclear bombs."

Carter frowned. "It's complicated."

"Then let's talk as we go." She motioned him to walk with her.

"I still haven't figured out the best way to explain what's happened. It defies regular understanding."

"Remember," Kate said, "I'm the one who saw a man turn into jelly. I've got an open mind when it comes to this topic."

Carter walked beside her across the parking structure, hands in his coat pockets, eyes down as if searching the cracked cement for somewhere to start.

"So, this Jason guy is your friend?" she offered as they ascended the stairs to level three.

The man winced. But he said, "Yeah. He and I, Bradley, and a few others were doing computer research at the university... three years ago, I suppose. I haven't seen him since. There was an accident."

"Three years? Damn, what kind of accident? Was he irradiated or something, and I saw the result?"

"Not exactly. Actually, I thought he was dead. If you saw Jason walking around, then a whole lot's happened that I don't know anything about."

Kate hoped Carter wasn't playing her. For someone who'd claimed to have all the answers on the phone, he was remarkably out of touch. On the other hand, he was the best thing going when it came to figuring what'd happened in the server room.

They reached level five of the structure, the one Kate was looking for. Before them, an expanse of empty parking spots fronted a blank wall and its single door bearing the BDR logo. A security camera perched above the entrance. A card reader flanked it.

But she didn't advance. She just waited.

"What's wrong?" said Carter.

"Listen, I need to know a lot more than 'yeah, an accident, I'm out of the loop' if you want my help."

Carter pursed his lips, but nodded.

"And," she said, "I need to prepare my kit. I posed as an office plant care specialist to get in last time, but that won't work on the weekend. You talk, I'll get plan B ready."

She set her pack down and rummaged for her card-spoofing shim. She and Raul had cobbled it together a year earlier. She'd been curious if a security reader could be bypassed by manipulating a reader's magnetic field to mimic a legitimate card. She'd about given up, but brought in Raul to see what he thought, and he'd managed to make it work. Raul had a way with electronics that sometimes seemed otherworldly.

"What's that?" Carter said as she produced the ugly thing trailing wires. He crouched down next to her, eyes alight with interest.

"It's our ticket into BDR. I have to calibrate it. But you're the one who's supposed to be talking." She rooted in her pack for a fresh 9V battery.

"All right," Carter said, and took a breath before beginning. "We were trying to improve computer processing power. Radically improve it, in order to render realistic electronic environments on the fly, quickly enough to walk around in them."

"In them?"

"We had a bank of virtual reality rigs. VR-goggles, haptic gloves, hydraulic harnesses, foot-plates…"

Kate imagined the set-up. She said, "Ah. Boys and their toys."

"Right." He grinned. "Plus a few women."

She'd found a package of unopened batteries and sawed at one end with her penknife. "Well, go on."

Carter said, "Peter Sanders, the lead researcher, developed a special chip. With it, he unlocked infinite processing through quantum recursion tunneling."

Kate snorted with disbelief. "Yeah… That's grade-A technobabble."

Carter shrugged. "Maybe. We didn't understand what the Hell we were messing with, that's for sure. And it bit us. We got mapped into a different network. Not just as avatars. Our minds transferred."

Kate plugged the battery into her improvised card-spoofer. The red LED blinked, indicating it was ready to go. But she wasn't. Carter wasn't making sense, which was worrisome. She said, "I don't understand."

He nodded, and said, "Because it doesn't make sense. I can only tell you what I know, which is what happened at the beginning. I have no idea what's happened over the last three years…" Carter's eyes focused past hers.

"C'mon. You can do better than going all emo on me. Spill."

"All right," Carter said. "Listen. This is what happened."

Then he told her a story about a VR experiment gone wrong, superposition chips, how dark energy was actually a trap that eventually claimed every intelligent race in the universe, and how he'd triggered that trap on Earth's behalf three years earlier.

10: ABROGATION
Jason Cole

Jason fiddled with his belt buckle. A lesser relic of Ardeyn, the red leather strap granted extra physical strength if he rotated the strap's buckle to the right, or resistance to psychic prying if the buckle was turned the opposite way. With each flip of the buckle's orientation, an electric tingle danced across Jason's stomach.

Gamma said, "There's a saying about Rome burning and Nero."

"Piss off," said Jason. The impact of Delta's sudden end on the other homunculi had obviously worn off. Jason's highest-grade clones made poor yes-men. He liked to pretend that he appreciated constructive feedback, but in truth, a lecture from a copy wasn't his favorite.

Gamma said, "Not until you get off your ass. Carter Strange might be back–"

"Don't call him that. It's Morrison."

"Whatever. Even if he's back, you can still do something about it. He hasn't reclaimed the Maker's mantle. At least, not yet."

"How do you know?" asked Jason. Anxiety made his voice higher than he intended.

"Because we're still here, instead of being chased by umber

wolves through the Night Vault, or simply eradicated, as *he* should've been."

Jason nodded, letting his gaze wander, pretending that the old fear wasn't racing through him. They stood in one of the tallest towers of his fortress Megeddon. But he didn't really see the landscape of Ardeyn rolling away to the north, or the tumult of the Strange to the south. His mind was fixed on all the possible scenarios the future might bring. Gamma was right about one thing, at least: the Maker, the self-appointed supreme being of Ardeyn, wasn't one for delaying justice, especially against rebel Incarnations like Jason. The Maker could be eying him even now, preparing to dole out justice.

"You think I should, what, make another deal with the kray?" asked Jason.

Gamma spread his hands with a slight shrug. "What else? An instance of Carter is active. Why or how doesn't matter, what matters is finding it."

The thought of dealing with the kray again was almost as terrifying as imagining the Maker showing up unannounced. He said, "I've got enough agents in Ardeyn to track him down without–"

"And what if he popped up on Earth, instead of here? If we finally managed to get someone through, who's to say the Maker, with all his additional resources, didn't manage the same? And maybe with better fidelity. His abilities outstripped ours by an order of magnitude, before we killed him. We *need* the kray on this one."

Jason rubbed his face. Several things could've triggered Carter's return, including Jason's constant probing for a connection with BITER. Hell, the USB stick Jason had made for Banks, with all its recursion programming, might've done it. For all he knew, maybe even something the kray had done precipitated Carter's reappearance.

Jason said, "No, no more kray. I can't afford to–"

"They could give you an entropic seed! Like last time."

The Betrayer blew out his breath. "If I give those alien bastards another inch, who's to say they won't grab a mile? Or everything?" If Jason opened the fences of Ardeyn as he'd done when he'd first betrayed the Maker, the entire Land of the Curse could be erased, including Jason and all his clones.

Gamma said, "If we get what we need from them and act quickly, it won't matter. We'll take back everything the kray steal, and more."

Jason frowned. "Who's 'we'?"

Gamma snorted. "A figure of speech."

"I'm sure. Don't forget who's actual."

Gamma wisely held his tongue. Because he knew, better than Jason himself, that Jason had already decided to ask those fucking kray for another favor. If the Lord of Megeddon was going to survive, he needed to break the rules again, damn the consequences. He needed to be War again, whatever else. That was the only way to be safe. The only way Jason could imagine not being afraid.

Jason descended from the tower, leaving Gamma behind. He made his way to the Xenobiology Foundry. A few reds puttered about the dissection tables, where a breed of burrowing crawler was stretched, skin flayed and its disintegration organ revealed. Upon seeing Jason, the reds set down their dissection scalpels and bowed. At least Delta's retirement was still fresh in *some* of himselves' heads.

"Where's Sigma?" he asked.

"Off-shift," a red mumbled. "Back in a few hours. Um, if you want, we can run a message to him?"

Jason considered. Then, "No. In fact, get lost. I want some privacy."

The reds scrambled to obey. Once Jason was alone, he turned to the cryotanks. Time to unthaw an ambassador from the Strange. Well, no, not an ambassador. The Strange was chaos and strife unending, separating domains unimaginable to humans. The kray were cockroaches in the walls of the cosmos compared to all myriad Strangers cruising the dark energy network. But out there, even cockroaches had access to computational wizardry that would dwarf anything in the so-very-finite domain of Ardeyn. The Seven Rules gave Ardeyn protection, but with that protection came limitations. It was an age-old compromise.

A dark bulk lurked behind the crytotank's frosted glass. A kray captured after its metamorphic "birth" inside Ardeyn was a difficult achievement, unless you didn't care how many clones were lost in the process. Though it took time to grow new homunculi, it'd been worth the investment of flesh.

Jason wished he'd asked one of the reds to remain behind to open the valve on the largest cryotank. The wheel stung his hands with frost. Oh well. He'd heal. And he wouldn't have to slay the red afterward for witnessing the emasculating event that would occur immediately afterward. Asking the kray for help yet again meant trading away more of his autonomy. But to ensure his success, Jason couldn't see any other way.

More than anything else, he wanted a stable connection back to his home, to Earth. Carter created Ardeyn to protect Earth from their bumbling intrusion into the Strange. Somehow, Carter's death unsynchronized the chronology between Earth and Ardeyn, trapping Jason and everyone else in Ardeyn even more completely.

Until Banks and Paldridge made a fumbling step toward actual quantum computing, enough that Jason had been to complete the contact with BITER. Unfortunately, the link was unstable. Making it permanent was his primary goal. And he only had a little time before the chance was lost.

Gamma was right. Jason needed the help only the kray could provide, even though their aid was insanely dangerous to accept. But if he didn't risk it now, he might lose all his future chances.

The raw computational power available to the kray and other entities of the Strange wasn't normally a threat to Ardeyn or Earth. The Seven Rules of Ardeyn fenced out any tampering, no matter how prodigious. But Jason was within Ardeyn's fence. And as someone on the inside, he could let the barriers down, so to speak, enough to accept gifts from those on the outside. In this case, he hoped, another entropic seed of the sort that the kray broodmother incubated.

An entropic seed was a computational spike. A singularity of calculation that approached infinity... Really, it was a magic wish. He'd used one before, when he'd "betrayed" Carter to his death during the Age of Myth. Using a seed was dangerous, because it splintered the protection of the Seven Rules, and broken rules were slow to mend in the aftermath.

But Jason needed one to salvage the situation slipping away from him. With it, he could permanently link Earth and Ardeyn. The power of the seed should allow him to accomplish at least that much. Even if he had to project himself to Earth directly.

With a firm connection, he wouldn't have to race deadlines. He could collect the other Rings at his leisure. He could take his time unlocking the Maker's ancient bastion: the Maker's Hall.

Once in the Maker's Hall, he'd fully revitalize the Rings of Incarnation, starting with his own. He'd be War again! Nothing would ever be able to threaten him again. It was the dream that'd started him scheming in earnest... but now it was almost academic. Because of course he'd also be master of the Hall, equal to the Maker in all ways. All Ardeyn would be his to command. It would be glorious.

He could go home. Return to Earth as he chose. He couldn't wait to meet some *real* people again. It'd been so long since he'd labored in this fantasy realm of caricatures, of make-believe beings. He imagined the sun on his face, a glass of cold IPA in one hand, and a cigar burning in the other, surrounded by friends...

New friends, anyway. All his old ones had turned against him, or were missing. Maybe he could introduce someone new to the idea of root beer floats like he and Carter used to enjoy.

He chided himself on entertaining, even for one second, such a sad, pedestrian, and melancholy goal. He had far grander visions of the future. Nothing would be beyond him, really, as the new Maker. If he wanted to, he could seed a recursion of his own into Strange, one of his own design, not fucking Carter. Maybe a world where demons *didn't* live beneath the crust. Or a world where you could soar through the sky as easily as thinking about it. A new realm. Nothing was too amazing to imagine.

Though even that paled before an even grander possibility. A fresh idea, should he manage to claim the Maker's Hall for his own, tickled him. Why not indeed? Why should he not try his hand at extending his influence into Earth itself? Out "there" in the world of normal matter, he might be able to leverage the computational power of the Strange to amazing ends. Maybe that's all the planetovores wanted to do – escape captivity and transform new worlds...

Either way, better him than them. What's the worst that could happen?

Jason double-checked that his belt was set to protect his mind. Before dread of what lay inside overcame him he grabbed the locking wheel and turned. Ice lanced his fingers. He only tightened his grip and spun the wheel harder, until the door creaked open.

Icy fog spilled out, revealing the carapace of the kray interpreter. Dead eyes stared at him with abyssal hunger.

11: ASPIRATION
Elandine, Queen of Hazurrium

"Elandine," Navar said, "Hazurrium isn't this way."

Elandine owed her First Protector more than royal inscrutability, so she didn't shrug; she reined to a stop in the shade of a date palm. Behind her, the captain, newly promoted after the death of his predecessor, called a halt to the twenty-odd members of the queen's detail. Elandine shifted in her saddle to face Navar on her charger and said, "I know that."

"Then where–"

"We're not returning to Hazurrium."

The qephilim's ears pointed askew from each other in surprise. She said, "And why is that, my queen? I know I don't have to tell you–"

Elandine said, "That's right, you don't. So stop."

Navar rumbled in frustration. "But your sister's internment–"

"Doesn't matter anymore," Elandine said. "See this?" She pointed to the ring snugly fitted to the index finger of her right hand, glowing red like the sunset.

"The Ring of Peace," said Navar, her voice uncharacteristically soft. "You're still wearing it?"

"It's awake," said Elandine.

The First Protector gazed at the queen for several heartbeats.

Then she said, "Your Majesty, you've lost me."

How could Elandine describe it? If she concentrated on the relic, burning letters scrolled across her vision describing wonders she'd thought permanently relegated to a mythical age when the Maker fashioned the world, during the Age of Myth.

Elandine said, "Functions my mother told me were lost may have returned. The Maker could be stirring. Amazing as that is, it's not what excites me. I care only that the Ring is working again. See, I plan on using it to bring Flora back."

Navar gasped. "Back? She's set to be interred into the Path of the Dead. She's in Hazurrium–"

"Navar," Elandine said, "we're going to the Moon Door."

Once every thirty-three days, the moon called Glitter passed between Flare's unblinking light and Ardeyn. When that happened, the moon's shadow was cast across the land beneath. At one spot in particular, Flare's light was blocked completely, so that night kissed the land by day. When that happened, the Moon Door opened.

"But, what... how... you can't!" said the First Protector.

"I can," Elandine said.

Navar got hold of herself and started again. "Even if Peace has remembered ancient functions, the Moon Door lies across a termination zone!"

She raised a hand to object, but Navar plowed on, saying, "What you're really suggesting is stepping through the Moon Door into the Night Vault."

"Exactly." Elandine savored the word.

"If umber wolves don't get you, the Court of Sleep will," Navar pleaded, her voice soft.

"I hold a Ring whose true name is Death. Elder qephilim of the Court will bow to its authority," Elandine said, "as they once did to she who wore it during the Age of Myth."

Navar said, "But you're not an Incarnation. You're a

woman with a magic artifact."

Before she could stop herself, Elandine shouted, "I'll drag Flora's spirit from the night tunnels, even if I have to kill every member of the Court of Sleep to do it!"

The First Protector's ears laid back and her eyes narrowed. But she kept any responses to herself. Say one thing for the First Protector – she knew enough not to push Elandine too much.

Though it was already too late. Anger had stripped away Elandine's earlier exultation, leaving behind smoldering coals. Elandine wanted to hit something. Why did she let Navar bait her?

The queen spurred her horse into a canter toward the black silhouettes that tumbled up over the horizon. They approached the Serpent Hills. It wasn't necessary to convince Navar who was right, or get approval. She only had to prepare the First Protector for what was to come. That, she'd accomplished. Let Navar stew in her wake.

The clopping of hooves on stone meant Navar's charger followed close. The calls of the queen's detail as they saw her sudden departure floated up from farther behind. She understood that from the First Protector's point of view, Elandine's actions were erratic. Her temper only exacerbated that impression. If she wasn't careful, Navar would think that Brandalun's affliction had come to Elandine, too, without the excuse of elderly dementia.

If the queen hadn't cut the conversation short, the First Protector might've brought up another of her favorite ways to chide Elandine. Another duty Elandine had failed to discharge. As queen, Elandine must either bear an heir, or name one. Each time she sauntered off into danger's teeth, Navar broached the topic, directly or indirectly. If Elandine failed to return to Hazurrium, the council would name a regent, and the line of queens of Hazurrium would fail. To prevent that, the shading council would likely name that wench Shari Marana, Elandine's cousin in Mandariel as the new queen.

Elandine spurred her steed to a gallop. Flora would be the heir, or no one. She just had to raise her younger sister from the dead.

Many hours later and some hard riding up a series of switchbacks saw the mounted company to the top of Lobahn Pass. The pass was one of the few easy routes up the southern arms of the Serpent Hills. Full night had nearly descended, and they set camp.

Elandine's sleep was troubled with images of her dying sister, and dawn's creeping orange fingers came too soon. She rubbed the tired ache from her eyes, glad to be rid of dreams of Flora.

Elandine dressed and left her tent. Her detail immediately began striking it. The queen's gaze fell into the plunging valley north of their campsite down to a twisted albino jungle. The sun's morning light limned the steep valley and white vegetation with shades of burning ember. The valley was a termination zone, where the Seven Rules sometimes bent and flowed like hot wax, making it a place only the foolish ventured. At the center of the uncertainty was the Moon Door. Elandine had never been. Her mother, however, had told her daughter the story of exploring the place so many times that it almost seemed as if Elandine had been the one to explore it herself.

"Now what?" said Navar, coming up behind.

"Now," Elandine said, "we chart a path through the zone, steering clear of anything dangerous."

"Then let's avoid the place entirely. Everything down there is dangerous."

Elandine laughed. Now that she was here and no one could deny her, her humor had returned. "Fair point, Protector. But that's our path. If we don't reach the center of the zone by noon, we'll miss our chance for another month. I don't mean to make Flora wander the Night Vault for even another day."

Navar's ears nervously flicked, but she made no response.

They descended on a path steeper and more tortuous than the one they'd ascended, leading their horses instead of riding. Brandalun hadn't described that aspect of the trip. When they reached the valley floor, morning was well along and Elandine was anxious, as well as soaking with sweat. "We've taken too long," she groused.

Pale and tortured trees clogged the valley, twisted by a lifetime growing under fluctuating Rules. They were also tall and strewn with creepers and hanging vines, which meant the central plateau she'd spied from higher up wasn't visible while they were beneath the canopy.

Ignoring the protests of Navar and her new captain, Elandine took the lead. She plunged into the undergrowth, swinging her sword *Rendswandir* to help cut a path. Over the sounds of her exertion, the humid air vibrated with the peculiar calls, some high and lilting, others deep and rumbling. Beasts of the termination zone jungle, she supposed, who would hopefully keep their distance.

Though she allowed herself to be spelled by others in her detail when she grew tired, it seemed to Elandine that their pace was no better than a wandering child's. When they finally broke into the clearing around the plateau, it was with only an hour to spare before totality. Carved stairs and gaping windows wound up the plateau.

The interior was supposedly a wrath haunt. When the spirit of a dead creature fails to find its way to the Night Vault, its fate is to become a bodiless being of rage and loss: a spirit of wrath. A wrath's touch rotted flesh and drained life.

Ribs, femurs, even a few skulls lay about the base of the plateau. Probably the remains of wrath victims who hadn't known to stay away, or who'd been lured by stories of treasure to be found in the Night Vault.

According to Brandalun, the stairs were at least as dangerous a route to the top as the tunnels and galleries that mazed the plateau's interior, because sometimes demons from the deepest places walked them. Meeting a demon on the stair was worse than meeting a wrath in the dark, Elandine's mother liked to say.

Navar pointed to the granite doors half-way around the circumference of the plateau, leading into the interior. The First Protector knew Brandalun's stories as well as the queen.

Elandine shook her head. "No. We don't have time to creep through the unmapped interior. That could take days. If I'm going to make it to the Moon Door on top of the plateau before noon, we have to try the stairs."

A babble of concern drowned out whatever objection lay on the First Protector's lips.

Several soldiers from her detail pointed into the sky. Glancing up, the queen saw a billowing gray cloud blowing in the wind.

Elandine asked Navar "What is it?"

"Bad weather? Unless…"

"Unless it's a breach!" finished Elandine. In places where the Seven Rules were weak, kray sometimes blew into Ardeyn, dispersed by the wind, using long strands of webbing like kites to carry them far inward from the Borderlands, or from a leaking termination zone.

"But there're so many! Hundreds!" barked Navar. "It can't be kray!"

In the queen's experience, no more than half a dozen kray had ever made it into Ardeyn at a time, and the destruction of even so few was an arduous task. On the other hand, she'd never traveled so far into a termination zone before, either.

"It's kray," Elandine said, knowing it with dry-mouthed

certainty. She grabbed the hilt of *Rendswandir* and squeezed the unyielding leather-wrapped metal. What was falling from the sky was nothing less than a catastrophe. Somewhere, a gaping hole had been torn in the protection granted by the Seven Rules.

12: CONFRONTATION
Katherine Manners

"Well, that's insane," Kate told Carter.

She'd finished calibrating the fake security card halfway through Carter's account, right around when the story veered into Lunatic-ville.

Carter shrugged. "I know. If you want off the bus, give me the USB stick. And hand over the card spoofer, too. Please? I'll take it from here. You can wash your hands of the whole thing."

She considered his offer. No one would fault her for leaving, not even herself. Finding Jason had been weird, but Carter's explanation was all kinds of fucked up.

But she said, "What happened next, after you, uh, printed back?"

Carter stuck his hands in his pockets. "I dropped the codebase of my defunct video game down the entangled link, into the primordial network."

Kate shook her head. He'd mentioned the game before, but she still wasn't clear on its significance. "Why the hell do that?"

"The starting grid code wasn't encrypted. It was like a big welcome sign pointing at Earth: 'Planetovores Welcome! All You Can Eat!' I hoped the finished code and its rules would fence out anything not part of the encoded setting. Ardeyn, Land of the Curse."

"Did it? Work, I mean?"

He nodded slowly. "The next thing I remember is waking up in a self-storage unit three years later wondering about my kidneys. Earth's still here, so it must have."

Her finding a melting man in a server room was almost pedestrian compared with the enormity of Carter's story. Kate's brain staggered and skipped, trying to grasp it. "So, someone built that crazy network? Where these planetovores roam?"

He shrugged. "I'm making lots of assumptions, but yeah, based on what I saw looking at the raw code in the starting grid. But a *long* time ago. My guess is that the network was created as a transport system."

Kate tried to imagine a transport system built of dark energy, but failed. She wanted to ask something more incisive. But all she could come up with was, "Really?"

"Maybe. I don't know for sure, but I've been thinking about it, and if it was a transport system, it explains the printing protocols already in place between the real world and the network layer. I didn't just whip that code up out of the whole cloth."

She nodded as if he'd made sense.

Carter pulled his hands from his pockets, mimed grabbing something with two hands, and breaking it in half. "My best guess is that this wonderful, amazing, alien transit system broke. Lots of travelers were stuck inside. Over aeons, terrible things evolved from what was trapped in the network. Desperate to escape, they eventually figured out a way to get out. A terrible way, which is why I came across planetovores. Or maybe planetovores went wrong in the first place." He shrugged. "Either way, based on what I glimpsed in the code, it looks like those things eat civilizations in the real universe of normal matter, every time they find one."

"Why? Why do these things want to eat worlds?" Kate flashed back to reading Jonah and the whale as a ten year-old. In her mind's eye, the whale, already old and bloated, grew with the ages. Over deep time, grew large enough to swallow the entire Earth. She shuddered.

"I don't know," said Carter. "Maybe they're just bad-ass aliens who survived being pulled into the network by earlier waves of planetovores. They could be emergent intelligences of the network itself, or something I can't even imagine. Probably all those things, and more. The dark energy network is *immense*."

Talking to Carter wasn't solving anything, nor were his answers proving to be easy to hear. In fact, the more she heard, the less reassured she felt. So she slapped the flash drive ring from Jason into the hand of the man with the mad story. Then she swiped the spoofed card through the reader. When the security door clicked, she pushed it open and asked Carter, "You coming? I haven't got all day."

Carter nodded, obviously surprised "Thank you." He made as if to go first, then motioned her ahead instead. A good sign, Kate thought – he'd remembered which one of them was trained at breaking and entering.

Ten minutes of sneaking saw them outside the door of a corner office. The frosted glass bore the title: Liza Banks, CEO. A yellow-orange glow filtered through the glass, as well as the sounds of more than one voice.

They put their ears to the door.

After a few moments, Carter whispered, "Can you make anything out?"

She shook her head. A lot of mumbling was audible as of at least two people talking, but nothing sensible. A male voice seemed excited, and another actually did seem a little bit familiar...

The door was yanked open.

"Don't move!" someone yelled. Kate squinted against the unexpected light. The voice belonged to a man with greasy hair holding a gun on her. Fuck. She raised her hands.

The CEO's office was richly appointed. A gargantuan flat screen monitor dominated one wood-paneled wall, displaying gray-white curls of static. An equally gargantuan desk crouched beneath the flat screen on carpet that probably cost more than Kate's annual income. Someone was tied into the desk chair with a bag over his or her head, so Kate couldn't see who it was. That wasn't too creepy.

In addition to the gunman and the captive, the office also contained a pudgy man with a neck beard. Finally, an impeccably put-together woman with horn-rimmed glasses stood near the gunman.

The woman gave a fake, perfunctory smile. She said, "Hello. Took you long enough to get from the garage to my office. Well, come in, but slowly. Don't try anything stupid. Fred has a twitchy trigger finger."

"You knew we were coming?" Carter said. Kate gave him a sidelong glance. Duh.

Fred the gunman gestured with the snub nose of his pistol, and backed away far enough to give her and Carter room to enter. She complied, her mind very much on her own concealed weapon as she shuffled forward. But it wasn't the time for sudden movements.

Carter followed her. They stopped where Fred indicated, along the office's back wall. Kate said in a tight voice, "Liza Banks?"

"The one and only," the woman said. "And you must be the precious detective. And there's the fellow we heard over the garage intercom spinning tall tales. Carter, is it?"

"You heard me?" said Carter. "I didn't see a mic. Maybe that makes things easier."

Liza shrugged, "We were wary already, on account of the other visitor who arrived before you. BDR is a popular destination today. If I'd known, I'd have put out appetizers."

As she spoke, Liza walked over to the captive sitting at the desk beneath the flat screen TV. She pulled off the captive's mask—

"Raul!" Kate yelled.

Raul's sheepish expression was hampered by a few fresh contusions. He said, "Hello, *mi chula*. Who's your new friend?" His eyes flicked to Carter.

As she'd feared, Raul hadn't bought her dog-walking excuse. She cursed herself. She should've said nothing. It would've been less suspicious. But she hadn't expected that Raul'd make a beeline for BDR while she dallied listening to Carter's story.

Liza said, "You know him? Makes sense. Though your coordination is terrible. We caught him trying to jimmy the doors to the executive lobby. We were just getting down to brass tacks, as Fred says, when we heard you on the intercom."

Carter said, "Then you know the danger the dark energy network represents! If you don't—"

Liza raised her hands, saying, "Woah, cowboy, slow down. I heard enough to concern me about your mental health, yes. And that you have something that belongs to me. Hand it over."

Neck Beard looked at Liza. He said, "Hold on. What if there's actually some kind of danger? My last set of tests returned results I frankly can't explain." He gestured to the static on the flat screen, as if that was some kind of proof, and continued, "Whoever this Jason is, he isn't providing us with the full story."

"That's why he sent the flash drive," said Liza with exaggerated exasperation. "He said that'll contain all we need to make the qbit chip and quantum computing a reality."

"You can't trust Jason," Carter intruded.

Fred raised the gun. "You. Shut up."

Carter glared, but shut up.

Kate finally got over the shock of seeing Raul. She said, "What's your interest in quantum computing? Are you trying to corner the market on VR, like Carter was?" The gunman didn't tell her to shut up, maybe because he didn't feel as threatened by a woman. A mistake a lot of men made.

Liza said, "Virtual Reality? Please. Dr Paldridge here," she gestured to Neck Beard, "promised me that his quantum computer would have an absurd amount of processing power, applicable to a wide range of schemes. But only if someone could iron out the difficulties. Someone like himself, with Jason's help. That kind of power could blow through any encryption in seconds."

Kate blinked. A pure money grab, then. She wondered if the woman had ever thought her scheme would come down to hiring gunmen and putting sacks over people's heads. To Kate, Liza Banks seemed nervous beneath her boasting exterior. Probably best not to test her though. Besides, she'd just remembered a story that'd been at the top of the security forums for weeks.

Kate shifted her attention to Neck Beard and said, "Mr Paldridge, is it?"

Neck Beard said "*Dr* Paldridge, but yes."

She continued, "Don't we already have quantum computers?"

Carter shot Kate a surprised look. She ignored him.

Paldridge bit his lip and said, "No."

"Some Canadian company has been selling quantum processors for a while now," Kate said. "I'm sure I just read about it online. D-Wave–"

Liza snorted.

Paldridge gave emphatic shake of his head and said, "Those

D-Wave machines are quantum annealers, not quantum computers. They're not even comparable to ENIAC. They can only solve a small subset of problems, not generalized quantum algorithms. I aim to bridge that gap."

All right then, the man seemed to know what he was talking about. Let's see–

"Enough chit chat," Liza said. "Hand over the device. Get it from them, Fred."

Fred advanced, pressing the gun to Carter's side. Kate instantly understood how Fred had sacrificed the distance advantage a firearm provided. On the other hand, Carter was obviously cowed by the brazen threat.

Carter said. "It's in my coat. That's what I'm reaching for. Is that all right?"

Fred nodded.

Carter's hand inched into the pocket of his pea coat, then emerged just as slowly with something balled in his fist. Kate considered going for her own gun while everyone's eyes were on Carter.

But Carter beat her to the stupid. He twisted suddenly, knocking Fred's gun hand with his elbow, trying to grab Fred's arm.

A gunshot tore through the office, louder than a car crash. Carter gasped, collapsing. The ring dropped from his hand and bounced across the floor.

"You shot him!" Kate yelled. Her ears were ringing, and her own words came out muted.

Liza's mouth hung open a moment in similar shock. She whispered, "Oh. That wasn't supposed to happen."

"What'd you expect?" Fred said. "He had it coming."

Liza swallowed. In a tight voice, she said, "Paldridge, bring me that." She pointed to the ring Carter had dropped. "Fred, see to the man you just shot. If he croaks, I'm shooting *you* next. Damn it."

Kate said again, louder, "You fucking shot him!"

Fred growled at Kate, "Try anything, bitch, and I'll shoot him again." Then he bent to the fallen Carter.

"Let me help," Kate begged. "I promise, I won't cross you." I won't cross you *yet*, she silently added. "I just want to make sure my friend doesn't bleed out."

Fred looked at the bleeding man, and seemed suddenly out of his depth. A second later, he motioned her over. She crouched next to the stretched-out Carter. A red stain was blooming on his upper chest beneath his shirt. Kate hoped it was "upper" enough that the bullet missed anything too vital...

Paldridge had gone pale and shaky, but he retrieved the ring as Liza requested and examined it in his cupped palm. The big costume jewel caught the light. He pulled the removable section from the ring and said, "What an odd flash drive."

Kate didn't have time to explain the extraordinary circumstances by which she'd come by the ring. She was too busy applying pressure to a bullet wound. She yelled at Fred, "Get a first aid-kit!"

Fred gave her a disinterested stare, but eventually said, "There's one in that closet." He pointed. "Get it yourself."

As Kate tried to explain how that'd require her to let up pressure on the wound, an electronic squeal howled from the wall-mounted display.

Another whine like tires spinning on asphalt followed it. The static cleared – not quite completely – revealing a man. He wore some kind of bulky black suit. Was it iron armor? Interference made everything jaggy. When the man spoke, his voice sounded as if it echoed up from a well. Kate couldn't understand him.

Banks went to the desk and fiddled with the keyboard of her computer. She said to the image, "Jason, you're breaking up. Please repeat."

Jason? Kate studied the monitor. The interference made it hard to tell, but the man did have brown eyes. But she'd seen him melt!

The figure said, "You've created the bridge. Congratulations. But it's a shaky connection, and I need you to finish the process I outlined to you. Why haven't you done it already?"

The CEO walked into view of the blinking camera over the monitor. She said, "Someone stole the flash drive. This woman," she pointed to Kate, "and her friend. But we've got it back. Dr Paldridge is going over it now."

Paldridge started. He said in a hesitant voice, "Uh, yes. Everything looks to be in order. Preliminarily, of course. I'll have to download and read through the specs. I imagine we'll want some modifications, based on what I find."

Jason wasn't looking at Paldridge. His eyes, fixed on Carter's bleeding form, grew wider every second. He suddenly screamed over Paldridge's ramble, "I *knew* it! Fucking Carter Strange, back in the flesh."

"He got shot," Liza offered, obviously unhappy at the admission.

"Really?" said Jason. "I doubt that'll keep him down for long. Or another one just like him, if this one croaks off. Thank the Maker I prepared for this contingency. Banks, put on the ring. Quick!"

"What? Why?" she said, confusion and perhaps a bit of caution in her voice. "What would that accomplish?" She glanced down at Carter, eyes narrowing. Kate imagined the woman was reviewing what she'd heard of Carter's story.

But she held out her hand to Dr Paldridge, who relinquished the ring to her waiting palm. Liza held it up before her, gazing through the circle of the band.

"Put it on," Jason repeated. "It's not as elegant as I'd planned, but that's why I talked to the kray."

Liza said, "Cray? The supercomputer company? You

promised no dealing behind my back, Mr Cole!"

Jason cocked his head, then chuckled. "No, never mind. You're still my first choice for business partner, Ms Banks. I need you to put on the ring because in order to unlock the flash drive, the ring needs a biometric signature." He grinned, unconvincingly, Kate thought. If Kate'd been the one holding the ring, she would've thrown it.

"Fine," said Liza. But she didn't put on the ring. Instead she hastened to where Raul was quietly taking in events from the comfort of his restraints.

"Hey!" Raul protested, leaning away as far as he could as Liza brandished the ring at him. "Stay back. If you're proposing, I don't accept!"

Liza spun Raul's chair around. After a bit of finger wrestling with the cuffed man, she forced the ring over the first knuckle of one of his fingers.

Raul stiffened as if the ring was electrified.

Kate launched herself to her feet. But the cold steel barrel of a gun in her side checked her mad dash.

"What's happening to him?" Kate yelled at the monitor.

"That ring is very special. Here in Ardeyn, it was once one of seven. Now it's merely a bridge. A way to make connections. That's what Desire promises, after all." He laughed. "So I'm using it to come across to see you," said Jason. Then static washed away the image.

Raul convulsed. He screamed. His head snapped back, and his eyes lit with pale blue fire.

Everyone in the room flinched back.

Raul slowly relaxed. He lowered his regard until he fixed Liza Banks with a burning gaze lit with evolving fractal sparks. He said, in Jason's voice, "It's a cliché, but true: if you want something done, you've got to do it yourself."

13: POSSESSION
Jason Cole

The pudgy computer scientist and Liza Banks inched away from Jason, almost trampling Carter, who blinked stupidly on the carpet. A circle of blood swelled by slow inches beneath him. And it *was* Carter. Jason could scarcely believe it. He'd been Jason's bogeyman for decades... Now look at him. Shot and dying, and Jason hadn't lifted a finger to put him there. It was bittersweet, how much he missed what they'd once been, and how much he'd come to hate and fear him later. Now he was about to expire.

Carter was obviously far less dangerous than the gunman, who couldn't decide if he should be pointing his weapon at Jason, or at a red-haired woman wearing a coal-black business suit–

The woman is Kate Manners, whispered a voice in his head. Then, *Who are you? What's going on with–*

Jason viciously suppressed the voice. The vessel knew things Jason didn't, but allowing it any autonomy would risk compromising his own control. It wasn't like he really knew what he was doing. The most recent aid he'd begged from the kray allowed him to make this crossing, but that didn't mean he understood how it worked. Thanks to the kray ambassador's entropic seed, he was "installed" in a human mind, but he didn't know for how long and just what his abilities were, if any.

Liza Banks *should* have been the vessel. But she hadn't put the ring from Ardeyn on her own finger, damn her, and now his hands were tied. Literally.

"Banks," he said, directing his gaze at BDR's CEO. "Untie me. Before Carter gets back on his feet."

Banks stared at him as if he'd sprouted a second head. Which wasn't far from the truth, he supposed.

"Raul?" said the woman his vessel had named as Kate Manners.

Jason ignored her. His initiative was crumbling; he had to get out of the bindings–

Raul surged with renewed fervor to throw Jason out. Jason had expected the vessel to remain stunned and uncomprehending while Jason rode him. But Raul wasn't having it. Keeping control of the body, and more importantly, the mind, was like trying to stand still in a hurricane.

Focus, Jason told himself. He visualized Raul as a tiny point of light, and his own control as an evening darkness. The light pulsed and flitted, but Jason finally caught it. It just required concentration. Then he flooded the vessel's bloodstream with adrenaline. The man's muscle fibers contracted with more than normal strength. Ligaments and fibers screamed. But the restraints, actually only a sweater someone had found to tie Raul down, tore with a snarl.

Jason stood, tossing aside the shredded polyester. He said, "Now then, as I was saying–"

The gunman turned tail and banged out through the office door. His footfalls receded in the corridor.

"That makes things easier," Jason said, a grin stretching the corners of his mouth. "I would've been pissed if my triumphant return was interrupted by a mook with a .45." No one knew Jason's limitations, and if he played his cards right, they never would.

Liza grabbed Dr Paldridge's shoulder, but her eyes never left Jason. She said, "Do something!"

"Um," said Paldridge.

Jason cracked his knuckles. "You can't put me back in a bottle, Ms Banks. But don't worry, I'm not staying long. Nor am I welching on our deal. I still owe you the secret to true quantum calculation. The time congruence between Ardeyn and Earth will slip if we don't fashion a stronger anchor. If that happens, you get nothing."

"Time congruence?" repeated Banks. She looked at Paldridge. The pudgy man opened and closed his mouth like a carp out of water.

"Never mind." Jason removed the ring and gave it a once-over. It was like Desire, yet unlike. It was no longer a Ring here on Earth. But it'd made the transition, and survived it, unlike his own clone. Jason twisted the translucent jewel to reveal the USB plug.

"Hold it! Don't move, Raul!" came the voice his vessel instinctively responded to: Kate Manners. Jason glanced up. Sure enough, Kate had brought a gun of her own to the party.

"I'm not Raul," he said.

"Jason, then," Kate replied. "I tried to help you before, when you were sick. In the server room. And you repay me by, by..." She shrugged, but the gun barrel remained trained on him. "... hijacking my friend?"

"Whoever you helped, it wasn't me," Jason said. "It was just an instance. Disposable."

"An instance?"

"Like a computer program running in multiple partitions simultaneously," Jason said. "Or you can think of the version of me you met before as a clone." Jason sang out, to the tune of I Think We're Alone Now, "I think I'm a clone now. There's always more of me running arou-ound."

No one laughed. He blinked. Why'd he done that? He was

supposed to be scaring these people, not serenading them.

"Ooo-kay," said Kate. "So, you're a clone, too, right?"

"No, I'm the original. My mind's entangled and translated here, not duplicated. The clone you met was Zeta, one of my lieutenants. Just between you and me, Zeta was always a bit too wishy-washy. Clones sometimes amplify my own most disagreeable traits. Happens like that sometimes."

Raul's inner voice said, *Chatty fellow, aren't you?*

He *was* oddly talkative, Jason thought. What had gotten into him? He rubbed his eyes. Maybe he was just hungry. Or Raul was. Either way, he decided the very next thing on his plate would be to order pizza. Pizza! His mouth watered at the thought of melting cheese, crisp garlic crust, and juicy slices of pepperoni. Right after–

"I helped your, um, clone when it needed a hand," said Kate, interrupting his train of thought. "Help me now – let go of my friend Raul."

Jason regarded Kate. Despite the gun she held on him, he liked talking to her. It was exhilarating. He hadn't really talked to another human being other than himselves for... he couldn't remember the last time. The kray certainly didn't count. Being cut off from Earth and living as a shadow of a broken Incarnation in Ardeyn for two hundred and some years had a way of changing a man. Maybe his aims *had* become too skewed, too fixed on revenge. Maybe–

The vessel's mind leaped for control, and knocked Jason aside. "Kate!" Raul said, "Shoot me! In the leg. Shock this *hijo de perra* out of my head!"

Jason reasserted control, forcing Raul back into silence, though not completely so. Raul was proving far more adept at resisting possession than should've been possible. Was Jason's erratic behavior – singing about clones, for fuck's sake – due to Raul's struggles? If so, then it wasn't going to stop until Jason vacated.

That give him an idea. Jason put up his hands and said, "No, hold on, don't shoot me, I'm back in control. Jason's gone!" How much he sounded like Raul, Jason wasn't sure. He'd heard the man's Mexican accent when he'd briefly reasserted control, and tried to duplicate it. An accent like that would be easy to overdo. But he only had to fool the woman for a few seconds.

Kate lowered her gun a fraction. "Raul?"

"Yes," Jason agreed. "And I know what to do." He leaned forward and slammed the USB stick into Liza Banks's laptop.

"Hey!" yelped Kate and Dr Paldridge almost simultaneously.

Kate continued, "You said that thing was crawling with malware! How do you know Banks's computer is isolated from the web?"

"I'm counting on the opposite," Jason replied. Glee stretched a circus clown grin across his stolen face.

Kate's gun snapped back into position. "Take it out," she ordered. "Now!"

Jason laughed. "Autorun code activated the moment I inserted the drive. It's too late! Shoot me if you want, kill your friend in the process, I don't care. I'll just skip town, so to speak. Meanwhile, the information I want to release is already self-propagating!"

Liza Banks said, "Wait, what? That wasn't the deal. Only Paldridge and my people at the institute were supposed to get that!"

"You and your friends have everything you need, Liza," said Jason. "Which is a head start. You'll get there first. Probably. Stable qbit chip production is something I can't rely on just one outlet for. If your institute friends fumble it, I'm screwed. So you have, at most, a few months before the worm I uploaded becomes active, after it's spent ninety days or so propagating all over the net. After that, who knows how many people will be able to make quantum computers according to this particular specification? I only need one to succeed."

And bridge the gap into the Strange, he didn't say. Once a translation gate connected Earth and Ardeyn, he could bootstrap that into a matter gate – a gate that would allow him to return to Earth in the full glory and majesty of an Incarnation. Or maybe even as the Maker, if all his plans came–

"Jason," a voice whispered, this one not in his head. It was Carter! The man was sitting up, looking at him. "Don't do it. I don't know what's happened to you, but do you really want to destroy your home? Do you really want to end the human race?"

Jason felt a moment of guilt, but anger washed that away. "Carter, I just want to say, fuck you. You've had this coming for a couple of hundred years, my time. From the perspective of War, whose Ring you gave me, you've actually had it coming for *thousands* of years! So let me assure you: revenge is sweet."

Carter said, his voice weak, "You know what's out there, in the dark energy network. Why are you doing this?"

"Because I want to be War again. You don't know what it's like… I want to be War without a master – the Maker – to call me to heel."

"But the dark energy–"

"Call the network what we decided on: it's the Strange. Just like what people in Ardeyn started calling you. Carter Strange, the Maker."

Carter only looked confused.

Could it be? Did the dying man before him have no memory of becoming the Maker? Fuck! Jason wasn't really getting his revenge. At least not directly. The disappointment was so palpable he almost felt slapped. Was this just a copy of Carter, one who hadn't fucked him over by trapping him in Ardeyn?

That's when Raul's mind struck again, stronger than ever. Jason's control slipped.

Ardeyn isn't the only world seeded in the Strange, whispered Raul's silent voice. *Other recursions exist. One is older than even humans. It's where I'm from. Ardeyn isn't alone in the dark energy network. And we won't let you destroy what we've spent so long cultivating.* With that came a mental jolt filled with images of an alien world the like of which Jason had never imagined.

"I don't understand," said Jason, or tried to. Instead, he lost his grip on Raul's struggling psyche. Entangled particles yanked him away, back down into the primeval network.

14: Emigration
Carter Morrison

"Jesus, I'm shot," I said, for the second or possibly twelfth time. The horrifying sensation of hot blood pouring down my back from the exit wound was worse than the excruciating burning below my collarbone. I was absolutely *going to* die. I knew it like Stephen King knows what lurks under the bed.

Kate yelled at the pudgy scientist, pointing with her gun barrel, "You! Help Carter. Put pressure on his wound."

Paldridge took a couple of hesitant steps toward me.

Banks announced, "I'm calling the police."

Kate's aim shifted a few millimeters, putting the CEO in her sights. "Don't, or we'll have two gunshot wounds to deal with," Kate said.

Banks swallowed, eyes fixed on Kate's unwavering pistol, and stayed where she was, wringing her hands and scowling. How'd this woman get caught up in Jason's crazy scheme?

Kate shifted her attention to the guy Jason had puppeted. Raul? Grayness around the edges of my thoughts made it hard to think. Paldridge distracted me from hearing what Kate told him because he started tearing strips from his lab coat and tying them around my wound.

"You're going to be all right," he said.

"I don't know what 'all right' means to you, but this isn't

it," I said. Even to my own ears, my voice was tremulous.

Kate led Raul over to where I was slumped. He was surprisingly unfazed by everything and even assisted Paldridge in completing my field dressing. Kate kept her eye on Banks.

When they finished wrapping me, I felt weaker than ever, but at least the jacket slowed the bleeding. On the other hand, blood was already soaking the bandages. The creeping redness coincided with a cold feeling in my stomach, inching larger every minute, turning me to ice...

"I'm going to pass out," I said, deciding at the last second to keep the conviction of my imminent death to myself. "So we need to figure out some stuff before that."

Kate's brow furrowed. "And we need a drink. Anyone but me need a drink? I mean..." Her eyes scanned down to my upper chest. "Sorry." The PI's face colored slightly.

"Raul, give me the ring," I said, "the one Ms Banks gave you."

Raul started, then hastily removed the band. He glanced back over to the laptop on Banks's desk. "The USB end is still plugged in. You want that too?"

"It's already done its damage," I said, "but yeah, I need the whole thing."

Raul moved to the laptop as Kate said, "You're going to the hospital, nothing else. Based on the amount of blood that's already come out of you, I'm surprised you're not already dead. Banks is right about one thing, anyway; we've got to call 911."

Manners wasn't wrong about the blood. Someone who'd lost as much as I had shouldn't be walking and talking. Maybe this printed version of me was tougher than Carter 1.0? Intriguing idea. But even if true, me 2.0 had shown himself not to be bulletproof.

"So, someone was in my head..." Raul poked at his temple. "Know anything 'bout that, amigo?"

"Yeah," I said. "Kate can fill you in with the whole story, but short and sweet: dark energy is a sea swarming with hungry sharks. When someone switches on a truly quantum computer, it's like dumping a bucket of chum over the side of your inflatable life raft. It's only a matter of time before something hungry swims up."

Raul nodded in recognition. "Yeah. That's about right." What an odd reaction.

Paldridge said, "What? That makes *no* sense. He's jabbering. Unless–"

Raul punched the scientist. Paldridge stumbled backward, yelping in surprise. His heels caught a carpet edge. He fell on his butt, and glared up at Raul, rubbing his face. But he shut up.

The gray haze thickened across my vision. I was just about out of time. "The ring!" I croaked.

"Here," said Raul. He clicked the two parts of the ring together and pressed it into my palm.

I examined it. It was eerily familiar, like something I'd glimpsed in a dream once. But I couldn't place it. According to Kate Manners, the band had printed to Earth along with Jason's first envoy. Which meant it was an artifact of Ardeyn. It was made of baryonic matter, but it was entangled with a world beneath the world.

That made the ring a sort of golden ticket. Maybe I could use it to try what Jason had just done, but in reverse. I had to stop Jason. And maybe save myself in the bargain, because me 2.0 wasn't long for the Earth.

I whispered, "Kate, Raul. Paldridge and Banks, you too. Clean up what Jason put out on the internet. Scrub it, and stop whoever tries to duplicate it."

Kate rubbed her eyes. "If it is a virus, or a worm like the one that took out those uranium enrichment centrifuges in Iran–"

"Idiot," snapped Banks. "He uploaded schematics for how to construct a quantum computer. *My* schematics!"

I didn't know if I could convince Liza Banks of the danger she was in. She wasn't interested in absorbing evidence that ran counter to her agenda. People get like that. When they do, they resist changing their minds, too invested in their old ideas, mistaking those ideas as a part of themselves. I was too mortally wounded to try to talk her to my way of thinking.

So I turned my attention to Kate and Raul, and said, "Banks is right about schematics, I'm guessing. The problem isn't merely a traditional computer virus or worm, it's the knowledge the worm contains. Knowing how to improve current quantum processor technology is most of the way to building one. Make sure that knowledge doesn't get out."

Banks cocked her head and butted in, asking, "You want us to become, what, code busters?"

My instinctive laugh at the term "code buster" became a cough. Banks was obviously not a technical person. When I got my spasming lungs under control, I said, "If you care about safeguarding yourselves, your friends, everyone – the whole Earth and everything on it, you'll do what I say."

"Right," said Banks in a speculative tone. She'd gone from angry to looking vaguely concerned.

I'd about run through my strength. Talking was done. Hopefully, they'd do what I said. Ultimately it wouldn't matter if they found every bit of loose code describing "superposition best practices" if, in the meantime, Jason brought on Ardeyn's apocalypse, collapsing the recursion. Without Ardeyn as a buffer, Earth would be exposed to the Strange, to the direct connection we'd unwittingly created three years ago. So my job was to stop him.

I fumbled on the ring. The numbness spread from my stomach, reaching all the way to my fingers and toes. I closed my eyes and pitched back. Hands might've caught me, or maybe not. Cold was the only sensation, except for the tingle of the ring around my finger, hot as a coal. I concentrated on it, and let the cold claim everything else.

A chasm opened beneath me. I fell into an abyss with sides as sheer as scissor blades.

15: SUSPICION
Katherine Manners

Kate watched Carter Morrison disappear. No sci-fi sparkle of lights or musical chord. Just blink, gone. Except for all the blood he'd left behind. That, and the ring.

She retrieved it without thinking. A spark of static electricity stung her palm, but she didn't let it go.

What the fuck had Carter meant about scrubbing out knowledge? He should know it was virtually impossible to remove information from the internet. When people were wounded and the oxygen to their brain slowed, they got confused. Except now she was the one who was confused. Maybe she'd taken a bullet, too, and hadn't realized it in the excitement. Kate started a visual inspection of her extremities, just to be sure.

"*Mierda*," whispered Raul. "Carter can translate. I wouldn't have guessed."

"*Translate*?" said Kate. "What's that mean?"

Raul pointed at the empty spot where Carter had been. "He can move between recursions by willing it. And so quickly!"

Oh, shit. Kate put the ring in her pocket almost absentmindedly. Now Raul was going funny, too. "Translate? Recursions? Explain that. Explain how you *know* that. Or... am I still talking to Jason?" She leveled the gun at her friend, wondering if any answer out of his mouth could satisfy her.

16: DECEPTION
Elandine, Queen of Hazurrium

A thick veil of blowing web strands settled across the jungle canopy. Each strand supported a single dark kernel. And each kernel, Elandine knew, would sprout a ravenous kray.

The descending mass's leading edge passed overhead, and she, Navar, and her entire detail came under its shadow.

"We're beneath it!" screamed the First Protector.

"Maker preserve us," breathed Elandine.

Even riding full out, they couldn't escape the krayfall. A few peacemakers tried anyway, spurring their steeds into a confused gallop across the broken plain, away from the plateau.

The poor fools were already dead, thought Elandine. Maybe she was, too, and all who stood their ground with their queen. Except she wore Death. It would suffice, or nothing.

Elandine raised her fist. On it her hope flashed. She concentrated on the Ring of Death, and a response stirred within its dark coil. It flashed like a black star, opening a sliver of its power to her. She flinched, as the shade of Death brushed past her. But what else had she expected?

Elandine called upon the serene stillness of the grave, inflating that quiet until it swept away up and around her. The descending kray seedlings passed through it, freezing solid. They pattered down around the queen and her host like hail, creating a perfect white circle at their feet. The visage of Death stared at Elandine with its lidless eyes, then faded. Profound tiredness sapped her breath, as if she'd just run a mile at a full sprint.

"Crush them!" gasped Elandine, ignoring the lassitude brought on by triggering the Ring. "Sweep them away. Quickly, before they thaw!" She brushed the rigid things from her garments and armor, stomping. Around her, peacemakers followed suit with barely-controlled alacrity.

The casements of the kray seedlings popped and cracked beneath her boot heels. She wasn't sure it was necessary – they might already be dead. She'd imprinted one of the Seven Rules directly upon them: in Ardeyn, all things are subject to Death. Amazing, really. She'd wiped the things out of the air, just by willing it! Death had done Elandine's bidding. It boded well for when she'd need that power to extract her sister from the Court of Sleep.

The queen's gaze swirled past the white zone of dead invaders, and her flicker of exhilaration blew out. Except in the relatively small zone around her, the seedlings had found purchase everywhere. They were surrounded. Kray scurriers were already shrugging out of discarded skins of bark, feathers, grass, moss, rabbits, and from the skins of the few men who'd tried to get away. An army of Strangers was popping up all around them, more than she ever would've thought possible. She and her detail had escaped instant death, but it wouldn't matter in another minute as the newborn kray converged.

"I'm sorry, my queen," murmured Navar. The First Protector knew the score as well as she.

"As am I, dearest friend." Fear, heady and fierce, tasted like acid in her throat.

A sea of monsters besieged them, roaring, slashing, spinning webs, and snapping their pincers. They twirled and surged like the surface of Oceanus or, Elandine realized, like dancers conveying the essence of Strange itself, twisting and repeating patterns beyond knowing. A kray along the front reared up, its carapace green and glistening as a favorite candy sold by Hazurrium street vendors, and gave voice to a trumpeting challenge that curdled the air. The sound was like nothing Elandine had ever heard or imagined.

But the pincered army remained outside the line of dead seedlings. Why?

"Listen," she said, hardly a whisper. "Listen to me!" she tried again, her voice louder as she pointed. "See? They fear to cross the line scribed by Death, and for good reason. Form up! We're not dead. Far from it. To me!"

The kray didn't know the boundary meant nothing. The effect she'd generated with the Ring was long gone. Given how tired snatching at Death's mantle had made her, she couldn't repeat the effect anytime soon. But she forced herself to stand tall, to look confident. To be their queen.

Soldiers' eyes were fixed on Elandine like she was an oasis in the desert. They wanted to believe survival was possible. They just needed a reason. All she had to do was provide one. Simple. And in turn, her dismay lessened as their anxiety fell away. People are eager to find hope. Including her.

The soldiers formed the lines and defensive groupings that'd been drilled into them, creating a defensive circle, facing outward. They were trained by Hazurrium's finest.

"The shells are moving." Navar's ears flicked sideways. It didn't need saying, of course, everyone could see it. A handful of kray among the thousands advanced on the boundary, and more lined up behind them. They weren't in a hurry. They came on stiff and steady, pincers held ready before them, eyestalks on Elandine.

Lines of webbing flapped over their heads. Strands that could cut through the Seven Laws like knives, before they finally burned away. She wondered how many web strands the army of kray could spin. Could such a large force cocoon the entire capitol city in their gauzy strands, and steal it away into the Strange? Imagining it made her feel sick. She sucked in a long breath. The battlefield was no place for distraction, her mother always said.

It was for killing. "Ashurs ready," she yelled, lifting her palms to the sky. The soldiers around her lifted their battle staves, sigils snapping with deadly soulmancy.

The advancing kray exploratory party didn't falter, or lose a step.

"They're not scared," muttered a woman with an ashur raised before discharge. More's the pity, thought Elandine. A human or qephilim company would flinch at walking into the sights of twenty-some battle staffs. But the kray didn't think like humans. They were of the Strange.

"Fire!" commanded Navar.

Rune ashurs spit death spells into the advancing horde with a sound like thunder. Kray carapaces shattered, ooze sprayed, and several gaps appeared in their line, here and there. But more advanced, trampling their fallen kin. Some of the replacements were noticeably larger than the fallen scurriers who'd advanced in the first rank.

Elandine frowned. An ashur sipped vitality from its wielder's soul, but in the face of the advancing sea of enemies, peacemaker strength would give out first. The shells had them outnumbered fifty to one.

She called, "Conserve your strength – choose your targets!"

Navar pointed, directing her attention to the side. A particularly massive specimen trundled into view, a kray the size of a small house. Frightened cries sounded around her. Ashur beams caught and sparked on the monster's carapace. It stumbled in the face of the onslaught, but came on.

"Maker, preserve us," she prayed, not for the first time. As if the Maker had ever heard or responded to a single entreaty in the history of Ardeyn…

She half believed stories about the Maker were just that – tales for children and credulous adults. Then again, she had Death. The heirloom ring was supposedly the Maker's gift to the first of her line. If she didn't believe in the myth of the Maker, why was she here with one of his implements? Why make for the Moon Door and attempt to petition the Court of Sleep if she didn't believe the Maker made it? The Ring of Death was tied to the Maker. A Maker who might have returned, given the Ring's newfound strength. Maybe all that was required was a petition of a different sort. A prayer from a believer willing to take a chance on a vanished god. If he would answer anyone, why not the descendant of one of his ancient Incarnations?

"Maker!" she screamed, Ring held before her. The behemoth kray lumbered closer. More ashur beams licked it, but their effects seemed less telling each moment.

"Maker, hear me. I am Queen Elandine of Hazurrium, and I pray for your aid! If you care at all for what you wrought, now is the time to intervene. If you've returned, show it. Help me!"

The Ring warmed on her finger. A bolt of pale light sparked into the sky like a flare, rising so high that it must've passed out of Ardeyn and into the Strange beyond. She gasped. The peacemakers stopped fighting and the kray paused. Even the big one hesitated, its eyestalks bending upward to take in the glowing trail.

A handful of seconds trickled past. One of the peacemakers pointed skyward. "There!" he yelled.

A creature soared overhead, leaving a streak of fire behind. It was like a lion wearing a metallic human mask, with eaglelike wings scratching the sky – a dlamma! They were rarely seen, and everyone who saw them counted it as a good omen.

The dlamma winged closer, revealing its rider. Black armor limned with glowing red designs covered the rider like a bulwark.

"Can it be?" yelled Navar. "The Maker?"

Elandine's breath caught.

The dlamma raced just above the snapping pincers of the shells. The creatures jostled each other as they leaped and sprayed webbing at the interloper, but the flyer moved too quickly for projected strands to catch it. The rider leaped from the saddle when the dlamma was still dozens of yards away. The dlamma flew on up, but the dismounted rider fell into the circle where Elandine stood. The ground shook and earth sprayed up in a cloud where he touched down. Peacemakers backed away from the newcomer, who remained as he had landed: down on one knee in the center of the crater of his own making. The kray were agitated, but didn't resume their attack.

Elandine swallowed. She'd prayed to the Maker… and he'd come. The builder of Ardeyn was before her. Unbelievable. His armored form hinted that he was man, not a qephilim, as some thought he must be. She moved closer.

"Thank you," she said, her voice hoarse, "for answering."

The figure finally rose. The helm covering the Maker's face was bestial and horned, save for the scarlet lines that glowed almost like fiery tears from his eyes, matching the flame burning on his staff, which he held in one hand. She'd never seen a likeness of the Maker before, but if she'd tried to guess how he might've looked, this wasn't it.

"Hello, Queen Elandine," came a male voice, normal as anything. "I'm here to help."

He turned to face the swarm of kray. Tired of waiting, they surged forward again.

Ashurs came up to shoulders, burning a new volley of webbing to cinders before most of the lines could reach the defenders. A few still got through. Cords touched the shoulders, the hands, and the boots of the queen's detail. Victims screamed in unbelieving pain. Louder yet came the Maker's roar as he raised his massive staff of black and red iron that burned. He dashed straight past the peacemakers, into the advancing kray, toward the behemoth. Trying not to think about what she was doing, she raised her own sword and charged down the lane the Maker had created with his passage. "For Hazurrium!" she screamed.

She slashed a few kray as she ran, but those closest to the Maker's path were mostly shattered and dissolving. Ahead of her, he waved the massive stave around as if it weighed nothing. Impressive, but nothing compared to what he did next.

The Maker split into more than a dozen duplicates! The newcomers flowed from him like water from a tap, each one armored in red or in green, none black like the Maker. In seconds, a small army of at least thirty Makers swept out through the sea of kray, fighting, killing, but also falling, and dying, and crying out in their own voices of pain. The Maker stopped spawning copies when he reached the behemoth. Battle was joined.

Elandine accounted herself an able swordswoman, especially given the power in her relic blade. But the man before her knew warfare like she knew the back of her own hand. Better. It was nothing short of magic.

She realized she'd stopped fighting. She closed her mouth and renewed her advance. As she did, the behemoth lashed out. The Maker grunted as he deflected a pincer the size of a dragon's wing on his burning staff. He spun away to smash an elbow into a normal-sized kray that'd slunk up behind. The thing's shell crunched through like a pastry.

"Watch out!" Elandine yelled as the behemoth's second pincer slammed down. He almost avoided it, rolling up and away through the air like an acrobat on a wire. Given his armor, such a move was a miracle in its own right. But not miraculous enough. The pincer clipped him with a sound like a hammer to the blacksmith's anvil.

The Maker went down. Elandine snapped out *Rendswandir* without thought, severing the pincer as it descended on the fallen warrior. Then the Maker was up again, fighting.

Together, over the course of a hard-fought minute, they brought the behemoth down.

"Thank you for that," the Maker offered, ever so slightly out of breath. She said, "I doubt you required it," then wished she'd stayed quiet.

Around them, the kray were dying. Her peacemakers, bolstered by the might of the Maker's red and green-hued avatars, were winning the day. Losses were steep, but it seemed clear the kray would be defeated. The few remaining just didn't realize it yet. It wasn't in their nature to retreat.

"So," she ventured, trying to read the Maker's visage, looking for eyes behind that armored helm to focus on. "Should I call you Maker?"

The head jerked to regard her. Then laughter echoed from the suit. Finally he said, "You might, you might indeed. And you have my thanks, truly. That thing might've actually had my ticket if you hadn't distracted it. You're quite the warrior, Queen Elandine."

"You're too generous."

He shrugged, his armored shoulders magnifying the movement. "Could be, could be. But enough. Do you have the Ring? I need it, if we're going to fix all this."

"Peace?"

"Death."

Elandine nodded, and lifted her hand. A feeling of lightness filled her up. She was in the presence of the Maker! He was real. He would fix things... he would help her get her sister back!

"There it is," said the Maker, his voice gleeful.

Elandine said, "With this, I could enter the Court of Sleep. My sister died. It wasn't right. With Peace – I mean, with Death, and you returned..." Elandine trailed off. She was babbling, not making it clear that she wanted the Maker to return Flora to life.

But the Maker said, "Of course! And I mean to help you. No reward is too much to ask. Resurrection is well within my power."

Elandine blinked, hardly daring to believe her ears.

"But first," he continued, "we've got to return your Ring to its *full power*. With my return, a portion of its strength is back, but not all it once possessed. Not enough for your sister, I think, until we repair it. So lend it to me." He mouth quirked as he continued, "I'll take it to the Maker's Hall, fix it up there, then bring it back here."

She was going to see her sister again! Joy washed away her fear and pain, and made her impulsive. Elandine removed the metallic band and dropped it into the Maker's gauntleted hand.

The Maker laughed. Something in his tone seemed off.

Elandine added, "As you know, the Ring was given to the first of my line. By you, of course." She laughed, feeling stupid, but she pressed on, "The Ring has passed from mother to daughter in an unbroken chain since then. Maybe I should–"

"Don't worry," the Maker said as he waved at something high overhead. The dlamma. It descended as the conflict burned out. Only a couple of the Maker's doubles remained, and they along with Elandine's peacemakers seemed intent on pursuing a last of the kray that, too late, tried to escape into the underbrush at the clearing's edges.

The rush of air pushed Elandine back a half step as the dlamma set down. The great metallic mask hiding the creature's face was red and savage, bestial almost. Not a look she would've guessed for the Maker's mount. The armored figure vaulted into the saddle. Events were rushing out of her control.

"Wait," said Elandine. "You said you'd bring it back here. Would you prefer to return it to me at my palace in Hazurrium? I mean, when should I expect you?"

"Actually, Queen Elandine, I have bad news. I won't be returning the Ring to you. Ever."

"What? But my sister! You said–"

"Yes, well, I lied, and not just once. I'm sorry. But I'm not the Maker. Not the original, anyhow. Though the job has recently opened up, and I'm stepping in."

Elandine gasped. "Who are you then?"

"You know me. People around these parts call me the Betrayer. I prefer Incarnation of War, or just War if you're going to be informal. Your great, great, great grandmother called me Jason." He laughed. "None of that matters any more. I've got your ring. Once I get a couple of others, I'll have what I need to break into the Maker's Hall and claim Carter's mantle for my own."

The dlamma leaped into the sky, bearing away the Betrayer, with Elandine's last hope clutched in his thieving hand.

17: NAMER
Carter Morrison

A furnace-bright point of fire raged in the sky, forcing me to squint into the glare and look away. Glass stretched away in every direction, like God's own solar oven. The heat tasted like burnt sand.

My sweat was already drying. Not good. On the other hand, when I let my fingers run across my upper chest, they felt no salty red wetness or gaping hole – all evidence of the gunshot wound was gone.

"Holy shit, I'm gonna live!"

The emptiness swallowed my shout. The glass didn't care. If anything, it seemed even warmer than before. That, and a strange lethargy clung to me, a feeling of hollowness in my belly that refused to depart despite the lack of wound. Was I going to live?

An inventory of my resources revealed a pale gray tunic under a blue coat. Cuneiform runes, vaguely familiar, stitched the coat's hem. Where had I seen those designs before?

My boots were impressively comfortable, maybe because of their leather soles. A pack hung off my shoulder. A few pouches, a satchel, and a bulging water skin were clipped to my belt.

I pulled the water skin's cork and sniffed. It smelled a

bit leathery and wasn't the least bit cold. Beggars couldn't be choosers. Not hydrating in this heat would see me dead within an hour, tops. Pressing my lips to the skin's mouth, I sucked down a gulp.

My mom used to set out pitchers of ice water for my friends and me in the backyard while we played basketball. That water had nothing on this. Yes, it was warm, but it washed away the taste of burnt sand in a lukewarm deluge. It promised life, and the hollowness in my stomach retreated. Enough water filled the skin to last at least a few hours in this unrelenting glare. Maybe long enough to see me somewhere less bright and oven-like.

The water from the skin revived me, and my brain, too. How could I have forgotten the runes on my tunic? I'd commissioned the creation of an alphabet for Ardeyn, Land of the Curse years ago. Roughly, the symbols on my clothing read *One Who Names*, or maybe *One Who Makes*.

With that recognition, I also knew that the flat, reflective plane all around me was the Glass Desert, a part of Ardeyn called Kuambis.

I was *in* Ardeyn, Land of the Curse! It was all fucking real...

Intellectually knowing a place existed was one thing. Seeing the sky go on forever, and feeling the searing heat of an actual desert was another. It made me a bit dizzy. Or was it sunstroke?

I experimentally stamped on the glass with my leather soles. It shimmered with vibration, sending a hard shock back up through my heel and calf. Rubbing the back of my hand across lips felt entirely authentic. The sweat forming in my armpits and on my brow were just as prolific as if I had been sitting in the middle of Death Valley in California. And why not? *Anything* could be emulated if nearly unlimited processing power was on tap, which was what the dark energy network provided.

I had no recollection of ever coming here before. Well, no, that wasn't entirely true. Something... Memory tickled my brain.

I *had* visited Ardeyn, after creating it. And when I did, I'd gained root access. I was Ardeyn's designer. I'd known where all the code was buried, so to speak. So I'd stepped into the ready-made role of Ardeyn's Maker, and offered to incarnate my friends the same way, if they wanted. They did. Why not? We'd been trapped. Alice, Mel, Jason, Sanders, and I had become like gods, thanks to me. Jason chose the Incarnation of War, Alice the Incarnation of Silence, Sanders Lore, and Mel considered the Incarnation of Desire, but finally settled on Death. Then–

A bead of sweat rolled off my eyebrow and stung my eyes. The insane recollection of handing out divine roles to my friends skittered away. Shit! I tried to dredge it up again. It shattered in my mental grasp like a soap bubble, like a dream facing daylight. Had it been real at all? If I was hallucinating from the warmth already, it wasn't a good sign. Another sip from the water skin didn't help.

I squinted into the glare reflecting from the glass stretching away to all horizons. The sun wasn't directly overhead yet, or I'd probably already be dried out as a prune. Splintery cracks, and occasional glass dust dunes interrupted an otherwise smooth surface. A deep scratch passed not more than a few dozen feet from me, stretching away in both directions as far as I could see.

"Oh, wow," I muttered, imagining the massive skate that had probably made the furrow.

When Ardeyn had been all code and art orders for animators, "glass pirates" had been conceived. They sailed on ships with iron skates instead of keels. The long groove in the glass might well have been laid down just such a skate. If I were lucky, maybe another glass pirate would sail by and offer me a lift to someplace with more shade. If I was unlucky, one would try to run me over for sport, or capture me so they could sell me as a slave in Kuambis.

Unless I could help myself first. Closing my eyes, I renewed my effort to recover the memory of my previous visit. According to Michael Bradley, I'd visited him after my supposed funeral, wearing some outlandish black outfit claiming that I had become the Maker. Why couldn't I remember more? I concentrated. Fresh images surfaced, but they were fogged and broken. Sort of like looking through the pocked, shattered surface of the Glass Desert itself to the bedrock beneath.

Otherworldly scenes spun past: the Seven Sentinels walking, kray pouring through a breach in the world, and the Incarnation of War – with Jason's grinning face – becoming a numberless army to defend Ardeyn. But nothing else. It was as if most of my mind had been cut away. Or as if it hadn't really happened to me at all. Nothing else Ardeyn-related flickered in the recesses of my brain.

Time to face facts. Except for a few random impressions, I was missing crucial memories of my previous time in Ardeyn. There was nothing I could do about that, at least not immediately.

On the other hand, I perfectly recalled waking up in the Seattle storage space, and everything after that, including the events at the BDR office. It'd be hard to forget a gunman putting a bullet through me. And Jason showing up, with a hate-on for me that, frankly, seemed insane. His time here had obviously unbalanced him. The worm he injected onto the internet was supposedly bursting with schematics for a quantum computer chip capable of pinging the Strange. Why would he do that? It was an insane risk for him to take. I'd been too shot to ask him why at the time, and then he'd slipped back to Ardeyn. I'd tried to follow using his ring, and save my life in the process—

The Ring! Sometimes I'm such an idiot. Jason had hinted it was the Ring of Desire. Once I figured out how to channel its power...

Where was it? It'd been the catalyst for flipping across the boundary into Ardeyn. But it wasn't on my finger. Nor was it in any of the pouches, pockets, or hidden compartments of my clothing, I was forced to admit after a thorough search.

The artifact hadn't made the trip back with me. Well, shit.

Picking a direction along the furrow in the glass, I began walking. The boots would protect my feet from burning, though care would still be required if I was going to travel across the desert. Stray splinters could cut the boots, and my feet within, to shreds.

After a few hundred yards, I shrugged out of my blue coat and hung it over one arm. If anything, the heat was even more oppressive without the coat to block it. The weakness was back, and growing dizziness made each step more of a risk than the last, comfortable leather soles or not. The heat was too much. I needed an edge, and quick.

"If you have anything of the Maker in you," I told my reflection in the smooth surface between my feet, "it's time to wake up." My reflection looked back at me stupidly.

My gaze shifted to the runes on my coat. I spoke the symbols aloud, "One Who Names." What did that mean? The phrase had the sound of a title. Maybe it was *my* title? We'd added a bit of true-name magic into some of the subsystems for Ardeyn during the beta. Did this fully realized version of our make-believe land have anything like that?

My gaze drifted to a crater-like blemish in the glass not far from the groove I'd been following. Lying in many pieces in the crater was what might have been a broken stone sculpture, I couldn't be sure. I wondered if it had fallen from the sky.

Kicking through the pieces, I found a few other bits of splintered wood, a rusted sword blade, some shattered ceramic that might have been part of a large tankard, and a metal sphere that must have been a cannonball. Did glass pirates have cannons? I couldn't remember, but evidence argued yes. That, along with what was obviously a belaying pin hinted the entire mess had fallen from a glass pirate ship.

I fished the cannonball from the jumble. It was silvery gray, and not especially large – just big enough to fit in my palm, rough and sun-warmed. Rust patches specked the sphere, and it wasn't perfectly round. But it was solid. The discoloration and irregular shape almost made the thing look like a metal skull. I addressed it, "What's your name?"

I felt only slightly foolish when it didn't answer. Mainly, because I sensed it had no name to give me. If it was to help, it needed a voice. I decided a name would help wake it. And not any old name, I felt with a thrill of certainty. A name that only *I* could give.

"Jushur," I named the metallic ball, though I didn't quite know why; it just seemed right. More words bubbled up, "Jushur is your name. I invest you with the gift of sight and knowledge. Wake from sleep, and greet your maker."

I didn't quite drop it when the iron sphere vibrated in my hand, and a voice answered, "Jushur is my name. I greet you, Maker." But it was a close thing. I did sort of juggle it.

Holy shit, I'd made a talking cannonball. I just didn't have the first clue *how* I'd done it. Best not look a gift horse in the mouth too early, though. Surprise made me forget what I'd taken as heat stroke symptoms.

"What can you tell me?" I said, recalling that I'd promised the inert thing the gift of sight and knowledge.

"Many things," Jushur replied. "All things are reflected here in the glass. What do you wish to know?" The voice was a whisper, and the vibration was creepy. I decided to ask my most pressing question rather than directions to the nearest shade. If the gift for gab bestowed was only temporary, I might only have one shot at finding Jason.

"Tell me where I can find War."

It whispered, "War is on the move. He returned to Ardeyn just this day, like you."

"Oh," I said. Of course, I'd already known that. The sphere might merely be reflecting my own knowledge back–

"He returned in another's guise, pretending to be one greater than he."

What the hell did that mean? A soft hiss in the distance sounded, but I tuned it out.

"Jushur," I ventured, "Can you tell me where Jason is now?"

"His mind is concealed from me." Well, crap.

"What else can you do?" I said.

"Only what your naming bequeathed me."

"All right, so you know stuff – you have 'sight and knowledge.' How wide is your knowledge?"

"Test me and see," came its whispered reply, like a dare.

A new thought struck me. I said, "Before Ardeyn, there was only a starting grid. The starting grid had, um, controls. Can you show me similar controls in Ardeyn?"

"No," said Jushur. I frowned. The hiss I'd noticed earlier was louder now and had gained a scratchy undertone, but I wasn't going to let it distract me.

I asked, "I once assumed the mantle of the Maker of Ardeyn. Do you know how I managed that?"

"No."

Jushur was an artifact of few words. Actually, the less an inanimate object spoke, probably the better. Especially something created by me in what was essentially a stab in the dark. Who knew what kind of dangerous shit I'd stirred up? My hair was damp with sweat from the heat as I scratched it.

"Jushur," I addressed the metallic lump again, "as your namer, I command your first allegiance. Is that clear? You answer only to me."

The sphere vibrated in my grip before it replied, "I will not betray you to the Betrayer, Jason Cole."

That had come oddly out of the blue. Moreover, the title bequeathed on Jason was like a fist to the gut. It was familiar, but I couldn't quite remember why. "The Betrayer? Jason's name here in Ardeyn is War. Isn't it? What're you—"

The sound of the scratchy hiss I'd been hearing for a while finally grew so loud that I could no longer ignore it. I turned.

A ship under full sail supported by a single massive iron blade beneath it was bearing down on me across the Glass Desert. I goggled. It sped toward me without slowing. When I threw myself out of its way, it was almost too late. The blade narrowly missed cutting me in half.

Glass pirates! I should've been watching for them. I'd designed the fuckers to be aggressive. I was following the tracks of one, for God's sake. Except I hadn't *actually* expected my own creation to manifest as something real, then try to kill me. Because I'm dumb. I'd have to cure myself of that quick if I wanted to live out the rest of the day.

The ship skated clear of my rolling body. Questioning shouts became excited cries of discovery and joy, as pirates at the rear of the craft spied me regaining my feet. The hunt was on, and I was the prey.

I considered my options. The pirate ship was executing a wide turn back toward me, its sails snapping to tack with the wind. Fresh shouts of delight echoed sharply off the glass surface.

The figures on the ship's prow wore brightly mismatched finery. I spotted a couple of eye patches and limb prosthetics, and an overabundance of weapons. In other words, they looked like pirates.

Most were human, but not all. One had a head like a jackal's. I noticed him because he screamed "Take him alive! The Citadel's paying double for fresh slaves!"

In Ardeyn, humans with jackal heads could be only one thing: qephilim. Qephilim were the angelic servitor race I'd imagined as having once served the various Incarnations. This one had obviously shed every ounce of its angelic history.

Jushur observed, "They mean you no good."

I resisted the urge to respond sarcastically, because Jushur was right. The ship was coming at me again. I stuffed my coat and Jushur into the satchel, then bent and retrieved the belaying pin I'd noticed earlier.

This time the craft slowed as it approached. Half a dozen pirates tumbled down ropes let over the side and smashed onto the glass, apparently unconcerned with the blazing warmth. I backed a few steps, but what else could I really do but confront them? It wasn't like I could outrun anyone in this heat.

One who dropped onto the glass was the qephilim I'd seen on the ship's prow. When I focused on him, I realized two things. He was actually a *she*, and I knew her name, despite never having met her before: Siraja. No time to wonder how I could possibly know that because they sprinted toward me.

"Siraja, hold!" I yelled. "Don't you know who I am?"

The qephilim's head rocked back when I named her, and she slowed. Those behind her did likewise.

"No. Who are you?" Siraja said. The tips of her ears swiveled forward as her eyes tried to pierce mine. The tiniest glow of light flickered in the air between her tall ears. "How do you know me?"

"Who cares?" said the bulky man at her side. He carried a hammer so large it almost looked ridiculous. Almost. Besides him and Siraja, three other pirates had come down onto the glass. One was tiny, one was dressed all in red, and last was a woman with braided hair that seemed to move of its own accord.

"I care," Siraja told the hammer wielder, whose name I suddenly realized was Kadir. Siraja continued, "I told you, we can sell this meat at the Citadel of the Harrowing. So—"

Kadir replied, "Dickspittle! You're not the captain's favorite any more, Siraja. *I* am. And I say we beat this sark-fondler into mash. He's got nice shit. Dibs on his boots!"

Before I could offer a reasonable objection, the brute charged me. Without thinking, I yelled, "Kadir, stop!"

Kadir slowed, surprised that I knew him, too, but he didn't come to a complete halt. On the other hand, instead of tenderizing my brains, his hammer missed. I took a few practice swings with the belaying pin. The rod whistled satisfyingly through the sweltering air.

Kadir came at me again. But Siraja raised a curved blade and yelled, "Kadir, you pock-faced rat! It's not your decision!" She hewed at him, not me.

The hammer wielder whirled to deal with the unexpected threat on his flank, which made it easy for me to deflect his swinging hammer with a backhand swing of my rod. The impact jolted my wrist and stung my palm, but it felt good, too. Real.

Kadir screamed to the others, "I told you! Didn't I say she'd try something? Get her!"

The tableau reset. Now Siraja stood at the center of a loose ring of her compatriots – the tiny fellow, the one wearing all red, and the woman with moving hair. Plus Kadir, a huge grin stretching his face.

I glanced up at the ship, which had stopped moving. A weathered name was visible on the prow: *Nightstar*. Several more figures stood watching events, with wagers passing between them. None of them were looking at me, but rather at Siraja and her predicament. I wondered if it was time to leave them to it.

"Mutiny!" growled Siraja, her ears and head glancing around to take in all those who menaced her.

"Oh come on," drawled the woman whose hair moved. Her name, I realized, was Mehvish the Strangler. Mehvish continued, "To be mutiny, you'd have to be part of the command structure. And you're not. Not anymore." The woman laughed.

A cold voice yelled down from the ship, "Hold." I glanced up. Another qephilim had spoken, a male wearing particularly fine clothing, and several gold rings piercing his tall ears. Captain Taimin – that was his name, I knew with easy certainty, despite having never seen him before. Apparently, knowing names was just something I could do here in Ardeyn. Perhaps I shouldn't have been surprised.

The pirates on the glass gave Captain Taimin their complete attention.

Taimin folded thick arms across his chest, arms sporting grandiose metallic bracers. He said, "Settle this squabble. I don't care how. Except for one thing: if Siraja comes back aboard the *Nightstar*, then Kadir may not. If Kadir returns instead, then Siraja must remain on the glass."

Taimin threw a two-finger salute, turned, and strode out of view.

"Well, well, well," said Kadir. The tiny fellow guffawed. The one wearing all red and Mehvish with the moving hair both grinned.

Siraja said in a cold voice, "You firepeckers have always been against me." Not even her captain had her back. She was alone. Which gave me an idea.

"Hey, Siraja!" I said. "If I help you sort this out, do the same for me? Vouch for me with your, um, crew?"

All the pirates looked at me. The one between me and Siraja – Mehvish – shifted her position somewhat so she was no longer bracketed between us.

"What can you do?" Siraja asked.

Declaring my ability to guess names sounded incredibly lame, even to me. So I hefted my heavy belying pin and adopted a martial position. "I can—"

The little guy's hands blurred, and a knife was suddenly protruding from my shoulder. The tiny fucker had thrown it. I screamed and dropped the rod. That was Siraja's cue; she spun, her curved sword extended. The little guy's head spun away from his body. His blood spattered on the glass, painting a zigzagging trail between his slumping form and the rolling lump of meat. My inner voice told me what his name had been, but I promptly forgot it, seeing as how it was no longer relevant.

A flurry of swinging pirate blades, iron hooks, and hammers erupted around me. One hand on my shoulder where the knife still protruded, I scrambled backward.

My ability to swing a heavy iron belaying pin meant squat in Ardeyn, where sorcerers and fantasy heroes walked. I was a fool to think otherwise. Running away seemed the only thing I could do, despite my offer to help Siraja.

Except, hold on. I was part of this world, now. Hell, I'd made it, at least in a manner of speaking. Shouldn't I be able to partake of the same abilities those heroes blithely employed? If my spotty memories and Bradley's story was any indication, I'd done it once before, and become the Maker with a capital M. I should be able to do it again.

Except I had no idea how. Yelling "Shazam" didn't seem to work.

Siraja bellowed, jerking my attention back to the fight. Only a few seconds had passed, but already she was bleeding from several cuts. The little knife thrower was down, but Kadir, Mehvish, and the guy in red still threatened. She saw my glance and yelled, "What are you waiting for? Help me!"

Right. Maybe something like what I'd managed before, when I'd made Kadir hesitate. I focused my attention on him. Kadir was his common name, everyone knew it. But as I concentrated and pushed deeper, his "true" name popped into my brain. All his strengths, all his weaknesses, all that he'd ever been was in that hidden name. Indeed, he was hardly more than a shell, acting according to a limited nature; he didn't have the spark of true consciousness. I don't know if that made a difference or not, but maybe it'd make what I was about to try easier.

I pronounced a portion of Kadir's true name. To anyone who heard it other than him, it was a nonsense word. To Kadir, it was the voice of thundering, burning command. Seeing that I had his attention, I said, "Drop your hammer!"

The hammer cratered onto the glass.

The sound seemed to jolt him out of his daze. He blinked and shook his head, then pointed at me. "He's a soul sorcerer. Forget Siraja, kill *him*!"

Oops.

Kadir grabbed for his hammer, but a residue of my command lingered, preventing him. Siraja engaged the fellow in red before he took more than a step toward me.

I lost track of the qephilim when a braid of Mehvish's hair lashed toward me, its tip uncannily cobra-like. I ducked, but a second braid grasped me around the ankle and yanked.

I fell on my left side. The braid kept pulling, and I slid along the glass, unable to stop myself. Mehvish's laughter scratched my ears. I tried to focus on her, searching for her true name as I had Kadir's. I couldn't get my breath, and the heat finally seemed to have soaked into my brain. Her true name eluded me. I needed help.

The winding length of animate hair yanked me across the glass. A friction burn seared my ass through the cloth. Before I could more than gasp at that, Mehvish kicked me in the side with the strength of a mule, and I lost track of everything else. Pain blossomed and I folded sideways, gasping. She kicked me again.

"Ever been strangled?" Mehvish asked. "How about drawn and quartered? What, won't talk? Answer me!" I gasped, trying to suck air into my lungs, and shook my head.

She drew her boot back and her hair rose about her like a storm cloud.

"No, never," I wheezed. Fuck, fuck, fuck, I was going to die here. Unless I got my shit together immediately. Where'd I dropped the belaying pin? I wondered if the talking cannonball in my satchel could hear me…

I gasped, "Jushur, kill this woman!"

Mehvish glanced around for who I might be talking to. I didn't wait to see if Jushur would actually help. The moment she was distracted, I renewed my concentration on her. She was different than Kadir. Far more complex. I riffled through bands of names and appellations that layered her like one of those Russian dolls. I realized she wasn't human, and in fact was much older than she looked. Like, hundreds of years older. Which was why I was having such a difficult time getting her number. She was too tangled to encapsulate, at least quickly.

So I tried the next best thing. "Mehvish," I said, and her eyes snapped back to me. "Stop, or I'll reveal what you really are to your friends. I'll tell your comrades and your captain. You'll be without a home once more, and without friends."

I had no idea how she'd react, or even if I was on the right track. If she ignored me, and instead kicked me hard enough, quickly enough, I wouldn't be able to scream out the truth about her. And why would a bunch of pirates believe some poor loser lost in the Glass Desert anyway?

But my threat shocked Mehvish into a startled stare. She glanced sideways, then back at me. She whispered, "Do not."

"Then go help Siraja, now, or you're done here." To my

own ears, I managed to speak with the dread authority of a storybook villain, with only a slight quaver.

Mehvish actually growled at me before she turned away. As she did, her lashing hair spread out into four separate twining braids. The braids converged on the man in red – Luwren was his name – and easily wrapped him up by his wrists and ankles. The hair obviously had an impressive power all its own, because Mehvish actually grabbed Luwren up and held him in the air with her animate hair. His scream of surprise turned into one of horrified agony a second before she pulled off both his arms.

All the conversation on the ship ceased, as did the jibes that Siraja and Kadir had been throwing back and forth at each other. Everyone was looking at Mehvish as she tossed Luwren's spurting remains. Then she pointed at Kadir, and said simply, "Go. I've decided that, actually, Siraja is a better fit for this crew."

Kadir and Siraja both looked surprised. But Siraja adapted first, and grinned. "Goodbye, Kadir. You can't beat me and Mehvish together."

"And me," I said, then coughed. I'm not sure anyone actually heard me.

Kadir said, "But you were demoted. I should be first mate!"

"Captain Taimin made his decree. Only one of us is welcome back aboard," said Siraja. "And that's me. Get going. Before Mehvish adds to her arm collection."

Kadir scowled. Then his shoulders slumped. He understood that he'd lost. He finally managed to grab the hammer I'd commanded him to drop. He flipped off the assembled crew still watching from the deck of the *Nightstar*, then walked away under the merciless sun.

I stood up.

"Are you coming?" Siraja asked me, then pointed to the pirate ship.

I nodded, though part of me wanted to follow Kadir and get away from these bloodthirsty thugs. Except I'd die from heat stroke if I didn't get more water soon.

So I said, "I thought you'd never ask."

18: REVELATION
Katherine Manners

Two Months Later

"Those dreams still bothering you?" said Raul.

"Now isn't the time," said Kate. The last thing she wanted to think about were her nightmares. The unfamiliar voices, finding herself lost in bizarre locations... Nope. Not the time for it.

So instead, she grabbed Raul's name badge and gave it a final once-over as the elevator ascended. She had faked up reasonable facsimiles of computer contractor IDs from a company in Portland, Oregon she'd picked at random from an online registry. They wouldn't stand up to detailed scrutiny if they were discovered in Garland Klein's private office, but she was reassured that a casual glance, at least, wouldn't blow their cover.

"We don't need to rush in," insisted Raul as the floors flashed higher on the elevator display. "I'm worried about you. You look tired."

Kate sighed. "All right, yes. I still get those dreams." More frequently than ever, she didn't add. Last night she dreamed she fell through her bedroom floor and directly onto a desert made of glass. In the dream, she'd burned her feet. The ring

Carter had left behind, which also featured in her dream, had spoken in her mind. The pain from her feet woke her before she was able to parse the ring's message.

Her soles still ached, but they hadn't been physically scorched when she checked in the morning light. And the ring, which she kept in a tiny plastic case, remained speechless. It was just another dream. Wasn't that what Dana Scully would say? She could imagine the hero of skeptics everywhere telling her exactly that. Kate sighed. Sometimes, though, she just wanted to believe. To be a hero, not someone who catches people cheating on their significant others.

So why was she feeling so off-kilter? Everything that happened meant that her chance to be a hero, to believe in something amazing, was happening all around her. *To* her, even. Was the fear of being disappointed still holding her back, after everything?

Raul broke her stream of consciousness with a cough. "We should talk about this. It could be related to your contact with Ardeyn, and the Strange–"

The elevator door slid open.

"Not now," she said, setting off down the corridor. At two in the morning, the September Project office in Portland, Oregon was deserted. Except for a few lamps shining from adjoining offices, it was also dark. Dream analysis from a friend, especially a friend who seemed as if he was dealing with his own brain issues, was a distraction they couldn't afford.

For once, Raul did as she asked and kept stride with her in silence. When they reached Gordon Klein's office, Kate applied the key card they'd stolen a day earlier at a coffee shop. The lock clicked open.

They strolled in like they owned the place. Luckily the corner office was deserted. Raul closed the door to the hallway while Kate flipped on the lights. The office was swank, the window blinds were lowered, and they were alone. Kate made a beeline for the desk. As her intelligence hinted, the safe was located in the first place she would've looked anyway: behind the large painting of Mount Hood behind Klein's desk.

Raul finished checking the auxiliary office, and gave her a thumbs up. Thankfully, they hadn't walked in on a secretary, cleaning person, or worst of all, Klein himself.

She leaned the painting along the wall and turned to the safe. Too bad it didn't have an electronic lock. She was far more confident of her ability to hack circuits than finesse tumblers. From her briefcase, which she'd settled on the desk, she selected her safe-cracking tool: a stethoscope. She settled in to try her luck.

Just as she was getting into the groove, Raul said, "These fellows certainly hit the ground running. I figured they would need another year to get financing."

Kate glanced up, biting back an irritated comeback. Raul was reading through the glitzy marketing pamphlets from the desktop. She'd seen those same pitches online, making claims about the future wonders quantum computing would offer. She doubted the pamphlets mentioned where the quantum breakthrough had originated. With a noncommittal "mmm," she returned to her work.

Safecracking by dint of old-fashioned lock manipulation wasn't easy. It required tremendous patience. If she failed, she'd have to resort to her fallback option – an explosive detonation. Which would draw whatever security lurked in the newly decorated offices of September Project, LLC, so she hoped it wouldn't come to that.

Raul watched her without further interruption for another minute before shrugging, dropping the pamphlets, and bending to his smartphone.

Kate still worried about Raul. That worry was probably the

reason she'd been so short with him lately. He *seemed* back to normal. But her trust would never return completely. She'd seen someone else look out from Raul's eyes. Instead of her friend, for a little while, he'd been Jason. *Supposedly,* he was back to being Raul again. Except... How could she know for sure?

"What?" Raul was looking at her. She realized she'd turned all the way around and was staring at him, not safecracking.

Kate sighed. Maybe now was the time after all. They were alone, and the safe wasn't going anywhere. "Raul, you said that Jason's gone. And maybe that's true. But look at it from my perspective. There's no way for me to test it, especially if he can draw on your memories and pretend to be you."

"Listen–"

"Let me finish! The thing is, you know a lot more about all this than you should. Even more than me, and *I'm* the one who brought *you* in. For instance, why're you so concerned about my stupid dreams? Do you know something? And why the hell do you think they'd have anything to do with Ardeyn or, what'd you call it, the Strange? What gives?"

"I told you," said Raul slowly, a pained expression on his face, "Jason let a few things slip, and I picked up–"

"Bullshit," said Kate. "I'm the one who found out about the September Project, not you. Why didn't Jason let that slip?"

"It doesn't work like–" Raul started.

"On the other hand," she gestured with the stethoscope chest piece she'd been using on the safe, "you have this unsettling new familiarity with all this, or as I heard you mutter last week, the 'limited worlds beneath Earth.' I guarantee you that stuff isn't on Wikipedia, because I've looked."

Raul rubbed his eyes. Finally he said, "They're called recursions, Kate."

"What are?"

"The limited worlds that Earth hosts. And you're right, I do know more about this than I've let on. I've always known."

"I knew it!" She'd spoken louder than she'd intended. Pitching her voice back down to a whisper, she said "You're still Jason!" Her hand dropped to her 9mm's holster.

"No. Jason returned to Ardeyn. But, I've *never* been exactly who you think. I'm... well, there's no easy way to say this. Like you said before, this isn't the time to go in–"

"It's the perfect time."

He glanced around Klein's office, swallowed, and said, "All right. Brace yourself."

"I'm braced."

"I'm not from Earth. I'm from a recursion. One that has hidden in the dark energy network – we call it the Strange – long before Ardeyn was created by Carter Morrison."

Well.

She hadn't seen that coming.

Raul said, "Say something. You must have... questions?"

He studied her, a hesitant smile on his lips, as her mind tried to make sense of the man's admission.

She said, "Oh, come on. So you're telling me, what, that you're an alien?"

Raul shrugged. "I've taken on Earth's context. I've been Raul for twenty years. I'm as human as you, Kate."

"Twenty years? Why? And what were you before?" Given everything else that had happened, Kate realized that she couldn't rule out Raul's story merely on principle. The "that's crazy!" ship had sailed several months ago, the night she'd met Jason's homunculus at BDR.

Raul said, "Do you understand what I'm saying?"

"No. Yes. Jesus Christ, Raul." The fuck of it all was that Raul was probably telling the truth. Of course, that didn't mean he wasn't a fuckhead who'd lied to her since the first day they'd met. He came from a world like Jason's, even if he wasn't Jason. How many fucking worlds were there "under" Earth, anyway?

He said, "I was—"

The office door beeped, and someone rattled the lock. Kate ducked. Her hand was already on Malcolm's holster, and she loosed the safety snap. Raul slipped around the desk and scrunched down next to her. He saw her hand on the gun and whispered "Wait!"

Kate waited by pulling the 9mm free. Ever since she and Carter had been caught flat-footed by Liza Banks's hired goon, she'd been putting in a few hours a week at a gun range in Bellevue. Her confidence with the piece had increased a lot. Though the way her heart pounded and hands shook, maybe she'd been fooling herself.

A voice outside the office said, "See? Empty."

Kate remembered that she'd left her briefcase sitting open on the desk. Worse, the normally hidden safe was plainly visible. The gig would be up if the office door opened. Shit!

"I heard a woman talking," another voice said.

"A woman? You wish."

Kate risked a peek around the desk. Two security guards loomed in the hallway light.

"Don't be a dick," one guard said. "Why are the lights on in there? They weren't an hour ago. We should check it out. Using the *new* procedure."

Guard Two said, "Fine."

It's not fine! Kate thought as she ducked back out of sight. What was the *new* procedure? Grenade first, inspect after?

But instead of chucking explosives, the sound of a single set of footsteps receded. As did the second guard's voice as he said, "If the freak is still here, she can do another scan."

"Her name is Soma," replied Guard One, apparently still loitering just outside the entrance to the office.

Raul's eyes found Kate's. He gave her a nod, as if that meant anything to her. Then he hopped up and over the desk, unlocked the office door, and eased it open.

Shocked that he'd revealed their position, she stood up before she could think better of it. She kept her gun concealed behind her back.

The nearer guard was watching his partner move off down the hallway. Before he realized he wasn't alone, Raul slipped up behind him and applied a chokehold. The guard made a soft noise and tried to pry Raul's forearm from around his neck, but failed.

Kate shook off her astonishment at seeing Raul move so aggressively. Today was apparently the day he'd decided to pull off all his masks. She whispered, "Pull him in here!" She hurried to the entrance and pressed her gun to the man's temple.

"Stop struggling," she hissed to the guard, "or I'll shoot." The man's eyes, already wide, locked on Malcolm. The fight went out of him, then consciousness as the chokehold restricted enough blood to knock him out. Raul pulled the limp form into Klein's office. The moment the guard's feet were clear of the door, she bumped it shut again. Raul settled him to the floor.

"We have to move, *mi chula*," Raul said. "I don't know where the other guard went, but it did not sound promising."

She nodded, studying the safe. No time for finesse or worrying about all Raul's lies. Kate pulled the shaped charge from her briefcase and removed the outer packaging. She slapped the charge onto the safe front where the smooth surface, she was fairly certain, hid the locking mechanism. When everything was set, she and Raul took shelter on the opposite side of the desk.

BANG!

Smoke and the acrid smell of burnt explosive filled the air.

Shattered knickknacks and shredded, smoking carcasses of books that had been on the shelves flanking the concealed safe now littered the carpet. She crept forward through the haze, careful not to step on anything sharp. The fist-sized, rough hole in the safe's surface was pretty much what she'd wanted to see. The safe door was slightly warped, but she pulled it open with a jerk.

Inside were a few scorched file folders and a smaller lock box. She grabbed everything and dumped it into her briefcase.

Raul waited for her at the door. He cracked it open and gazed into the hallway. She paused until he gave the all-clear.

Five seconds passed, and he didn't move. Then another five. The hair on her arms stood up.

"Raul? What is it?"

Still no response. She held her breath and approached the door. Raul was as immobile as a statue. Dread caught at her limbs, but she pulled the door wider anyway.

A woman stood in the hallway, and her eyes met Kate's. The woman's clothing was oddly *wrong*. Far more alarming was the haze of blue light that swirled around her head. It reminded Kate of false color images she'd seen of magnetic field lines migrating across the sun. Not something you expect or want to see flaring around someone's head.

The woman said, "Here's your security leak. Two people. One's from Ruk, but I've got him." The woman was talking to the guard who'd walked off, who stood nearby. He was obviously more nervous about the blue-light woman than concerned about seeing an intruder standing in Klein's office.

Kate aimed her 9mm at the woman and asked, "Who are you?" She hated how her voice shook. And what was a Ruk?

"My name doesn't matter," the woman replied, unfazed by the gun pointed at her. "I stop oppressors and thieves, like you, and make them sorry. Although..." The woman's hand went to her temple. "You're not just a thief, are you?

Something about you is interfering with my talent. Or maybe I've just stayed too long..." The authority in the woman's voice faded as she said the last.

The woman gestured with her other hand. Kate's muscles seized. She tottered and almost toppled. The blue-light woman was doing it, somehow. Kate concentrated on squeezing the trigger. Something prevented her. So she redoubled her efforts.

The woman yelled, "She's fighting me! She's quickened, and I—"

The gun went off. Mobility suddenly returned. Her first shot had been wild. The guard threw himself to the floor. The woman looked shocked, and her weird aura was gone.

"Try that again, bitch," Kate said, "and I put a bullet in your brain."

Raul groaned, and pitched forward on his face like a marionette released by its puppeteer. In the time it took Kate to glance his way and back, the woman snatched a small object from her belt sash.

"Drop it!" screamed Kate.

The woman complied. The object, shaped something like a snow globe, smashed on the floor. The shards blossomed into a rip in space, a literal opening to somewhere else. Kate saw an unfamiliar city skyline in the cavity. The strange woman stepped through the hole while Kate gaped. Then the opening collapsed to the sound of distant thunder.

Kate blinked. Except for cracked hallway tiles, nothing remained of the other guard, the woman who could immobilize people with a glance, or the doorway to elsewhere. Had she seen into another world? What had Raul called it; another recursion?

Their regular coffee shop, much as she loved it, wasn't a discreet location for discussing their burglary at September Project. Plus it was still closed at five in the morning, which was when they'd made it back to Seattle after driving north up I-5 from Portland. So Kate brought Raul back to her condo. She'd got it cheap after the bottom fell out of the housing market in '08. The condo was comfortable enough, if small, and offered them reasonable privacy.

Raul's daze lifted after she'd set him up with a chicken salad sandwich and some ice tea at her kitchen bar. She helped herself to a second sandwich.

"So, you want to talk?" Raul said. He looked resigned.

Kate chewed a bite of sandwich, then swallowed. "Yeah. Starting with that woman, the one with the blue aura. She was from a recursion?"

"She was."

"The same place as you? Ruk, she called it?"

"No, someplace else. A different limited world. I have no idea which one. Hundreds, maybe thousands of recursions are hosted around Earth. Most of them born from the power of human imagination – from human fiction. She might be some character in a kid's story come to life, or maybe inspired by a fusion of several stories, seeding someplace wholly new."

Kate's head swam with possibilities. But she didn't want to let herself get distracted. She said, "But you're from Ruk?" She wondered if she could believe anything he said. She wanted to, but trust had been breached.

Raul nodded.

"I'm pretty sure there are no novels or movies about a place by that name. I mean, if you said you were from Middle Earth, or the Federation..."

"Ruk, like Ardeyn, was crafted purposefully," said Raul.

"Ah," said Kate, as if that explained everything. It didn't, of course. "C'mon, stop making me pry it out of you. And why'd you say you were an alien?"

"That was your word."

"So you're not an alien?"

Raul waggled the hand not holding his sandwich. "It's complicated. Ruk has hidden in Earth's shadow since before humans fully evolved. In Ruk, reality operates under a different set of laws. Amazing feats of science are easy in Ruk. We've mastered the secrets of biosculpting and genetic engineering. To say we're alien isn't really correct. Rukians are almost indistinguishable from humans, and purposefully so."

Kate shook her head. Ancient people on Ruk had made themselves look human on purpose? Or was he suggesting that Rukians had made human ancestors on Earth look like people from Ruk? She decided not to pursue either line of inquiry in case she didn't like the answer.

Instead she said, "So, Ruk is a recursion like Ardeyn, a tiny world? But instead of magic spells, you've got warp drive and killer robots?"

"Well. Yes, in very broad strokes, that's correct," said Raul.

"If Ruk has been around so long, why not reveal yourself to people on Earth?"

"It's not our way. We're a cautious people. Plus, only a tiny percentage of Rukians can pass between recursions, just like on Earth. Recursors are what we call people with that ability. All are rare, special people."

"Then why are *you* here? Twenty years, you said you've been Raul? I thought you were from Mexico City!"

Raul smiled. "We're a fractious people. Some among us are even dangerous. A faction called the Karum is particularly outspoken in its desire to sever Ruk's ties with Earth, violently if necessary. I came to Earth to keep an eye out for Karum activity. I was installed as a sort of sleeper agent, you might say. One of a few."

"Oh great. How many Ruk natives are creeping around Earth?"

"I don't know. Less than a dozen, probably. It's been mostly quiet. We couldn't have guessed that the threat to Earth would come from an upstart recursion force-seeded three years ago."

"Who's 'we?'" asked Kate.

"An organization on Ruk that believes that Ruk is best served by Earth's continued safety, called the Quiet Cabal. It's the faction that sent me here, to guard against the Karum. Now it seems like Ardeyn is the bigger threat."

"Huh," she said, and finished her sandwich. She hadn't really tasted it. Their conversation absorbed her attention. At least she was no longer ravenous. Which somehow made it easier to believe everything Raul said. It pissed her off. It didn't mean she trusted him.

She said, "All this time you've been an alien agent, here to safeguard Earth. And you never told me. I thought you were my friend."

"I *am* your friend. But I also have a job to do. I'm surprised you didn't suspect something, especially when I went into hiding."

"Why would I?"

Raul said, "You didn't think it odd when I went underground and removed myself from society?"

"I just thought you were an eccentric. It's quite a leap to say, 'Wow, Raul sure is weird. I wonder if he's an alien from a parallel dimension.'"

"Ah, true." He looked sheepish.

Kate slapped the table with her palm. "How was it that you came to be *my* friend? How could you've known that I'd one day get involved with this?"

"*Mi chula*... I sensed something about you. You are touched by the Strange. Quickened. Like I am, like Carter Morrison must be, and as the woman at the office who tried to fry my brain most certainly was."

Kate rocked back, "What the hell do you mean by that?"

"Quickened" had been what that woman said, too. The memory of Kate's limbs locking up returned. The helpless feeling, now that the direct danger was passed, made her queasy. She wished she hadn't eaten her sandwich so fast.

Raul said, "Some people, whether they're from Earth or a recursion, are connected to the Strange. That connection allows them to travel between recursions, to take on the context of each new recursion they enter, and even call on amazing abilities. People who can do that under their own power are quickened."

Kate didn't know what to make of Raul's explanation, but she didn't like the subtext. "You say you're my friend. But really, you stayed near me because you were watching me like a lab rat. To see if I'd start using Strange powers." She stated it as a fact, studying Raul to see his reaction.

"It wasn't like that!" he said.

She kept her gaze on him.

Raul blushed, then he said, "All right, yes, at first it was like that. But think about it, Kate. I could have watched you from a distance and you'd never have been the wiser. I stayed in contact because you *became* my friend." He glanced away, embarrassed.

"Jesus, Raul. I just don't know…"

She wanted to trust him. She *had* thought of him as a confidante for years. His admissions now threatened to invalidate everything between them.

An uneasy quiet fell as she struggled to come to a decision. It was tempting to just trust him, because that was easiest. But easy didn't mean smart.

Finally Raul volunteered, "We should try to figure out the nature of your quickened abilities. You held off that woman remarkably–"

Kate held up a hand. Raul stopped. "Let's see what was in the safe. We can worry about whether I'm quickened later," she said. One thing at a time, she told herself. Her plate was already full.

She set the briefcase on the kitchen bar and opened it. Inside was her stethoscope and other tools, plus the scorched file folders and lock box she'd taken from the September Project safe.

She grabbed the files, Raul the lockbox.

Coming cold to someone else's records and organizational system was always a pain. She laid out the documents, collating them until she eventually figured it out.

"Damn it!" she said. "They've split their quantum research between locations. Portland was just a fucking HR office."

"We already knew they were doing the actual research somewhere else," said Raul in a distracted voice. He was still fiddling with the lock box.

"Yeah. Well, getting to these places isn't going to be as easy as driving to Portland. One's in Brazil, and the other one... well it's some place I've never heard of. And according to this document," she waved a piece of paper, "we need to go to the one in Brazil before you can use the key to get to the other place. Whatever *that* means." Kate sighed.

"Where in Brazil?" asked Raul.

"City called Curitiba, at the Federal University. Shit, do we have to get a visa to travel to Brazil?"

"We'll check. Where's the other place?"

She shook her head. "These files call it the Sister Foundry. It's located somewhere called Megeddon."

He flinched, almost dropping the lock box, and stared at her.

"What?" she said.

"It's pronounced 'meh-GED-on,'" he said, his voice rough.

"Fine," she said. "Is Me*geddo*n in Brazil, too?"

"No. Megeddon, the Fortress of the Betrayer – Jason Cole, in other words – lies in the recursion of Ardeyn."

19: RINGMASTER
Jason Cole

A psychic sledgehammer smashed into Jason's mind. He bellowed a sort of obscenity-scream. Worse than the pain was how his eyesight grew dim. Most disturbing of all was the explosion of brain cotton behind his eyes, so invasive that when he reached for War's facility to duplicate himself, he couldn't find it. Icy fear stabbed Jason's stomach. He whirled, lashing out blindly with his staff. He struck something that grunted with a deep, earthy tone.

He backed away blinking. He hoped his retreat was in the direction of the dragon lair's exit. Jason had entered the crumbling opening high on the side of the dead volcano thinking to slip in unnoticed. No such luck. At least whatever faced him probably wasn't the dragon itself, because the tunnel was too small to contain Merid's bulk. Unless she could shrink herself. Maybe the dragon knew a spell that could reduce her bus-sized bulk enough to fit into tunnels only humans could normally navigate. Seemed unlikely, but...

"Merid?" he ventured, slashing blindly. "This is a misunderstanding. I came to propose an alliance! If you have the Ring of Silence in your hoard, there is an opportunity for both of–"

A rough voice interrupted, "Merid will not treat with you, Betrayer."

Jason's eyes cleared enough for him to see that his foe was no dragon. But... A hiss of surprise escaped Jason.

A metallic mask set with a single ruby-red viewport covered the face of the creature advancing on him. Elaborate horns sprouted from its head behind the mask. He recognized it: a monitor. He supposed he shouldn't have been surprised. Monitors were what remained of qephilim who once served the Incarnation of Silence. When Silence disappeared, monitors remained. They were like ghosts haunting Ardeyn, watching all that happened in quiet, oversized contemplation. They disengaged from every other interaction, friendship, or cause. They didn't intercede. And didn't normally fight, preferring to flee violence so they could watch it from a safe distance. They waited for a sign from the Incarnation of Silence.

Relief flooded him. It had surprised him, that was all. And a monitor wasn't truly a match for War. It was probably already retreating. Once Jason's vision completely cleared–

The monitor wasn't moving off. The single red eye on its mask was fixed on him. Under the influence of that all-seeing gaze, Jason discovered he was unable to call up the office of War and spawn duplicates.

It wasn't fair! Jason was just getting used to the abilities the partly re-powered Ring of War offered. To have those functions yanked away so precipitously sickened him.

The creature charged. Jason swung his staff at its face. The monitor shifted, and he smashed down on one of its shoulders instead. Bone creaked, but the creature barely slowed. The monitor hit Jason like an avalanche, and swept him out of the tunnel and into the cold, crisp evening air, high on Mount Merid. He didn't see the rocks on the path until he stumbled over them and fell. His head bounced off a boulder, and everything swam.

Part of Jason – the part that was War – screamed internally. That some creature could get the jump on an Incarnation, let alone the Incarnation of War, was unthinkable. For his part, Jason realized he'd gotten cocky. War's ring wasn't fully recharged. And apparently, its power was still easily subverted.

The monitor hit Jason while he was down, smashing him in the chest so hard he heard a rib crack, then snugging a wide arm around Jason's neck in a stranglehold. Jason ceased straining after War's abilities. If he wasn't fully War again, at least he remained the Betrayer, damn it. And he could fight, dirty if need be. Determination made him growl. He bit the arm trying to squeeze his head off. Dry flesh tasting of dust and old leather filled his mouth.

The pressure fell away. Jason leaped to his feet, careful to avoid pitching himself off the narrow path he'd followed up to the volcano's summit. The last bits of cottony streamers departed his vision. He watched the monitor retreat to the tunnel entrance, blocking it. Its breath heaved and its shoulders shook, but its unwavering gaze never left Jason.

"You're Merid's doorman?" Jason asked. "I thought she preferred other dragons as her servants."

The monitor remained silent.

"Or maybe she doesn't realize you're up here, keeping guests from her parlor. You've been watching, haven't you? You've seen me collecting Rings of the lost Incarnations. So you waited up here to keep the Ring of Silence safe. I'm right, aren't I? Merid probably doesn't even know she has such a valuable treasure. I bet I'd be doing her a favor if I told her she has a lackey for Silence watching–"

The monitor thundered forward, easily covering the distance separating them. Jason was braced, but still went down when the bulk smashed into him. They rolled, and

Jason lost his burning staff. The monitor's horns gouged Jason's sides. He elbowed the creature's neck, trying to smash in its windpipe. The flesh was more like wood than skin and bone. But something crunched, so he brought his elbow down on it a few more times, snarling in satisfaction. A horn slashed him, deeper than before, but the hot whip of the laceration wasn't enough to stop the memory of War, the Betrayer, or even Jason Cole.

Unfortunately, they continued rolling. So instead of trying to crush the thing's skull between his two straining hands, Jason let go, latching onto a thorn bush instead. Thorns cut deep gouges down his palms and forearms, but the bush's roots held.

The monitor realized its trajectory too late. It tried to grab Jason as it tumbled onward, but he kicked it. The creature flipped over the edge of the drop without a sound.

Jason levered himself to his feet. His wounds stung, but without the monitor's mystical eye on him, the residual power of War was returning, numbing him to pain and hurt. He walked to the edge and gazed down the mountainous drop.

He spied the broken remains of the monitor. It'd bounced a few times on its way down, and had fetched up a few thousand feet below on an outcrop. It wasn't getting up any time soon, if ever.

Jason retrieved his staff. War's power surged from the Ring on his finger, through his body, and into the implement, kindling its head to bonfire brightness.

"Let's try this again," he said, facing the unguarded entrance. "Anyone else want to try and stop me from coming inside?"

No takers appeared. He entered, ready for another ambush that failed to materialize. The passage quickly descended in tight spirals. In the light of his conjured flame, Jason saw the tunnel rock was striated with crazy jags of green and purple sediment. He wasn't sure it made any kind of actual geological sense. Not that any of that mattered in Ardeyn. Everything in the realm was, at its core, fake.

He considered the state of his plan as he moved downward. Stealing the Ring of Death from Queen Elandine had proved both easier, and harder, than he'd anticipated. If he hadn't intervened, the queen and her Ring would've been kray-chow. That number of kray inside Ardeyn's borders was beyond unusual, but then again, the Moon Door was known for being a place where the Rules were flimsy. Something to do with allowing mystical access to the realm of the dead. He shrugged away the irrelevancy.

The other Ring he'd obtained since then hadn't required nearly so much activity or risk to his life as finding Elandine had.

Following the gentle pulse of his own awakening Ring, War had plucked the Ring of Commerce from the dusty collection of an antiquities dealer on the shores of Oceanus who had no sense of its true worth. With his own Ring of War, plus Commerce and Death, he needed just one more ring to bring his collection to four. Of course, he'd had another ring – Desire – for many years, but he'd had to sacrifice it in order to get the whole ball rolling in the first place. He was just glad he didn't need all seven! Four Rings was the magic number required to regain entry into the Maker's Hall.

And Merid had the Ring of Silence.

The tunnel finally emptied into a massive subterranean chamber lit by hundreds of torches. Jason was surprised to see the expansive space contained several human-sized wagons gathered around a lantern-lit caravanserai. A dragon's head with gray plumage stretched above the walled courtyard, and Jason stopped moving.

It hadn't noticed him. He could hear the murmur of its

speech from where he stood in shadow on the chamber's periphery. It was bartering with unseen traders for water, amusements, and spices.

He realized the gray wasn't Merid. His spies reported that her plumage was iridescent with reds, golds, blues, and greens. The gray must be a servant. One of several who dealt with human agents who in turn scoured Ardeyn for treasures. This entire chamber was obviously merely a satellite room set aside for such interaction. It lay exterior to Merid's actual lair, which must lay deeper.

At least five other passages, all of them larger and more obvious than the one he'd used to gain entry, exited the cavern. As he considered which one to take, someone tapped him on the shoulder.

Jason spun around, his staff whipping through the air with lethal velocity. He barely managed to stop himself before he brained the woman who'd somehow snuck up on him so completely. She wore iridescent robes of shifting color. Her eyes glittered with a vitality more than merely human. A smell like cinnamon and burnt oranges filled his nostrils. He knew instantly who she was. Apparently Merid *did* know how to shrink herself into a tunnel meant for humans: she could become human. The power to change form was a power some dragons possessed.

"Merid, greetings," he said.

"You know me, then," she said. "And I certainly recognize you, Betrayer. Not that I needed to. Your scuffle with that interloper in my chimney was so loud it would've awakened me from a dead sleep."

Jason was prepared to try to take the Ring of Silence by force, if required. But he was caught off guard, literally. And Merid seemed in the mood to talk. Maybe even deal? Might as well give it a try, he thought.

He bent at the waist and swept his arm in a formal bow. "I

am War. I seek an audience, Great One, regarding a matter that could prove incredibly advantageous for both of us."

"So courteous. Which I admire, especially in someone I caught trying to sneak in."

"You were clever to catch me, Merid. And brave to do so alone, given my... reputation."

She laughed uproariously. He almost took offense. She said, "You're confident! I appreciate that. And I enjoy an actual conversation from time to time. My servants and agents, whether human, dragon, or qephilim, are no fun. They believe that if they disagree with me, I'll bite their heads off."

Jason nodded. He faced similar issues. Especially among his more brainy homunculi, since he *did* tend to murder them if they gave him too much lip. His clones weren't really *him*, so it wasn't really murder. If she did the same among her own, he couldn't blame her.

Merid touched his elbow and guided him toward the caravanserai. "I suggest we enjoy some strong coffee and smoke while we talk. What say you, Betrayer?"

"Sounds wonderful." He'd spent two months pursuing his plan since he'd returned from Earth. One more evening wasn't going to derail him. They walked through an arched entrance in the caravanserai.

In addition to several bright lanterns high on iron posts, the courtyard was decorated with colored lamps that hadn't been visible from outside. A pig-like creature roasted over a kitchen fire, sending a magnificent odor of cooking pork into the air that almost made Jason forget why he was there.

The gray-feathered dragon and the small huddle of humans around it looked up at their entrance. The humans didn't noticeably react, but the gray dragon flinched. *It* at least knew who Merid was.

"Please retire to your rooms and roosts," Merid ordered.

The gray repeated the request, and the humans obliged with only a token protest. They finally retreated to the various rooms dotting the courtyard's inner wall. The dragon flew directly up into the darkness of the vast chamber. A couple of people shot him quizzical looks as they departed, but none voiced their questions.

Merid walked Jason over to a large cabinet, where they gathered utensils, mugs, and a nargilah with two tubes. "Do you take smoke?"

"I've been known to indulge."

After some choice cuts of the pig prepared over polenta in a spice sauce, a bowl of surprisingly exquisite tobacco, and iced coffee, Jason decided that Merid was truly a delightful conversationalist. Her reputation as one of the most terrifying creatures in the Daylands was obviously something she maintained as a front... though he detected an inner core of fire beneath her courteous exterior. The part of him that was War wondered what it would take to bring it to the surface. War anticipated testing himself against a dragon of the first brood. He blinked, and red dreams of tooth and sword retreated to the back of his mind.

Jason inched forward slightly and said, "So, did you know a monitor was watching you?"

Merid took another deep breath from the nargilah tube. She blew it out to create a smoke sculpture of a dragon in flight. She said, "Of course. It was doing only what its sad kind always do. Watching. Until it attacked you." She said the last accusingly.

"Unexpected," he agreed.

"I heard what you said to it. Perhaps you were right, and it hoped to safeguard something of great value."

There went *that* advantage. "So you know why I'm here. I'm hoping we can come to an arrangement."

"I'm not in the habit of distributing items from my

collection. Each piece has its place. And the Ring of Silence, which I heard you name to the monitor, is one of my most cherished pieces. I well know what it is. I have it in a fabulous diorama."

War thundered, but Jason pushed thoughts of violence back. He said, "Hear me out. I can make this worth your while."

Merid looked at him with a skeptical tilt to her chin and eyebrow. "Go on," she drawled.

"I have recovered nearly all War's strength," he said, shading the truth. "Why? Because my Ring regained a measure of its ancient magic. It's not the only Ring of Incarnation to do so. I've learned that the other Rings have regained a portion of their élan as well."

"Really?" The glitter in Merid's eye went from joking to avaricious.

"Of course," he said quickly, "only heirs of the original Incarnations can unlock the power of the Rings. Which means that to most alive in Ardeyn today, they are merely baubles." That was also true enough, though Jason actually suspected that anyone originally native to Earth could claim the power of a Ring of Incarnation. Thankfully, he was the only native of Earth he knew of still alive in all the Land of the Curse.

The dragon said, "Immensely *valuable* baubles, all the same."

"If you can find the Incarnation of Silence or her heir, maybe. But trust me, Silence is long gone, and she left no heirs."

"She?"

"I knew her secret name: Alice." Jason gnawed his lip. He wasn't sure if he should've volunteered that information. It was a gamble. He hoped Merid could sense that he was telling the truth, and not press the issue. He doubted that even a dragon as powerful as she knew the *true* nature of Ardeyn's inception. The dragon presumably thought she was thousands of years old, just like all the Incarnations. Better she keep that belief. He didn't know how she'd react if he let her in on Carter Morrison and his game-made-real.

Merid said, "How odd. Alice, eh? Not that it matters any longer. When you betrayed the Maker, did you also slay this Alice, or as the rest of us called her, Silence? But what if some of her great, great grandchildren come asking after their lost trinket?"

He hadn't killed Silence, or any of the other Incarnations. Just that bastard Carter. Well, not even him, as Carter's reappearance proved. Though Jason had certainly tried. He'd plunged the spiked end of his burning staff into the Maker from behind. Jason watched Carter die. After that, things got confusing. He didn't really like to think about the considerable amount of time he'd lost. When he finally came back to himself, the power of War had left him, and the other Incarnations were missing. He wondered if they'd simply disintegrated. If so, he was lucky the same thing hadn't happened to him. Of course, he'd been prepared, unlike the others. For years he tried to discover what'd actually happened to them, but finally grew tired of the search. If any remained alive, as he had in his reduced state, they were keeping their distance from him. The fact that so many Rings had turned up absent their owners suggested they were simply dead.

Merid didn't need to know any of that. So he shrugged and said, "Indirectly, I suppose I did kill her."

The dragon-in-woman-form nodded thoughtfully. "That band on your finger is presumably the Ring of War."

Jason raised his left hand and made a fist, displaying the red metal loop. He nodded, and couldn't restrain allowing a brief smile to twitch across his lips.

"I'm so happy for you," Merid said. "So, what's Silence's

Ring to you then? Unless you were lying, it won't work for you. I can't imagine War was an 'heir' of Silence by any stretch of the imagination."

He shrugged. "I have a different use for it in mind. As you know, the position of the Maker is vacant. What you may not know is that the Maker had a secret citadel, a place where he could rest his weary head after a long day screwing things up in Ardeyn. It's called the Maker's Hall. It contains potent spells and rituals that will grant me all that I need to fully empower my own Ring, and become as I once was: War, in truth, and not merely in name."

"Don't fancy being called the Betrayer until the end of time?"

He ignored her jibe and continued, "Of course, the Maker's Hall is sealed. It will open only to the Maker's hand. Or, to one who holds any Four of the Seven."

Realization of what he implied burned in Merid's eyes. She wasn't slow. Which was why he needed to keep as close to the truth as possible, without revealing his entire plan. She'd probably object if she suspected he intended to step into the Maker's role, using War merely as a stepping stone.

"What's in it for me, War?" He decided it was a good sign that she'd addressed him by his old title, finally. She was beginning to believe.

"When I enter the Maker's Hall–"

"When *we* enter the Maker's Hall, you mean," Merid interrupted.

Jason considered a moment. Allowing Merid into the Hall would introduce complications. But he couldn't put her off immediately, or their talk was at an end. He said, "We can work out those details, of course. What I'm actually offering you is one of the Rings of Incarnation. Enchanted so it would work for *you*. You could have your choice of them, except for the Ring of War, of course." He chuckled.

Merid sucked in a breath, and he knew he had her.

"An Incarnation. That would be something."

He smiled and nodded.

"And all I must do is give you the Ring of Silence?"

"Lend it to me, if Silence is the Incarnation you wish to become."

Merid pondered. "Maybe. Though Lore or Desire could also prove diverting, each in their own way." Telling her that Desire was lost in an inaccessible realm didn't seem politic at that moment.

"Do we have a deal?"

"Yes, we have a deal," she said. "Except for one wrinkle. Earlier today when I discovered War on the summit of the volcano, asking after the Ring of Silence, I grew concerned. So I sent it away for safekeeping until I could determine why you'd come."

"What do you mean?" His voice rumbled, but Merid didn't so much as flinch.

"Before I met you outside the caravanserai, I sent the Ring of Silence west by dragon wing. Given your reputation, you might've tried to take it by force of arms. Being clever, I thought to put it beyond your reach."

"You're telling me–"

"The Ring of Silence is not here. I sent it out past the Borderlands for safekeeping, into the Strange."

20: REGENT
Elandine, Queen of Hazurrium

"Sark are heading this way, Your Majesty," said the scout. "They know we're here."

Elandine bit into the yellow fruit whose name she didn't know as she listened to the scout's alarming report. Juice exploded in her mouth, slightly sweet, but mostly bitter. Appropriate, she mused.

Navar had warned against choosing a regent in haste. Once again, Elandine regretted her hot-headed decision to ignore the First Protector's advice. To Navar's credit, no recriminations had been offered. Yet.

Opportunities for I-told-you-sos would present themselves after they emerged from this latest unfolding disaster. Assuming they made it through, and didn't disappear into the fetid Green Wilds without a trace. Since Elandine's expedition had no business being anywhere *near* the Green Wilds, no one was going to come looking for them in the tumult of giant trees, poisonous snakes, and numberless sark anytime soon. Especially with a regent sitting on Hazurrium's throne with what Elandine pictured as a secret, smug smile on her face.

Damn it, this was all Brandalun's fault! If her mother hadn't dashed off to pursue her latest cause, whatever the hell it actually was, Elandine wouldn't have been wearing the crown. Why couldn't Brandalun have finished out her reign with dignity and wisdom, and let Elandine grow into the position for a few more years?

But things were as they were. What a rude awakening to learn that merely having that title of queen didn't protect one from a series of wrong – some might call them disastrous – decisions. Being angry helped her through the bad times, but it was no substitute for steering clear of poor policy in the first place. Damn Brandalun!

After War duped Elandine and escaped with the Ring of Peace, the queen fell into a depression the like of which she'd never previously endured. She finally gave in to the inevitable. She retreated to the queendom of Hazurrium to lick her wounds and to mourn her sister Flora.

At least, that'd been the plan. But the passing months didn't dampen her flame; they fed her anger. Say one thing about Queen Elandine, say she holds a grudge like none other. So after the worst of feeling sorry for herself had passed, Elandine allowed the rage to ramp up once more. She vowed revenge on the Betrayer. Deposed Incarnation of War or not, no shading piece of dragon shit was going to get the better of the Queen of Hazurrium!

So she'd raised a host of peacemakers, pardoned criminals, and the cream of the adventuring companies Hazurrium was famous for hosting. Doing so dangerously weakened the standing force that guarded the city. That hadn't been her worst error. Because right before leaving, she gave in to her councilors' recommendation. She installed someone to rule in her stead in case she was gone for an extended period. Regent Shari Marana. Shari was Elandine's cousin, and a noble in her own right in the neighboring kingdom of Mandariel. As regent, Shari had promised fidelity and honor in the queen's absence.

Instead of doing any of that, Regent Shari had somehow arranged for Elandine and her host, shipping across the blue stretches of Oceanus, to sail directly into the teeth of the most wicked storm to lash the great sea within the memory of any living sailor.

Some might call it bad luck. Of course, they didn't know the "gift" Elandine had received in the throne room prior to her departure from Hazurrium. Regent Shari had bowed, respectful and fawning as any handmaiden. She'd described how her agents had made a secret rendezvous with the Oracle in Telenbar. Everyone knew the Oracle's predictions were never wrong. The trick was getting her to provide a prognostication in the first place. Somehow, Shari had managed it. So caught up in the preparations of departure, Queen Elandine never questioned the veracity of the document containing the Oracle's supposed prognostication. She'd been taken in by Shari Marana's downcast eyes and her explanation that the gift was merely something *any* subject would offer her queen setting off on a dangerous quest.

The document laid out a timetable describing when the most auspicious sea crossings might be made over Oceanus for the next few months. It described when good winds and weather would be assured for Elandine and her army to take ship. Elandine, already feeling the sting of too little time, was happy to shift her original timetable a few more days, in order to sail through the prognosticated "window" when they could expect the best winds and weather to see them across the sea in record time.

Who would've guessed waves could grow so tall? It was as if Oceanus had gained a malign will of its own that night. It tried to shake off all who inched across its wind-torn, wave-lashed skin. The queen's armada was shattered.

The storm had been more terrifying than the fight during the krayfall at the Moon Door. Then, at least, she had been able to fight for her life. Against the angry sea, swords mattered little. One could only scream imprecations. Of course, all words, prayers, and curses had been instantly drowned in the wrack and boom. Half the ships Elandine led out of Hazurrium went down with all hands, including the vessels transporting their mounts.. The survivors were blown west, only to break up on the rocky cliffs of Oceanus's southwestern shores.

So Elandine had assembled the survivors. All told, including herself and Navar the First Protector, she counted just over a thousand able warriors still strong enough to test the walls of Megeddon. The remaining survivors, those too hurt or too depleted in spirit to continue, she ordered to the queendom's nearest outpost instead of back to Hazurrium. As much as she wanted Shari Marana to know that her scheme had failed and that the true Queen of Hazurrium yet lived, she'd decided to lay low. If all her enemies thought her dead, when she finally gathered her forces, she could strike with devastating surprise.

But of course things were already off to a bad start. The salvaged carts containing supplies enough to feed her much-reduced force continually broke or got mired in the rough, roadless terrain. Three warriors had succumbed to some kind of poisonous asp, ten had come down with shakes from forest fever, heatstroke culled dozens more, and now the scout had returned with news of sark headed their way.

"How many?" Navar asked the scout, a woman dressed in gray and brown leathers with a scar that ran from the edge of her left eye across her face.

The scout shrugged. "A dozen." She appeared not the least impressed at being asked to give her report directly to Queen Elandine and the First Protector in the royal pavilion. On the other hand, the royal pavilion was hardly more than a large tent. The scout added, "But there could be more. Those curs can cut through the forest like water past rocks in a stream.

If I'd gotten closer, they'd have seen me, certain as winter."

Elandine had fought sark before. Vicious, debased, and graceless, the fallen qephilim were hardly more than animals, and rumored to be driven by the quiescent will of the Sinner himself. It made her shiver to think on *that* connection overlong. The idea that sark were once qephilim at all seemed absurd on its face. But Elandine knew it was true. They'd lost any grace they might have once possessed, and wore only clothing made from the hides and scalps of their victims. They'd forsaken dignity, and possibly even their sanity.

"How soon will they arrive?" Elandine said, putting images of the vile creatures from her mind.

"Assuming they keep moving at their current pace and speed, they're less than an hour from our camp."

Navar saluted the scout. The scout squinted at the First Protector in confusion, and gave something that was halfway between a wave and salute in return. Had the scout been a peacemaker, she'd have known she'd just been dismissed. But she was from one of the companies who'd joined the expeditions in hopes of finding fabulous loot in Megeddon, and just stood there.

"Thank you," said Elandine. "Please alert your troops and any other unit leaders you see to expect company."

"Sure," said the woman, finally realizing the situation. Before ducking out under the flaps, the scout snatched a piece of fruit from a silver platter. The platter had been set by Elandine's seneschal, who remained more concerned with maintaining etiquette than the reality of their situation.

Navar studied the floor of the tent, staying silent. But not for long; by her posture, Elandine knew what was coming. So Elandine got the jump on her First Protector. "Don't say it. We're pressing forward."

Navar's ears flattened fractionally. Only because Elandine had spent so much time with her did she recognize it: the First

Protector's body language screamed disapproval. Elandine felt slightly ashamed of all the horse dung she made the First Protector swallow. Navar was only trying to live up to her duties. But so was she.

"Listen. For all we know," said Elandine, "the Betrayer was behind Shari's duplicity. Either way, War's spies have likely reported to him that Queen Elandine and her retinue are dead. Which means his guard is down. We can't let this opportunity go past without seizing it! You would do the same were you given to rule over the queendom."

"Our forces are only a quarter of what they were."

"And still twice what we need if we strike from surprise."

"Maybe."

"It's a maybe we won't get to try again any time soon. If we're successful, we will do more than secure the Ring of my ancestors – we will cleanse Ardeyn of the Betrayer! All the Daylands will be the safer for his removal, not merely Hazurrium. You know it's true."

Navar shook her head and said, "I've offered all my arguments. I won't offer them anew, because I know your mind is made up. My apologies."

Elandine smiled. "None necessary."

"Let us see to the approaching sark threat. If we survive that, we can assess our best route through the Green Wilds. We'll need to resupply before venturing across the Glass Desert, or skirt it. We did not count on that as our original route."

Elandine nodded. She said, "If our enemies knew we'd survived in the first place, they won't guess we'd track south through the tangled paths, or that we'd spill out onto the killing glass. We have an advantage. We should use it."

She stood, grabbed her sword, then paused a moment to admire the fine runes glittering along the blade. Without the Ring of Peace, her power was lessened, but *Rendswandir* remained as deadly as ever. It was particularly good at dispatching sark. And scheming regents. She said, "I wonder what that bitch Shari is doing right now?"

The First Protector deigned not to answer.

Elandine girded the sword to her waist. "Round up a detachment to ambush those damned sark before they reach us."

"Of course."

Elandine put a hand on Navar's arm before she lifted a flap to exit the pavilion, then pointed at the platter. "You should have one, while they're still fresh. The taste is tolerable. Satisfying, even."

"Later, Your Majesty."

"Your loss." Elandine enjoyed another few bites of the yellow, bitter fruit.

21: NIGHTSTAR
Carter Morrison

The crew of *Nightstar* delighted in setting rats on fire just to watch how far the shrieking things could run across the glass before expiring. Nightly degradations occurred down in the prisoners' hold, where desperate captives were shackled. Hazing was also popular; new crewmembers were ambushed in some dark corner of the ship and beaten within an inch of their lives, while onlookers laughed themselves sick.

Captain Taimin wasn't present for any of these particular episodes, or half a dozen similar incidents that occurred daily on his ship. But he might as well have been the one holding the torch, the whip, or the rope. His implicit permission for every and any atrocity perpetrated by his crew gave the worst among them an excuse to indulge in depravities they were unlikely to have attempted on their own.

That's how I saw it, and for me it wasn't academic. I fucking hated Taimin, despite not having seen his face in the couple of months since I'd come aboard. Things would've been bad enough, but several of Kadir's comrades remained on *Nightstar*. They were none too happy that their friend had been forced off the ship. They'd selected me as the target for their dissatisfaction. From their perspective, Mehvish was too scary to hassle, and Siraja had come under the captain's eye, potentially as his new first mate.

Which left me. And who was I? A stranger found on the glass who should, by all rights, be shackled down with the other captives to be sold as a slave the next time *Nightstar* visited the Citadel of the Harrowing.

Siraja saw to it that I had a hammock and a daily allotment of the slop that each pirate was due. She also provided me with a safe in her own cabin where I kept Jushur. I worried that if I kept that odd object on my person, on in my bunk, someone would steal it.

But Siraja was also kept busy by her new duties, so I hardly ever saw her. Mehvish made it clear I was not to come anywhere near her, or our deal was off. Which left me pretty much on my own. At first, that seemed ideal. I figured that I'd spent the first week or so just trying to understand how things worked on *Nightstar*. And more importantly, trying to delve into my newly revealed Ardeyn-given talents and memories. Then, once things settled a bit more, I'd planned on getting the hell out of Dodge.

Things hadn't proved so easy. Finding more than a few minutes of time to myself was insanely difficult. Several pirates shared my bunk on alternate sleep shifts from me, so I couldn't retreat to the hammock for private time other than during the five-hour sleep shift I had to myself. The bosun seemed to know exactly where I'd next try to hide from him, so as to avoid some backbreaking job or other that he delighted in handing out. And keeping ahead of Kadir's many comrades was a full-time job in itself.

And that's when I learned about the hazing.

Limper, one of the pirates who shared my hammock on alternate sleep shifts, was a greasy, smelly man. He walked as if perpetually drunk, though his rolling gait was actually due to an injury, and thus his name. Of course, he always *was* inebriated, which didn't help.

Limper was also the keeper of the maps. Instead of taking his place in the hammock we shared when my turn came around, I followed him up to the main deck. I was almost dead on my feet and too tired to think straight, but I'd finally realized he'd know *Nightstar*'s route better than anyone. Which meant he'd know the ship's closest approach to the edge of the Glass Desert.

Limper made his wavering way to the stern, and I followed. I wanted to talk to him when no one else was around. I didn't want to invite curiosity about my interest in our route. Someone might guess my actual intent to escape my "duties" as a privateer.

I caught my quarry at the very rear of the ship, along a sort of narrow catwalk that skirted the sterncastle. The sun had set a few minutes earlier, but the warmth radiating up from the glass below was still palpable.

Limper had out his charts, maps, and a sextant. I was surprised a sextant worked in Ardeyn, but there it was.

"Hey, Limper, got a minute?" I said. Only after addressing him with the name everyone else used did my newfound facility for knowing what people are called reveal his birth name: Alizado.

Limper – Alizado – flinched, jerking the sextant away from his eye.

Seeing me, his eyes narrowed. "You shouldn't be here."

"I know, I should be sleeping. Shit, I'm tired. But I wanted to talk to you first. I hear you're a master with the maps, no one better. I was hoping you could help me." Yes, I was resorting to flattery.

He scowled. "As if I'd help *you*. Get away from me, demon!" Not the response I'd expected, and it knocked me back on my heels.

"Hey!" I said. Not particularly eloquent, but better than the response I'd swallowed, "I'm not a demon!"

"Bad enough I got to share my hammock with the moontaint who got Kadir, bravest son of the Maker, thrown off *Nightstar*. Not my choice. But I don't have to stain my ears with anything out of your mouth. Or look at you." He turned back to his equipment.

Another member of Kadir's fan club. How such a bully had won over so many friends I couldn't imagine, but there it was. Limper wasn't going to willingly speak with me, let alone help me. Unless… I helped him see the merit of my cause.

And really, wasn't Limper just an outgrowth of the code I'd written to create Ardeyn? Yes, he was. Which meant I could directly tweak his attitude. And in doing so, I argued with the part of me suddenly concerned with where this was going, I wasn't so much overriding the will of a conscious being as making a few adjustments to eliminate bugs.

Right? I promised myself that I'd wrestle with moral implications later, and concentrated, looking for Limper's *true* name. Alizado was only part of the greater truth making up the man.

A hand fell on my shoulder and squeezed hard before I discovered anything more about Limper. The hand spun me around into the foul breath of someone three times my size. It was Big Toma. Bad news. Another Kadir stalwart. In fact Big Toma was still openly bitching about Kadir's absence. No one else would dare talk so openly against Captain Taimin's decision. But Big Toma was either too stupid, or too sure of his own strength – or both – to keep his tongue in check. And now he had me in one of his oversized hands.

Big Toma said, "You're that new prick, right? Just joined the crew. What's your name?" He grabbed me around the neck and squeezed.

"Cart-ooph!" I wheezed with what air I had left. He'd caught me off guard. I wasn't getting enough oxygen.

"Cart? That's a funny name. Well, Cart, you ain't faced the Red Mast of Valor, have you? You can't be one of us if you ain't gone through what the rest of us done!"

"Yeah!" Limper chimed in. "I shattered my leg 'cause of the Red Mast, but I survived. I proved myself. This little fish's gotta do the same."

"Yup," agreed Big Toma. He turned and padded back around the sterncastle, dragging me behind him like a piece of luggage. Trying to breathe with his fingers still clutched around my neck made me wheeze. He only squeezed harder when I tried to pry them loose.

People around the ship looked up as Big Toma pulled me into view. I was like a doll to him, and I worried he was about to try to pull out my stuffing.

"Hey!" I gasped, or tried to. It came out as a croak, "Get Siraja! Or Mehvish! Or the captain – Toma isn't acting on orders!"

A cackle of laughter went up. A dozen eager, grinning faces congregated as I was hauled across the deck. Amid the gabble of their voices, one phrase was repeated often in eager tones: "Red Mast of Valor!" Fuck. I had no idea what that was, but any sort of hazing that left an able-bodied man with a limp for the rest of his life was not something I wanted to face.

Big Toma finally stopped amidships, beneath the mainmast. The mast was a rusty-sort of red color, which until that moment, I'd failed to realize.

When my captor let go of my neck, it was only so he could jerk me up by my ankle. He lifted me entirely off the deck, upside down. I could only cough and gag. With his free hand, he wrapped the end of rope hanging from the mast around my leg several times, then pulled the cord tight. The world went topsy as blood rushed into my head.

Big Toma tied the line off with an elaborate sailor's knot to the cheers of the onlookers. The wrapping dug painfully into my calf.

No sense of decorum, dignity, or the barest idea of a plan remained in my head. I was near to blubbering. "What're you doing?" I gurgled.

"Making sure you don't fall, little birdie," said my tormenter. "You're going to dangle from the spar where the sails hang for a while. Time to show us your valor, birdie!"

The phrase "hang him from the yardarm" whispered through my brain. I'd always thought it was something they did for executions... Oh.

"No, don't!" I screamed. But I was already being hauled skyward, head down and feet to the sky.

The deck fell away in a series of jerks, each one tightening the rope's grip around my leg. More blood pooled in my head, making me feel even more thick and ineffectual. Paradoxically, the sense of fullness and loss of agency also calmed my panic. I clamped my mouth shut and stopped begging. It wasn't doing any good.

I tried pulling my knees up toward my chest as I bent at the waist. The bumping and jerking made it almost impossible, but I managed to bend and strain upward, getting a hand on the massive knot Big Toma had tied. My leg was already growing numb. The mass of rope around my leg wasn't so much a knot, I saw, as it was a tourniquet. If this was what had happened to Limper, I was surprised he hadn't lost his entire limb.

Having reached a height nearly equal to the topmost spar, Toma tied off his end of the rope around a deck stanchion. He yelled up, "Get comfortable. There you hang till sunrise, birdie!"

Apparently, calling me "birdie" was considered the height of wit, based on the roar of delight the lout got each time he said it.

Tuning out the laughter and crude suggestions below, I tried to figure out how to undo the knot. Hanging upside down, leg going numb, and blood pooling in my brain were factors working against me. Not to mention that it was dark. My fingers fumbled over tight coils and loops of rope I could hardly see.

My heart was pounding and I could hardly breathe. Was I dying?

And yet through my panic, new knowledge trickled into me. Just as I'd somehow known the names of nearly everyone I'd interacted with so far in Ardeyn, I knew this rope. More than merely the rope, in fact. Unless my blood-flooded brain was feeding me hallucinations, I *knew* the mast, the air I was breathing, even the gravity that pulled me downward. The laws of Ardeyn momentarily shuddered into view before my awestruck eyes like illustrations of moving gears within gears within gears... I gasped.

The vision was like another key in the lock of my memory. Or at least, the memory of someone I might have once been:

The Maker handed out Rings to those who became newly embodied Incarnations of Death, War, Lore, and Desire. To them was given a chance to be gods of a fresh reality merely by accepting simple bands of metal. It was that, or face annihilation. When Ardeyn first formed to buffer Earth from the Strange, planetovores were already half-way through the rift. We'd had to stop them. And together, we *did*. But the details were faded to begin with, and grew hazier the more I strained after them.

"Holy shit," I croaked. I'd been something amazing. Something unimaginable... well, actually something straight out of a comic book. The memory of the experience was overwhelming. The vision crashed. Tears welled in my eyes, but rolled up my forehead.

Maybe a version of me had once been something amazing here in Ardeyn.

But I was just a guy hanging from the yardarm for the

amusement of a boatload of jeering pirates.

Except a little something remained after my unexpected recollection like a tickle on the back of my brain. I focused on the rope. When I did, I suddenly understood a bit more of its underlying essence, and the simple geometries of the knot Big Toma had tied. It wasn't as impossible to decipher as it first seemed. I pulled the tangle of cords there, pushed here, and prodded *there*.

The knot fell open like a solved puzzle box under my fingers.

The rope loosened. My leg came free and gravity jerked downward. I grabbed for the mast, and found a tangle of line to hold as I flipped end for end. Maybe a little bit of the élan I'd used to untie the knot was still in my hands, because I can't otherwise imagine how the flip and pull didn't rip me free of my purchase and dash me onto the deck. I did sprain my wrist for my trouble, and the pins and needles of the blood returning to my leg was quickly becoming fiery. If Jushur hadn't been safely stored with Siraja, the sphere would've shaken loose and probably shattered planking on the deck.

"Better stay up there, birdie!" someone bellowed from below. "Your time isn't up!"

Twilight approached, but I could still see a dozen faces looking up at me. One of them, standing on top of the sterncastle, was that bastard Captain Taimin. It was too dark and far for me to see his expression – not that I could read a qephilim's face – but his body language was plain. He was amused. He'd watched the whole thing go down, and hadn't done a thing to stop it.

Did I mention Captain Taimin wasn't my favorite?

The qephilim saw my regard. He whistled to get his crew's attention and said, "You've had your fun! The new meat faced the Red Mast of Valor, better than most of you. Now let him down without harm. Or you'll be the next one sent aloft.

And it won't be your leg the rope is tied to!"

General grumbling followed this command. I waited for some outburst from the huge man who'd run me up, but even he kept his tongue. I peered down the mast. His glare transmitted undisguised hatred. Crap. I was going to have more trouble with Big Toma before all was said and done. But not right then, because he ducked his head, and walked away.

I climbed down under my own power, but only after my leg woke enough for me to feel the stubby rungs on the side of the mast. By the time I was back safely on deck, it was almost completely dark. Several lanterns and a few torches provided warm light. Most of the crew had dispersed. Taimin hadn't moved, and when I looked at him, he said, "You're more competent than you look."

I replied, "Or luckier."

"Maybe. Either way, I wonder if my ship is the right place for you." His ears swiveled on his head.

My heart sped up. Was he offering me a chance to leave, or threatening to take my life? With Taimin, it could go either way. He remained quiet and watched me, and I realized he was waiting for some kind of answer.

"Well," I temporized, "I admit the incident with the hanging from the mast has soured me a bit on *Nightstar*. Most of your crew dislikes me; they blame me for Kadir being sent away."

"Kadir," he said in a musing tone. Then, "Come to my cabin. I have a job for you and a couple of others. If you manage it, I'll let you leave *Nightstar* alive, not in slaves' chains, at the next port we put in."

He turned and went into the forecastle structure where he kept his cabin.

I stumbled up the steps, favoring my tingling leg, and followed him inside.

The captain's cabin was lushly appointed with gold, silks,

and leather. Surprisingly large, too, making me wonder if it was larger on the inside than outside. Such magic was certainly possible in Ardeyn.

Besides Captain Taimin, the palatial chamber held Siraja, my benefactor, and Mehvish, she of the twining hair and deep secrets. I couldn't read Siraja's qephilim features, but Mehvish's eyes held as least as much disdain for me as Big Toma's had. I wondered if I'd fallen out of the pan and into the fire.

"Carter," said the captain. "Interesting choice of name. Did your mother choose to name you after that ancient myth, Carter Strange, or did you take it because you thought to make yourself seem more than you are?"

I sputtered.

Taimin didn't notice my response. He didn't really want to know, he'd just been offering niceties, such as they were.

The captain continued, "I've got a special task for you three. You can think of it as an opportunity if you like, because if you succeed, all of you will get something you want. Carter will go free. Siraja will become my First Mate in truth. And to Mehvish, well, that'd be telling."

"Opportunities aboard *Nightstar* are always welcome, Captain," said Siraja, ears attentive.

"I'm sure. But I want you to know that the assignment is also punitive; if you fail, you'll certainly die."

"Why punitive?" I said.

"Because you three cost me my last first mate, and that has repercussions. I never thought Siraja had it in her to defeat Kadir. My mistake. Which makes me look weak, and I can't have that. I should have killed all of you the moment you came back aboard."

Mehvish hissed, "But here we are still alive..."

"Don't interrupt. But yes. Resources are scarce on the Glass Desert. I'd be a fool to waste your lives, especially if I can put them to use."

The direction this was going worried me.

Siraja lifted her lip lift to reveal canines.

"You mean to send us into the Singing Crater!" yelled Mehvish suddenly.

In response, the captain smiled like the cat who ate the canary.

"Singing Crater?" I said.

"You'll see," said the captain. "Tomorrow."

22: COMPVTATION
Katherine Manners

The orange taxi pulled up outside the sprawling Federal University of Parana, Brazil. The main structure reminded Kate of the White House back in the USA. Lots of white columns, windows, pomp and circumstance.

"Obrigado," Raul told the taxi driver, handing over several colorful bills. The car sped off, leaving Katherine wondering which door they should enter by. Various signs seemed promising, but she couldn't read them. Before she applied for a visa to visit Brazil, she hadn't even known that Portuguese was the country's official language. She was embarrassed to remember she'd assumed it was Spanish.

A man with black-rimmed glasses and neatly trimmed gray hair noticed them from the steps. He yelled, "Olá!" and waved them over.

"Is that Claudio?" said Raul.

"Must be," she said. They waded through the sea of students to the steps.

Liza Banks had provided their contact, one Claudio Rodrigues, who worked in the Federal University computing lab, spoke English, and was amenable to showing an "American silicon valley investor" around the newly founded, next-generation computer research facility the university was building.

"You must be Ms Manners!" said Claudio, beaming.

"And you're Senhor Rodrigues?"

The man's smile widened with delight. "Yes, indeed I am. I am so glad to make your acquaintance. But please call me Claudio." His command of English was so perfect that his accent was hardly noticeable, but when he said Claudio, the name sounded to her ears more like *clowd-joe*.

Claudio looked at Raul. "And this is?"

Raul smiled, turning up the amperage to match their host. He extended his hand and said, "Glad to meet you. Vick Tanzler. I'm hoping what you've got here is as exciting as what we've been led to believe. Because I've got angel investment cash gathering dust in an index fund. An *index* fund, dude! Boring. I can't tell you how awesome it would be to put those greenbacks to work on something exciting. Something like I hear you've got cooking down here in Brazil!"

Kate's mouth fell open. Raul's Mexican accent was gone, replaced by an over-cooked LA surfer accent. *Awesome?*

Claudio blinked a few times, apparently as taken aback at "Vick's" enthusiasm as Kate.

Kate jumped into the breach and said, "Didn't Liza tell you? Things were moving so fast I guess our wires got crossed. Mr Tanzler has joined our group. You can probably see why. So yes, if we like what we see, then we're ready to move with investment papers immediately. Maybe even today?"

"Oh." Comprehension dawned. "Oh! Well that would be wonderful! Though the formal tour of the facility isn't scheduled until tomorrow–"

Raul clapped Claudio on the shoulder and said, "I didn't get where I am by wasting time while the sun's up, dude. All of us only have so much time on this Earth. And I only want to spend part of the days left for me on business, know what I mean?"

"I guess. Well, maybe not–"

"Dude – listen." Raul squeezed Claudio's shoulder for emphasis. "Is there any way you could let us take a peek early? Like, right now? I'd really appreciate it."

Kate suppressed a flinch at hearing yet another "dude" emerge from Raul's lips. She even gave Claudio a conspiratorial wink. Claudio's earlier enthusiasm snuck back onto his face. Their combined effort to sway him seemed to be working. Claudio said, "Well, sure, why not? I have a key card. I suppose it wouldn't hurt to give you a preliminary tour."

"You're a prince, dude."

Claudio gave a nervous laugh, then said, "Follow me."

Kate and Raul fell into step behind their new guide. Kate elbowed Raul in the ribs and whispered, "Lay off the surfer persona."

"Why?" Raul whispered back. "He's buying it."

"Because otherwise, I'm gonna punch you in the face, *dude*."

Raul grinned.

Claudio led them through a series of hallways flooded with students and teachers. Kate smelled books, fried food, and that indefinable scent of aged leather and dust that fill so many places of learning.

Her cell phone rang. She plucked it from her purse and saw Liza Banks's name. Kate answered, "Hello? Make it quick; we're heading toward the facility right now."

Banks voice came over the line, "You work fast. Well, I wanted to let you know that things are moving forward back here, too. We might even have a new asset for the initiative!"

"Um, remind me. Which initiative are you talking about?" Banks had cooked up several. Ahead of her, Claudio paused before a heavy metal door and started going through his pockets, presumably looking for keycard to fit the reader.

"The *Estate* initiative," Liza said, exasperation clear in her tone.

"Oh, right." Liza, Paldridge, Raul, and Kate had discussed dozens of scenarios for scrubbing the quantum code from the "internets." Kate had also revealed – with Raul's reluctant blessing – Raul's claim to be from an alternate dimension. Or, a "recursion" as Raul insisted on calling it.

Instead of being shocked and feeling betrayed like Kate, or even being even the least bit incredulous of his claim, Liza Banks got excited. She'd been specially taken with the idea that Raul was part of a secret organization that dealt with cross-recursion difficulties. Banks suggested Earth needed a similar sort of body, a group with more structure and resources than the ragtag team that she, Paldridge, Raul, and Manners represented. Kate had agreed in principle, but said that it was something to worry about later, after she and Raul dealt with the active research project in Curitiba.

Apparently, Banks hadn't listened.

Raul leaned his head close and whispered, "Everything all right?"

Kate shrugged, and shushed Raul with a finger to her lips. Meanwhile, Claudio found the card he was looking for, and swiped it through the reader. The red light on the reader turned from red to green.

Banks said something, but screeching hinges from the opening metal door was too loud for Kate to understand.

"Repeat that?" Kate asked, following Raul into a narrow hallway beyond the door. "And make it quick."

"Hertzfeld, I said. No last name, like Cher," said Banks.

"I missed something. What're you talking about? Listen, this isn't the best–"

"I put up a webpage, like we talked about. Seeded with code words only someone familiar with the Strange and recursions could've possibly have interpreted correctly. A guy named Hertzfeld saw the website, and our secret message. He's a science-geek type. Maybe a touch autistic. Anyway,

I've got Paldridge checking him out now, to see if he's legit, or just a crackpot who got lucky."

Kate whispered fiercely into the phone, cupping her hand over the mouth and receiver so Claudio wouldn't hear, "You put up a webpage describing... all this?" Kate was appalled. "And we didn't talk about doing any such thing!"

"Well, maybe it was Raul and me who discussed it. If you've got internet, point your browser to the Estate Foundation dot org and tell me what you think!"

Kate put her hand over the receiver and shot Raul a poisonous look. Raul looked confused and mouthed, "What?" She wanted to tell him this was all his fault, but Banks continued, possibly a bit defensive, "So, let me know, OK? We're not standing still up here while you guys are cleaning up code outbreaks in Brazil."

It was too late to worry about Liza Banks running with scissors without Kate around to, what? Supervise? Truth be told, Banks had come around in a big way. Maybe it was time that Kate recognized that. Maybe everything didn't rest on her shoulders.

The thought was kind of nice. She had to admit that their cause was incredibly important, and was very much in need of competent help. As much as they could get.

Kate finally said, "That sounds great, Liza. Good thinking. Can't wait to meet Hertzfeld, if he checks out."

"Excellent. So how, how are things going in Brazil?"

"We're just about to find out." Claudio glanced around and nodded, obviously half-listening to her conversation on the phone. He probably thought she was talking to her investment partners back in the USA. So she said, "Yes, Senhor Rodrigues is a prince, like you said, Liza. I'll let you know how our preliminary look at the facility goes in an hour or so. So far, so good!"

"He's listening, isn't he?" asked Liza.

"Yep."

Banks said, "OK, bye. Good luck," and hung up. What Kate assumed the woman had meant but didn't say, was "Good luck destroying the facility."

"Goodbye." Kate slipped her phone into her purse as Claudio led them up to another security check. This time, each of them had to submit to having their picture taken by a wall-mounted sensor. "Just to maintain a record of visitors," Claudio explained. Then they proceeded into a larger chamber, one with no other obvious exits.

The chamber had been recently retrofitted. The detritus of quick construction was everywhere. Kate recognized electrical, phone, and data fiber cables, pallets filled with construction materials, and the smell of new paint once common to internet startups before the bubble burst.

"Sorry, it's cold in here," said Claudio. Several computer workstations, mostly powered down except for one display featuring a naturescapes screensaver, were crammed around the edges of the room, leaving the center open. Claudio led them across the chamber toward the far wall. "It's even colder in there, where we've got the machine running." Their guide gestured to a wide viewing window set in the wall.

Raul and Kate moved up and peered through. A chunky piece of hardware was installed in a custom rack, occupying most of the sealed room. A subtle vibration, presumably from its operation, tickled Kate's soles. A jumble of cables splayed out from the base, and slithered to various outlets and other ports along the walls.

"Impressive," said Raul.

Claudio nodded. "You want to see what it can do?" His eyes sparkled with excitement.

"That's why we're here," Kate said.

The three gathered around one of the monitors. Claudio entered a password at the prompt too quickly for Kate to catch it. The screen saver cleared, replaced by a clunky input interface.

"Everyone who works in the field tells you that quantum computers are the secret to creating unbreakable encryption," began Claudio, who navigated through a series of menus as he talked. "Or maybe, the secret to *breaking* normal encryption." He laughed, shaking his head. "Others explain how quantum computing unlocks vast new processing power to use on various problems, so that we can finally model complex rocket equations, actually predict weather, or make self-driving cars even safer."

"That's mostly theoretical," said Kate. "Lots of companies have made claims, but few have delivered anything." She was goading Claudio purposefully.

Claudio glanced at her and winked. "Watch this!" He tapped in a few more commands, and one of the screens next to him lit up. It showed what was, apparently, a real-time camera feed of the room in which they were standing. She looked around. She didn't see a camera. From the perspective, she figured it must be concealed over the door where they entered. She waved, and her image on the screen waved in synch.

She said, "I don't understand. You can control spy cameras with your computer?"

Claudio laughed, "No! Well, yes. Like I said, breaking normal encryption is theoretically pretty easy for us. But what true, unlimited quantum computing actually offers is almost limitless processing power for use in simulations. What you're looking at on the screen isn't a camera feed. It's a *simulation* I'm running on the computer based only on the real-time sound cues we're providing, a layout map of the lab, and the pictures I had the system take of us as we entered. It's *extrapolating* everything else. Isn't that incredible?"

"Extrapolating? Like, how I'm moving my hand right now? How I'm twiddling my hair? How could it possibly do that? You're having us on." Despite her protests, Kate's skin prickled. What if he was telling the truth?

"With the right starting conditions, we can simulate and extrapolate in real time. It's uncanny. And as I'm demonstrating, worth your investment."

Raul looked worried. "How far beyond this room have you extended this simulation?"

"How far would you like me to pull back? We've done some limited tests, and have managed to simulate the first floor of the university. But hypothetically, we could increase the scope by an order of magnitude. Maybe even more!"

Kate said, "I can't believe that a piece of hardware, however advanced, has the horsepower to accomplish even a fraction of that."

"Before working on this project, I'd have agreed with you," said Claudio. "But then we, um, learned of an entirely new way to control nuclear and electronic spins in diamond crystals. That allowed us to create a next-generation of quantum computing chip. Now that it's running, it's almost as if we've tapped into some larger network! The more processing power we ask for, the more we get."

It reminded Kate of Carter's story, the one about his VR simulation going so disastrously wrong. "Shut it down," she said. "We've seen enough."

"But I was just—"

Raul yelled, his old accent back, "Turn it off, you fool! Every second it runs, we risk forging a permanent connection *directly* to the dark energy network!"

"Do as he says," a new voice behind them instructed. "Shut it down. Then explain why you're running unsanctioned simulations in here, let alone with strangers present?"

A bulky man in a suit stood in the center of the room. He

wore red sunglasses. Pale amber light hazed the air around him, making the room behind him seem blurry and unreal.

Claudio gasped. "Mr Coleson! I didn't know you were here today."

"Answer my question," replied the suit, taking a step closer. Kate reached for Malcolm before remembering she hadn't checked her pistol on the international flight. Too much could've gone wrong. Unfortunately, things were going wrong in a different fashion now.

Claudio typed a command on the workstation keyboard and the simulation on the screen died. Raul, who obviously understood more than her, literally breathed a sigh of relief.

Kate decided to ignore the haze for the moment. She addressed the newcomer with red shades. "Mr Coleson? Would I be correct in assuming you're the one who supplied the schematics to the university? Presumably you found those schematics somewhere online?"

The man's scarlet gaze settled on her. Something about him was sort of familiar. His mouth quirked up one side of his face in a sardonic smile. "Nope. Claudio here found those himself. I only appeared on the scene, so to speak, after he turned on the machine the first time. Let's just say that I serve the interests of Jason Cole."

"Who's Jason Cole?" asked Claudio. Everyone ignored him.

"Coleson – Jason Cole!" hissed Kate "It's *you*!" The man's features strongly resembled the face they'd all seen on the screen in Liza Banks's office. Although, not exactly.

"No. Not the *original*, anyhow."

Then she understood.

"You're another fucking copy!" she accused. She remembered how the man she'd encountered in the server room of BDR so many months earlier had slumped like hot candle wax into a slurry of pink goo. He'd been a sort of clone-envoy of Jason from Ardeyn. "So, when are *you* going to melt?"

He laughed. "Not going to happen. Think I'd risk a trip and maybe end up the same way? Nope, thanks to the new regime operating here, I'm every bit as real as you are. I've translated. Assuming Claudio doesn't fuck everything up."

"Hey!" said Claudio.

"We're going to shut you down," said Raul.

Red glasses said, "Fine. We don't even need this place, not anymore. We've perfected translation initiation from our side. Witness the mouth of this translation gate." He gestured behind him.

Kate's eyes flicked to the vertical hazing in the air. Shit. Coleson was intimating that the lightshow was, what, some kind of physical gate into Ardeyn? And that they could open gates back "there" and reality at will now?

"Why are you telling us this?" asked Raul. "You know we're here to stop it."

"Because you *can't* stop it," Coleson said. "And I'm bored. You try talking only to yourself for decades at a stretch and tell me if doesn't drive you insane with boredom."

"Listen," interrupted Claudio. "What the hell are you talking about, Coleson? What's this business with a translation gate? And what the hell is that?" He pointed an accusatory finger at what Coleson called the translation gate.

Coleson glanced at the university man. "I'm not talking to you."

Raul said, "I'll tell you this for free, Coleson: you've got to keep this machine off, and destroy it. Both Ardeyn and Earth are vulnerable while it's on. Tell your boss he doesn't really understand what he's messing with."

Coleson shrugged, "Knowing Jason – and trust me, I *know* him – it's possible he doesn't understand. But it's a gamble we'll have to–"

"Hey," said Claudio. "You're all having me on, right? What

are you talking about? Where's Ardeyn? Through the, um, gate?"

"For the love of Christ, shut up, man," Coleson told Claudio. "Can't you see I'm trying to have a conversation?" Coleson pulled a gun from his suit and shot Claudio. He swung back to Kate and Raul. "Now where were we?"

Raul yelled "Take cover!" as he followed his own advice, ducking behind a monitor.

Kate dove behind a workstation.

"Hey, now why'd you go do that?" Coleson yelled. "It was rude. Don't you want to talk anymore? Fine. You were starting to bore me anyway."

Shots, fired in rapid succession, echoed like cannons in the small room, followed by the sharp din of shattering glass. Shards of broken window hit the floor around her. After a few seconds of utter silence, she peeked around the edge of a partition.

Claudio was slumped on the floor, blood pooling around his unmoving form. Shit! He'd seemed like a genuinely nice guy.

Raul crouched behind a workstation two down from Kate. He produced what looked like a slender silver flashlight from his pocket. He pointed one end at Coleson. A ray of purple light flashed from it. The ray missed Coleson, but only because he leaped like a man-sized insect from one side of the room to the other. Upon landing as easily as a ballet dancer, he spun and fired his gun yet again. This time, one of his shots grazed Raul, who fell back with a yelp.

Fuck. They'd all be dead in less than twenty seconds at this rate. She had to do something! But what? No gun; that'd been established. But she had the ring that Jason had sent across with his first, failed clone. The same ring he'd used to get inside Raul's head.

Maybe if she flashed it, she could trigger some kind of

hesitation on Coleson's part. He was a clone of Jason, after all. Then she'd try to tackle the bastard. She pulled the ring from her pocket and slipped it on.

It was oddly cool to the touch. Unexpectedly, the contact calmed her. Somehow, she knew it was all going to be all right. She just had to concentrate on what she wanted. So what did she desire? She wanted Coleson gone, that's what.

So she focused on the man. It suddenly struck her just how out of place he was. He shouldn't *be* here. He'd just stepped through a portal from some other world – a world that wasn't even actually *real!* It wasn't right. The hairs on her arm rose like they sometimes did when she watched electrical storms.

Before her better sense could convince her she was committing suicide, she rose, pointing at Coleson with the hand wearing the ring, and said, "You're not welcome here."

A confluence of fundamental forces – she wasn't sure what else to call them – jolted him from all directions, curling out of dimensions normally too small to be seen. Coleson went rigid, as if held in place by a massive electric current running through him. His wrongness, she knew, his presence on Earth when he was native to Ardeyn, added to the effectiveness of what she'd done. Whatever that was.

The weird bubble of calmness she'd been acting in popped. What the fucking hell? She glanced at Raul.

Raul said to her, "See? I told you didn't need a gun, *mi chula*. You're quickened."

"I didn't do that," she said.

"Well, *I* didn't do it," said Raul, his tone reasonable.

Kate looked back at Coleson. He was still rigid and vibrating, but she sensed that whatever effect she'd triggered, it wouldn't last long. They had a minute at most. Or maybe far less. "What should we do?"

"What we came to do." Raul produced another device from his pocket. A miniature grenade? "This should do the trick." Raul pressed a contact on the side. He tossed it overhand through the broken window, at the machine that still vibrated there. An iridescent green explosion of light consumed the grenade, the computer, and half the side-room. The roar of the explosion was loud, but not as loud as Kate would've expected. It was over before Kate even thought to move back.

The computer was simply gone, as was the floor in a roughly circular area around where it had been. That's when Kate realized that she hadn't been flung back by a grenade blast, a blast that had essentially happened only about fifteen feet in front of her. Grenades normally killed within fifteen feet, and sometimes a lot farther.

"Cypher," said Raul, as if that explained things. It didn't.

Then he walked up to the blur hanging in the air. It was noticeably smaller than before. "C'mon, *mi chula*. We must to go through and destroy the sister facility. Before this translation gate collapses. It could take us months to find where we need to go if we don't go through now."

Her head was spinning, but she knew exactly what Raul was proposing, so she didn't ask him if he was insane, pretend she didn't understand his intent, or otherwise try to fend off the inevitable. Because she suspected he was right. But if she thought too much about it, she still might not agree.

But first...

She picked up Coleson's gun, and aimed it directly at Coleson, who still wasn't moving. Her finger touched the trigger, then fell away.

What had she done to him, when she'd pointed at him? Now that she had a gun, part of her wanted to shoot Coleson, not so much because he probably deserved, but because she wanted to negate what had just happened, what she'd just done.

She wanted the crazy to go away.

Raul looked at her. "I don't blame you for not shooting a

defenseless man. Nor will I think any worse of you if you do. But decide!"

"Fuck it," she whispered.

Kate lowered the gun and jumped with Raul through the rapidly closing translation gate.

23: EXPEDITION
Jason Cole

The last hints of Ardeyn's atmosphere whispered away. Jason plunged into a sea of spiraling fractal patterns iterating upon themselves like snakes forever eating their own tails. A shock of bluish-purple color dazed him. Flashes of gold, orange, and blood-red light seared his retinas. He blinked repeatedly. The twists and turns of the shapes shimmering all around him seemed chaotic, but when he followed any single edge, his mind picked out maddeningly complex patterns that threatened a headache like nothing he'd previously experienced. If Jason hadn't been mounted on the dlamma, he would've foundered.

Merid had sent the Ring of Silence into the Strange to keep it out of his hands before she and he reached detente. He didn't fully trust her, so he'd suggested they retrieve the Ring together, despite the fact that Jason had never previously dared to enter the Strange. If the kray found him in their domain, without the Rules of Ardeyn to enforce their mutual agreements, they'd consume him in an instant. Well, probably not instantly. He was War, after all, even out here. It was the kray matriarch he feared. The longer he stayed out here, the more likely she'd come for him.

But he *needed* the Ring of Silence. It was go after it, or give up on a century of effort. Even so, he might not have risked the trip if Merid hadn't agreed to guide them safely. In return for the Ring, he'd promised to reward her generously after he entered the Maker's Hall.

The dragon had warned that his senses would be confused in the alien environment. So he'd been ready. He just hadn't realized that the Strange was going to be like *this*. The visual phenomena were gut-churning. But it was the unexpected *odor* that left him gasping.

Jason smelled a dusty, slightly mildewed basement bedroom. The odor triggered his childhood memories with the vividness of a bullet through a window. He was back in his bed in his parents' drafty house, hearing the sounds of the ghost that had tormented him.

Remembering which were "real" memories wasn't easy for Jason anymore. He suffered from recollection overload. In addition to his actual childhood experiences, all those imposed by the Incarnation of War's fake history also flooded his head. Not to mention all memories he'd earned the old-fashioned way in the last two-hundred odd years he'd been marooned in Ardeyn.

The rare times Jason tried remembering being a kid in Kansas, the memories cross-circuited. Instead of green grass and trees, he saw one of a hundred apocalyptic battles between dragons, qephilim, humans, dlamma, demons, and Incarnations that had happened during the Age of Myth. Sometimes he remembered plunging a burning blade in the Maker's back. Or he'd recall some other detail of his existence as an Incarnation that had nothing to do with the ranch-style house where he *actually* grew up. When it came to his mother, Nancy Cole, or his father, Avery Cole, Jason came up almost completely blank. He could barely remember their names, let alone their faces, how they'd treated him, or any formative childhood lessons they'd provided. All except for the ghost thing, of course.

Avery, whatever his other strengths or weakness might have been as a parent, also apparently thought that instilling a healthy fear of the dark was important for his child. To that end, he occasionally snuck downstairs and went into the room next to Jason's, where the washer and dryer, the furnace, and the extra freezer were located. Avery proceeded to make "ghost noises" from the other side of the wall. He groaned, growled, and sighed like a lost spirit. Avery did this after Jason had already gone to bed, of course, not long after Jason made the perilous run from the light switch back to the protective blankets of his bed. He'd known the noises were coming from his father, not a ghost. He wasn't stupid. But the ghostly groans had terrified him anyway. He'd been a kid.

Normally, such old memories – when he could pull them up at all – were faded like paper left in the sun. Colorless and drab, they lacked sting.

But not this time. This time, the memory of being afraid in his bed brain-slammed Jason. The sound of his father pretending to be the ghost was all he could hear. The darkness under the blankets – and their particular odor – was all he could see and smell. The sounds terrified him, pulling an answering cry of negation from him in a hoarse whisper.

"War?" came Merid's voice, dragging Jason back to the moment. He was still astride his dlamma, its wings spread wide, using them to surf the dark energy boil. Next to the dlamma flew Merid, transformed into her real shape: a massive dragon, with brilliant feathered wings more than twice as far from tip to tip as the dlamma's.

Jason was *in* the Strange. After what Carter had described on his first exposure – an endless, shuddering expanse deeper than any real sky, an infinite wheeling eternity where hunger stirred – Jason'd decided to never chance it himself. Yet here he was, smelling that same smell as the basement beneath his bed, remembering those same traumas he'd dismissed and forgotten as silly childhood fears...

"Are you leaving me already? What kind of failed Incarnation are you?" Merid said, drawing him back from his recollections a second time. "Whatever you're seeing or feeling, it's not real. It's an effect of this realm on the mind. I told you to be ready."

Jason concentrated on gathering his strength. The warmth of embarrassment flushed his face. It was a feeling he hadn't endured in years.

"I'm fine." He focused his eyes just ahead and above the dlamma's head, where a void between two larger fractals created a zone free of mind-bending patterns. The dlamma seemed unfazed by what lay all around them, as did Merid.

"You were making sounds like a child. At least, I think it was a child," said Merid, her draconic visage swiveled on her long neck to regard him quizzically.

"Maybe. But the fit has passed," he said. "How is it that you and the dlamma aren't affected? This place seems designed to tear minds asunder."

The dragon's scaled lips drew back into something probably meant to be a smile. "For my part, I'm still surprised one of *those* would agree to bear you, of all people." Merid's closer wing dipped, indicating the dlamma.

Was she avoiding his question? Maybe she was trying to direct his thoughts away from the precipice... So he decided to go with it. "What, you think all dlammas are champions of the weak and downtrodden in Ardeyn?"

The dlamma bearing Jason flew on without giving the least indication that it understood their conversation, though of course it could. Dlammas originally were the steeds of qephilim who fought against the human dragon riders serving Lotan during the Age of Myth. At least, according to the prehistory of the fake recursion Jason called home.

"Even the ones who no longer uphold the Seven Rules – the twisted ones – seem unlikely to serve a master, however powerful," pressed Merid.

"So long as I allow it to hunt one of my homunculi every month or so, it agrees to bear me."

"Interesting!" Merid said. "And now I understand. Did you know, usually when I meet a dlamma, it's a fight."

The dragon turned its gaze on the dlamma as they winged through the void, as if challenging it. It ignored her completely. Jason stilled his instinct to pat the dlamma on the neck, which he knew from personal experience would cause it to buck him off. Here in the Strange, would that be lethal?

"Maybe you can fight later," Jason said. For the hundredth time, Jason mentally checked his connection to his Ring, and through it, the directional fix he had on the Ring of Silence. It still lay ahead. If Merid was leading him into a trap, at least it was baited with what he needed.

"How far?" Jason asked.

Merid shrugged, which was a sort of full body movement for her. She said, "It's not so much distance as time. Locations are relative out here. Everything is constantly changing. Finding a way between them requires that you mentally memorize beacons and signposts, and concentrate on reaching them."

Jason craned his head around and looked behind him. He'd expected to see Ardeyn growing smaller in the distance. Instead, he saw only more of the Strange, stretching away to infinity behind them. As he considered whether or not to comment on the feeling of being utterly lost, he spied a hazy, translucent bubble in the far distance. Ardeyn was hundreds of miles across, but the sphere was hardly a fraction of that, and growing smaller every minute as the dlamma and dragon flew on. He focused his gaze upon the sphere, committing it to memory.

Merid's head twisted round, and her lips drew back into another smile, though he was beginning to have his doubts about the expression. "That sphere," Jason said. "It's Ardeyn's beacon, yeah?"

"It'll serve that purpose," she said, and her smile fled. It reappeared on Jason's face, his first one in the Strange. At least that was one thing she couldn't hold over him.

"Not to be pedantic, then, but how *long* until we reach this hidden enclave of yours?"

"It's variable. Several more hours at least. Perhaps we can pass the time by you telling me more of this Earth I've heard you speak of, and what's kept you so busy at your Foundries."

Jason rubbed his chin. "I don't recall telling you anything about Earth."

"Yet, I seem to know about it. Maybe I learned about it from my spies." She laughed.

Jason seriously doubted Merid had anyone on the inside of his operation. Everyone was *him*, for fuck's sake. He wouldn't betray *himself*... Then again, he was kind of a dick.

And sometimes the clones created using the body vats were unreliable. He looked forward to the day *all* his power returned, and he could scrap those homunculi completely. His lieutenants in particular had it coming.

"Well, you got me there," Jason said. "So fair's fair. Explain what else you've learned about this insane place we're flying through. If you've got a lair out here, you must've been out here before. Most critters of Ardeyn remain stuck in the narrative of the Land of the Curse."

"'Stuck in the narrative'? Fascinating way of putting it, I'll have to remember that. But *I* woke up. Maybe partly because of your own actions, upsetting everything when you slew the Maker. I discovered the land I lived in was only one of many limited worlds, all adrift in the Strange."

Something about the dragon's explanation bothered Jason. He was certain she was leaving something out. But he nodded along.

She continued, "One world isn't so limited, is it? The world *you* come from. Earth."

"Just how *did* you learn about that?"

"You're not the first version of yourself who I've had the pleasure of speaking with. You've cast so many of yourselves away over the years. Luckily for me, most versions of you are fairly compliant, when enough pain is applied."

Jason reined the dlamma to a stop, so that they hung drifting in the void. Merid flew past, then dipped one wing to curve her flight so that she entered a wide orbit around them.

"What's wrong?" she called. That damned "smile" was back on her muzzle.

"How many of my homunculi have you interrogated?" he asked with a sinking feeling. It was a stalling tactic. She probably knew his entire plan. And she'd lured him out here for a reason; probably not the one he thought.

"I've lost count. The odd thing is that, despite all of them being copies of you, they were all a little different. They all died differently. Some defiantly, some pleading, others in stoic silence. Isn't that fascinating?"

"Yeah." Jason craned his head back along their route, looking for the sphere he'd earlier spied. It was gone, too far behind him. But he'd marked it as a beacon, as the dragon had described. He hoped that would be enough.

Merid continued. "So I wonder how *you* will die, now that your time has come."

"You can't hope to beat me in a fight, Merid, for all your strength. I am War, and a measure of my Incarnation has returned to me."

To demonstrate, and to see if he could draw on the power of War while in this crazy realm, he threw off a handful of armored duplicates. None of them had mounts to support them, so they hung in the emptiness around him like paratroopers in free fall. He swallowed a sigh of relief. Their heads began swiveling in unison, tracking the dragon.

Merid fluidly widened her orbit, then said, "You're confident because you don't fully understand what it is to be a dragon. On the other wing, a dragon does not like to leave things to chance when she doesn't have to. It's not how I gained my current position, by being sloppy. And it's why I brought you out here, where I have friends who are especially interested in you. What is it you call them? The kray?"

"You didn't."

"Oh, I did. They promised to give me anything I wanted, if they could have *you*. And look, here they come now!" The dragon pointed with a claw.

A stain was growing in the void in the direction they had been traveling. He'd noticed earlier, but had assumed it was yet another oddity of the network best not studied too closely. He focused his senses. The stain leaped into clarity: it was composed of thousands of swarming kray, swirling in their direction through the void like a school of starving razorfish. And he didn't doubt that behind the vanguard, their matriarch followed. Somewhere in all that alien flesh, he sensed the Ring of Silence.

"You bitch," he said to Merid, not quite able to keep his voice even, but not from fear. It was rage. She'd ruined everything.

Jason reined his dlamma around and whispered, "To Ardeyn, as if your life depended on it." The dlamma, tucking its wings, banked sharply enough that Jason nearly fell off, then surged back the way they'd come.

Merid easily paced them, leaving the handful of homunculi he'd summoned behind. He mentally commanded that they blunt the kray advance, for all the good it would do.

"Fleeing won't save you," Merid said, from his left. Her wings had no trouble sculling through the void of the Strange as she paced his dlamma.

He knew it was probably pointless, but decided to try. He yelled, "Why do you think the kray want me? If they kill me out here, where none of the Seven Rules apply, they render the agreements I've made with them null and void. Those agreements are... complicated. If I'm killed out here, it'll probably breach Ardeyn's Seven Rules. Nothing will prevent the kray from pouring into the Land of the Curse. They won't stop until they've consumed everything! Including you."

"As if I would trust anything you tell me," she replied. "The title 'Betrayer' did not come to you for nothing." Then she breathed a sheet of fire hot as the sun at him.

His dlamma veered. The fire only singed them. Still, the skin along his back, beneath his armor, blistered. The dlamma's wingtips smeared trails of smoke.

War's aura kindled like a bonfire from the pain of his blistering skin, overcoming and magnifying him like the director of a thousand-piece symphony orchestra. Well, two hundred-piece, he had time to marvel as the exultation of the drums built. Then he was no longer Jason. He was the Incarnation of War.

He jumped away from his saddle, aiming at the dragon. The dlamma kept winging onward without so much as a look backward.

War drew his staff. It burst into flame at least as bright as Merid's breath. The dragon, banked upward to avoid his leap. His trajectory carried him through the void as if he had wings of his own. Merid wasn't fast enough to completely evade his surprise attack. She roared as his fiery weapon crashed down on one wing and went tumbling away as the momentum of his own attack carried him onward.

War realized it wasn't the *wings* of either the dlamma or the dragon that allowed them to travel through the Strange. After all, the approaching kray armada had none. It was will. And of that, War had plenty. More than any dragon, however ancient and powerful. Before there were dragons, he had strode Ardeyn as the manifestation of battle.

War's trajectory abruptly curved. He came around, exhilaration burning through him like a forge fire, then accelerated like a bolt from a ballista toward Merid.

The dragon, one wing hurt, still managed to react almost instantly. She extended her head and loosed another stream of fire. War didn't flinch; he accreted dozens of lesser selves around him with a thought, creating a barrier of flesh.

Which immediately began burning away like ablative armor, individual components screaming in searing agony. War felt the unbearable pain of his duplicate selves dying, but he didn't let his dive toward Merid falter. On one level, he didn't care. On the field of battle, soldiers died. But on another level, it shocked him. For an instant, his sense of self – as Jason – sparked back into existence. Like fire taking light, Jason's mind bloomed back to full control. Jason wavered even as he brought his staff around, connecting with Merid's head. But not lethally, as the blow would've otherwise been. He'd allowed himself to think, damn it all, and War's aura faded away into the background once more. With the power of the Ring only partially renewed, he didn't know when he'd be able to call on it again.

But Merid didn't know that. She backed off, wings suddenly frantic, head unsteady from his blow. Then she fled without another word or thought of trying to distract him.

The kray's advance now blotted out a quarter of the emptiness, and the scent that had nearly undone him was replaced with a sort of termite reek. They were too close. If he lingered any longer, the advancing wave would envelop him. His dlamma, understanding the better part of valor, was already far ahead of Jason, following the fleeing dragon.

Words whispered out of the void behind him, from the massed throats – if they had throats – of the kray. Or maybe it was in his head? He heard, *War of Ardeyn, all your promises are due. We call them in now, as is our right. As we agreed. Give yourselves up to us!*

"No!" screamed Jason, terror pouring like ice water down his spine. "That wasn't our agreement!" He'd never needed to be War so desperately as then, but the Incarnation seemed farther away than ever. Could dread give you a heart attack?

Our agreement was open to change, as you agreed when we gave you the last gift. The one you used to touch your home in the universe of the real...

"Just give me more time. Let me return to Ardeyn. Finish what I've started." Sweat beaded on his lip, trickled down his back within his suddenly too-warm armor.

Why should we?

That was a good question. "The universe of 'the real' you called it. If you let me go now, I will open the way for you." Of course, he wouldn't actually do that, not really. Would he?

The kray didn't answer. Their advance didn't stop. But it slowed. As if to give him time...

Time to betray not only everyone in Ardeyn, but everyone on Earth...

No. Jason frowned. The kray were easily manipulated, as he'd just proven, again. They wouldn't get Earth – his home planet didn't deserve to be destroyed by inhuman monsters. If anyone were going to take over the planet, it was going to be him.

At that thought, a flicker of War's mantle pulsed once, bequeathing a gift before falling nascent once more. Jason recalled the secret of moving in the Strange that War had divined: the will to make a change.

Jason shot away from the advancing kray front. His fiery staff left a smear of sooty ash across the void.

24. EXPLORATION
Carter Morrison

A massive crater pocked the Glass Desert. Shards of silvery glass larger than houses surrounded the cavity. They were still sharp. Siraja had explained that it'd once been a blister that'd shattered. The resulting hole was called the Singing Crater because of the strange music that emerged from the cavity. The pirates sometimes heard it from miles away at night, high and fluting.

"Who makes the music?" I asked her as *Nightstar* wove between stands of broken glass. The ship was close to the crater's edge. We stood along the railing, watching the shards slip past. The sun was already well up, but a low cover of clouds kept things tolerably cool. Even though we were near our destination, I couldn't hear any harmonies.

"No one knows. Maybe we'll find the performer," she said, without much conviction.

"No one's gone to check before now? I find that hard to believe."

"Many have tried," she said. "What became of them…?"

"Let me guess: they never returned."

She smiled. "Not always. Sometimes only parts returned. One of the princes in Mandariel sent a party of explorers into the crater five years ago. A few days after they were sent, the explorers' right hands were found piled in a heap on the floor of the prince's bedroom."

"That can't possibly be true. It's just a pirate's tale. Right?"

She shrugged. She did that a lot, but I didn't take it as a slight. It was a kind of casual gesture normally shared only between friends. Early on, she may have regretted stepping in to help me. But since then, I liked to believe we'd become friends, or at least friendly acquaintances.

"Regardless," I continued my thought, "if so many people are willing to risk their lives – and dismemberment – to find the sound's source, the music must be exquisite."

"It's mysterious, certainly," Siraja said. "But explorers and greedy princes care more about the legend." She looked at me. I stared back. Her head was almost perfectly smooth, like polished ebony, and reminded me of nothing so much as a bust of the god Anubis. But here in Ardeyn, no one had ever heard of ancient Egypt, except for me, Jason, and maybe some of the others I'd stranded here, if they were still alive. Despite her nonhuman features, I could read her expression. I'd been here that long. She was looking at me as if she expected me to know what the hell she was taking about.

So I shook my head and said, "All right, I'll bite. Tell me about this legend."

"Yes, please finish your story," Mehvish urged Siraja. Startled, I jumped a little.

Where the hell had she come from? Mehvish hated me, I was certain. Sometimes she called me "the half-wit." Once she'd suggested that she'd like to add my hair to her collection, whatever that meant. Given that she was supernaturally good at disappearing then reappearing while I was distracted, the whole hair collection thing freaked me out more than a little.

Instead of jumping in surprise, Siraja flicked an ear at Mehvish. "According to legend, the Glass Desert is all that remains of the Maker's Hall. It was once a vast castle of glass.

It was the Maker's citadel in Ardeyn, but was slagged and melted when Lotan burned hottest during the Age of Myth."

Oh. Right. Stupid me, I knew that because I'd written a lot of the fake history for the Land of the Curse. *Fake no more, Carter,* I reminded myself. It was surreal.

Siraja continued. "The legend says that beneath the desert, in bubbles and hollows, explorers can discover artifacts of the Age of Myth. Stuff that was once kept in the Maker's Hall. But especially greedy types say that these are just the merest sprinkling of the true treasures waiting to be claimed, if one could find a surviving entrance to what remains of the Hall's interior."

Suddenly, the idea of exploring the Singing Crater sounded like the best idea I'd ever heard.

And here I was smack-dab in the center of the Glass Desert, which I'd completely forgotten was the Maker's home in this world's pre-history. Could it be a wild stroke of luck?

No. Nor mere coincidence. Yes, I'd translated blindly into Ardeyn. But I'd obviously arrived at the site my older self thought of as home: the Maker's Hall. At least, what was left of it. Or maybe this was the place where my older self left Ardeyn... when the Maker was killed by Jason. I frowned.

Anyway, I wasn't going to look a gift horse in the mouth. If I could get into where the Maker version of me had done all his mojo, maybe *I* could make things right, take care of Jason, and eliminate whatever contamination he'd delivered to Earth on his Ardeyn-built flash drive. I wanted to ask Jushur what it thought of the idea and my chances, but I'd made a point of not talking to the sphere since I'd come aboard the pirate ship. The last thing I needed was for it to spook them, and give everyone yet another reason to hate me.

A cry went up from the crow's nest. The crew of the pirate ship furled sails. Before us, not more than a half a football field away, was the crater's edge. Broken shards lay in haphazard heaps around it, in piles reaching dozens of feet high in places, forming a foreboding barrier without room for the ship from to approach closer. I didn't see any easy footpaths, either.

"This is the only way in?" I asked.

Siraja shrugged.

Captain Taimin marched up, idly stroking the length of his muzzle like some men rub their beard while thinking. Spying us, he nodded in satisfaction.

"You have three days," he said. "If you're not back by then, we'll skate off and leave you to whatever end you find below."

"And what, exactly, should we bring out of that death trap, should we be so lucky?" demanded Mehvish.

"Something worthy of your captain," said the qephilim. "I leave what that might be to your imagination. Don't come back at all if you can't find something suitable."

Since I was hoping to find something of the Maker and never return to the captain's wretched ship, I didn't ask him to be more specific. If I discovered what I hoped, I wouldn't need Taimin and the *Nightstar* to escape the Glass Desert. Hell, maybe I already had all I needed to find Jason and defeat him, or leave Ardeyn and return to Earth, hidden somewhere in my swiss-cheese memory. I half-closed my eyes, trying to remember... But my recollections were as slippery as fish.

Mehvish prodded me. "Have your wits deserted you completely? What's wrong?"

I blinked. "I was just thinking of a song I used to know," I lied. Mehvish wasn't going to give me an inch, that was clear, even now when our lives depended on us working together. Once we were off the ship, I decided the three of us needed to have a heart-to-heart about the situation.

"Is everyone ready?" asked Siraja. Mehvish turned slightly. I saw she wore a pack, just like Siraja and I. My pack held rope, water, food for a few days, a utility knife, parchment

and a charcoal pen, and a mirror. All things I'd requested –
and received – from ship's stores in preparation for our trip.
Really, all items I'd pack for a camping trip.

A wiry privateer lowered a rope ladder over the side. I
followed the others down its length, the rough rope thick and
scratchy in my palms. We stood in the shadow cast by the ship,
so the sun reflected in the glass didn't burn us like ants under
a microscope, though the heat was still uncomfortable. A
trickle of sweat inched down my back beneath my undershirt.

"Which way?" I said. The forest of shards around the edge
seemed impenetrable from where I stood. I'd hoped a path
would become clear once we'd gotten down on the glass.

Siraja shrugged again. Perhaps my earlier estimation of
what her shrug meant had been off. Friendly or not, it was a
gesture I was beginning to despise. She said, "We walk around
until we see a path," she announced.

Mehvish glared without offering an opinion. I had nothing
better to suggest, so I said, "Lay on Macduff." I doubt she got
the reference, though she didn't bother to ask what I meant,
either.

Instead Siraja moved to the left leaving behind the cool
shadow. Mehvish and I followed. When the sun hit me,
my skin prickled as it pulled taut and dry. After we'd gone
a few dozen yards, I glanced back at the ship. A handful of
heads were silhouetted up on the railing. A hand went up
and waved, and raucous laughter floated across to us down
on the reflective surface. The pirates watched, and no doubt,
were laying odds on how quickly we'd meet our end. But
after only a few more paces, towering shards blocked the
view. Hopefully, it was the last they'd ever see of us. Even
if I didn't find my salvation in the crater, maybe we'd avoid
returning to *Nightstar* courtesy of heatstroke or a razor-sharp
glass avalanche.

We walked in silence for several minutes. Though the

heaped glass was dangerous, at least it sometimes shaded us from the sun. Other times, reflected light was so bright we could hardly see our way forward.

"They sent us out here to die you know," Mehvish finally observed in a perfectly calm voice, as if she was commenting on the weather.

Siraja stopped. She shook her head in negation, though not with the hearty confidence of someone who knows she is right. Shit.

"Listen," I said. "Taimin is crap, yeah. But he doesn't strike me as someone who'd throw away perfectly good crew out of spite. There must be some hope of us finding a way in, or he'd have saved a lot of trouble by just letting us off in any old place on the glass."

"He'd have done it by dragging," intoned Siraja.

"Right," I said, "dragging!" I didn't know what death by dragging was, but I could imagine. I continued, "A public execution would generate a lot more solidarity, and fear of the captain, with the rest of the crew. Whereas sending us off on some quest where no one can see us die robs him of that spectacle. If we die out here, everyone will just forget about us and move on. Which means the captain, that twisted fuck, thinks we've got a chance. And we do, if we can all work together, and put our differences behind us. At least on this mission."

"A sound plan," Siraja agreed. Then she actually grinned at me. Which is sort of terrifying on a qephilim's face. We both glanced at Mehvish.

Mehvish grunted, then drank from her water skin. I could tell it was already mostly empty. Mine was the same. When she didn't disagree, I decided to take it as agreement, however reluctant.

"So," I said, "let's get serious about getting past this rim of broken glass to the crater itself."

"That's what we're doing, idiot," said Mehvish.

My hands didn't quite clench into fists. Instead I said, "Right. But we need help. I'm running low on water already. Isn't there some kind of – I don't know – a story or myth about the Maker? Maybe one that talks about the Maker's Hall? Like, how the hell did the Maker get in and out of it?" I risked spilling my secret desire, but these two needed a little motivation.

"I've seen the Maker's Hall," Mehvish said. "When I was young."

"The Maker's Hall was destroyed during the Age of Myth," said Siraja. "And I doubt you're that old, for all the stories they tell about you."

Mehvish continued, as if Siraja hadn't interrupted, "Once, when all the moons were painted across the sky in a perfect line, I saw the Maker's Hall. I saw it reflected in the Glass Desert, tall, terrible, but beautiful, shimmering like a ghost."

I swallowed. "What did it look like, exactly?"

"Mounting, shining ramparts reached for the sky. I saw a single entrance, a gate whose opulence outshone a dragon's hoard. I was with my mother. She said that if we dared, we could attempt to enter, and there seize the power of the Maker himself." Mehvish stopped speaking, but her braids twined of their own accord.

"Did you try to enter?" asked Siraja.

"No. Creatures of broken glass rose up and chased us off."

I'd bluffed Mehvish before, when I got her to switch allegiances and back Siraja instead of Kadir. I'd only been able to suss out that she wasn't a native of Ardeyn. She was a Stranger. I'd known instinctively that if I branded her with that term, the pirates would've turned against her. But for all my assurance, I really didn't know anything else.

So I wondered who Mehvish *really* was, who her mother had been, and where they'd come from, if not Ardeyn.

Neither she nor anyone like her had appeared in any of the original code, I knew that with relative certainty.

Before I could give in to my curiosity, the sound of piping flutes distracted me. Siraja, Mehvish, and I all glanced in the direction of the unexpected melody. A sort of lullaby, maybe, one whose words danced just on the edge of memory. After only a few bars, it faded back to nothing. We looked at each other, then hastened forward.

Another hundred yards brought us to a sloping pane of glass with a shape reminiscent of an elephant's flared ears. On the far side, there was a gap that lead inward, toward the edge. It was the first one we'd seen.

Siraja said, "That looks promising."

"It looks unstable," judged Mehvish.

"What do you think, Carter?" asked Siraja.

Mehvish was right. The first pane was tented against a series of crumpled glass shards, which we'd have to pass under to get through. If we brushed against it, the whole thing might come crashing down on us. Even if we were careful, a strong wind seemed likely to collapse it.

On the other hand, the heat was doing me in. The passage was dark and out of the sun...

Concentrating on the glass, I tried to determine if it had any sort of inner essence or name that I could question or command. Nothing. I closed my eyes, focusing harder. Nope.

"It's just a heap of rubble," I said, opening my eyes. "I don't know how safe it is."

Mehvish snorted. "Your little trick of knowing secrets not working?"

"Remember, we're a team. Team members support each other, not belittle failure."

Mehvish actually laughed, and Siraja smiled again. Progress? Maybe.

The music came again, louder than before. It was definitely

coming from inside the crater, echoing through the tunnel of glass debris. Words accompanied the music this time, but not ones I could understand.

"This has *got* to be the way," said Siraja, and ducked into the opening. Her body blocked the light at the far end. After a few seconds, her voice came back, hollow and faint, "Come, it's fine."

Fuck dithering. I followed. The air was noticeably cooler in the tunnel, which was a welcome relief. I hoped the shadows didn't hide a jagged piece of glass as I inched carefully forward.

The tunnel didn't collapse on me and I made it through. Siraja waited for me on the other side. She was perched at the edge of a massive hole in the glass in an area relatively free of debris. The cavity was circular, stretching at least a half-mile in diameter. Churning white mist filled it, hiding the crater's bottom. Presuming it had a bottom.

Mehvish emerged from the tunnel. She moved to put Siraja between herself and me. She sniffed, then crinkled her nose as if in disgust.

Though I couldn't smell anything, I decided not to ask what she'd sniffed. Instead, I carefully swept my gaze around the periphery, looking for some way to safely descend into the cloying whiteness.

I bent to retrieve a loose piece of broken glass, then spun the fragment down into the mist. A dull crashing noise echoed out of the whiteness, probably not more than a couple of seconds later.

"Now our presence is known!" hissed Mehvish.

"By who?" I countered, but feeling guilty all the same.

She had no answer. But she'd been right to reprimand me – tossing glass into the pit had certainly announced our presence if anyone was hiding down in the mist. I can be an idiot sometimes.

About two hundred yards farther along the rim I spied what

looked like a pile of dead animals. "Look," I said, pointing.

Siraja followed my finger. Her eyes widened. "A chimera! A dead one, though. I didn't think they ever flew out over the desert."

At her words, the image resolved in my head. Instead of three animals, I realized it was one creature with three heads – one goat, one lion, and one freaky looking lizard face. Its long, green tail dangled into the crater, and its end was obscured by the roiling fog.

"What killed it?" I said, hoping no one suggested that the mist was poison.

I watched Siraja, waiting for the shrug. She didn't disappoint.

"We should go check it out," I said.

"How do you propose we get across to it?" said Mehvish.

The area where we stood was relatively clear of shards, but if we wanted to move along the edge in either direction for more than a dozen yards, we'd be faced with jagged barriers sharp as, well, broken glass. Finding out what had killed the chimera would be useful information to have, probably, but I didn't fancy slicing open a femoral artery on a trek across the sharp mess to find out.

"Maybe later," I finally said.

Siraja said, "Then let's head into the crater. We're wasting time up here." She dropped her pack and removed a thick coil of rope. Loop after loop, the qephilim unfurled one end down the side of the great cavity.

"Any idea how deep it is?" I asked.

"We're going to find out," Mehvish answered as Siraja continued letting the rope out. "Stop asking questions we can't answer, or I'll push you over." The qephilim's ears twitched at that last. Did she think Mehvish was funny, or was she annoyed, too?

Just my luck to be partnered with someone who might

actually want me dead. And I wasn't really all that sure about Siraja's regard.

Too bad Jushur wasn't more able-bodied... What the hell. I pulled the sphere from a pouch and addressed it. "Jushur, advise me."

"On what?" the sphere responded.

Mehvish gasped. Siraja paused in her work to regard me.

I said to the metallic orb, "We mean to descend this cavity, and through it, to enter the ruins of the Maker's Hall. How should we proceed?"

Jushur's form rotated creepily in my hand, as if to take in my companions, the crater, then slid back to me. "Anyone may enter the ruins," it said. "They lie scattered beneath this hard plain. But only the Maker may enter the original Hall. Him, or at minimum, Four of the Seven Incarnations acting in concert. Since the Maker is dead, only the Incarnations, or their implements, can enter. Gather those Rings, and you will succeed beyond your wildest hopes. Call the Rings, and they may come."

"You keep an artifact of sorcery," said Siraja, her voice high with surprise. "Why didn't you use it to improve your station on the *Nightstar*?"

I was too busy considering Jushur's response to answer. The object knew my relationship to the Maker; I'd told it. Which meant that it didn't think I had enough Maker in me to successfully enter whatever remained of the Hall. On the other hand, it thought I could "call" the implements of the Incarnations. Rings, apparently. What did that–

Circles sizzling with powerful magic, seven in all, seven for Seven Incarnations, cascaded across my vision. The Rings the Maker – that *I* – had given to the Incarnations as the catalyst for their power. Rings of War, Death, Silence, Commerce, Law, Lore, and Desire!

The memory faded, like ice-cream dropped on sun-warmed sidewalk. Before it completely melted, I seized it with everything that I could dredge up of my newfound ability. I *fixed* that memory in my mind by naming it as mine. I would not forget it. If the Maker knew it, so should I. The Maker was gone... but maybe I could reconstruct a workable facade of what he'd been, memory by memory. What *I* had been. If I could accomplish that, maybe I'd be able to enter the Hall without calling the Rings.

On the other hand, a little insurance couldn't hurt. Maybe trying to call them was exactly what I should do.

"Carter, are you–"

"Hold on," I told Siraja.

Would it work? Probably not. On the other hand, if I didn't try, how would I ever know? Maybe I could even tune the entreaty to exclude War from hearing. Last time Jason saw me, he'd been happy to see me shot.

Concentrating on images I'd just glued to the inside of my brain, I whispered, "Come, Rings of Incarnation. It is I, your Maker, calling. Return to me, in my hour of need. If worn, then I command you, the wearer, to find me. The Ring will know the way. If I speak instead to a mute band – find me. Find a wearer, and lead them to me."

I was pretty sure nothing was happening.

Screwing my eyes shut, I meditated on all seven implements at once, and called again, repeating my message silently in my mind. I imagined the Rings, or whoever held them now, or anyone who had once held or *would* hold the rings of Incarnation, receiving my summons. Unfortunately, I couldn't exclude War after all – it was one of the Seven, and couldn't be ignored.

The strength of my hope pulsed away like a shock front, shattering the heaped glass around me and pushing Siraja and Mehvish back a step. Mehvish would've fallen into the crater if a braid of her hair hadn't snaked out steadied her.

"What in the name of the Lotan's burning scrotum was that?" Siraja yelled. "Are you trying to get attention of every soul sorcerer and glass dragon in the entire desert?"

Oops. "It was an accident," I said.

"Your accident could mean all our deaths," said Mehvish.

My face warmed. She was right. I didn't really know what I was doing. If there were any enemies in the crater below, then they probably felt my fumbling attempt at magic, and now knew we were here. Although the blandly white fog remained as enigmatic as when we first saw it.

Sadly, no Rings had dropped out of the sky or appeared in my waiting palm. If they *had*, I would've shown them to Mehvish and Siraja and been vindicated. As it was, I decided to study my boots.

Siraja tapped me on the shoulder. She'd said something in a quiet voice, but I'd been too absorbed in feeling bad about myself to catch it.

"Sorry?" I said.

"The musicians are back," she whispered. The sound floated up from the crater softly, with just a bit of echo. Quick and sharp, I heard strings, both played and plucked, drums, and the same flute from before fluttering up and down the scale. No voices. Though I tried, hearing the sound without visual cues apparently wasn't enough for me to name it with my residue of Maker's ability.

We just listened. The music continued for several minutes, then died away.

"I'm no expert," I said, stowing Jushur again, "but that sounded sad."

Mehvish nodded slowly, her eyes downward. Siraja's ears flicked and she said "I've tied off the rope. Let's descend and see for ourselves. I'll go first. Carter, you're next. Mehvish, bring up the rear."

Siraja was braver than me, that was obvious, and I was glad

not to be the first down the rope. Ashamed at the thought, I vowed to see things through, whatever we found.

The qephilim put together a sort of harness using a long scarf. Watching her, I realized I needed something similar. I fashioned something I hoped was workable from extra rope in my own pack. I checked the knots twice. If I screwed up, I'd have no one to blame but myself. It occurred to me that maybe I should try to enchant the makeshift harness as I'd done to Jushur. But the idea of a talking harness was too bizarre. One semi-sentient found object with unknown capabilities was probably one too many to carry around already.

Good as her word, the qephilim descended the rope first. After she was a good ten feet down the line, I tightened my makeshift harness, secured it around the descending rope, and put my weight on the line. Too bad I was fresh out of carabineers.

Mist closed in overhead as I descended, until Mehvish, silhouetted by the bright light as she stared over the edge, faded in the pearly whiteness. Just as I lost sight of the strange woman, she raised her hand and waved at me, as if in farewell. Damn it, was she backing out? If so, I prayed she would just walk away and not cut our rope out of spite.

Siraja's occasional sharp breaths, grunts and clack of boots on stone rose from beneath me. My own hands grew hard to see as the mist thickened the deeper I went, so applied myself to paying attention to the small details of my descent, putting Mehvish out of my mind.

Finally, my feet touched down on dark stone and a thin layer of broken glass. Untying the rope from my makeshift harness was a moment's work, and I stowed it in my pack. Even with the harness, ascending was going to be a lot more challenging than coming down. Something to worry about later. The mist was less thick at the bottom, but still prevented me from seeing more than a dozen yards in any direction.

Siraja had moved just far enough from the end of the rope to give me room to come down.

When Siraja saw I was finished stowing my gear, she pointed to the crater's center. A collection of heaped boulders, rounded and obviously artificial, resolved from the fog. The nearest one was only a few feet away.

"Where's Mehvish?" she asked quietly.

"Should be right behind me," I whispered, deciding not to tell her about Mehvish's odd wave in case I'd imagined it. I shuffled to the nearby boulder heap, which turned out to be farther away than I'd realized, and larger. The fog was screwing with my perceptions. Close up, the pile I'd approached reached a good hand span over my head.

A figure in a white cloak and hood stepped around from behind the boulder heap. I stifled a yelp.

"Who are you?" I asked, my voice a fair impression of not sounding like someone who'd almost crapped his pants.

The figure threw back his hood. He was well into his seventies. The hand he'd used to reveal his face was covered in tattooed swirls and loops; the other held a flute the color of bone.

"I am the one who watches for intruders," he said in a weary voice. "Call me Greeter. Who are you, and why are you here?"

"That's our business," Siraja snapped.

"Rude," sniffed Greeter. "You hope to pilfer the Maker's vaults. Unless you're complete fools, you have a new strategy, one that hasn't been tried a thousand times before. Tell me, and perhaps together, all of us can succeed. My brothers and I will share with you what we find. Keep silent, and die here." The old man finished with a disquieting croaking noise. Laughter?

"So the rumors are true," said Siraja as she moved up to stand next to me. "Soul sorcerers infest the crater like roaches in a roadside inn."

Not the honey-sweet diplomacy I would've chosen. I jumped in, "Cooperation is possible, Greeter..." I trailed off as I realized that, actually no, I really didn't like the idea of allowing a pack of limb-severing soul sorcerers into the Maker's Hall, assuming Siraja's earlier story had been true. I needed to know more about him.

"But?" prompted Greeter, the ghost of a smile on his lips.

What was his name, I wondered, and focused on his lined, haggard face. His eyes were a faded blue like old denim. Greeter flinched, but a backwash of psychic energy slapped me like an open hand across my face.

I staggered, but didn't quite bellow in surprise. Was he warded somehow?

The old man's smile was gone. "I suppose we'll have to kill you then."

Siraja charged Greeter. Her sword stroke missed, but he retreated a step. As he did, his white robe, hood, and wrinkly skin of his face inflated, puffing out like pale balloon. Shaggy white fur sprouted everywhere as he grew taller and taller, until he towered over us. It happened fast, too fast for me to do more than gape and blink. Instead of a man, something like a giant gorilla with white fur stared down at us. White, except where its fur was stained red as if with gore from previous kills, especially around its mouth and clawed hands.

The white ape kicked Siraja out of the way like she was a straw-stuffed puppet with straw. Holy shit. She rolled to a stop and didn't move. Had the ape thing just killed her?

Then it came for me. I ducked under a massive fist and ran between its legs. The mist was clearing, which was the only reason I saw something dart toward me from the side. I dived sideways, just avoiding an attack from...

Fuck. One of the piled rock heaps stood up, a slab of animate stone about the shape and size of a person, and tried to sucker punch me. The second I saw it move, its name blazed in my brain: it was a golem. This one had once been a soldier for the Incarnations during the Age of Myth–

"Rauwr!" screamed the transformed Greeter, who hadn't forgotten about me. Seeing it had my attention, the ape's bestial features stretched into a horrible grin.

Siraja was probably dead and Mehvish had never come down the rope in the first place. I was faced a huge hairy gorilla and a stone-cold killer alone. Yep, I was gonna die.

"Greeter!" I yelled, deciding to use the name he'd given me instead of trying to dig deeper again. "Your name is now mine. Stand quietly, or lose it forever." I was bluffing, of course. I still felt the pain from the first time I'd fished for his true name.

Puzzlement scrunched the ape's face, but Greeter didn't immediately attack me again. Surprise that my ploy had worked at all kept me mute a few moments. Stumbling over my next demand would erode my claim.

Siraja, battered but still kicking, raced out of the mist and stabbed the ape in the back. Its shriek was deafening. I wanted to clap my hands over my ears.

A stone fist clipped me and I stumbled back from the golem, forgetting the ape and qephilim. I gazed at where eyes would've been on a living creature. A horrifying expanse of blank stone stared back. I desperately wished it was gone. A name occurred to me, and I said it, stuttering over the syllables in my fear. A name antithetical to animate stone, like antimatter to substance; I un-named the golem.

It exploded.

I lost at least a few seconds in the flash and roar. When I blinked back to the moment, the ringing in my ears drowned out whatever Siraja was saying.

"What?"

"Get up, Carter!"

I pushed myself upright, wincing at the oozing cuts the broken glass covering the crater floor had inflicted on my palms and fingers. Most of the mist was gone, maybe blown away by the golem detonation blast. I saw Greeter was back to his old shape: a trembling old man in bloodied robes. Maybe the golem blast had destabilized his spell.

Of Mehvish, there was still no sign, though the rope we'd used to descend dangled down the crater wall. At least she'd left us a way to escape.

"Behind you," said Siraja. I glanced round and saw the retreating mist had uncovered a dark crack in the crater floor. I wasn't sure if the three additional golems and at least twice that number of soul sorcerers, all wearing white like Greeter, had just emerged from the crack, of if they'd been standing in the mist all along, watching the fight.

As I opened my mouth to lie, plead, or say something – anything – to deflect what I feared was going to be my end, the fist of a fresh golem pounded me into the glassy scree.

25: TRANSLATION
Katherine Manners

Kate passed through nothing. For a moment she *was* nothing, except need. She wanted form again, substance, and purpose. She flailed, but without limbs. Screamed, but had no voice. Discordant clanks and bangs pelted her. Distant and faint at first, they grew louder and more insistent as she focused on them. Then a sound like an avalanche vibrated through her, and just like that, Katherine Manners stepped into Ardeyn.

She knew she was in Ardeyn, just like she knew her name was Kate. Memory unfurled, as if she'd always known that spirits of the slain are drawn to Ardeyn's subterranean Night Vault, that the Maker and his Incarnations were dead, and that magic came as naturally to some people as weaving did to others. After all, she herself could shepherd the dead, calming spirits and guiding them–

"What the hell is wrong with me?" she whispered.

"You translated," said a large man standing next to her. A large man, but somehow also Raul. A Raul about half a foot taller and wearing altogether more colorful clothing than a few seconds earlier, including two matching short swords with scarlet hilts. Before they'd stepped through that blurred continuity hanging in the computer lab of the Brazilian university...

"I'm dreaming. Or I hit my head," she proclaimed. Kate glanced down. The gun she'd almost shot Coleson with had become the hilt of a slender blade. Bracelets adorned her wrists, rings her fingers, and in place of her jeans, boots, and top, she wore glistening yellow robes stitched with elaborate symbols.

"You are neither dreaming nor mentally damaged, *mi chula*," said Raul. She concentrated on him, wondering if he was a dream, soon to fade away with the rest of her delusion. Nope. And he really *had* grown in height and width. And gained two swords and elaborate leather armor that looked like it was right out of a movie set.

Raul held out his hand, and after a second, she took it. "It can be a shock the first few times. As it happens, this is the first time I've been to Ardeyn myself. In fact, it's so new, I'm probably the first from Ruk to come here..." He trailed off.

"New? It's hundreds of thousands of years old!" she countered.

He cocked his head. Kate realized she was drawing on memories, the same ones that'd trickled into her consciousness the more she looked around. She *knew* Ardeyn had been created who knows how many millennia ago by the Maker. But of course she *also* knew that Carter Morrison claimed to have seeded Ardeyn just a few years ago.

"I imagined everything would be more like a video game," she said. "Blocky and maybe even pixelated. Not... like *this*."

Raul nodded solemnly and squeezed her hand. "Integrating the reality of a recursion takes time. You need to acclimate to the idea that this is *real*. Judging by the glyphs decorating your shawl, I'm guessing that you've developed a knack for, mmm, calming spirits?"

Kate's eyes were drawn to the largest ring on her left hand. Unlike the rest of her jewelry and belongings she'd left behind on Earth, the ring Jason Cole brought to Earth had followed her back to Ardeyn. It had translated, too, taking on a new context. Whatever else it was, it also now served as her spirit focus.

"Spirit focus," she whispered, the words both familiar and new to her. Of course! She could shepherd the dead. In fact, the ghostly soul of a long-dead warrior now resided within the Ring, waiting for her to call it forth...

"I might be going crazy," she said, her voice matter-of-fact.

"No," Raul said, and patted her shoulder. The way her sudden familiarity with Ardeyn slipped into her brain was almost more unsettling than the content itself. It was unbelievable. At least, it would be unbelievable, if she hadn't called on similarly crazy abilities even before leaving Earth. Like when she'd jolted Coleson with energy that'd left him dazed, which was right before they'd stepped through – *translated* to – this new place.

"Stop," said Raul. "Breathe. Stop fighting it. Just concentrate on your breathing."

She did as Raul suggested, taking five long breaths.

"Better?"

"Yeah," she said as much for her own benefit as Raul's. Saying it out loud would make it so. "I'm done losing my shit."

They stood in a metallic alcove. The cavity opened directly on a wide, but dimly lit industrial catwalk that circled a metal-sided pit. Purplish light leaked from whatever lay at the bottom.

Along the catwalk opposite the pit, wide arches opened on a dozen or more separate chambers at semi-regular intervals. The distant buzz of what sounded like table saws, the glittering flash of welding torches, and a low-level murmur of many voices reminded Kate of a factory floor. Figures moved along the catwalk and between the various doors, but none had taken any interest in Kate or Raul. She wasn't sure why they hadn't raised a hue and cry when she and Raul appeared, but she was happy to let the status quo roll along a while longer.

The ring that had come along for the ride from Earth tingled on her finger. Not unpleasantly. Maybe it was reacting to coming home again?

"I have a question, Raul. This is the ring Jason first sent across, the one I found in the BDR server room. It came with me from Brazil." She showed it to him. "It's a spirit focus, here in Ardeyn. But it's also the original ring. What does that mean?"

Raul took her hand and squinted at the piece of jewelry still fitted to her finger. He frowned. "I don't know. Some artifacts can translate, but they're so rare I've never seen one. Usually only cyphers move between worlds with recursors."

"You can explain cyphers later. For now, tell me about this."

Raul made a tsking noise. "It must have serious power of its own. I guess I didn't think about it before... I mean, Jason originally sent this ring from Ardeyn to Earth. Which is actually sort of amazing. Even Ruk science would be hard pressed to duplicate that, had we been somehow cut off from Earth."

"Do you think it's a problem? What if this thing has magically clued in Jason that we've invaded his base?"

"It's possible," said Raul. "So let's move quickly. We need to locate the other half of the gate."

"Good thing everyone's ignoring us," said Kate.

Raul nodded.

"And why is that?" she said. "Isn't this supposed to be Megeddon, the heart of the Betrayer's evil... -ness?" She gestured to the two nearest vaguely illuminated figures walking along the catwalk. The figures stopped short of their alcove and turned into an open doorway. The two workers looked oddly similar to each other. And familiar.

Raul explained, "We've taken on Ardeyn's context. *And* we've translated directly into Megeddon, so we've taken on the veneer of those who belong here."

"Really? Then why don't we just walk into–"

"But only for as long as we do nothing to draw attention to ourselves. The second we do something disruptive, everyone will know we don't belong."

"Yeah, otherwise it'd be too easy," she grumped. "All right, which way?" Nothing resembling the interface they'd jumped through was evident.

"The gate has to be nearby," Raul said. "Otherwise we wouldn't have appeared here. I'm surprised we don't see it, truthfully. Let me ask."

Raul waved down a lone figure wearing a black leather duster walking along the catwalk in their direction. The purple light from the pit reflected from the figure in a particularly unsettling fashion. The newcomer seemed to truly notice her and Raul for the first time, and veered to approach them.

As he drew closer she realized the oddity was with the man himself, not the unsettling light. The skin of his face and exposed hands wasn't really reflecting light from the pit, but refracting it. She saw his jaw, his brain as if behind hazed gelatin.

The refracting light hid it until he stopped before them, but the man's features exactly resembled those of Jason Cole. Not to mention Coleson, who'd they'd left behind on Earth. In fact, he was a perfect ringer for the translucent Jason duplicate she'd met on Earth. Kate's heart began to beat erratically in her chest and throat, fluttering like a trapped bird.

"What are you doing in here?" demanded the lookalike, his voice a match for Coleson's, an accusing finger jabbing as if he would pin them in place with it.

"Don't you know?" said Raul, advancing a lazy step. Kate's ring tingled again, even as a new cocky surety infused Raul.

"We were told to expect a tour of the facility by someone who looked just like you. Though he was less, mm, see-through."

The man may have blinked, though with his lack of skin pigmentation, Kate wasn't certain.

"A homunculus brought you to the Foundries? Why?"

Raul said with easy confidence, "We're emissaries from Mandariel. We're here to seal the nonaggression pact between our nation and Megeddon." Raul raised a fist. "And to discuss what to do about our common enemy, Hazurrium."

Knowledge unfolded behind Kate's left eye like an incipient migraine. Hazurrium, also called the queendom, was a prominent power in Ardeyn, and currently ruled by Queen Elandine. Mandariel was a much younger nation, ruled by the Twelve Princes. The two powers were not especially friendly.

The look-alike shook his head, obviously confused. So was Kate. What the fuck was Raul trying to do?

"Listen," Raul said. "The Betrayer *himself* asked us here to explore whether such a pact made sense. But ever since we've arrived, all we've gotten is delay after delay. The *first* interesting thing that happened to us since we've arrived was being asked if we'd like to look around, what did you call them?" He snapped his fingers, "Oh, the Foundries, right. Then we were abandoned here until you came along. What's your name?"

As if compelled by Raul's sudden request, the duplicate Jason said, "I'm Gamma. First Lieutenant of War."

Kate guessed that Raul was being more than deceptively persuasive. He was actually exerting some kind of mental influence as he spun his lies. Unbelievable. Yet here he was, chatting up a clone.

"And where *is* War?" said Raul. "He was supposed to meet us."

It took everything Kate had not to glance at Raul like he was a lunatic.

"He is attending to private matters," Gamma replied. A sour expression on the duplicate's face revealed that he wasn't exactly happy with whatever Jason was doing. Or maybe he didn't know. Either way, Kate was relieved that the Betrayer – or Coleson – wasn't around to end to their charade.

"Then it falls to *you* to show us around the Foundries," declared Raul, an approving smile breaking on his face. As if he couldn't help himself, Gamma returned the expression. Kate managed not to snort. She wasn't sure who she was more viscerally disgusted with – Gamma for being yet another version of Jason-fucking-Cole, or Raul for being such a fucking liar. Had Raul ever led her on in the same way? He'd be sorry if she discovered he'd tried the "not the droids you're looking for" tactic with *her*.

Both Coleson and the duplicate she'd met in the server room so many months ago – they'd been like Gamma. A person molded from the identity of someone else. Server-room Jason had died – melting away – before she'd understood anything. He'd apologized, though she hadn't then known why. Separated from his "parent," maybe he'd had second thoughts about his role in Jason's plot, about leaving behind the ring containing the Trojan horse quantum code. Kate idly traced the curve of the cold band on her finger with her thumb.

And now before her stood one more duplicate, his mind yet another instance of Jason's. Was he in lock-step with the original, or was he like a twin: a completely separate person in his own right? Server-room-Jason hadn't struck her as someone who would have been so easily misled. Then again, he hadn't had to deal with Raul's "super power" for twisting brains into pretzels. She felt a little sorry for Gamma, despite everything.

Gamma motioned them around the mouth of the monstrous pit. Kate glanced down. Amethyst light glittered far below, winking in code she couldn't decipher. "What's this?" she asked.

"War has many projects," Gamma threw over his shoulder. "If this one ever comes to fruition, we'll have no need of alliances or treaties; we'll have all the power we need at our fingertips."

"War mentioned he'd developed some kind of connection to a higher world," Raul said. "To a place he called Earth. Is this the portal?"

Gamma stopped in mid-stride, turning. Confusion wrinkled his face. "War told you about BITER? But that's..."

Raul cranked up the persuasion, "Yes, that's classified. But War wants Mandariel's friendship. He mentioned it – BITER – as a sign of good faith. Being called the Betrayer means you have to work double-hard to engender trust among your would-be allies."

Kate glanced into the pit again. The purple light at the bottom looked nothing like the portal they'd used to arrive in Megeddon. She couldn't say that aloud without blowing their cover. So instead she said, "This doesn't look like the... the BITER portal War described to us."

Gamma's look of stark incomprehension, perhaps even betrayal, softened. "That's because this isn't BITER. Like I said, we're taking it slow on the Pit Reactor. One mistake could blast Megeddon from existence in a flare of loose chaos."

Kate and Raul eased back a step.

The ghost of a smile lifted Gamma's mouth. "Well, if War wants you to see what's in the Contact Foundry, so be it."

Kate said, "The Contact Foundry?"

"BITER is in the Contact Foundry," answered Gamma.

Raul said, "That's the spirit."

The clone led them another half turn around the pit, then ducked under a large arch. Inside, two massive crystal screens – three-stories tall if they were a foot – faced off across the length of the room. The tall surfaces rapidly flashed scenes, each lasting no more than an eyeblink: A city skyline. A highway system streaming with cars. A farm. An airport. On and on, and all of them from Earth.

At the center of the space, midway between the two screens, a blurry smear hung in the air, like the one that'd formed when Coleson appeared in Brazil. Except this one stuttered, randomly appearing and disappearing. Noise, like the static from a dead channel, issued from it each time it appeared.

A handful of clones, their skin apple red wearing armor nearly the same color, rushed about on scaffolding suspended along the edges of the display surfaces, pulling oversize levers and turning dials as if racing each other for a mad science prize. A handful of clones lay broken on the ground at the base of either monolith, burnt and unmoving. Pale smoke spiraled up from one of the bodies.

"What's happened?" Gamma demanded of the room. Except for some anxious glances from a few reds, no one answered.

Gamma walked farther into the chamber, toward the stuttering discontinuity. "Answer me! Where's Sigma?" he asked.

One red homunculus threw a lever, then glanced around long enough to gasp, "He went to investigate intruders on the other side of the link. He wasn't gone more than a minute when the portal slipped. There was an explosion. The connection has destabilized."

Raul glanced at Kate. She silently mouthed the name, "Coleson," at him. He considered half a second, then nodded.

Gamma spared them a quick, "Excuse me," and rushed to help the reds. Kate and Raul found themselves alone, standing a dozen feet from the discontinuity.

"If we jumped through this, I supposed we'd show up back

on Earth," Kate muttered.

"I expect so, yes," he said. "It's a gateway. A translation gate. Though I wouldn't chance it at the moment. It looks... ill."

Kate studied the flickering hole in existence, then shifted her gaze to the crystal screens. They'd destroyed the quantum computer on Earth to unbalance Earth's connection to Ardeyn. Here in Megeddon, the quantum computer's analog might well be the twin imaging devices over which the clones swarmed.

"Let's break those." She pointed to the screens. The gate was only a byproduct of the flickering surfaces. The magical mechanisms keeping the gate open must lay inside them.

"Agreed. But right now?" asked Raul. "It's crowded in here. Perhaps we should wait until odds shift in our favor."

"We might not get another chance," she replied. "Use your mind control ability to tell everyone to leave."

He gave her a measured look. "It's not *mind control*. It's the ability to make people think I'm someone other than I am, or fast talk my way out of some situations. Anyway, it's hard for me to affect more than a couple of people at once."

Kate grunted noncommittally.

"And if you're wondering; no. I've never fast talked *you*, Kate. You'd remember."

He knew her well. She decided to believe him, but not let him completely off the hook. "For your sake, I'd better not find out otherwise," she said. Then, "Focus on Gamma. He's the one in charge here."

Raul sighed. He studied the transparent clone of Jason who was directing his red-hued siblings on the scaffolding. "How should I play this, I wonder?" he muttered. Then he walked over to Sigma and tapped the clone on the shoulder.

"Not now!" Sigma said.

"War has a message. He says—"

"I thought you were an envoy from Mandariel?"

Raul shook his head impatiently. "That's just my cover. We're actually agents War employs beyond the walls of Megeddon." Even from where she was standing, Kate's brain prickled at the surge of invisible persuasion rolling off Raul. Gamma must have felt it too, because he began to stammer, all the while looking at Raul as if the man had just declared he was Santa Claus.

"Listen, this is War's message," Raul continued. "You need to head to the west wall immediately. War's waiting there. He needs you. He's hurt; he just survived an assassination attempt, but more assassins are coming. And take your friends!" He pointed at the other clones.

Gamma nodded slowly. Then all expression drained from his face. "No," he said. "I don't think so."

"I said—"

Gamma punched Raul in the face. The prickling sensation ceased as Raul's head rocked back. The clone followed up with a roundhouse kick to Raul's midsection.

"Hey!" she yelled, and tried what she'd done to Coleson in Brazil. Last time, it just sort of happened. It was like trying to remember a word just on the tip of her tongue that was just out of reach.

No. It wasn't a word, it was a feeling, a sensation like conviction. And then she had it.

Electricity curled out of nowhere and zapped Gamma. The clone's clear skin hazed where lightning burned him. But it didn't put him down. Slowed and hurt, he continued advancing on Raul, expertly jabbing, kicking, and elbowing like an MMA fighter. Given that he was a clone of War, it made sense that he was adept with weapons of all kinds, even his empty hands.

For his part, Raul gave up ground in measured steps, circling rather than letting Gamma back him up against a wall. Kate's lightning bolt had distracted Gamma, at least. Enough for Raul to unsheathe his red-hilted short swords, one in each hand. He wove blades in swift patterns between himself and the clone. Gamma stopped advancing, but a happy grin split the duplicate's face. That probably didn't bode well. Crap.

Raul cut and parried Gamma's panther-quick strikes, shouting, "I can keep this poser busy, *mi chula*. Destroy the gate generators!"

He *did* look as if he could handle himself, so Kate decided to believe him. She turned to the nearest screen, wondering what she should try first. A grenade would be handy, but she was fresh out. She could try the lightning again, but a tightness behind her eyes when she tried triggering it for a third time suggested she needed wait a bit, unless she wanted to burn out her mind.

A couple of the red clones on the scaffolding shot her worried glances as she approached, but continued their frenzied work. They seemed convinced they could salvage the connection if given enough time. Maybe that's what she should do: distract them from affecting repairs – or whatever they were doing – long enough for everything to fall apart.

She lifted the ring, the one Jason had called the Ring of Desire, but which now served as the focus of her power in Ardeyn to shepherd souls. From it she called the warrior spirit that nestled within. She learned his name even as it passed her lips, "Darneth, come forth. Aid me!"

Thick mist steamed from her ring, forming the ghostly image of a figure in armor wielding a phantom blade. "As you command," the spirit whispered. She shivered. It was damn spooky, despite everything.

She gestured to the nearest clone and yelled, "Eliminate that one!" Darneth's hollow gaze lingered on her for an instant, as if in protest of his fate. Then he complied, rolling upward to threaten the red she'd pointed out. The homunculus heard her, too. It turned from whatever desperate task that had consumed it to defend itself.

The spirit moved slowly toward the clone, then paused in midair, light from the screens flickering through it. It wasn't attacking, which was fine. Her goal had been to distract. Not that she'd have minded if Darneth had followed through. But she'd never met Darneth before, had never helped ease his spiritual pain, nor commanded him either: she hadn't built up any trust with him. She sensed, through the vague connection they shared, that he wasn't willing to risk his own continued existence by becoming corporeal enough to attack, and be attacked in turn.

Kate glanced at the next nearest homunculus, whose attention remained fixed on his controls. The tightness behind her eyes had eased somewhat, so she released a stroke of lightning, striking him in the back. She couldn't help feeling slightly guilty at–

Screeching and smoking, the red spun around. Hate filled his eyes, and he leaped from the scaffolding to close the distance between them, smoke streaming from its wound. If the red hadn't misjudged the distance, it might've gone badly for her. But the red smashed hard onto the floor at her feet. It didn't get up.

She stared at the body, her mouth hanging open. He was dead. She'd killed him.

"Katherine!" came Raul's warning.

He still sparred with Gamma, and from the wet blood spotting his clothing, he'd taken a couple of serious hits. Why had he called out to her? She glanced around to see a newcomer enter the Contact Foundry.

A thing, half crow, half leprous Jason clone, stood in the entrance. A fell light flickered between the feathers of the thing's wings, forking into the floor. A caw burst from its clacking beak-mouth. The insidious sound made her brain ring like the clapper in a bell.

Then it went for her.

She dodged left, putting the flickering mouth of the translation gate between herself and it.

The monster came on, unconcerned about the discontinuity in its path. It opened its mouth, and tentacles with even tinier mouths writhed within. She screamed; she couldn't help it.

It brushed the translation gate as it came for her. Scarlet light outlined the fluctuating hole in space, emitting a blast of heat intense enough to curl her eyelids.

The beast's hungry caws turned into a steam train whistle of pain. Half the creature was pulled through the gate... but the other half remained behind. That half slumped in a spray of red fluid that spattered and sizzled on the gate's white-hot margin.

"The connection's degraded!" a red on the scaffolding yelled, his voice horrified.

"Fix it," barked Gamma, his attention divided between Raul and the unfurling disaster.

Kate glanced at what remained of Mr Crow who wasn't clever enough by half. Nope, it wasn't getting up, whatever it was. She backed away from the wildly fluctuating gate, then hurled another eye-searing bolt at the red who looked most intent on his work. The jagged light cut deep into the clone's side. It staggered mutely, then dropped over the edge to lay unmoving. The sound the body made hitting the floor made her feel slightly sick.

Pain speared between her eyes. As if she'd run the fifty-meter dash, fatigue pulled at her limbs and a wave of dizziness made her stagger. If she kept hurling her unearthly power, she was going to burn herself up.

She needed some kind of weapon.

Hands shaking, she rifled through the belongings of the red who'd tried to tackle her. A crash and an answering cry of pain from Raul's made her fumble and drop the short sword she'd pulled from the clone's belt, so she grabbed the rod that was sheathed next to the sword. The moment her fingers touched the rod, they tingled. She left the sword where it lay and straightened. A nugget of knowledge opened in her mind – the thing was a kind of war wand employed in Ardeyn called an "ashur." She sensed that the ashur was an ideal way to break stuff.

She spun and pointed the liberated wand at one of the crystal screens, currently displaying a satellite view of a large city on Earth. She concentrated, and the wand spat a line of green energy at the nearer crystal panel. It was like the time she'd smashed a window with a hammer to break into an abandoned motor home – the crystal shattered with a peculiar barking crash, shards raining down on the closest reds.

Her spirit, Darneth, returned. It whispered, "If you remain where you stand, you'll die." So speaking, it wrapped itself around her like a swaddling cloak, as if trying to hug her. Or protect her.

White light enveloped her, even as what she imagined as a human-sized fly-swatter smashed her across the length of her body.

"I'm all right," she rasped, hoping it was true, though she wasn't sure to whom she spoke. She was sprawled on the ground, her limbs entwined with a duplicate who'd fared much worse in the explosion than her. It could've been the one she'd looted, or a different one. How did the fucking things tell each other apart?

Pain needled through her joints and neck as she tried standing. "Less all right than I thought," she amended, and stayed on the floor.

One panel was gone, as were all the reds who'd tended it. A crater-like blast pattern scorched the floor where the translation gate had hung in the air. A zigzagging crack splintered the face of the opposite panel.

She couldn't see Raul or Gamma, which worried her. Fresh rubble lay between her and where they'd been fighting at the chamber's edge. They'd been farther from the gate detonation than she'd been. Raul was all right, she told herself. Unless that rubble – was it from the ceiling? – had fallen on him.

Pushing through the sharp spikes of pain she was ready for this time, she got up.

Darneth was gone – the spirit's misty shape was nowhere in the chamber, as was its sense of presence she'd earlier detected in the ring. Darneth had wound itself around her to protect her. The spirit hadn't been willing to fight for her, but it had tried to save her. And now... she wasn't sure where it was. A hollow feeling made her swallow. Funny, because in a way, Darneth wasn't real.

Except he was. This was all *real*. At least, it was as real as life on Earth, which was made up of particles, waves, and maybe tiny vibrating strings even deeper down. Whatever dark energy mechanism was imposing order and structure to everything around her was just as comprehensive in fashioning an instance of unique reality. Which meant that the reds she'd killed directly, and those who'd died in the subsequent blast she'd caused were also real. Clones or not, they'd been *alive*. But no more.

She bent double and retched.

26: REFLECTION
Elandine, Queen of Hazurrium

Seven moons fell among the brilliant stars along their nightly course. Each lunar sphere was named for a Rule, or perhaps an Incarnation, for they were one and the same. The glimmer of false dawn edging both horizons meant it was near middle-night, when the sun swam beneath Ardeyn, illuminating its craggy, barren underside.

Though Queen Elandine and her host were closer to the Daylands' western edge, nothing blocked their sightline eastward across the empty Glass Desert. The hard plain had already radiated away the heat from the day before, rendering the night surprisingly frigid. The darkness and the morning hours of the next day still offered at least nine or ten hours of travel time across the desert's reflective surface. Not long after that, as the risen sun crested toward noon, without clouds it would grow so hot that they'd need shelter. Which was a difficult proposition out on the glass. Only fools would choose to go in that direction. Yet it was their course, because that way lay Megeddon.

Elandine carefully reached into a wicker cage and pulled out a tiny bird. Wings fluttering, it chirped at her. "Hello," she told it. "Are you ready to find the way forward?"

The bird chirped again. The queen smiled. The creature

263

had been a lucky find, considering all that had happened since they'd surprised the sark in the Green Wilds.

Surviving the sark attack had been her number one priority. And thanks to their planning and the skill and bravery of her people, they'd done exactly that. The sark had been woefully unprepared for an army of Hazurrium's finest. Surprised and likely terrified that they were the target of a much larger invasion, the creatures pulled back into their Green Wilds lairs. A three-day passage, without any further encounters with the debased qephilim, saw her army to the southern edge of the forest.

Their good luck failed – a particularly rabid sark tribe infested a ruined fortress overlooking the crossing of the Drudessa River, which was some considerable distance from the boughs of the Green Wilds. No one had expected any further trouble with sark so far from their haunts. When about half her army was across the river, stretched out and vulnerable, the savages boiled out of the fortress on the opposite bank in a perfectly timed ambush.

She'd lost at least twenty peacemakers. But in the end, a thousand warriors against a single tribe of sark, no matter how bloodthirsty, ended with the sark's elimination. Flora would've been appalled. Though her mother would've been proud of the queen's tactics, Elandine was sure. If she'd been around to see them.

Elandine had ordered the wounded tended, and sent a small unit into the fortress to scout for any additional danger. They returned a few hours later claiming the creatures would be no further trouble and carrying salvaged sark treasure she allowed them to keep for their effort. All except for the little bird in her hand, which they'd given her.

It was a sere dove, pearlescent with a delicate beak. Unlike most of its avian kin, it knew the pockets, cracks, and wrecks littering the desert. The sark probably kept it for the same use she had in mind.

Elandine raised the creature. Its scaly feet pinched her thumb.

She said, "Seek your path eastward. Fly!"

The sere dove took wing. She half expected it to wheel back toward the sark fortress or northwest toward the Green Wilds. But whether it was trained or because that was simply its nature, the dove fluttered southeast, out across the reflective plain.

"Sound the horn," she told Navar.

The First Protector complied, sending a long, high call ringing across the assembled ranks. Her forces moved out, with their queen in the lead, her eyes on the dove. They walked into the night, reflected stars and tumbling moons at their feet.

As the sun's disk broke over the horizon like a molten gold coin, guilt stabbed Elandine. She hadn't spared a second for Flora's plight since well before the Drudessa River crossing. After spending so many months almost prostrate at sorrow's altar, it seemed like a kind of betrayal that she hadn't given Flora's memory its due recently. Going over her death again and again somehow kept the woman part of the present, and not merely a shade of the past.

Except, not thinking about it was easier... a thought that made her feel even more guilty.

But she *did* have other things to think about. Hazurrium couldn't stand for the embodiment of its power, the symbol of rulership, to be stolen without an answer. Their standing as a primary power in Ardeyn was at stake. Keeping this expedition on track required nothing less than Elandine's full attention.

And yet, wasn't it to snatch her sister back from the Night Vault that she was *actually* challenging the Betrayer, why she led her forces across the most desolate part of Ardeyn? Elandine knew of no other way to effect that escape other than with the Ring of Death.

Oddly, she could still feel it on her finger, a phantom band like a severed limb, cold and serene in the face of all calamities.

Given all that she was doing to recover that Ring and thus Flora's escape from death, Elandine reasoned, she didn't have the time to grieve.

Shielding the blinding dawn and its equally blazing reflection with one hand, Elandine gazed across the reflective plain. She'd lost sight of the bird hours ago, but not before establishing the ruler-straight direction of its flight. Sere doves flew between oases, and an observant traveler who following one's path could pick their way across the desert, including armies led by observant queens.

She didn't need to find water or food – her forces carried adequate provisions. Just a crack, hill, or even a lone dune of encroaching dust from the Borderlands that was large enough to shelter her forces during peak heat if they dug in.

No cave, dune, structure, or other protective feature leaped out at her as she scanned the landscape. That wasn't a complete disaster, because they had a few hours before the warmth really picked up. But it concerned her, because it would take about that much time to walk as far as she could currently see. It was even farther if they turned back. They had to go forward.

Navar watched, a question in the angle of her ears.

Elandine said, "Onward!" and Navar blew the horn, signaling the short rest was over. The army marched on into the sunrise.

Less than an hour later, with the sun well up, the sweat trickled under her armor and stung her eyes. She wiped her forehead with the cuff of her sleeve, managing to keep an exasperated profanity from escaping her lips. Everyone looked to her for strength, not complaints.

That's when she spied a narrow crack in the glass ahead and to the left. She pointed it out to Navar, who ran ahead to check it out.

Ran, instead of rode, because they lost their mounts when her ships foundered in the storm. That loss wounded her pride as much as anything else, but Elandine knew that for Navar, it was worse. The First Protector had formed a close bond with her charger, and its loss weighed on the qephilim heavily. Not that she'd ever say. The regent in Hazurrium had much to answer for, not the least being the death of horses. All would be accounted for when Elandine returned, she promised herself for the hundredth or thousandth time. The dull anger that burned when she thought of the regent was one of the goads that kept her moving forward.

"This may serve!" called Navar, and motioned for Elandine.

She joined her and looked down a much larger space than she'd expected. The crack was narrow, but it opened up into a hollow, darkened space a few feet beneath the glass. A rubble of boulders actually looked as though it would make a passable stair. Cool air and the faint scent of water came up from below.

"This is where the sere dove was leading," she said, hoping it was true, and that it was large enough give everyone a chance to rest in the shade. If it wasn't, they'd devise a schedule to rotate the army into the coolness unit by unit.

"I'll call up a team to investigate," said Navar.

"We don't have time – the sun is going to bake us if we don't do this quick. I'm going to check it out–"

"My queen!" protested Navar. If it wasn't Navar's job to protect the queen, Elandine was pretty sure the First Protector would kill her one of these days.

"I'll keep a force of peacemakers at my elbow," Elandine

said. "You stay here and prepare our forces to descend immediately, one unit at a time."

Navar shut up and did as Elandine commanded, and the queen was grateful for her forbearance.

Elandine called over the captain of the nearest peacemaker unit and, as Navar began forming up the tiny army on the glass, the queen ventured down into the coolness with twelve peacemakers ranging out before her with lanterns, crossbows, and drawn swords.

She descended several tens of steps. The underground space grew wider and wider. Her apprehension about whether her forces would fit evaporated. The scent of water sharpened, and the air grew even cooler.

They found a subterranean forest, of a sort. Instead of trees, great glass pillars stretched upward, trunks wider than any four humans could encircle, spreading away into a darkness that was lit here and there by glints of light from above. Dust caught in the shafts danced like fireflies.

"Your Majesty," the lead peacemaker called. "Over here."

Joining the peacemaker, a man named Ghali, the queen saw that he was squinting into the depths of a glass pillar. "What is it?" she asked.

"I thought I saw someone moving within."

Elandine resisted asking the peacemaker if he was certain. He wouldn't have wasted her time on anything less.

"Describe it," she said instead, bringing her own lantern to bear on the surface. The light penetrated a few hand spans, but the pillar grew milky and opaque.

"I thought it was my own reflection at first," Ghali said, "but then I realized the face was too thin and pale, the armor too raged. Perhaps it was a rogue spirit."

Some spirits didn't find their way to the Court of Sleep, but instead lingered on the surface. It wouldn't surprise her if a place as deadly as the Glass Desert was haunted by more than its fair share of the uneasy dead. If she had the Ring of Death...

If. If dreams had wings Elandine would fly back to Hazurrium, strike the false regent's head from her shoulders, and ask her departed sister Flora to the royal veranda for sweet cakes and strong coffee. If.

Instead she said, "You're probably right, Ghali. Keep watch. If sere spirits haunt this delve, they may grow unquiet when the rest of our forces descend. Or, maybe they will flee so much attention."

"Let's hope for the latter, Your Majesty," Ghali said.

Elandine arranged for another peacemaker to give Navar the all clear, so the First Protector could bring down the host. She knew it was getting warm topside. Then she continued to press into the hollow. How big was it, really?

Thirty or forty paces further in, she found a spring bubbling up to form a shallow pool. A stream slipped away from the pool, running down between sharp edged glass boulders and reflective pillars. She directed the beam of her lantern to follow the stream's uneven path down–

The phantom Ring on her finger vibrated. The sensation was so unexpected she froze for a full second before jerking her hand into the light of the lantern. Her finger was bare.

When her eyes came back up, she was looking directly into the empty gaze of a grinning skull! No, it was a reflection in a glass pillar; the figure was standing behind her.

Elandine spun to face the thing that had ambushed her. Nothing was there.

"Lotan's hoary nethers," she cursed.

When she snapped her glance back to the glass pillar, the skull was still there, and it had grown a hand that was reaching for her. She flinched away, and the thing's bony fingers, glowing with searing heat, grazed her. She *felt* the contact, smelled the burning metal of her breastplate, and a faint surge of heat.

Yet she couldn't see it at all with her own eyes – only by its reflection.

"Good enough," she grunted, unsheathing her sword. She swiped *Rendswandir* through the air where the reflection told her the spirit should be. The runes on her blade flared gold as she struck *something*, and a suggestion of a shape briefly occupied the empty air before fading back to invisibility.

A scream of rage followed, sepulchral for all that it aped the passion of life. Shouts from the direction she'd come, of peacemakers realizing their queen had gone forward without them, followed.

Fighting a foe you could only see by its reflection was damn difficult, she decided when she sidestepped *into* the thing's next burning touch instead of away. This time the scent of burning material included skin, though it took a moment for the pain to follow. When it did she almost dropped her sword.

Suddenly Ghali was with her, eyes alight with alarm, searching for the foe she faced.

"Look for its reflection!" she yelled, and swung at the grinning spirit. Misjudging, her sword whistled through empty air. She checked the sheet of glass, frowning to see two more spirits fade into the image, one human and the other qephilim. They hissed, the sound like blowing sand.

Elandine tried reason. "We are not treasure seekers or soul sorcerers here to trap you. We're only shelter seekers, fleeing the noonday sun. I beg you, allow us to share the coolness for a span, and then we will be gone."

The new spirits paused, looking uncertain, if that was possible. But the original's reflection only laughed louder, hollow and echoing in the underground space. Where had it gone? Its reflection in the original sheet of glass had vanished.

A searing line of pain drew itself down her back. She rolled forward, realizing the thing had positioned itself so she hadn't been able to see it in the glass. Thank the Maker her relic breastplate was light enough she could move as if unencumbered.

The peacemaker Ghali, standing farther up the broken trail among the glass pillars, had a different vantage of the fight. He screamed, "I see you!" and lunged.

From Elandine's perspective, his thrust cut emptiness. But the sere spirit's laughter choked off. When Ghali withdrew his blade a haze of spectral light flared around the steel, then dissolved to ash. The tortured spirit was sent to its rest, she hoped. Even if not, it wouldn't bother them for at least another revolution of the seven moons.

She fixed her eyes on the remaining two spirits. Brandishing her fist as if she yet wore the Ring of Death, she decreed, "Leave us, or your fate will prove the worse. I will erase you, I swear by the Incarnation of Death!"

A thrill of potency electrified her as she spoke, starting from her bare finger. The echo of the power she'd worn for so long seemed to reach from the past and give her words truth. The two remaining spirits fled as if blown away in a sandstorm.

After a pause, to make certain it wasn't a ruse, Elandine relaxed. She glanced at Ghali, and couldn't quite restrain a grin. "I think that's done it, then," she said.

"My queen, it seems so."

Navar and a riot of peacemakers stampeded down the steps and surrounded her, blades drawn, eyes blazing with indignation and vigilance.

Elandine could tell from Navar's expression that she was furious, though she held her tongue. Probably only because Elandine and the First Protector were among her forces, and it would be unseemly. But the queen knew that she was in for a dressing-down when they were alone next. Not that she didn't deserve it, of course. Shame threatened to warm her cheeks. She considered appointing the peacekeepers who'd followed the First Protector as the "queen's personal detachment" for the foreseeable future, just to put off the dressing down as long as possible. She didn't need to hear it. She already knew Navar was right.

"How fares the bivouac?" Elandine said.

"The army is descending in good order," replied the First Protector, her ears flicking with annoyance. "I'm sure you can hear them, Your Majesty." The qephilim gestured upward and back.

True, the clamor of a company banging and clanging its way above into the wide space was unmistakable. Voices issuing orders and boots on stone grew louder. She saw the yellow-orange glow of fresh lanterns shinning blearily through the translucent columns.

"Your Majesty..." began Navar. Damn it, Navar wasn't going to wait until they were alone after all.

Elandine held up a hand. "Later."

"Please," she said, "I saw something... odd as I rushed to defend you–"

"I know, Navar. Believe me."

"I trust you *do* understand the foolishness of your lone advance, you're not an imbecile. But that's not what I'm talking about."

Elandine blinked, and cleared her throat. Navar was of course suggesting exactly the opposite. She ignored the jibe and said, "Then what?" she said

"When you commanded the spirits to leave, I'm certain I saw a flash – the same light I saw when we were beset by the Moon Door. You called on the Ring of Peace then to quell the kray, and the band flashed."

Elandine well remembered that moment, when she'd asked the serene stillness of death, and froze descending kray seedlings before they touched her and her host. But... "I don't have the Ring anymore." She raised her hand to demonstrate, and wiggled her bare fingers at the First Protector.

And yet... She looked more closely at her ring finger. She'd felt a phantom of the power the newly wakened Ring had contained a few times. Was it possible what she'd experienced was no mere memory?

She concentrated, attempting to recall exactly how the sensation had come to her. She imagined the cool band encircling her finger. A cold tingle – real or imagined she didn't try to determine – answered. Faint, oh so faint. But maybe something real. Like an umber wolf sneaking up on an oblivious pilgrim, she carefully examined the feeling.

A ghostly voice floated across her, of someone speaking. A man, speaking. She didn't recognize the voice, yet it was familiar, as if something inside her had been waiting to hear it since forever. It whispered, "Come to me, Rings of Incarnation. It is I, your Maker, who calls you. Return to me, in my hour of need. If worn, then I command you, the wearer, to find me. The ring will know the way. If I speak instead to a mute band – find me. Find a wearer, and lead her or him to me."

The message didn't repeat. But suddenly, certainty clutched Elandine with a crystal clarity she hadn't felt about anything for far too long. She knew where the Maker was, and this time, she knew it wasn't a sham. It was no seeming, or fraud. How she was able to discern it, she couldn't say. She just knew that *this* time, the Maker really had returned to Ardeyn. And he was calling all the Rings of Incarnation to him. Including the Ring of Peace. Of... Death. The band that should be hers.

No doubt the Maker had the power to force the Betrayer to return the Ring to its rightful owner, if she proved unable. But would the Maker return Death to her, if she made a claim?

The only way to find out was to ask. She knew the way. For once circumstance smiled upon her. He wasn't far.

27: HOMECOMING
Jason Cole

He lost sight of Merid hours earlier in the insane boil of unzipping fractal solids and multicolored hues. The kray still pursued him, though at a horrifyingly leisurely pace, as if they didn't actually want to catch him. Which was fine by Jason. But his ability to move through the Strange was gradually deteriorating. The place scraped his mind like sandpaper.

Which is why when the dlamma appeared out of nowhere, having circled back to look for him, a weight of tension and fear loosened his body. He was pretty sure the kray hadn't already caught him up because they were just toying with him, not because they couldn't.

He grabbed the pommel and pulled himself into the saddle. The dlamma spread its wings, and they surged with a velocity Jason could hardly hoped to have matched. He was going to survive after all, it seemed. No thanks to that bitch Merid.

The massed horde quickly fell from sight, lost in the sickening swirl. He didn't spend too long looking because it reminded him too much of staring into a suppurating wound.

And yet... He still sensed the massed horde of kray advancing. Even though they'd fallen completely out of sight, the feeling of their lingering presence remained. He hoped it was his imagination.

"Thank you," he told the dlamma. "You have War's gratitude."

It nodded. Maybe the dlamma had realized Jason needed help, not only in escaping the kray, but also in finding the interface back to Ardeyn. The translucent membrane was difficult to see out in the Strange, because the Strange was a fucking mad house, and the interface was a mere blip in the maelstrom. He reminded himself, the Strange didn't "contain" the Land of the Curse. Instead it hosted it like a computer network hosted a program. As real as Ardeyn sometimes seemed, *this* was the raw medium that gave it that semblance.

Ahead, the empty space they'd been rushing toward suddenly contained a curved pane of hard glass, one they were about to smash directly into. When the dlamma winged onward and into it, he forced himself not to flinch.

Firm pressure enveloped Jason, a giant fist squeezing every inch of him to fit into some more bounded, confined shape, one of rules, responsibilities, and hard consequences. The pressure eased and he blinked. Ardeyn stretched before him, familiar and *normal*. The corners of his mouth tugged up.

They soared over the Borderlands from Ardeyn's southern foot, just miles from his fortress of Megeddon. Even from this distance, he could see the sprawling walls, the tall ebony towers, and the searing volcanic extrusions tapped to power the Foundries...

Odd he could see it all, actually. "I don't understand," he said. "Merid said that when we returned, it would be in same location we left – which was in the Borderlands west of her lair. Yet..." He gestured at the scene ahead.

The dlamma's shoulders gave a subtle shrug, and it surprised him by speaking, "I have skills Merid lacks, when it comes to traveling back and forth between Ardeyn and the Strange. I can re-enter a recursion from the interface and come out almost anywhere I choose, if it lies along a specified boundary."

Jason grinned. Allying with the dlamma continued to pay dividends. This creature aided him for inscrutable reasons of its own, not because it feared him. It had a spark of knowing that was lacking in others of its kind – it knew Ardeyn was a world bounded by a much wider, stranger reality. It possessed skills that even he, once an Incarnation of Ardeyn, was still learning. Making it a pet or taking its aid for obedience would probably piss it off, and that'd be the end of a beautiful friendship.

Indeed, with the dlamma's help, perhaps he could finally deal with Merid... But only after he'd taken care of a few other things. For instance–

Blunt pain, like indigestion gone horribly wrong, stabbed through his bowels.

Jason grunted in surprise. He could count on one hand the number of times he'd felt physical discomfort, even during his mostly mortal existence over the preceding two centuries he'd been trapped in Ardeyn. He carefully rubbed his abdomen, checking for a stray spine or dart. Maybe a kray or the dragon had managed to stick him in all the chaos...

Nope. No visible wound or discoloration was visible.

But still he felt wrong, like he was going to be sick all over the dlamma's back.

Jason tried to will the nausea away. He didn't have time to diagnose the problem. The sensation was probably related to his anxiety about the kray armada, out there in the void. An armada that possessed the Ring of Silence, denied him.

Without at least four rings, he would not be entering the Maker's Hall anytime soon. The pain inside him gouged at his liver, and he winced.

"You see it too, then," said the dlamma, misreading his physical reaction.

Jason's eyes snapped to the towers over Megeddon. He realized that the pillar of dark smoke rising from the center of his fortress wasn't normal. Not by half.

He scanned, both visually and with his enhanced senses, trying to discern the cause of the disturbance. No dragon was present, thankfully. Nor any kray he could detect – not even seedlings. But something bad had happened, somewhere within his Foundries. And... someone new had come into his realm.

His breath caught. That part of him that was War sensed a power that was familiar, from the days of old, from before the Betrayal.

"The Ring of Desire has returned to Megeddon," he murmured, uncertain. But how could that be? The closer they came, however, the more certain War became. Desire was back, somehow.

Jason didn't know what to think. He hadn't made the Ring of Desire part of his plans moving forward after it served its purposes on Earth. Which had been shortsighted, given its evident return. But hell, he was willing to learn from his errors, as any good soldier did. In fact, the more he turned it over in his mind, the more Desire's surprising return augured that his plans could proceed apace without the Ring of Silence. Let the kray have it! He wouldn't be lured out past the Borderlands a second time.

But how had the ring he'd repurposed to deliver quantum code on Earth returned to Ardeyn? Was Desire's reappearance related to the pillar of smoke rising from his fortress? His gut said it was connected.

Unless the kray had got ahead of him, suggested the part of him that liked to dash his most cherished dreams.

"Faster, damn you! I mean, please go quickly as you can, my friend," he told the dlamma.

The dlamma sped toward the brooding walls of his home – hopefully, his home for only a little while longer, until he quit it and returned to Earth on his own terms. As they flew, Jason idly massaged at the lingering pain in his side.

•••

Something both better and far worse than he'd imagined had played out in the heart of Megeddon in his absence. Among the press of reds stumbling mindlessly through the thick smoke around the edge of the Pit Reactor, no kray hunted, which was a relief. But the heaped rubble and even thicker smoke spilling out of the Contact Foundry made Jason's heart jump into his throat.

He bounded forward and passed through the smoke.

"What the hell is going on in here?" he roared as he took in the disaster.

Debris, mixed with the corpses of his red homunculi were everywhere. Worse, BITER was a wreck of shattered crystals steaming noxious black vapor as they continued to disintegrate. A century of work, obliterated…

And the translation gate focus that had shimmered in the center of the chamber, the gate he'd managed to connect to Earth, was gone. The connection was severed.

He got his breathing under control by rationalizing. It wasn't a *complete* disaster; he'd already accomplished his initial goal of bringing Earth back into sync with Ardeyn. With that in place, moving between the locations should prove far easier, especially for someone like him. He'd just proved he could move between worlds hosted by the dark energy network. Could the world or normal matter be that much more difficult to breach, now that it was synched?

Not once he had taken the Maker's attributes for his own, he decided.

Jason finally spied the intruders: a man and a woman, standing still as statues over the dead body of one of Jason's lieutenants. He knew who they were. For fuck's sake, he'd actually puppeted the man around on Earth, which he'd temporarily entangled with the Ring of Desire using the entropic seed he'd gotten from the kray.

Raul, the man pretended his name was, though that was a

fucking lie; it was actually something like Url-shoon or some similar mouthful. When he'd possessed Raul, Jason had seen into the man's mind. There, he'd glimpsed an alien world called "Ruk" the likes of which he could never even have imagined. Insane biotech science fiction craziness run amok...

Raul had warned him that Ardeyn "wasn't alone," and that War's plans wouldn't be allowed to succeed. And here Raul was. The man's threats hadn't been idle. He was obviously responsible for the destruction visited on Jason's fortress. Which implied that maybe there *was* such a place as Ruk, twin to Ardeyn in the dark energy network. He decided not to worry about that complication just yet.

Jason knew the woman, too. She'd been on Earth with Raul.

Aloud, Jason said "Katherine Manners." She glanced at him and – holy shit, she was wearing the Ring of Desire. Shit. *Shit!*

Did she know its full potential? Did she have any inkling of what she could do with it on her finger? Like all the other Rings, it hadn't returned to full power, but he imagined a reasonable portion of its old strength had returned. He reached out to see if any of the entanglement created by the entropic seed remained, but that link was gone.

"Jason Cole," Kate said, looking at him with wide eyes. Scared eyes. Which suggested she didn't know what the Ring of Desire could do, after all. Relief made him smile.

"Call me War," he told her. "Why'd you destroy my Contact Foundry?"

Anger replaced the fear in her eyes and face. She sputtered, "Why? To save the world. Because you tried to leave Earth vulnerable against the Strange! And... the *things* that live there!"

As she spoke, "Raul from Ruk" nodded along casually. But to War's trained eyes, the man was actually poised to go for Jason's throat. Raul was dangerous, maybe even to an Incarnation. Jason glanced round and saw a couple of reds he could call to his defense, if it came to it. Or he could summon the mantle to War and create a small unit of duplicates about as quickly. But either way, Jason, his homunculi, and his duplicates would be vulnerable to Desire's will, should she show forth that particular Ring's mind-bending power. Desire's demands had always been War's biggest weakness, if half-remembered fragments of ancient memory could be believed.

His regard dipped to the band on her hand against his will, then flinched away. Jason decided to play along a while longer, and continue to assess the situation. He needed that ring off Kate's finger.

"Endanger the Earth?" asked Jason. "Did Carter tell you that? He's brain-damaged by everything that's happened to him. He has it all wrong. If you're getting your intel from Carter Morrison, think again."

"You're lying," said Kate.

"Am I? Says who?"

Raul cleared his throat. "Says me. You're risking this recursion, and Earth, and Ruk, plus every other limited world connected to Earth with your insane machinations. You *do* know that, right? Or are you actually ignorant of how excessive quantum computing attracts the attention of alien entities in the dark energy network?" Raul curled his lip in contempt.

Fuck it. Jason smashed his elbow into the man's throat with bone crushing force. Or he would've, if Raul hadn't been ready for him, probably trying to elicit exactly such a response. Instead of crushing the man's larynx and so resigning him to death by suffocation, Jason's elbow was slapped aside and down, pinned briefly across Jason's own chest.

With the hand he wasn't using to restrict War's arm, Raul

stabbed at Jason with a scarlet-hilted short sword. Jason's own reflexes took over, and he shifted back and away, breaking the pin and evading the sword in one move.

Surprisingly, Raul didn't follow up. Instead he speared Jason with amazingly clear eyes and said, "Wouldn't you rather just have a nice, comfortable rest? All this fighting, all this striving. It's so tiring! Come on, let's call it quits and sit for a bit. What do you say?"

For a half moment, the man's mental twist actually had the ghost of an effect. Luckily the influence Raul exerted fell far short of what'd be needed to compromise War… but Jason pretended to go along with it anyway. He allowed his mouth to go slack, and his arms drop to his sides. He said, "You know, I *am* tired. Trying to take over the world isn't easy."

Raul nodded. "I can only imagine. Why don't you go over there and have a seat? Perfect place for a nap." He motioned toward the nearest wall.

Jason made a show of yawning, and took a few steps that way.

Kate whispered to Raul, "What're you doing?"

The moment the man's attention shifted to his friend, War's mantle surged up in Jason like rising magma. He multiplied from a single figure into a company a dozen strong, each clad in ebony armor and wielding weapons that kindled to roaring flame.

The intruders would pay for their insolence. In one voice, he and his company demanded, "Give up your Ring, or die." Their fingers pointed at Kate like ebony knives.

"Oh, holy Jesus," Kate said, reflexively hiding her Ring with her opposite hand. Raul stepped in front of her, drawing a second short sword from his sheath. He held the blades with reasonable skill. Not that it was going to do him any good against War.

Jason laughed. Or maybe it was War. Did it matter? The

power of his Incarnation was cresting again, and while basking in that mastery, failure was unimaginable. The Ring of War glowed scarlet, brighter than he'd seen it since before the Maker's death, bathing his duplicates, the floor, Raul and his swords, and even Kate who cowered from the light's intensity.

The band on Kate's finger flickered into a glowing life of its own, as if taking light from the fervor of his own mantle. Not red like blood splashed across the battlefield. Her light was violet. War remembered that color. The Ring of Desire emitted the hue of purity, lucidity, ambition, delight... and devotion.

War frowned, understanding his tactical error. By invoking his own aura, he'd catalyzed the somnolent power in the mortal's Ring. A power now rising into awareness. War had to deal with things immediately before Desire realized he'd just given her a human host.

With as little effort as closing his fist, War launched his company into a charge. His soldiers fell on Raul and Kate, burning weapons slashing, crushing, and stabbing.

28: DESIRE
Katherine Manners

Kate was so terrified she thought she might pee. Maybe she did. It didn't matter. She and Raul were about to die.

She'd sensed Jason's change before it happened, like a tsunami of invisible energy. As it rolled over him, Jason's expression and posture fell away and the Incarnation of War melded into his place. And he grew. Shadows fled from his presence. The scarlet light burning from his Ring was more than illumination – it was the clang of steel on steel, of warriors screaming battle cries, and of soldiers dying on battlefields thousands of years ago.

His soldiers – versions of *him* called into being as she stared slack mouthed – charged. They at least retained human size. But there were so many! She scrabbled for the ashur. Without the spiritual cloak Darneth had provided, she felt naked.

The soldiers crashed into Raul. He deflected three attacks in a stunning display of swordsmanship. One duplicate fell, and hazed away in a swirl of sparks. But at a cost. A red-hot blade sliced across Raul's shoulder, a mace cracked his forearm, and a dagger protruded from his stomach, its hilt still burning with War's flame. Raul screamed, staggering.

"No! Stop!" Kate yelled. Her voice was a ring of violet radiance that swept away from her in all directions, and she stumbled. What…? Dizziness swamped her. She went down on one knee, opposite hand slapping onto the tiled floor for balance. On that hand, her ring blazed. It was the source of the violet light, and her dizziness. It was…

Revelation bloomed: it was the fucking Ring of Desire.

A window snapped open in her mind. Through it, years swept by. Of Ardeyn when it was young, of the Maker and his Incarnations… an Incarnation such as herself. She was a physical manifestation of the Seven Rules of Ardeyn, which kept Lotan the Sinner bound. They'd struggled for millennia, during the Age of Myth. Of course! How had she forgotten?

She'd been like a god. It was beyond wonderful! But was it real? Dana Scully would prescribe Kate a hefty dose of anti-hallucinogens. Because no, of course it wasn't *real*, it was all a fiction given the guise of reality, her lurking sense of disappointment whispered. It was–

Raul cried out, breaking Kate from her insane recollection. He was still fighting, protecting her while she crouched on the floor. Blood pooled on the floor beneath him. He staggered and groaned with each parry and sword thrust.

But half War's duplicates had stopped moving completely, their eyes glowing not red with War's authority, but violet. Violet with clarity and devotion. To her. To Desire. She knew they would do as she demanded, at least for a little while. But how?

She let her fear of disappointment lapse, and the Incarnation of Desire's mantle swept over Kate. Everything was different. Pain, fear, uncertainty, loss, and most importantly, fear of disappointment – were transformed to various textures of glorious existence. When last Desire walked, a newness had come into the Land of the Curse. War, the Maker, and some of her fellow Incarnations were changed, gaining memories of other people from another world *completely different* than Ardeyn. Excitement at the prospect of learning more had enflamed her, then, though Desire herself hadn't fused with the mind of a mortal host. She relished that change in the others, though, anticipated what it might mean.

Then War, who'd always been her favorite Incarnation, murdered the Maker. Remembering the cut, the hot blood pouring from him, then nothing else until this moment, soured Desire's delight. Anger warmed her, though it was an emotion she felt so rarely that she hardly recognized it. It seeped up from the one named Kate whose body Desire manifested within. Anger burned away second thoughts and second guesses, and scared mental voices like Kate's, making her certain.

Here was War again, once more sending his duplicates to slay, as he'd slain the Maker. Not again, vowed Desire.

With a thought, she turned those duplicates of War she'd already bedazzled upon their fellows. The ones who'd been trying to hack through the swordsman's – Raul's – faltering sword defense turned and hurtled back toward their hulking master. Raul sank to the floor, gasping and bleeding.

Desire raised her voice and said to War, "Why did you forsake me, darling?"

War froze, avoiding looking directly into her eyes. He was vulnerable to her, but he knew it. He wasn't an idiot, more was the pity. Instead of answering her directly, the incarnation clenched his fist and threw off another company of duplicates that smoked out of him, hornets from a kicked nest.

She sensed the minds of War's army kindling as they formed, each merely a clipping of War's complete consciousness. Which was why they were even more susceptible than their progenitor. The Incarnation of War, for all his defenses, had a soft spot for her. Everyone did, but War in particular had willingly set aside his defenses on more than one occasion during their long struggles. She'd welcomed him then. As she welcomed his army now, with arms wide and a smile like an amethyst sun and the smell of lilac.

More than half instantly came under Desire's influence, and she wasn't even trying. Her own glamor dizzied Desire, swept her up, and made her laugh in delight as fighting ignited in War's ranks, soldier falling upon soldier. The emotions they generated belied her knowledge that the duplicates weren't fully real. When they killed each other, the cold, sharp stab she sensed was almost the same as when a normal Ardeyner perished. Except no spirits came free of the duplicate's flesh, and their bodies dissolved moments later like fleeing fireflies. The mind they possessed cast no shadow in the afterworld.

Which was why Desire felt only a tug of remorse when she commanded each new wave of soldiers War hatched to kill their brothers. "I can keep this up all day, darling," she told him, betraying no hint of that minor regret.

He pretended not to hear her over the clamor. She knew her words had registered. War's sole reaction was to spawn yet *another* company and hurl them toward her. Desire smiled indulgently. He'd always been headstrong.

"War," she said, "you can't win me back by showing off. You never could. Remember our time in the Green Wilds?" She called up the sweet memory, and projected it with another violet wave. Every one of the duplicates, and War himself, paused to recall those golden hours so long ago. Memories of most creatures grow cold and shift with time's passage. Not so for Desire. Hers grew only more grand and magnificent as time marched on.

War groaned, struggling to hold onto his army, and losing. To a one, they turned on him.

"Lotan take you!" War hissed. He dissolved his traitor army with an angry slash of his fiery staff.

"That's no way to greet a lover," she said, "even one that you spurned." War glanced at her, and finally, deliciously, their gazes locked.

War stood long strides from Desire, but she could see his eyes. He certainly saw hers. She only had one chance at this, and Desire didn't intend to waste her opportunity adding War to her retinue. Already his pupils were larger than normal, but as the moments passed and they stood unmoving regarding each other, the dark circles expanded. He was coming fully under her spell. Already, she doubted he remembered his own name. Soon, he wouldn't be more than–

Desire and Kate both blanched when Raul's life snuffed out.

All deaths saddened Desire, but for Kate, it was like being kicked in the stomach.

Desire's mantle shredded and was gone.

"Raul!" Kate sobbed, spinning away from War. She rushed to the crumpled body. "No, no, no, please…"

The Incarnation's easy mastery of exotic minds and wills, even those of the dead, was gone with her Ring's mantle. But Kate retained the sensitivity to spirits she'd gained when she'd taken on the context of a shepherd when entering Ardeyn. A shepherd of the dead. Darneth had been her sole charge. And she'd lost him.

Now Kate sensed that same tentative energy before her that Darneth had demonstrated, a gray cloud on the edge of blowing away. Rather than a forgotten warrior of some previous age of Ardeyn, it was *Raul*. She could feel the man's identity in the memory of his ephemeral eyes.

"Can you hear me?"

The vague shape, ceased its slow dispersal. "Raul?" she asked it. "Stay with me."

A man's face smoothed out of the rough smoke around the eyes. Raul's face. He blinked, colorless. His hands moved, affectless. But she could hear him. He said, "Where am I? It's so cold…"

"You saved me," she said. "From War's army." Which was

true, as far as that went. If he hadn't intervened, the very first charge of duplicates would've cut her into so many bloody ribbons. After that, though, Kate had found the power to save herself from War...

She glanced round quickly, realizing she'd turned her back on the Betrayer! But whatever whammy Desire had slapped War with still had Jason blinking and shaking. Yes, it was Jason, she realized, chiefly because he'd returned to his normal human size.

Desire ... The memories and mindset of the Incarnation who'd possessed her were unbelievable. Inconceivable, really. Feelings so intense, so beyond her experience, she didn't know what to think. Devotion, curiosity, clarity, and erotic desire! Erotic and downright... scandalous. Of course, to Desire, "scandal" was a word significant only to mortals. Seeing things simultaneously as Desire and as Katherine Manners was like double vision. A splitting headache threatened to descend on her with each heartbeat. She dismissed Desire's memories, physically flinching back. To do otherwise risked insanity.

Maybe that's what'd happened to Jason – when Jason merged with War, and gained War's memories of battles, stratagems, and strife going back thousands of years, he'd lost his mind. Maybe she should strip the Ring of Desire off her finger and throw it in that Pit that Gamma had shown them.

But... The Ring had also become her spirit focus, when she translated into Ardeyn. And the outline of a plan that came to her, right then, required that she keep it, and fucking hell, keep Desire, too.

"Raul!" she said, "I can save you! Or at least keep you safe, until we figure something out. Listen... Curl into my Ring, like Darneth. He's gone. There's a place for you. Will you do that? Can you?"

For many long seconds, Raul's shade did nothing. The

expressions of life no longer flickered across his face. Micro-expressions, tells, all the body language a living creature communicated simply by being physically present were absent in Raul's shade. She had no idea what he was thinking. Or if he was thinking. Was he confused? Why didn't he listen?

"Raul, we don't have time. Please!" She offered the back of her hand, as if he was a gentleman in a period piece, who would take it and lightly brush his lips.

Instead, Raul's uncertain outline melted into so much swirling vapor. He smoked into the Ring.

29: EMANCIPATION
Carter Morrison

In stories, especially novels and on TV, the main character is always getting knocked out, or even fainting. In reality, it's really hard to "knock" unconscious a healthy adult, unless you've come dangerously close to killing the poor bastard, or inflicting permanent brain damage. If you've beaten someone so badly that they go into a coma... well, figure it out for yourself.

On the other hand, after being punched in the back of the head by a golem, it's sort of surprising my skull wasn't crushed like an egg. Then I *would* have been unconscious just long enough for my brain to completely starve from lack of oxygen. By mere fact I was able to consider it, it was obvious I'd escaped that outcome. What I'm trying say is that, for the record, I didn't go unconscious.

But fuck if it didn't hurt.

Pretty much I was a puking, mewling mess. Barely able to move my fingers, resisting wasn't an option when they dragged me and Siraja into that crack at the bottom of the crater. Plus, I was bleeding. A *lot*. Apparently, that was something they had right in stories – head wounds bleed like the promise of no more tomorrows. A coppery sweet taste in my mouth sickened me, so I spit, but avoided actually retching. Much.

Wiping my mouth was impossible, because iron manacles pinched my wrists and clanked tight when I tried. My arms were stretched above my head. While *not* being unconscious I blearily recalled being dumped in some sort of cage.

Scooting myself closer to the bars provided enough slack in the chains so I could sit up straight. The ache in my head threatened to split it open, and nausea followed. I gasped, waiting for the dizziness to recede. When it finally did, the awfulness of my situation was fully revealed.

Rather than a cage, I was in a cell, one of several sunk into the stone around the edge of some larger cavernous chamber. The restraining bars were embedded in the solid stone. There were some stand-alone cages, too, hanging from the rocky ceiling.

A large area between the cages held a massive sculpture resembling some kind of mythological flying beast. Light spilled from its interior, flickering from several fist-sized holes piercing its side. A muttering buzz also issued from the object, which reminded me of thousands of roaches swarming over each other.

The cells held prisoners besides me. The closest was Siraja. She sat, hands bound behind her, facing the main chamber and the buzzing statue, manacles secured to the bars. She turned her head and blinked at me a few times, but offered no audible comment. The leather armor I'd grown accustomed seeing her in was absent. My own outerwear was missing, too, as was Jushur. Crap.

"Are you all right?" I asked the qephilim.

Siraja gave a cautious nod, but remained quiet. Her eyes and ears flicked from me back to the main open area containing the cages.

My talent whispered to me that she was indeed hale, save for a few bruises and an all-consuming anxiety. She was much healthier than me, in fact. My head was foggy and simultaneously felt as if it was in a vice: probably a concussion. A stabbing feeling near my abdomen whenever I shifted meant some bruised or even busted ribs. Could there be some internal damage? Best not to think about that, I decided.

If someone hadn't relieved me of Jushur, I would've asked it what to do.

Though I bet the sanctimonious thing would tell me to see to my own wounds. If I could break a rope, or mend it by naming it, it would tell me that I could rend flesh, or repair it, too, even if it was my own. Easy for it to say.

Although, imaginary Jushur had a point. After all, the sphere was a product of my own creation and will. As most things here in Ardeyn were... Even if it'd all grown far more real than anything I could've ever imagined when I'd started coding the Land of the Curse so many years ago.

Anyway, according to the context of this place, all I needed was a name to conjure with... And I knew my own name.

"Carter Morrison," I whispered to myself. The words burned my lips as the sound emerged, then spread until I was engulfed in a conflagration of sensation. It wasn't exactly searing pain, though not far off. A yelp escaped me as what felt like fire seared my skin. I'd just made my final, most lethal mistake.

Then cool relief followed. There was no burning, no bonfire with me as the kindling. Nor any hint of the pain from broken ribs, the foggy feeling from the concussion, or any other hurt.

Huh.

Flush with success and perhaps slightly high from the sensation of perfect health still tingling from the tip of my head to my toes, I named the manacles, loosening them so they fell off, and then next cell door lock, triggering it open. Whoa.

"Carter!" hissed Siraja.

"Hold on," I said, and ambled over to the winged vessel

and glanced into one of the many vents. OK… not roaches. Tiny little lizards, each burning like a red-hot ember in fire, scuttling over each other and some larger, burnt object. Something vaguely human shaped lay curled inside, with a few blackened bones poking out.

"Oh jeez," I croaked. "Is that a person?"

A rough voice answered, "If Mehvish is the spy who stayed up on the rim when you descended, then no, she got away. We sacrificed this slave in her place." The speaker stepped around from the opposite side of the vessel. The tattooed, wrinkled face and white cloak of Greeter, back in human form, smiled at me. He still clutched his bone flute, but had added a circle of white metal at his temples. A crown?

"You," I said. I'm witty like that.

"You have no power here, namer." He pointed to the white circlet. "This protects me from mental influence or attempts to compromise my loyalties." Not a crown, then, but something of power.

"What protects it?" I said, as the circlet's name found me.

Greeter frowned, even as I asked the metal to stretch so that it slipped off his head. It settled loosely around his neck.

His first reaction, the same one he'd relied on when he'd ambushed us on the crater floor, was his downfall. If he'd just removed the circlet, he might've beat me. But that's not what he did; he triggered his ape-otheosis with a snarl.

Greeter grew, but I held the circlet's size in place with a whisper, so that whatever magic the soul sorcerer used, it didn't affect the stiff band as it did his cloak and other equipment.

A strangled growl became a gasping whisper as the massive white ape, scrabbling at his neck with oversize claws, stumbled about the cell-lined chamber, knocking into the free-hanging cages dangling from the ceiling. I scrambled back so I wasn't crushed underneath when the huge creature finally toppled over. The winged vessel wasn't so fortunate.

The container overturned with a clatter, spilling scurrying fire lizards everywhere, as well as the charcoal body, which broke into pieces.

Siraja yelled, "Carter, you toad fondler, look what you've done!"

Red embers, each a tiny creature, raced everywhere like ants when some dipshit kid kicks the colony over. Except these things were each as hot as a poker.

Turning, I hustled to Siraja's cell, jumping between momentary clear spots on the floor, between scrabbling red dots. Sudden sweat stung my eyes and dryness tightened my throat; the little bastards gave off a lot of heat.

The little fuckers sensed me, crawling after me as I closed on Siraja.

There were too many to individually name; I could maybe tell a handful to run away, but hundreds of others would take that time to burn us into carbon footstools. I had the vague sense that had I been the Maker, I wouldn't have been bound by such a restriction. But the Maker, I was not.

A handful of lizards spilled into the qephilim's cell. She leaned away from them, but her manacles kept her pinned essentially in place. The movement drew the fire lizard's attention, plus more still outside the cell. Which gave me an idea...

I shifted my attention to the toppled, winged vessel. What was the shape supposed to represent? Memory kindled from art sketches I'd approved. It was in the crude likeness of a creature of Ardeyn: a dlamma! A winged lammasu I'd adapted from Sumerian myth for the Land of the Curse.

And so I named it, but with a twist in the same way I had named Jushur, when I'd fashioned it from the refuse I'd found in the Glass Desert. Then, I'd had time to create something lasting. For this, I needed something quick before Siraja and

I were overwhelmed.

Naming it, I told it to run, as far and as fast as it could.

The vessel jerked, its ungainly limbs – suddenly suffused with pseudo-life – struggling to right itself, wings spastically flapping in a crude approximation of something actually alive. The lizards near me and the qephilim responded, and flowed toward the spectacle, while we froze in place.

The faux-dlamma trundled away from me, seeming even larger now that it could move, drawing the fire lizards, despite that it'd previously served as the vessel containing them. They were too stupid to care. Or maybe they wanted revenge.

The lead fire lizards in the wave leaped after the tottering statue, scorching its exterior, but otherwise having little effect. The thing dashed itself down the length of the dungeon and into the far wall, breaking through into a larger space. I felt the enchantment I'd woken in it shatter as the statue disintegrated from the impact.

The lizards apparently liked what they found in the chamber beyond because they didn't return the way they'd come. Then I heard distant cries of consternation from that direction. More soul sorcerers was my guess. Time to go.

A few moments of fumbling with the mechanisms got Siraja out of her cell and manacles. The qephilim rubbed her wrists, keeping a wary eye on the new hole in the wall. No one yet appeared to backtrack the source of the ruckus. That would presumably soon change.

"How many soul sorcerers do you suppose are creeping around down here?" I asked.

Siraja shrugged. "The stories don't give good numbers. There can't be too many because sooner or later, they'd form factions and turn on each other."

"Whether it's five or five hundred, I vote we avoid meeting any more of our hosts." Of the three other exits to the prison other than the freshly smashed hole, one seemed sort of familiar. "They brought us in that way."

"How can you be sure? I was blindfolded. And you were unconscious."

"I was *not* unconscious. I just had to rest my eyes."

The qephilim's ears waggled. She said, "Then we should go the way you remember."

"You are too gracious," I said, grinning.

First we checked to make sure no one else was caged in the chamber. The other figures I'd spied turned out to be dried corpses. Neither of us was keen on investigating further, so we left them.

Torches set in wall sconces wound along the passage leading out, providing smoky light. A side chamber gaped halfway along it, which I did *not* remember. Of course, I didn't actually remember having all my stuff taken, so...

We glanced into the side chamber, which turned out to be small. Two walls were stacked floor to ceiling with cubbies. Dusty bundles clogged most of the cavities, but two contained loose piles without layers of filth covering them. Jushur's metallic curve winked in my torch light in the cubby on the left.

We reclaimed our stuff. Besides my magic talking sphere, the cavity held my clothing and everything else I'd been carrying, including my pack. Despite how my clothes smelled a bit stale with sweat, it was a relief.

"Everything's here," Siraja said, "including my weapons and coin. That's surprising; I'd imagined these sad old sorcerers would find whatever visitors bring them to be diverting, at minimum, if not needful."

"They can probably conjure all the entertainments and sustenance they need. Otherwise they'd have died out centuries ago."

"Or they just hadn't gotten around to sorting through our stuff yet. We've been down here less than an hour."

We returned to the passage. It remained clear, so we set forth along it, heading away from the prison.

A dozen yards later, we came to a four-way intersection. One more thing I didn't remember. Crap. Torches only lit two of the ways – straight ahead, and the path to the right.

"Which way?" Siraja asked, her ears waggling once more.

"I forget."

"Sure."

Waggling ears on a qephilim, I decided, might just be laughter.

"Why not ask your magic cannonball?" she suggested.

Why not, indeed? The sphere was cool and rough in my hand as I addressed it, "Which way should we go?"

"To find what you seek, turn left, Maker," it replied.

Jushur had never given me that title before. But time was short, and I didn't waste time trying to figure out what had short-circuited in what passed for the object's magical mind.

Siraja gave me a fishy look. She'd heard what it called me, too, but didn't comment on it as she grabbed a torch. We trooped along the lightless left-hand corridor for a few minutes before worry suddenly grabbed me by the lapels. Surely we hadn't come so far after the sorcerers had ambushed us? Embarrassed, I kept my tongue for another couple of minutes.

Siraja didn't. "Are you certain this is the way?"

"Jushur, you heard the qephilim. I don't recall coming in this direction."

The sphere remained silent. I gave it a shake, as if that would do any good. It didn't.

"Look." Siraja pointed farther along the corridor. The flickery light of her torch revealed the corridor's end. The far wall wasn't blank stone – it was heavily inscribed with symbols that danced around in an ever-widening spiral procession. They looked worn and old.

"Dead end," muttered Siraja.

"We'll see," I said, as I searched for the wall's name. If nothing else, I wanted to know what the symbols on it meant.

The qephilim continued, "The talisman isn't great with directions. Of course, how could it know which way to go in the first place? It has no eyes."

Ignoring her, I concentrated on the wall. The symbols were slippery. Changeable. They weren't like other things I'd tried to name so far. Something like heat haze rising off a highway distorted their meaning. I concentrated, and without considering whether it was a good idea, touched the wall.

Immediately the symbols jumped to clarity. Information trickled into my brain: the symbols were magical components in a system designed to allow access for certain creatures, or blast into so many drifting motes of burning ash anyone who tried to get past who weren't on the safe list.

For a wonder, we were already on the "safe" side of the passage. Safe if you didn't include the crazy soul sorcerers, anyway. Getting out, the direction we were apparently heading, didn't seem to be fraught with risk of annihilation.

"Jushur had it right all along," I said, and pressed the symbol that should open the way.

The entire wall faded like mist, revealing a space unlike the one we'd just taken. Instead of squarely carved passages through stone, the area beyond was natural: a twisting, irregular corkscrew of a cave passage ascended via a series of flowstone formations. From somewhere far above, faint light filtered down.

The way was steep and twisty. We scrambled, crawled, and shuffled sideways in silence, but with each foot gained, my mood brightened, as did the light ahead. I couldn't restrain a grin as I glanced Siraja's way. "We got away," I said.

Her ears moved apart. Maybe amusement, maybe skepticism, or a little of both.

"You know," I said, "We've known each other for, what, two months? Three? You're my only friend in all Ardeyn."

Siraja's ears moved wide apart. Skepticism, then.

"OK, OK, you're the only person I've met here who hasn't either tried to kill me, promised to kill me, or laughed when someone else did their best to kill me."

She shrugged. "I suppose you have one or two redeeming qualities. But don't let it go to your head. I may one day decide I'd like to kill you." Then her ears waggled.

Laughing felt good. But my curiosity was peaked. "I know nothing about you. How'd you come to be working on the *Nightstar*? You're not like the other pirates. What's your story?"

Siraja grunted, and started upward again.

We continued in silence for several yards. Definitely not the reaction I'd hoped for. Making friends with jackal people wasn't as easy as it looked.

After another dozen or so yards of progress, she said, "That's a story I've not told before, and one we don't have time for now. The short version is that a series of bad choices brought me to the *Nightstar*."

"Understood," I said. "Sorry to pry."

She paused, shaking her head. "No, you've earned the right, Carter. If we get out of this alive, I owe you that."

My smile returned. "I look forward to it."

"But you'll have to tell me your story in return. You're hiding many things from me."

"I am?" I said somewhat guiltily.

"Something of even more import than my own circumstance, I judge."

Yeah. That I was the author of this entire world. Siraja would find that a *fascinating* claim. Or rather, an insane one. She'd dismiss me as a lunatic on the spot, and maybe she'd be right to do so. I was a shadow of a shadow of the Maker.

Finally, I said, "Frankly, you wouldn't believe me."

"Why did your magic ball call you the Maker?"

She obviously wasn't going to let that slide.

"What would you think if I told you that I've, um, acquired a few of the Maker's memories and lesser abilities?"

Siraja didn't quite snort. "I'd say have another swallow, drunkard."

"Exactly. Who'd blame you? Not me. But that doesn't change the fact that it's true. It's why you found me in the Glass Desert."

Her ears pointed almost directly away from each other. "Right, because the Maker decided he'd like to be a pirate."

"Funny."

"That was meant to be sarcastic."

Telling her everything was probably the wrong move, but screw it. "I'm not the Maker, I told you. But, I can do some of the things he could do. It's why I came to Ardeyn, to stop the Betrayer from breaking the walls of the world. To do that, or wake the true Maker so he can stop the Betrayer, I need to get into the Maker's Hall."

Siraja nodded as I wound down. When I finished, she said, "Chaff. I said there was a lot of chaff to you. That tale goes beyond the boasts of a man in his cups, and ventures into the realm of pure insanity."

"You saw me animate that statue back there after calling it by its true name."

"A sorcerer with a lucky spell could've done the same."

I nodded. "Perhaps."

"You're having me on. You're an adventurer who lost his crew, that's all. One with a bit of sunstroke from too much time spent on the glass before we found you. You're mostly harmless. Mostly."

I sighed. "I tell you what. If I ever *do* wake the Maker's power, I'll make you your own ship. Maybe you'll believe me then."

She snorted, but offered no more rejoinders. Arguing wasn't going to convince her. The qephilim hadn't even considered the possibility that I was telling the truth. My exuberance at our escape frayed. Indeed, now that I considered how fully I'd failed to achieve my objective of entering the Hall, I realized I'd come full circle. Each step was a pace farther from where I needed to be.

Gaining direct control over the situation required that I enter the Maker's Hall. And I'd failed. A group of demented old men and their servitors had nearly killed me and Siraja. They *had* killed who knows how many people in their creepy dungeon, most recently a sacrifice "in place" of Mehvish. Mehvish was an entirely separate mystery, one I didn't have time to worry about just then. But I was glad she'd apparently escaped.

My plans – both those carefully laid and the ones I'd come up with on the fly – had done nothing to stem Jason Cole's mad schemes. My thoughts churned as I tried to devise a new plan. If I could appeal to the soul sorcerers on a logical level, if they could be made to understand what was actually at stake, they'd have to let me try, right?

Somehow, I sensed that logic might not win them over. But I had to try, otherwise, I was just a coward. A stinking, self-saving coward.

On the other hand, dying wasn't going to solve anything. Forcing myself to turn back and face the soul sorcerers wasn't an option. The urge to flee had me in its grip like an addiction. I'd already given in.

We exited onto the surface of the Glass Desert through a crack just wide enough to wriggle through. The sun was doubled as it dipped to touch the reflective plain. The glass was hot, but its daytime furnace intensity had already faded. Behind us, the great shattered blister of the Singing Crater threw shadows hundreds of yards long across emptiness. The

Nightstar was nowhere to be seen.

"How long did Taimin say he'd wait for us?" I asked.

"Three days."

"It can't have been more than one," I mused.

"Perhaps he had other matters to attend to."

"Yeah," I said, gazing around. "Or maybe he was chased off." I pointed, even though I felt like curling into a ball.

Siraja actually hissed when she saw the figures emerging from the shade offered by the standing shards around the crater. They'd seen us first. A group was headed our way. Here I thought we'd escaped from the goddamned soul sorcerers, but no. We'd just walked into the teeth of their power.

Although... I didn't see any white apes, elderly people in robes, or golems.

Instead, the strangers wore chain armor with deep blue surcoats featuring a design across the chest: a gold circle set within a field of black speckled with stars. My knack for names breathed fresh knowledge into my brain: The symbol was the Crown Banner, reserved for the Queen of Hazurrium. The circle depicted the queen's implement of rulership, the Ring of Peace.

"Holy shit, Hazurrium," I breathed. In the defunct MMORPG, the queendom was a shining land of beauty and peace, the quintessential realm of noble humanity. Everything I knew about the place was two hundred years out of date. What had happened in the all that time? I was about to find out.

Five figures moved to the fore as the group approached. The shortest seemed the one in charge: a woman in magnificent armor wearing a crown. A sword rode her hip, and confidence lit her face. Her name was Elandine, my talent whispered. She ruled the queendom. Which was significant, for some reason. Then I had it: Elandine was directly descended from my friend Mel. Melissa Perkins.

The recognition made me gasp. I'd taken the mantle of the Maker, Jason Cole had chosen the Incarnation of War, Alice the Incarnation of Silence, Peter Sanders had become Lore... and Mel had taken up the mantle of Death. Though mostly in name – the role she'd really preferred had been that of Hazurrium's queen. Oh, the parties she'd thrown...

Elandine had Mel's likeness, all these generations later.

The queen fixed me with her great-to-the-somethingth grandmother's eyes and said, "I heard your call, Maker. I came."

30: COMMITMENT
Elandine, Queen of Hazurrium

For the creator of the world, the Maker looked rather shabby. But the supernatural call had led here. This ramshackle man was the source, she was certain. What she was less sure about was whether she should've responded in the first place. His haggard stare, torn and weathered clothing, and qephilim companion – whose scars and flamboyant dress screamed glass pirate – made him resemble the sort of person routinely turned out of Hazurrium for disorderly behavior.

The man she'd just greeted as the Maker coughed. Then he said, "I'm Carter Morrison. I'm *not* the Maker. But–" he raised hand to forestall the exclamation already springing to her lips, "but what he was... is part of me. And this is my friend, Siraja."

The qephilim pirate snorted.

Elandine didn't care for what the raggedy man was implying. "What he *was*? I've traveled across half of Ardeyn to find the Maker, not some pretender."

Her statement wasn't strictly true, of course; her mission had started as one of revenge, before the call came. But as usual, anger made her tongue quick and somewhat inexact. Although the name Carter sounded familiar. Not the Morrison surname, though. Carter *Strange* was the name she remembered from stories her mother used to tell her. Carter Strange was the name the Maker took when he traveled among mortals. Of course, if this fellow was a fraud, he'd simply incorporate those myths into his charade. Maybe he perpetrated some kind of elaborate deceit, possibly up to and including manufacturing the call to the Rings...

Elandine let her hand drop to the hilt of her sword. "Explain yourself," she commanded.

He saw her not-so-subtle movement, as she intended, but his expression didn't falter. "I'm saying I *was* the Maker. And that maybe, with your help, I can be again. I need to get inside the Maker's Hall, and to do that, I need the Rings of Incarnation. Which means you have one of the Seven. If you heard my call, you must." He looked at her hopefully.

Of course she *didn't* have the Ring of her ancestors. Shame colored Elandine's face, which only made her angrier. "If the Maker is dead, with only you and your pirate friend to keep the memory alive, maybe that's best. What's so important that you need to enter the Hall? For all I know you simply want to steal the Maker's knowledge. You wouldn't be the first to try and abscond with the power of an Incarnation."

"Listen. Everything is at stake. My world, and Ardeyn, too, and every other connected realm. Otherwise, Jason – you probably know him as War – will shatter the walls of existence and let horror consume everything."

The heat that had been building inside Elandine, sharpening like a spear thrust aimed at Carter suddenly shifted and found a new target. She screamed, "War! The Betrayer, you mean. That sodden, earthwanking, pissguzzling thief!"

The raggedy man flinched. His pirate companion, who seemed to be having a hard time with their conversation in the first place, took a step back. Elandine felt Navar's calming hand on her shoulder. She closed her eyes and counted to five.

"So you *do* know Jason," Carter said into the silence.

"War – the Betrayer – stole the Ring from me. He helped me in a desperate hour claiming that *he* was the Maker. In my need, I lent the Ring to him." Her face felt warm.

"Holy crap," murmured Carter, looking crestfallen. "How did Jason pull off that con?"

"Con?" Elandine frowned.

"Con – short for confidence trick. A swindle. How did he fool you?"

She chewed her lip, debating whether to tell him or walk away. Explaining what she'd been up to, she realized, might not sound completely sane. On the other hand, this man was claiming he'd once been the Maker. In the balance, who was he to judge her? Finally she said, "When the Ring's power swelled recently, I decided to use it to storm the Court of Sleep, and ask for release of my sister Flora, recently slain, from those who judge the dead. When the false Maker appeared, I was betrayed by my hope and desperation. I'm not going to make that mistake a second time."

So saying, Elandine drew her sword – it made a *shhhhh* sound as it came free – and in one continuous motion, placed the point at Carter's neck.

"So, convince me you're who you say you are, and not just another thief sniffing after power," she said.

The qephilim pirate finally spoke, raising her hands placatingly. "Excuse me? We seem to have gotten off on the wrong foot. And unless I've forgotten everything I know about heraldry, you appear to be Queen of Hazurrium, out for a stroll on the Glass Desert with a small army. That's downright peculiar, given that you're hundreds of miles from your land. Is the queen who *you* really are?"

Elandine didn't let the sword tip waver, but gave a tight nod. When the pirate put it that way, it did sound faintly ludicrous.

Siraja continued, "Excellent. Which means I shall address you properly from now on, Your Majesty. Easy enough. This leads me to my next point: I *also* only just learned Carter's claim to be the fallen creator of Ardeyn. And like you, Your Majesty, I found his claim suspect."

"So you don't believe him," Elandine said. "Why do you travel with him?"

"That's a long and complicated story, but leave that for a moment. I said I found his claim suspect. But in the time since he's suggested his mad provenance until now, I've been considering the possibility. I've compared the claim with everything I know about him and seen him accomplish since we've been together. I've reviewed all his peculiar abilities."

"I'm right here, you know," said Carter, his eyes flicking between Elandine, down to the queen's sword, and over to the qephilim.

"I'm talking to the pirate," said the queen. Then, "Go on, pirate."

"My name is Siraja, Your Majesty."

"Go on, Siraja, and make it quick, if you please. What peculiar abilities?"

"Abilities like how he knows the name of anything, anything at all, just by looking at it," Siraja said. "Or how, once he knows a thing's name, he can command it, or change it. Or even give it life. That's how he freed us from the soul sorcerers we just escaped. By animating a hollow statue to create a distraction. And I realized, just now when you showed up here calling him Maker, that those would be exactly the sort of abilities I'd expect the creator of Ardeyn to wield. He might be telling the truth." The pirate ceased talking, and fixed Carter with a nonplussed look, as if surprised at her own words.

Elandine stepped on the hope that flickered behind her heart. She said, "Fascinating. Assuming you're not simply in on his elaborate sham."

"It's all true, I swear it," Carter said.

"Then show me," commanded Elandine. "Show forth your power. Name my sword." Her weapon, a sword of power wielded during the Age of Myth, had a secret name that only she—

"Your sword has a secret name, which makes it harder for me to know it, but—"

"Stop," she yelled, suddenly realizing that the man might actually succeed, and worse, blurt out her weapon's name. The blade was powered, to some degree, by the mystery inherent in its origin and name. "Whisper it to me."

Carter stepped close, and said into her cupped ear, "*Rendswandir*. It was forged during the War of the Fall for its first wielder Garsan. Garsan slew the Dragon of Shades on its deadly edge." He stepped back.

Elandine gasped. "How? No one but I know the sword's secret name…"

"Apparently, no longer strictly true," Siraja said.

Carter looked vaguely rueful and said, "It's a knack, but I don't know how it works. And sometimes I remember things that didn't happen to me."

"Then to who?"

"To the Maker. Part of him is in me. Which is why I think I can wake him again, or at least his tools."

"What sorts of things do you remember?" asked Elandine, fascinated despite herself.

"Flashes of stuff I don't understand very well. Fields of combat thick with monsters and angels, of vast spaces underground, of souls being judged… And certainty. Certainty of a sort I've never felt before, as if—"

"Souls being judged?" Elandine interrupted again. "Was it the Court of Sleep you saw?"

"Maybe," allowed Carter. "But it's all—"

"If I help you get into the Maker's Hall, do you promise to release my sister Flora from whatever fate she was handed by the Umber Judges, they who judge the souls of the dead? On your name as the Maker?"

Carter looked confused. "I shouldn't make such a promise. I don't know how to return the dead to life."

"*You* may not," said Elandine, hope tugging the corners of her mouth upward, "but if you really can wake the Maker, *he* will know. Do you promise?"

Carter looked at Siraja. The pirate said, "Like Her Highness says, if you're really the Maker, then what's beyond you? Or, him, I mean."

Carter nodded, returning his gaze to Elandine. "If we get into the Hall, and I can claim the Maker's power as my own – and *after* I resolve the issue of saving the world – then yes, I will do all I can to help your sister."

"Glorious!" whispered the queen. She glanced around to see the army of Peacemakers arrayed at her back, and Navar. The First Protector's ears flicked worriedly, but for once, she held her tongue.

"So," said Carter. "I can point you back the way down to the spaces beneath the glass, where a coven of soul sorcerers is ensconced. They're tough, but I doubt they could stand up to your army."

"Why would we go down there?" Elandine wondered, her mind reviewing happy memories of Flora, and anticipating the look on her face when she was pulled from Death by the Maker's decree.

"Um," mumbled Carter, becoming unsure.

"Because all we need do," continued Elandine happily, "is wait for the others to arrive."

"The others being?"

"If your call reached me, it reached everyone who still has or recently carried a Ring of Incarnation. Once they are assembled, you'll have your key. With them, you can summon the door to the Hall, without need of cleaning out the vermin ensconced below."

Carter looked doubtful. "You think it'll be that easy?"

Elandine shrugged. "Well, of course when the Betrayer arrives, we'll have to kill him and take his Ring *and* the one he stole from me. I suppose other arrivals could prove similarly annoying."

The First Protector finally broke her silence, "Your Majesty can't be suggesting we attack the Betrayer!"

"Why not? We've got the Maker-in-Waiting right here! Plus me and my army. And as the Maker here reminds me—"

"Please call me Carter," he interrupted.

"As *Carter Strange* here reminds me, I've still got my blade. Its edge remains sharp enough to cut the throat of a fallen Incarnation."

31: HAUNTING
Raul of Ruk

I'm dead, Raul thought.

Not that he cared especially; concerns seemed far from him. Probably it was the nonchalance the dead were famous for, he mused. All around him, it was black. Well, not so much black as *void*, if nothingness could be said to have a color. People, even people in Ruk, imagined the void of space as black. And in the universe of normal matter, where things like photons and optical nerves were real, perhaps darkness really was black in outer space, from a certain perspective.

From Raul's current point of view, optic nerves and photons were distant concepts. He was, he reminded himself a second time, dead.

Another thought occurred to him: thoughts don't normally occur to the dead. Maybe he wasn't actually–

Nope, he was dead, as they said on Earth, as a doornail. Jason Cole – War – had done it for him. He'd perished before he could use a curative cypher or the one that might have removed him from harm's way by flying him straight out of Megeddon. He was no longer alive, it was true.

But he was also in Ardeyn. Which made all the difference.

The rules worked differently in the Land of the Curse than on Earth or in Ruk, or any other recursion Raul had personally visited. As policy, Ruk's Quiet Cabal rarely traveled to fictionally or mythologically seeded recursions around Earth, out of fear of igniting the spark of cognizance in the inhabitants. And that went double for recursions created by fictions that included spirits that survived bodily death; those were the sorts of stories likely to contain beings of "magical" power, including all manner of demons, demigods, and probably even deities. No one wanted to risk one of those creatures gaining the spark and worse, becoming quickened.

But here he was, in this surprise recursion of Ardeyn, which should never have been, where the soul survived bodily death. He was proof.

Raul was glad that ghosts didn't have emotions, otherwise he'd be freaking the hell out, to use another Earthly phrase. When he'd first translated to Earth, he'd acquired Spanish automatically, becoming as fluid as a native speaker. He'd had to learn English by dint of concentrated study. Since then, he'd become something of a connoisseur of both languages during his decades long stay on Earth. He particularly enjoyed the colorful sayings. Not that any of that mattered now.

On balance, he was beginning to wonder about his no-emotions assumption. For instance, he obviously retained a sense of curiosity, because he wanted to know very badly where he was. And if he was going to be completely truthful about it, he was becoming attached to even the limited existence he still apparently retained. Though that paled before the cold worry that soaked through him when he wondered what had become of Katherine Manners.

"*Mi chula!*" he whispered. And just like that, the void suddenly spat him out, and he was with Kate.

Last time he'd seen her, she'd been in the Foundries facing off against War. He'd tried to save her. As a senior agent of Ruk's Quiet Cabal, Raul figured he stood a chance against Jason. But in the context of Ardeyn, Jason was also War, a demigod of combat. And before an Incarnation, Raul had failed to prevail.

"Raul," said Kate, as her eyes focused on him. They were red as if she'd been crying. "I'm so sorry."

He reached to comfort her but his hand passed right through her shoulder. The sensation was like waving through cool fog. He drew back and studied his hand. It seemed normal enough – and solid – to him. He wondered how he looked to Kate. Ghostly and pale? The fiction-made-real meant that yes, that was probably how he looked.

"Where are we?" he asked.

"In a storeroom just off the Contact Foundry." Burlap-wrapped parcels cluttered the small room. The single exit was barred with a thin metallic rod.

"Kate, staying in the enemy's stronghold is foolhardy!"

"Tell me about it. But I don't know where to go! But we're safe for now. I'm safe, anyhow. What about you? You're the one who... died."

"Remarkably good, considering." His voice sounded almost exactly the same to his own ears, other than having acquired a slight resonance. Some might even call it a ghostly resonance.

She glanced into his eyes. "Fuck, Raul, I didn't know what to do! I saw you bleeding out, and before I could really even think about it, the part of me that believes she's part of this world, that shepherds the dead, reached out to you. Offered you a place with me. If that was wrong of me, I–"

"Seriously?" he interrupted. She'd provided him a place to anchor. If he concentrated, he could feel a cool current, as if he was standing ankle deep in icy water. Here with Kate, he knew, he could ignore it. But without her, he'd have been swept away into the Night Vault on a colorless wave of nonexistence...

He continued, "If I'd been stabbed that many times in Ruk or on Earth, that would have been the end, forever. So thank you for thinking on your feet, and offering a hand. I feel overwhelmingly odd, but that's hardly surprising. And when you think about the alternative..." He shrugged.

Kate scrunched her eyes in sudden thought. She said. "Hey. Is a ghost-you enough like the real you to translate back to Earth and arrive as the living version of you?"

He blinked. "I don't know. I suspect not, but I suppose we could try and see what–"

Kate said, "No! At least, not before we look into it further. Do some experiments first, so we don't kill you." She waved her hands as if at some imaginary space where experiments on ghosts and dimensional travel could be conducted. "What if we try and you turn up on Earth as a corpse?"

Raul nodded. What he understood of context-keeping during translations between recursions hinted that if a dead person translated into a world where standard physics held sway... well, he hoped he'd make a pretty corpse. He kept his doubts to himself. Instead he said, "What do you propose?"

She pointed at her Ring. "This is even more important than we first thought. Jason originally sent it to Earth, in contravention of everything you've told me about translating. To survive that trip, it had to be something exceptional here in Ardeyn. It can move between realms, which is why Jason used it in the first place, and why I found it in that server room on Earth."

"Agreed. Usually, only cyphers can–"

"I figured out what it really is. One of the Rings of Incarnation. It's Desire."

Raul had acquired enough frame of reference upon translation into Ardeyn to know exactly what that meant. If a ghost could gasp, he would have.

Kate continued, "And War accidentally woke it. For a little while, it was as if *I* was the Incarnation of Desire."

"I don't remember..."

"You were dying."

"Ah." He wanted to clear his throat, but found he lacked the means. Instead he said, "So, you're suggesting this Incarnation has the means to return to life those recently dead?"

"I... don't know. But I'm going to try."

"Wait!" urged Raul, suddenly nervous for a reason he couldn't name. "Where's War? Won't he be back?"

"I don't know. Desire bested him somehow, made him stand down. Then you died, and I was distracted. After that, he was gone. Not much time's passed since you reappeared. Five minutes, maybe."

"We need to find out where he is, and go somewhere else, so he doesn't turn *you* into a ghost too.'

She shook her head. "If he shows up again, Desire can handle him."

"Desire? You talk like it's a separate entity. You're wearing the Ring. Doesn't that mean you control the power of the Incarnation?"

"Sort of. I can't quite explain it." She waved away his question, and continued, "It doesn't matter. Let's see if we can do anything for you."

He recognized that intractable tone. "Fine," he said. "But I'm keeping watch. Jason might have left for reasons of his own, but he or one of his duplicates could turn up again at any moment. These Foundries are presumably central to his operation."

Kate wasn't listening. She'd raised her hand, the one wearing the Ring. The *Ring* of Desire. Raul eyed it with newfound wariness. She closed her eyes in concentration.

About ten seconds passed before he realized sapphire and silver flowers, just coming into bloom, sprouted from the storeroom floor. Funny that he hadn't noticed them before. The delicate scent of lily-of-the-valley mixed with the nostalgic odor of lilac relaxed him, though he idly wondered how it was he could smell. The blooms were thickest at Kate's feet, where the petals flowed into a blue gown, sewn with silver thread.

Had Kate been wearing that all along? If so, he hadn't appreciated how magnificent it was. He'd always known she was wonderful, but now her beauty outshone the sun. Her red hair was a bundle of braids wound about with silver wire, and on her finger sat a wide band that burned with divine grace.

His earlier suspicion that spirits in Ardeyn could feel emotion was confirmed. At least in the presence of *this* woman, the emotion of desire transfixed, and perhaps would have frozen his heart, had he had one.

"¡Híjole!," Raul muttered. Spanish was better for expressing surprise than English or Rukian.

Ruk... Which was his home recursion. Right. What the–

Raul startled from his spell. He managed to croak, "Kate? You in there? That Ring of Desire, it's not fooling around."

Desire slowly blinked, and looked down at her Ring, ignoring Raul completely. She said, her voice both like Katherine's and something far more, "I hear the Maker speaking. His voice is so faint. Oh, praise be to Him; He is not slain! War tried, but failed."

"That's good," mumbled Raul. "But–"

She cocked her head, as if straining to hear. "He summons us! All the Incarnations. He needs us. We must go to him. And I am late! Too late? He called days ago, and I tarried, unknowing. Just as War failed to hear."

Her eyes closed. The divine light that had shone down on her from some higher realm faded. Raul realized there were no flowers, no overpowering floral fragrance, or a god whose presence could madden those who saw her. There was only Kate, who looked confused.

"I wonder if it is wise to call up the power of that Incarnation ever again," said Raul quietly.

"You might be right," Kate replied, rubbing her temple. "It was hard to push her back this time. But I learned something. I know where Carter is, and where War has gone. Carter's trying to get into the Maker's Hall."

"Carter? He's here?"

"Him, or someone who thinks he's the Maker, anyway."

Raul frowned. He said, "This Maker's Hall. It's like Ardeyn's version of Mount Olympus?" Earth mythology was something every agent of the Quiet Cabal learned. It came in handy in knowing what recursions to avoid.

"Presumably. It's the same place Jason wants to break into to steal the keys to the kingdom. So to speak. And if Desire knows where Carter is, so must War. And Jason. He's been trying to accumulate the Rings of Incarnation for the same purpose: use them to open the Maker's Hall."

"How do you know what Jason's been up to?"

"Desire learned much gazing into Jason's eyes. She could read his deepest desires. That's one of her gifts." Kate coughed.

"Right... So. If it *is* Carter, he must have called the Rings of Incarnation because he wants to get into the Hall, too. Meanwhile, Jason knows Carter is back in Ardeyn. The same way as you?"

"The same way as Desire just did, yes. If I concentrate, I can still almost feel what Jason is thinking."

"Maybe you shouldn't do that," Raul cautioned.

"We need to stop Jason," Kate said. "He's planning on overpowering Carter, taking all the Rings for himself, and claiming the power of the Maker!"

Raul would've felt queasy if he had a stomach. "Jason is a psychopath."

"He doesn't think any of this is real," Kate said. "Plus, bearing one of these Rings as long as he has can't have been easy for him."

"Regardless," Raul said, "he's got to be stopped. He's at least partially quickened, if he was able to send the Ring of Desire to Earth in the first place, BITER or no. If he gained godlike power in Ardeyn, he wouldn't be long satisfied in this realm. He'd turn his eyes to Earth. We need to get help."

"From where?"

"From Ruk. From those who sent me to the world of normal matter in the first place: the Quiet Cabal."

"But you might blink out of existence if you leave Ardeyn. Or if I leave, what happens to you? Besides, I don't know the way."

"I can tell you what you need to know to translate—"

"No. You'll die."

"I'm already dead, *mi chula*."

"I'm not going to argue about it. *We* are here. Within the context of Ardeyn, we have the power to oppose Jason."

"He's the Betrayer; he's War!"

"And I can call on Desire."

Raul knew, as he'd known before, that it was futile to keep talking when Kate's tone settled in that particular stubborn pitch. But he offered one last argument, "If the Betrayer doesn't kill you, Desire might subsume you. That might be even worse. You'd lose your mind and personality. Your soul..."

"If Jason gains his heart's desire, everyone on Earth will be wiped out, or overwritten with clones of Jason's making. It's me, or billions. Seems like an easy choice. Don't you agree?"

Raul didn't want to admit it, but Kate was right. He said, "And if Earth is devoured by Jason, it wouldn't be long before all the recursions that Earth hosts would come to the same end, probably by a breach from the Strange itself. All the limited worlds would be wiped out. Including Ruk."

"So help me, damn it! Is there some kind of translational ability that will get me to Carter?"

"You'd know it if you had something like that. But you've got that Ring. Can Incarnations fly? Like angels?"

Kate blinked. "I don't know. I'd have to call her up again to find out."

"Wait on that. I might have something." Raul pointed at his own corpse, which Kate must have dragged into the antechamber with her. It lay battered, torn, and pale in a dark bloom of blood. He'd avoided looking until then, just in case the experience didn't sit well. He'd been right to do so; seeing himself splayed out like meat on a butcher's block was awful. Luckily, he had no time for drama.

Kate followed his gesture, moving to the blood's edge.

Raul directed, "Check in my stuff. I carried a couple of cyphers with me from Earth. Grab them both."

Kate bent and removed the pouch from the corpse's belt with quick fingers. Raul half expected to feel something when she did, through some kind of sympathetic relationship. But apparently the connection between what he'd been before and the ghost he was now was severed.

"Are these it?" Kate dumped a handful of gold coins, a rolled bundle of lock picking tools, a small dagger, an amulet, and a vial of elixir into her palm.

Raul said, "Grab the vial and the amulet. The rest is just leftover residue from my translation. They're meaningless."

Kate dumped the coins, keeping the amulet, the vial, and Raul noticed, the lock picking tools. She shoved those into her satchel, then examined the remaining items. Her eyes grew wider. "You know, I can feel that there's something different about these."

"Anyone who's quickened has the same ability," Raul explained. "The ability to sense objects birthed in the Strange – like cyphers. Stow the vial. It's the amulet we want."

"Should I put it on?"

Without thinking, he reached for it to show her how

to activate the function. His hand passed through her and amulet.

"Better just tell me how it works," she said.

"It's an instant shield," Raul said. "It has a special traveling property. I've been itching to try it out, truth to tell. Put on the amulet, then press the circular image on the front, with the wing design."

Kate lifted the chain over her neck. "What's going to happen?"

"You'll gain the means to rapidly travel," he said. "I don't know the specifics. That's how cyphers work."

"Then you better tuck in. I don't want to leave you behind." Kate raised the Ring of Incarnation. "It's your new focus, until we figure out how to translate you back to life."

Raul glanced one last time at his corpse. He hoped Kate's confidence wasn't misplaced. Then he allowed himself to disincorporate. The void claimed him once more, except now that he knew his situation, he found that he wasn't actually in a place of emptiness.

Concentrating, Raul recognized that he remained "with" Kate, except he was bodiless and without form. It was like he was... haunting her. Everything was a bit fuzzy, but he could still sense what was going on around her.

Kate examined the amulet a few more moments, glanced at the corpse, then away. She mumbled, "Time to fly the fuck out of here."

She unbarred the door to the antechamber and activated the cypher. A full-sized iron shield popped into existence as the amulet melted away in a mist of fractal designs. Blazoned on the shield's front were feathered dragon wings. Kate flinched away, but the shield remained before her, hovering protectively.

She shrugged, then inserted her arm into the straps and said, "Take me to Carter Morrison, where he waits upon the Glass Desert."

The shield warped and grew, reaching to wrap her in a protective envelope of thin iron. In a second, it transformed into a craft that resembled, so far as Raul could determine, a carved metal dragon. Twin portholes for eyes allowed Kate to look out. She was already cursing in surprise as the enchanted conveyance swept its wings back and rocketed forward on a jet of dragon-heated air. The wing edges struck sparks and terrific echoes from the walls of Megeddon as the craft careened along corridors and up every set of stairs it found, moving higher and higher within the fortress. More than once, homunculi had to throw themselves flat to avoid being splattered across its front.

Then they burst free from the structure like an arrow fired from a giant's bow. They sped high above the Betrayer's lava-lit citadel of doom, gaining even more velocity. Raul barely had a moment to take it in; already the craft was rolling into a new trajectory.

A mirror bright line of radiance blazed on the horizon. With obscenities spewing in their wake from a thoroughly rattled Katherine Manners, the craft winged west, toward the eye-watering glow.

32: SHORT CUT
Jason Cole

The moment Desire's attention lifted, Jason fled from Megeddon's Foundries like a cockroach let out from beneath a glass. He didn't race along the corridors of his fortress out of fear. He wasn't afraid of Desire. Exactly the opposite. But events of the prior minutes had convinced him that no matter whether he addressed Desire while wearing the aura of War, or as merely Jason the Betrayer, he was vulnerable. Whatever affair the two Incarnations had enjoyed in their fictional relationship before he'd stepped into the office of War was a chink in his armor he couldn't repair. At least, not without due preparation. Preparation he'd just discovered he had no time for.

While he'd stood bedazzled by Desire's divine smile, War heard Carter Strange call for the Rings of Incarnation.

Jason's metallic, oversize boots clanged on the stone stairs as he sprinted up to the aerie. He was delighted to find the dlamma hadn't left for wherever it called home. The creature had landed Jason there less than an hour before. Two red homunculi were wiping it down. Evidence of a repast was spread out on the stone, red and rare like the dlamma preferred.

"Are you rested?" Jason asked. "I need your help again.

Something has happened. Desire is here! Can you believe it? She's incarnate! Though that's not what I need your help with. Still, I can't help wondering–"

The dlamma said, "You are babbling."

Jason counted to five. He congratulated himself on his self-discipline for not smashing the flying thing into paste for its impertinence. He concentrated on all the fond thoughts he'd recently entertained regarding the winged beast. He said, "Allow me to rephrase," he said. "Please fly me to the center of the Glass Desert. Immediately. Will you?"

The dlamma regarded Jason for several long seconds with its expression unreadable behind its mask. It finally replied, "I need a restorative more vital than this meal." Its eyes flicked to the red mess. "But yes. I sense you would not ask were the need not urgent."

"Urgent?" He coughed, catching himself yet again. "Yes, that's exactly right." Jason removed from his belt an elixir, one of the special class of potions and similar trinkets that turned up unexpectedly now and again. "I'll spare you the details, if you're not interested," he continued, handing over the vial. The dlamma grasped it in surprisingly dexterous feathers and sucked the vial dry. A shimmer of vibrancy flowed across its wings and tail feathers, and its eyes sparkled. After that it bowed, allowing Jason to mount.

As he secured himself with leather straps into the saddle, Jason explained, "Suffice it to say that a sad pretender to the Maker's power is back in play, and we need to work swiftly to stay in the game."

The dlamma leaped, wings fanning out. They were back in the air. Instead of flying west, the creature winged straight south.

As Jason opened his mouth to make the obvious comment, the dlamma said, "We can cut hours off the trip by skimming along the exterior of Ardeyn in the Strange, then re-entering at a point closest to our destination."

"We can?"

The dlamma continued, "Of course. Remember our homecoming? We talked about this very thing."

"Of course," Jason admitted. He was embarrassed to have forgotten. But to be fair to himself, before his trip with Merid, he'd avoided thinking about the dark energy network as policy.

"But now that I do remember, why not go *up*?" he inquired. "Ardeyn isn't spherical."

"The air is mostly confined to within ten miles of the surface, true," the dlamma replied. "But the boundary where the Strange begins is much farther above and beneath the land mass than where the air gives out, presumably to leave room for the sun, moons, and all the stars to exist within."

"Right," Jason said. He'd occasionally wondered if those celestial objects lay out in the Strange. Apparently not. But it didn't matter. The dlamma was flying. He trusted it to take him where he wanted to go.

The creature flapped on, eating up the miles. Sitting on the dlamma's saddle, he could do nothing except think. The Borderlands rolled beneath him as they approached the Edge. He had some time to consider his situation. He'd been far more reactive of late than he preferred. Events had been pushing him, rather than the other way around, and he didn't like it.

Jason pulled out the chain on which he kept the two other Rings he'd collected besides his own: Death and Commerce. Both were weighty, thick with significance that shone from them almost like illumination. He contemplated the bands, thinking that if he had known better, maybe he would not have sent the Ring of Desire off to Earth. Back then, he'd had two Rings – War and Desire – and he'd known where to find Commerce. Maybe he could've tracked down Death on his own, giving him the four needed to open the way. He could've used them as the key...

No, probably not. Before Ardeyn had been pulled from the Schrödinger-like null space where it'd nestled in the Strange out of synch from Earth, his own Ring of War, not to mention the Ring of Commerce, and the Ring of Desire had possessed only a ghost of their previous power. Too little to have opened the Hall, his research had proven. Besides, he hadn't known for sure where to look for the Ring of Death. Stealing it had been a happy accident.

As he'd planned in sending the Ring of Desire across, laden with spells-cum-malware, Earth and Ardeyn had reconnected. He'd been thrilled to learn that two hundred years hadn't passed on Earth as it had here, but only three.

The reconnection brought Carter back, which Jason hadn't expected. Carter's renewed existence, in turn, rejuvenated the Rings to their current potential, which while not yet full, were surely at least half their original strength. Strength enough to open the Hall.

Starting with getting his revenge on the man who'd trapped him here for two hundred years. But this time he wouldn't kill Carter. No. He'd learned his lesson. He needed Carter alive to keep the Rings revitalized. Carter obviously didn't have all the Maker's power himself yet, or he'd have gone into the Hall. Which was why he'd called the Rings.

Jason wasn't exactly sure how it would all go down. It was all a tangled mess. But Jason was committed to surfing that chaos and coming out on top. Of course, if he managed to enter the Hall and claim the Maker's mantle, Carter would be superfluous. Worse, a threat. As the dlamma flew, Jason imagined different ways he might end Carter's existence permanently, or at least painfully.

Ardeyn's edges were ragged, half-dead, and partly crumbled into drifting earth motes called skerries. As the dlamma winged out into the void toward the superficies, the discomfort in his stomach that'd plagued him as they'd left the Strange sharpened. Jason remembered the kray who'd pursued him out of their domain. "What if the kray are waiting?"

"I am fast," the dlamma replied.

"You better be."

They passed into the Strange. As before, the roiling infinities stretched Jason's mind to breaking point. Closing his eyes offered scant comfort. Somehow the medium was able to press through his eyelids and impart their immensities directly into his consciousness.

The dlamma swerved sharply, almost throwing him; only the leather restraints kept him in the saddle. Jason's eyes snapped open instinctively.

The kray armada was all around them, a carapaced swarm of thousands falling through the Strange with pincers extended like fighter-plane guns. The dlamma swerved again to avoid a flight of five kray no bigger than dogs, then dove like a stone to get beneath a kray as large as a house.

The monsters had obviously not ceased their advance after he'd escaped their pursuit by entering Ardeyn. Had they known he'd emerge again? "Get us out of here!" he screamed to the dlamma. The winged beast was already juking and corkscrewing like a rebel alliance ship dodging tie-fighters. His command was only more noise amid a rising scream of hunting kray.

The pain in his belly was worse than ever. He pushed it away. The leather straps keeping him in the saddle jerked savagely each time the dlamma made a course correction, adding to his discomfort. How had the kray known to wait for him, when he himself hadn't known he'd return to the Strange more than a few hours ago?

A kray pincer clipped the dlamma. He and the dlamma tumbled, though neither uttered a shriek. Jason prepared to call for the mantle of War, but his mount pulled out of the fall, which perhaps not coincidentally put them at least a hundred meters from the closest kray. They flashed through a region of thin blue fractals stretching away like curling puppet strings. Beyond the kray outriders that'd ambushed them, a far larger kray mass boiled and surged like a flying ant hill above them. A nebula of darkness swirled at its core, and from that darkness, Jason sensed an all-consuming malevolence.

Even if Ardeyn wasn't really "real," the planetovore that commanded the kray in that advancing apocalypse was every bit as authentic and palpable as Jason himself. Not for the first time, he regretted he'd ever had dealings with the damned things. Those bargains had literally lessened him.

The dlamma took advantage of the clear space around it and looped back in a wide curve toward the interface with Ardeyn. A flight of kray tried to get in between them and the superficies. Jason batted them away with his staff using War's strength, spattering both himself and his mount with gore, and the dlamma zipped through the opening.

With a familiar psychic squeeze, they passed back into Ardeyn. Relief made him gasp. He half expected to see Megeddon on the horizon, but as the dlamma had promised, beyond the Borderlands was only a sere flatland of polished glass. The Glass Desert.

He glanced behind them, back the way they'd come.

The barest hints of the Strange were visible beyond the tumbling earth motes, but the boundary would keep out their pursuers. Kray always tried to find a way in, but the Seven Rules inevitably kept them fenced out.

"You have my thanks," Jason told the dlamma as it returned to its earlier, slower pace. Sweat slicked its back, and heat came off it like a furnace. Any lesser effort would've seen them fall into the kray's clutches.

They flew on into the desert along the route Jason pointed out, based on his intuitive sense of where Carter had called from.

Hours later, the ache in his stomach was back. "By the Maker," Jason muttered, rubbing. It was worse than ever. Was he going to be sick?

The sensation grew, until it burned in his belly like someone holding a torch to his skin.

He hissed at the uptick in agony and bent to visually check if he'd taken a wound he'd failed to notice. Lifting the stiff leather of his armor, he saw not the least blemish.

"How...?"

Then he realized the sensation wasn't actually coming from his stomach; it was referred pain. The actual injury was somewhere else. The burning escalated, like acid bubbling inside him, as if one of his organs had split open and spilled its contents into his veins and arteries. He felt something shatter, and nearly fell from the saddle. Darkness stabbed across Jason's vision like reverse lighting, and he cried out.

As did the dlamma. Its flight became erratic. It screamed, "What have you done, Betrayer? Why does the sky darken and crack in our wake? The interface between Ardeyn and the Strange is failing – and I feel the walls of the world shaking!"

"What walls?"

"The walls – the Seven Rules that keep out Strangers, you fool!" screamed the dlamma.

"Oh no," whispered Jason as a new agony spasmed through him. He understood.

All his deals with the kray over the years – all the pieces of himself he'd traded away for their aid. He hadn't only been trading on his own soul. How could he? He was also an Incarnation of the Maker, a manifestation of one of the Seven Rules.

Every promise he'd made, every lease on his independence he'd traded away for reality seeds, artifacts of the dark energy network he'd been too afraid to search out for himself within the Strange, and favors large and small, all had been trades on

Ardeyn's sovereignty, too.

When he'd finally seen the kray, naked and unfiltered in the Strange, they'd called all his promises due, in their massed mental voice. He thought they'd wanted him then and there.

But unlike what he'd told Merid, if the kray had eaten him out in the Strange, unconnected with the realm of his birth, the kray would've lost all the ground they'd gained by helping him and exacting their promises. If he'd been outside Ardeyn, the Land of the Curse would've remained barred to them upon his death.

Those fucking monsters had played him. After declaring their covenant due, they'd let him get away. He'd done as they'd secretly desired, his relief blinding him to what they really wanted. The kray wanted him to return to Ardeyn.

He'd been the final key in the lock.

Jason gazed back at the sky, from where they'd come. Bruised storm clouds swelled there, boiling in a way that reminded him of how the fundament of the Strange moved. Lightning dark as crow wings stabbed and played beneath, and where it struck the ground, geysers of disintegrated stone and glass from the desert sprayed up. Reality was becoming liminal, fragile.

"What can we do?" screamed the dlamma over a peal of basso thunder.

"We... *I* can stop this. I am *War*, damn it. I'm an Incarnation, by the Maker. I should be able to stop the kray's advance!"

Jason didn't really believe his own words, but he didn't have to convince *himself*. He had to convince the shadow of War that haunted his soul to emerge once more, and take charge.

Or...

A new thought crystallized. It wasn't quite a plan; it was more of a desperate ploy. He pointed.

"That way, dlamma! Carter waits. He'll help. He won't have a choice."

33: REUNION
Carter Strange

Pre-dawn light filtered in through tent fabric. For several delicious moments, I didn't know where I was – other than in a tent – or remember how I'd gotten there. I relished the feeling for all of four seconds.

"Carter, get out here!" The voice belonged to Queen Elandine and came from somewhere outside the tent. My waking daze crumbled, and I remembered everything.

Crap. It couldn't have been more than a few hours since I'd been offered a tent to get some rest.

I rose, slipped on my boots and outer robe, grabbed my magic sphere, and followed Siraja outside. The sun was still below the horizon, which meant it wasn't scorching hot. But the light was increasing fast.

The tent was set in the lee of a wall of glass shards that ran away west. The shards had apparently formed when one massive segment of the desert ground into another segment, throwing up a sharp rampart. The queen's protector, Navar had picked the spot last evening because of its "defensive posture." The soul sorcerers hadn't come boiling out of their crater to track me down yet, so we hadn't had to test whether the blade-sharp splinters truly offered a formidable barrier.

A storm was rolling up from the south, its reflection

in the glass doubling its already prodigious size. It was wrong somehow, but my attention was dragged to a closer disturbance. A detachment of the queen's guards clustered around something on the glass, blocking my view.

Shoving through the press, Siraja at my heels, I saw what had so ruffled the peacekeepers: two strangers.

One was a noble-winged dlamma, its humanlike face hidden in a ritual mask. I sensed the mask also served as its name, which translated to something like "Far Voyager."

The other stranger dismounted the dlamma as I approached. He was a large man wearing armor forged of black iron. His helm sported impressively proportioned backward-swept spikes. He wielded something that might have been a mace, a staff, or a spear, or all three at once, that flickered redly at one end.

"Jason," I said, knowing him despite his extravagant costume. Just as I'd known him on Earth when Jason, the psycho, had possessed Kate Manners' friend Raul. Jason Cole stood before me, but his name echoed with the sound of swords clashing and the smell of blood spilling. He was also War.

"Carter Strange!" yelled Jason, doffing his helm. Revealed was the face I recognized from our years together, when we'd been colleagues, if not friends. Dark lines etched his brown eyes, his hair was too long, and the barest hint of a sneer twitched on his lips. How I hated that face.

I raised Jushur defensively. Of its own volition, it took flight and hovered near my head. Around me, the queen's troops also brought up their crossbows, all fixed on Jason.

The surrounding guards stepped aside, admitting Elandine and Navar. The queen immediately drew her blade.

Siraja just looked at me, a question plain on her face. She wanted to know what my play was going to be. I wish I knew.

I opened my mouth to say something anyway, hoping the

mere act would pull something useful out.

The queen beat me to the punch. Spitting each word like a trebuchet bullet, she addressed Jason, "You have something of mine, War. Give it back. Even you can't defeat me and my army, not when the Maker stands with us." Her eyes flicked to me when she said "Maker." I was glad it was still too dark for anyone to see my checks flush.

"Your Majesty," said Jason, "believe me when I tell you how sorry I am that I lied—"

"You stole the Ring of Peace! After you promised to save my sister!" She took a step closer, but restrained herself from hewing Jason or commanding her troops to attack. I worried she wouldn't wait much longer, though.

Jason coughed, then responded, "Despite all that, I believe we can come to an accord." He licked his lips, smiled a sad smile. "As it happens, I need Carter's help with something. It's rather urgent. Have any of the other Rings come to you yet, Carter, since you made your call?" His eyes darted hopefully around the camp, as if he was looking for a stray Incarnation loitering behind the mess tent.

"So you can make off with those, too, you thief?" Elandine yelled, anger stretching her voice tight.

Surprising that Jason hadn't attacked us outright. A good sign? On the other hand, Elandine was moments from violence.

"What do you mean you need my help?" I said. "Last time we talked, back on Earth, weren't you gloating that you finally had your revenge? Didn't you laugh when you saw I'd been shot?"

Jason rubbed the bridge of his nose, sighing. "Look, it's all true. I admit everything. I'm an evil prick. But it doesn't matter."

"Doesn't matter?" I yelled, momentarily forgetting I'd been the one who was trying to calm the situation and figure out what War wanted before Elandine tried to cut his liver out.

"Nope," Jason said. "All that is bygones. Don't know if you've noticed, ol' buddy, but the Seven Rules of Ardeyn have been breached." Jason gestured at the wonky storm still piling higher on the southern horizon. "In about ten minutes, we're all going to be ass-deep in kray."

My eyes found the storm again. I focused on the black thunderheads that visibly swelled as each second passed. The wrongness I'd sensed before remained. In fact...

"Oh, no," I breathed when I saw what lay behind the clouds. The storm was an atmospheric reaction to an incursion. It was a kray invasion of Ardeyn, with every monster precipitating cloud formation by its unwelcome presence. Kray swirled in that storm, thousands strong. I could sense something like exultance mixed with unending hunger. But they were only the vanguard for the thing that followed after them, easing itself a little at a time through the crack in the bulwark of Ardeyn I'd thrown up three years earlier to protect Earth. I tried to name it, understand it, but failed so completely that the feedback of my defeat sparked a blinding headache. I grunted and grabbed my head, squeezing my eyes shut but unable to keep the memory of what I'd seen crawling behind my eyes.

"Are you all right, Carter?" I heard Siraja ask through a migraine-like aura.

Was I? The initial pain spike was already subsiding, replaced by a burning anger at what I suspected must have happened. Anger was easier to bear than uncertainty, than fear. Fury damps out other internal voices. It's a form of certainty. And it seemed certain that Jason had killed Earth.

"We can still fix this," he said. "We can–"

"You think I'm stupid enough to trust *you*?" I snapped, as my vision cleared. I focused only on him. "For all I know, you're the one who caused this. In fact, given how you were fucking around uploading quantum computer manufacturing instructions to idiots on Earth, I'm sure of it."

"No," he said, but he sounded like a liar to my special sense. I didn't believe him. On the other hand, why wasn't he arriving *with* these invaders as they poured into Ardeyn? Seemed exactly like the sick thrill ride War – and maybe even Jason – would get off on.

Then the truth, a black rose blooming, sprouted and it disgusted me. "I know what happened – you tried to *deal* with the kray, didn't you? They gave you something that gave you access to Earth. But then they double-crossed you, too. Betrayed the Betrayer."

Jason said, "I didn't–"

"You did, except you didn't know they'd take everything on offer, and then some. There're here to eat Ardeyn *and* you, isn't that right? To consume it all, and then rush up the renewed link you forged with Earth and take that, too."

"I didn't know," Jason said, almost pleading.

I shook my head in contempt. "You asshole. I made you an Incarnation. I gave you everything you could've dreamed of here in Ardeyn. And in return you–"

Jason interrupted, his voice suddenly loud and hot, and no longer defensive. "No. Screw that, Carter. You gave me nothing. You *trapped* me here in this fucking dream world. This nightmare that would never end, and told me how happy I should be. You caged me in a make-believe place filled with shadows of actual people and told me it was better than real life. You locked me, Sanders, Alice, and Melissa in here! Like we were animals in a zoo, explaining that it was OK because the cage looked *so* realistic. Well, we knew, you bastard. We knew. It's a fucking fake. *You're* the asshole, Carter. You betrayed all of us first."

The storm swelled. Even as true dawn gathered beneath the horizon, the portion of the Glass Desert beneath the kray armada remained dark. In their approaching shadow, I couldn't sustain my own anger at Jason. For the first time, I had an inkling of what had driven my old friend to such crazy lengths. If he didn't view Ardeyn and the advantages I'd given him and the others as real and meaningful, then of course it must have felt like a trap.

Arguments I could've used to convince Jason that this place was every bit as real as Earth, that he had it all wrong, on and on, gathered behind my lips. And stayed there. The kray were minutes away. Besides, Jason was two hundred years – from his perspective – down the road of convincing himself of his worldview, one where *I* had betrayed him. Rushed observations and arguments by me were not going to make him suddenly realize he was looking at everything wrong, that everyone he'd hurt or killed to get where he was had been real enough to feel that pain and death, and, oh gee, can't we all just be friends now?

He was still a killer, even if he didn't want to admit it to himself.

But killer or not, didn't he have at least something approaching a point? Had our positions been reversed, and Jason locked me in someplace I regarded as a facade of reality, who's to say I wouldn't have reacted the same?

So instead, I sighed and said, "Jason, I apologize. I disagree, and I think your tactics are shit. But I can see things from your shoes. Being trapped someplace you don't want to be sucks. You didn't deserve it, and didn't ask to spend two centuries here. I'm sorry."

"Damn straight!" he yelled. Then he blinked as if confused, apparently not quite sure where to go next. My capitulation had lanced some of his rancor and knocked him off-balance.

"So, explain more about what you said earlier," I said. "About needing my help? Do you have a plan to turn back the kray?"

Jason fumed a second longer, glanced at the storm, then reluctantly nodded. He'd come this far, I could almost sense him thinking, and he'd be damned if he was going to give up now.

"I do have a plan," he said. He seemed suddenly, if it was possible, afraid. As if he feared what the kray might do to him personally. Served the psycho right.

He pulled something that clinked from a pouch on his belt, displaying it on his palm. Two rings lay there, threaded on a leather thong, and a third gleamed from his index finger. Not rings; Rings. I gasped.

"Three Rings, Carter. We have three. Unless one of the other Incarnations...?"

I shook my head no.

He continued, "Had I known the kray were breaking through the interface, I'd have tried to extract a fourth Ring that's... residing in my fortress. Sadly, no time remains for us to retrieve it. I'm hoping we don't need it. With you – the sorry excuse of what remains of the Maker – there's a chance we can open up the Maker's Hall and fix everything. We've got three Rings plus whatever Maker you can manifest. We can re-seal the Borderlands. Eject the kray."

I concentrated on the Rings, and knew them instantly. Jason wore the Ring of War. On his palm was the Ring of Commerce and the Ring of Death.

Elandine had moved closer during Jason's recital of my crimes against him. Now she said in a voice devoid of all emotion, "Hand over my Ring."

I think she was as surprised as me when he untied the cord and passed her one of the heavy bands. The queen couldn't quite bring herself to thank Jason for returning what he'd taken from her, so she looked at me instead. "Is there any truth to what the Betrayer says? Are we all about to die?"

"If we can't stop the kray, yes. Everyone in Ardeyn."

"And you can use my Ring, and the two he has, to open the Hall?"

"Maybe."

"And doing so will save us?"

"Only if we're insanely lucky," I admitted.

The sad truth was I didn't know the answer to any of the queen's questions. If Jason was wrong, there was a good chance we were about to die out on the glass. I addressed the hovering sphere, "Jushur, can we open the Maker's Hall with only three Rings and myself?"

"You can try. I cannot predict the future. Not even the Maker could."

"We need a little more assurance than that," I complained.

"I have none to give," Jushur said.

"Well," I said, "unless someone else has a better plan, I say we try it. Better let me hold Commerce."

Jason handed it over. It was even heavier than I expected. None of the friends I'd accidentally trapped in Ardeyn had been interested in being the Incarnation of Commerce, yet that Incarnation had also walked the Land of the Curse, too. Commerce hadn't possessed the spark of consciousness allowing it to realize its true nature. It believed it was a demigod of Ardeyn and nothing else, unlike the Rings who I'd given human hosts. Or me, when I'd made myself Maker.

"Should I put it on," Elandine said, "or just hold it?"

I spent a second studying her and the Ring. From it I sensed a cold wind, a whiff of rotting flesh, and a sound like a stone sarcophagus lid slamming. "Jason's wearing the Ring of War. You might as well wear the Ring of Death. Doing so might strengthen your connection, and improve our chances to open the way."

Jason made as if to protest.

"What?" I asked.

He turned to Elandine. "With Carter's revival, a measure

of each Ring's potency has returned, as you know. Try not to let the office of Death overwhelm you. Her agenda might not be yours."

Elandine just glared at him, then slipped on the Ring.

"It's cold," she said.

Then she added, her voice deeper and more resonant. "But cold is Death's realm, and I am returned."

"Oh-kay," I said, glancing at Jason. He hadn't been kidding. "Try to keep it together Elandine. Join hands everyone." So saying, I slipped on the Ring of Commerce.

The queen and Jason didn't want to hold hands. I remained with my hands out until they – War and Death? – acquiesced. War was on my left. His hand gripped mine in an overly aggressive clench that actually hurt. On my right, Elandine. Her clasp was as light and cold as a dusting of snow over a tombstone.

I sensed the resting aura of Commerce, not conscious, but not quite absent, either, as a dizzying flurry of numbers carved on tablets, bales of silk, and the feel of hard coin. I sensed that I could inflate that aura around me, if only briefly, and glory in the truth of sums. But that wasn't my path, nor would it provide us the answer we sought.

For the Maker, there was no Ring that served as a badge of office, no Ring of Creation. Had it been so, this would've been so much easier. Of course, Jason would've have found and stolen something like that a long time ago.

The office of the Maker was conviction. It was an unshakeable trust of knowing yourself as the architect of Ardeyn, first in words, then in lines of code. And finally, in an act of wanton desperation when I'd impressed it on the dark energy network.

I squeezed my eyes shut. My teeth creaked as I ground them together. The hands I clasped in mine were solid evidence of my creation, as was the glass below my boots, and the very air I breathed. It may have been simulated by the dark energy network, but it was simulated as well as reality itself was simulated by atoms of normal matter.

For all that, conviction eluded me.

Certitude had always been hard for me – I was more of a doubter, especially of my own capabilities. Usually, I pulled off a little magic trick by flipping my usual uncertainty into a humorous shield, finding something to laugh about in almost any situation, especially if I could point out how I'd screwed something up. Jokes were my defense for my failure of confidence; they were faux-conviction. Ha, ha.

Except now that it'd come to it, nothing was funny about my inability to grasp the Maker's power. The version of me who'd done it must have lucked into it. I wasn't up to the task. If anything, the more I chased it, whatever *it* was, the further–

"Why do you try to kill the seed of the Maker within you?" intoned the queen, her voice echoing as if from a mausoleum. I opened my eyes and glanced at her. Elandine was there, but also stood there was Death. Instead of armor, Elandine wore shadow. She retained *Rendswandir* at her belt, but in her possession, I knew it for an implement whose merest touch would slay any living thing. I shuddered.

War added, his voice far more than Jason's, "If you cannot defeat your own doubts, you do not deserve to be the Maker. All we have left is to fight, and die, on this final field of battle." War's grip loosened as he prepared to disengage from our circle.

"Stop," I told War. In that moment, as I instructed the Incarnation, a trickle of what the Maker had been came to me. I seized it before it could slip away, and willed that my home of old show itself.

The sun burst over the horizon. The Maker's Hall was revealed as a reflection in the surface of the Glass Desert.

Plunging falls, colossal images of noble qephilim, and beyond that, an astounding series of mounting, shining ramparts that seemed to go up forever...

The image wavered in the very substance the rising ramparts had once been constructed of, before the final battle with Lotan's armies. The Maker's Hall, a stupefyingly immense glass castle, had been slagged and melted when Lotan burned hottest. Lotan had ultimately been defeated, but the glass castle slumped, becoming the Glass Desert.

Though how any of that could be literally true, I hadn't the first clue–

The Maker's assurance retreated like a wave after it breaks. I'd been touched by greatness, but only for a moment, but one lasting long enough to produce an image of the Maker's Hall.

"As I recall it from old," uttered War.

"A vision from the Age of Myth," agreed Death.

"It's just a reflection," I protested. "How do we get in?"

They both looked at me like I'd pointed out a turd in the punch bowl.

"Well?" I said. The reflection wavered at our feet. Access to what it represented was closed, and worse, not even really there. My naming sense reported that in its current state, access to the Hall lay beyond our ability.

Death's visage dispersed, leaving Elandine blinking into the glaring sun. "We're out of time." She released my hand.

Jason did the same, muttering, "Nice knowing you, Carter. Actually, no. It pretty much sucked."

The storm was a pale cloak being drawn across the empty plain toward us. It was maybe thirty seconds away. The queen shouted to Navar and her army. They raced to deploy into defensive positions behind the fence of glass shards where our camp lay. Flickers of Death's shadow followed in her wake.

Jason turned to face the oncoming storm, lifting his helm

to cover his head. He literally swelled in size, becoming more a creature than a man. It was his true guise as War, something that I vaguely remembered as if from a childhood dream. Around him, his army of lesser selves appeared in ones and twos, then fives and tens, and more.

Siraja had watched our failed attempt to enter the Hall. I sensed her disappointment in the lay of her ears. "This is insane," she said. "We will all die." But she drew her blade, and set herself to defend.

The dlamma called Far Voyager flew away, moving swiftly in the opposite direction as the oncoming storm, fleeing the field. I couldn't say I blamed it.

I faced our onrushing foe. The southern half of the Glass Desert was gone. It was hidden under a line of clawing mist, a thunderhead fallen from the sky. The rising sun's brilliance was dimmed to that of a hazy silver quarter, over which shapes flitted like bats across the moon. Except they weren't bats. They were kray.

Then the storm engulfed us.

My mouth went dry and my hands shook as the mist washed over me, overwhelming me. Sharp sounds were muffled as fog made it hard to see farther than a few dozen yards. In that murk, the kray swarmed like wasps. They were alien terrors bent on destroying us.

Before I knew it, I was on the ground, my head ringing from smacking into the glass. Had a kray knocked me over? No. My own feet had tripped me up when I panicked. The monsters wouldn't get me if I brained myself first.

My arms were locked over my head, so I forced them down. Pressing them onto the cracked glass beneath me, I pushed myself back to me feet. I forced myself to draw a few calming breaths.

Maybe all wasn't lost.

The invading kray were in Ardeyn. Though breached, my

world still imposed rules. Though infected, Ardeyn still–

A kray's shape resolved from the haze and darted at me. "You cocksucker!" I screamed as it knocked me over. Before this moment, the thing had been nameless. Now it had one, even though accidentally bestowed. But in Ardeyn, names have power, if you know what you're doing.

Rolling to avoid a pincer stab, panting and wheezing, I choked out a different name, one that conflated its new name to stone.

Gray and lifeless as a statue, it dropped on the glass and smashed into three parts.

"Yes!" I whispered, feeling almost jubilant. This wasn't beyond me, if I could keep my fear in check, and make a plan.

The haze thinned, allowing me to see much farther.

Sword blades and arrow tips flickered as Elandine's army hewed and peppered the onrushing force. Seeing that they hadn't merely been erased by the mist, as some panicked part of my brain had apparently decided, made me stand taller. A score more invaders died the final death at their hands even as I watched. Lone soldiers who'd broken from cover to keep kray from overrunning the queen's archers spun and hacked with sharp blades. Sometimes a carapace was pierced and the soldier moved onto another foe.

Elandine strode back and forth along the line of archers. Her shadow deepened once more even as I watched, until she was a pillar of darkness. Death walked Ardeyn again, and I could feel her chill from here. Her implement scythed out, and in ones and twos, kray who'd managed to get past the skirmish line of blade-wielders crumbled like ash at its touch.

As effective as Death was, War was more awesome. He was a multitude, fielding nearly as many warriors as the soldiers in Elandine's army. They fought with more abandon, more ferocity, and with less concern for their own safety. And each time one died, another stepped from War's flesh, fresh to the fight and a master in the arts of blade and battle. War himself was a bulwark. He lay about him with his flaming implement, smearing kray into so much burning offal with each blow. Watching him, despite everything, filled me with elation.

By chance or design, Siraja and I stood in the pocket created by War and Death. When I saw a stray kray slip through our defense, I named it stone. I was amazed anew each time one smashed onto the glass, leaving a small crater of crazed cracks.

Siraja muttered, "I can't believe we're still alive."

"Stay with me," I said, "and we'll get through this." She spared me a doubtful sidelong glance.

"It's only luck we haven't already died," Siraja said.

"Listen, did you see what I did back there? What the queen and War are doing? We've—"

"Look what comes for us now!" She pointed.

I looked. Dread edged my earlier confidence.

Resolving from the fog, a mass of scrambling kray charged across the glass, each twice as large as a man. The flitting, flying ones we'd been downing with so much success were annoying insects compared to the galloping, horse-sized crab-spiders coming for us. Even larger ones, rumbling like tanks, were visible as dim shadows through the mist behind them. More uncertain yet, though too large to dismiss, the hint of something vast heaved closer, cutting through the mist like a supertanker cleaves ocean swells. A kaiju-sized monstrosity whose complete dimensions were cloaked in gray mist. An infrasonic *boom-boom, boom-boom, boom-boom* vibrated up through the glass, matching the many-legged strides of the half-sensed thing. Each clap hammered at my courage. It was the central entity I'd failed to identify when I'd first tried to name the storm. My elation tumbled back toward fear. This was nothing less than our end.

War's forces wavered and shrank, even as the Incarnation's height diminished to more human proportions. A voice that was purely Jason's yelled, "It's the fucking matriarch. She's coming for me! I gotta get out of here."

Oh, fuck. I had no time to wonder what he meant by "she." Jason's fear was toxic to his ability to manifest War. Without War, we stood no chance. Well, we stood even less of a chance than the zero chance we currently faced. I had no illusions; our odds were grim. But, fuck it. Jason was going to have to face up to his crime, and fight on, like the rest of us, to the end.

Then again... What if the kray were *literally* here for Jason? At least, as step one of their plan. If he died so far in their debt, one of the Seven Rules would more than simply teeter and bend as had already happened; it would dissolve. That would release Lotan at the core!

But before the Cursed One could do more than blink, the kray would crack Ardeyn like a virus bursting an infected cell. Rather than spewing kray back out into the Strange, they'd instead infect the connection between Earth and Ardeyn, pulling their planetovore matriarch behind them.

"War," I named Jason. "You are an Incarnation of Ardeyn. You are one of the Seven. Fight! I command you, in the Maker's name." Warmth bloomed in my chest as I spoke. I *knew* that I had again successfully triggered my ability. I just didn't know how.

Jason receded, and War come once again to the fore. Perhaps more so than at any previous time. The armored man swelled to his former towering height and then some. His army of multiples expanded outward from him like a ripple spreading outward from a stone dropped in water. A rush of kray who'd moved to take advantage of the weakness Jason's doubt had created along the left flank was quickly overrun. War was back, and I knew he would fight until he could do so no longer.

From the right, where Elandine's army was deployed,

Death in her shadowed caul gave me a nod of congratulations. Almost like she might've given the real Maker.

"Impressive," said Siraja. "Now open the doors to the Maker's Hall. Because even an eleven-foot tall demigod and the incarnation of Death can't stand long against that." She pointed out into the mist at the monstrosity.

She was right. I resolved to try again, using the time War's return had brought us.

A kray dropped from directly overhead, slamming into me and Siraja. The impact smashed me to the glass. Siraja spun away staggering, but stayed on her feet. The kray ignored her, and lowered one massive claw to snip off my head. I tried to name it, but the stars behind my eyes and the lack of air in my lungs meant I was only able to gasp. The pirate stepped forward and plunged her sword into the kray's side. Goo sprayed and the monster squealed. Then its many legs buckled and I army-crawled from beneath it before it toppled to the glass.

The qephilim pulled me up just in time to face four more who'd somehow got around War, Death, and their respective armies. Our foes numbers had increased so much that even with kray dead piling up like snow, there were still too many.

Strands of webbing arced high through the air. Where strands fell among the soldiers, screams rang out. The webbing was like acid, in that it burned away the substance of Ardeyn. I growled a wordless curse, then named all the webbing I could see. It dispersed into a rain of white flowers that normally only grew along the mountain tops. The kray responded by launching another volley.

The fight descended into a free-for-all. There wasn't time to try to open a way into the Hall again. If I didn't concentrate everything on staying alive, we would be dead in seconds. My nails bit into my palms as I clenched my hands into fists. Panic and fear would only get me killed now. I screamed as I lost myself in the frenzied, hazed battle to save the world.

34: DISSOLUTION
Elandine, Queen of Hazurrium

The kray had no souls. At least, they didn't before they entered Ardeyn. One of the ground rules for Land of the Curse demanded that any intelligent creature who perished there must leave behind a record of its mind and goals, its accomplishments and failures; its soul.

Thus did Death reap the kray, pulling their newly minted souls from their bodies like pits from an olive. If they'd been natives, she'd have sent them to be judged by her faithful kindred in the Court of Sleep. To her was given the power to expunge from any creature its spark. The kray who'd come into Ardeyn had life. Which Death gladly wiped away, as she relinquished their confused, fledgling souls to nothingness.

Even so, the part of Death that remembered it was Elandine marveled at herself. Never before had *Rendswandir* moved with such lethal fluidity. Flick, flick, stab, snap; four dead kray. Slash, touch, spin; five more dead kray. Everything was a blur, hypnotizing Elandine and fueling Death's vigor. Rarely had the Incarnation unleashed her power in such a tide, not since the great battles during the Age of Myth, when humans had fought on the side of Lotan. Then, she'd mowed the humans down with an implement even grander than this one. A scythe of magic and will that she wished was with her now. She'd been sleeping too long, though, to remember where she'd laid it down. *Rendswandir* would have to do.

Behind her, the Peacemakers delivered death to the foe, too, though not as efficiently as she. Death aided them, in as much as by killing the kray, those particular kray didn't attack the humans. But beyond that, she found it difficult to intervene when a kray snipped off a screaming human's arm, leg, or head with massive pincers, or zipped a convulsing qephilim into a cocoon of reality-wiping webs. When it comes to dying, Death had no favorites. She reaped the souls of her dying allies without sadness or rancor. It was their time, and they would find their fate handed out by the dictates of an Umber Judge.

Death frowned as she slew, and her aura of dissolution flickered. Elandine's consciousness pointed out that if they were not victors here today, the Court of Sleep would also be wiped away, if Ardeyn was destroyed. Lotan would be loosed–

A horse-sized kray lunged forward, trying to disembowel her with a slashing pincer across her stomach. Death skipped back so the tip only grazed her, then charged back when it wheeled past. But the thing was quick; quicker than she expected. It almost got the pincer back in front of itself as a defense before she stepped in and cut off the entire limb with a stroke of *Rendswandir.*

The small kray scurriers were easy to kill, but the larger versions that had finally reached them required more effort. This one had five more snapping chitinous claws, each as large as a wagon.

The First Protector – splattered in kray ichor and strands of kray webbing – sidled up to the queen. "Your Majesty, are you all right?" Navar said. "Shadow took you, and I–"

"Navar," Elandine said, breaking from the spell of the Incarnation for a moment. "Help that squadron! Believe me, I no longer need a protector. Not when Death walks with me."

Navar's ears flattened, but the First Protector nodded, and

348   MYTH OF THE MAKER

did as she was bid. Navar was ever the faithful servant.

A new wave of kray rushed their line. She saw War step forward to blunt their advance. He did so by flooding the enemy nearest to him with his duplicates, each of which hacked and hewed until the kray went down. Elandine realized that, as Death, she could do something... similar. She just had to let go completely. So far, she'd refused the Incarnation *complete* control. Elandine was a queen, and the last time she'd given up her power to someone else, she'd regretted it. It might have cost her the kingdom of Hazurrium.

Of course, Hazurrium was lost anyway, scheming regent or no scheming regent, if they couldn't pull victory from what was apparently a disaster. She wasn't a pessimist, but she didn't like their chances. If there was ever a time to sacrifice everything to achieve a goal, this was it.

She hoped that when it was all over, perhaps Death would repay the favor and allow Elandine to retrieve her sister...

But, no. Hope wasn't what Death required to reap. Hope was Death's antithesis. The end of all things brought all things low without fail, smashing through emotion. Hoping to avoid death was like promising to throw the moon. Empty words. And yet mortals hoped, and in doing so, somehow against all logic, kept Death at bay for months or even years longer before she finally, inevitably, arrived.

Wishing didn't make things so. The only certainty was dying. Elandine thought of her sister Flora, and her fierce hope to rescue her from death. It was a vain hope, a foolish hope, and moreover, a barrier that prevented Elandine from giving up her autonomy to Death. All things died, even her sister. And her hope that anything could ever be different.

The queen released control to Death, without reservation. Then the queen was no more, not even a voice.

The Incarnation of Death fully manifested for the first time since before the Betrayal, since before she'd melded with the mind of a living human named Melissa. The Incarnation had never really forgiven the Maker for forcing her, a manifestation of one of the Seven Rules, to make way for another. She assumed War had felt that sting even worse, which led to Betrayal. Not that it mattered now. Death was returned. And she vowed never to leave again.

Though... Elandine's idea regarding bolstering her strength remained. Death concurred. With a wave of her implement, she pulled the souls of all the dead humans who'd perished in the defense – a sum of some fifty spirits so far, and growing with each minute that passed. It irked Death that when War's soldiers died they left behind no soul for her to claim. Their essence flowed back into him. The kray souls, too, proved resistant to command. She didn't doubt with study and concentration she could bend those alien consciousnesses to her will. But time waited for no one, not even Death.

She would have to confine herself to human and qephilim spirits. It would suffice.

Death assembled five small squadrons of the dead, misty white and ethereal, but so freshly deceased they didn't realize they no longer walked as living creatures. Their memories of weapons and armor were reflected in their appearance, and their abilities. They existed to do her will.

Another large kray broke through the line of Peacemaker defenders, sending humans and qephilim flying. Reflexively, she sent one of her freshly formed deathless squadrons to take it down. The ghosts swarmed over the Stranger like ants.

She grinned as the large kray shriveled under their life-draining blows. Her only regret was that it would take more time than remained to Ardeyn to slay every invading kray. Actually, the term "regret" was strong for what she felt. She was a philosophical Incarnation, and knew when the inevitable was upon her.

Even Death must finally die.

35: ACCLAMATION
Jason Cole

The enemy charged across the glass with no regard for their lives. They raced into the embrace of blades, hammers, swords, and arrows of War, in his multitude. His army was equally fearless. When kray and his army clashed, neither flinched, even as blood and ichor sprayed, heads and limbs were relinquished, and bodies were ground beneath booted and pincered feet.

The ability to overcome fear was a crucial quality in a soldier. His warriors, those he generated now as easily as speaking words, had no sense of self-preservation. Each one fought like a demon. Which was why the army he fielded today was so far superior to the sad homunculi his host had been reduced to using over the previous two centuries. The homunculi shared all the frailties and misgivings of the mortal from which they'd been copied: Jason Cole.

War was disgusted at what he'd been forced to endure. Subsumed by a being of flesh, a weak-minded, grasping, bumbling fool – it was humiliating to remember. Why War had not risen up sooner and submerged Jason, he couldn't imagine. Something to do with the will of the Maker, perhaps. He sneered, even as he smashed flat a kray that'd tried to bite off his ankle.

The only brave thing Jason Cole had ever done was to slay the faux Maker, and force the alien pretender from the Land of the Curse. Of course, War had a hand in moving Jason to that decision. Without War's subtle manipulation, they might all still be leashed to the pretender. Sometimes rule by the Sword was the only option.

The epic conflict kept his irritation at bay. Despite the magnificent glory of it all, it irked War that, through Jason's folly, he found himself allied with Death and, worse, the returned pretender! The only saving grace was that the pretender was far less capable than the first time he'd appeared in Ardeyn. He possessed a flickering spark, War sensed, of the Maker's flame, but nothing else. The greater part of him was missing.

Locked away, no doubt, in the Maker's Hall–

A chariot-sized kray rushed War, its open mouth screaming some high pitched roar. War snatched one outstretched pincer, spun the massive creature about, and flipped it thirty feet through the air. Its descent was broken by one of the bladelike glass splinters along the line Death defended.

The Maker's Hall, War continued his thought, where Jason had so badly wanted to go. Where they still needed to go, if the kray invasion was to be pushed back. If they found entry, War and everyone else in Ardeyn would be saved. And the pretender would again become the Maker.

War called up Jason's spark of consciousness so he could interrogate it about Carter Strange, but Jason wasn't having it. The mortal, who'd sought so long to strip himself of fear by losing himself in War, had finally succeeded. The act of resignation was perilously close to suicide, which sickened the Incarnation. He let Jason fall back into darkness.

He spared a glance over his shoulder. Carter Strange and his qephilim stooge were still there, but instead of continuing their efforts to enter the Hall, they'd been forced to fight for their lives against the thickening press of kray that had slipped past him and Death. Perhaps he hadn't been as diligent as he could've been in keeping the kray away from the pretender.

War laughed when he saw an even larger concentration of kray racing forward across the glass. These weren't horse-sized or chariot-sized; they were large as houses. He sensed each would offer him a challenge worthy of any he'd survived during the Age of Myth.

"Fight! *Fight!*" he roared to his warriors, expelling a dozen or more each second, for all the good it seemed to do. Half died, impaled on pincers or wrapped in dissolving webbing, within moments of their birth.

Yet it was glorious. They died in the heat of strife, blood raging and exultant. For indeed, today was as good a day as any to die. Sometimes, wars are lost.

36: FERVOR
Katherine Manners

Following her tumultuous departure from Megeddon, the tiny vessel leveled out as it arrowed west. Kate stopped cursing after her heart rate resumed normal speed. Not long after that, she fell asleep, exhaustion pulling her down into gauzy nothingness.

She must have slept most of the night through because it was dark outside the next time she opened her eyes. Red streaks of approaching dawn glowed through the portholes, which reminded her of submersible viewports. Not that she'd ever been in a submersible.

She bent closer. The glass was cold on her cheek. Below, the ground raced past in a smear of darkness streaked with gray blurs. Above the horizon, the sky grew lighter.

The interior of the craft was too small to stand, but Kate could sit up without grazing her head on the metallic ceiling. She rubbed her neck, and the sleep out of her eyes.

"Hello?" she said. "Raul?" Worry struck her that she'd never see him again. Maybe without her awake, his spirit had slipped away for good. What if–

Raul's hazy shape materialized next to her. If he hadn't been immaterial, he wouldn't have fit. His body glimmered like an old night light, enough to light up the interior of their vessel.

"Good morning, sleepy," he greeted her.

She was intensely glad to see him. She decided not to share her momentary worry. "Hi, yourself."

"You know, this thing is damn cool," said Raul, gesturing around him.

Kate was confused at Raul's apparent surprise. "You should know – it was yours." She stopped short before reminding the man she'd taken the cypher from his corpse.

"Cyphers are plentiful," Raul said, "if you know where to look. But the method for finding exactly the kind you want has eluded even Ruk scientists. And they've been looking into it for a while. I didn't know for certain how this would manifest."

She snorted. "Well, it seems to be the right one for the occasion."

"I kept it back in case I ever needed to make a quick getaway. You're lucky I like to be prepared."

Kate doubted he'd been prepared for death... Damn it, stop that, she silently remonstrated. Too late. She wiped a bit of moisture from her eyes.

Raul inquired, "Are you all right?"

"I've been thinking," said Kate.

"Never a good sign," Raul replied.

That particular exchange was one of their comfortable traditions. She smiled to hear Raul's usual rejoinder. He was the same old Raul. She said, "If this Maker's Hall is everything myth says, we should try to get in, too."

"After we stop War," said Raul.

"Yes, after we stop War," agreed Kate. "But right after that, we go in, hopefully on Carter's arm. Get him to show us the controls for 'magic resurrection' or whatever it's called here, and put your spirit through the process. We can get you back."

Raul's eyebrows rose in surprise and he stroked his nonexistent chin. "Sounds great," he agreed. "But it's not the primary goal."

"But it's *a* goal," she insisted.

"Promise," he added, "that Jason comes first. Don't be a hero on my account."

She grimaced. The idea of saving Raul had already pushed aside her concern over Jason-fucking-Cole.

"Why not do both?" she said.

"If you save me but lose the world in the bargain, I'll only live as long as you and everyone else. Which will likely be only until the Betrayer – or Jason, or whatever that *puta madre* ends up calling himself – gets what he wants. He intends to bring the power of the Maker to Earth. That won't work out well, probably not even for him, ultimately."

Raul had a point. The man could be single-minded, and sometimes wrong, but usually his advice was sound. This was one of those times she couldn't fault his logic. "All right, I promise," she said. She meant it, even though it felt a little like giving up on her friend.

Raul's specter grinned.

Rather than meet his eye, she leaned to peer out the front viewport. They'd reached a height over Ardeyn that, although probably not as high as jets on Earth flew, was still several miles over the plain.

"Would you look at that storm?" she said. Thunderheads piled together, one towering tier crowding the next, glittering with flashes passing between them. They marched in from what seemed like the edge of the world. The storm hadn't yet covered the Glass Desert, over which she realized they must have been flying since before she woke. But the cloud system's rapid pace suggested it would manage that feat within a few hours, and after that, go on to cover a much bigger swath of the landscape. For some reason, the idea made her uneasy.

The craft's nose dipped precipitously. They began to

descend. Kate mentally traced an imaginary line of their course through the viewport. They were too high for her to make out much, but the area they aimed for seemed to be just in advance of the storm's leading edge. Was that where Carter was? Had to be, unless their flying cypher was malfunctioning.

"We're coming down," Kate said. "We're heading right into the teeth of that storm, so..." So, that meant nothing to someone who had no physical form.

Raul sat with her, his face also taking in the raging clouds. His head cocked. He said, "Katherine. That storm isn't natural It is of the Strange! Where it touches, Ardeyn is being eroded. Perhaps consumed!"

What the hell was Raul talking about? Kate narrowed her eyes in concentration. The sun rose in the east, directly ahead of them. She shaded her eyes with one hand. The light streamed over the lip of the world, sending illuminating shafts into the flanks of the storm. The storm didn't care, but then Kate saw what Raul was talking about. The clouds of water vapor concealed something awful.

Kray, whispered the part of her that had taken in Ardeyn's context. Or maybe it was Desire. Either way, if kray in this incalculable number were streaming across Ardeyn, it suggested one reasonable and apocalyptic interpretation: the world was ending.

She caught the hint of a kray taller than a skyscraper lumbering through the clouds after all the others. "Oh, no." It was horrible. But it was wondrous, too. Like nothing she'd ever imagined before.

"This can't be happening," Raul whispered. "Those things are going to eat Ardeyn to the ground. If they do, they could find a way to Earth. The big one is something that shouldn't exist, even here."

Use me, a fervent voice demanded. This time, there was

no uncertainty regarding its source. Desire still encircled her finger. The Incarnation wanted free rein once more.

Last time she'd let Desire call the shots, Kate barely got her mind back. Letting Desire loose again was something she'd unconsciously decided to avoid. The last time Desire had possessed her, the personality in the Ring seemed reluctant to let go. It *desired* Kate. Next time, it might not ever let her go.

But... the vision through the window was essentially a rendition of Hell. If Raul was right, a Hell that wouldn't be satisfied with Ardeyn, especially not now that Ardeyn was freshly connected to Earth. Could she sacrifice her mind, her will, her *life* to help save everyone else? There was no guarantee that Desire's aid would do anything to stop the disaster she saw unfolding below her.

She dragged her attention away from the Godzilla-plus-sized monster. From the vantage of their approach angle, they'd plunged into the storm. They were close enough that a desperate fight on the glass's surface resolved. A small army of human-sized figures faced off against a far vaster army of spider-lobster-monsters that came with the storm. Among the defenders, she sensed War, Death, and Commerce, her Ring's siblings. Of the Maker, however, she wasn't sure. But there was something...

They all fought upon the image of a magnificent fortress reflected in the glass, which shone all the brighter in the glass for the storm's gathering gloom. Its breathtaking grandeur put the walls of Megeddon to shame. Even though she knew it was only a likeness, the image was like a promise of the Maker's Hall returned. It wasn't manifest yet... But it would be, if she arrived in time.

Damn it. She was going to do it, wasn't she? Trust in the consciousness that inhabited the band on her finger. A personality that valued things only as much as it wanted them. And it wanted everything. Maybe even to save the world.

Before she could give herself an out, she acted.

Save Ardeyn; help the Maker! Kate instructed her Ring.

Nothing happened.

Something restrained the Incarnation bottled in the Ring. Part of her wasn't even really surprised. That part of her that always feared to believe in the impossible, in case she was disappointed. To play it safe. To be cynical.

"Kate?" wondered Raul.

She looked at him. Her cynicism was what had kept them as friends, and nothing more, for years. The fear of disappointment had done that.

And now it was keeping Desire from manifesting.

Naming the thing meant she could master it, or try to. So she told herself that it was OK to believe, OK to want the impossible. It's worth taking risks with your heart.

Then Desire was smiling. It was an expression so dazzling that the tiny craft confining her dissolved in its radiance. The consciousness of Katherine Manners and her otherworldly haunt faded away in the same blast.

Desire knew the exultant shriek of wind in her hair as she plunged, spread-eagle, toward the Hall's entrance. She was a falling star, serving as a new sun in her brilliance. All beneath her paused to glance at her speeding descent. In their hearts, desire kindled, and her power redoubled.

Even the kray, in their alien way, wanted her. Probably for food, but hunger was also aspiration, and it strengthened her. The sensation of being wanted was as intoxicating as it had ever been. She would never give it up again, Desire decided. In fact, in the warmth of that appropriation and her fast-dwindling view from on high, she decided that *she* would take charge of Ardeyn. The Maker had had his time. His time was done.

Four Incarnations were required to form the key to the Hall's lock. Three waited below, as did the one who had once been the Maker. Desire made Four.

She plunged down like a fiery fist, punching the Glass Desert with the energy of a meteorite strike. Every erg of that power was channeled into the creation of a keyhole. The key created by the presence of the Four turned.

The Maker's Hall opened for the first time since the Age of Myth concluded.

37: EXALTATION
The Maker

A plunging star burned a descending arc across the sky, aimed right for me.

Desire had arrived. The moment Desire's aura snapped into existence as a blazing streak overhead, the grim brooding of Death, the brash challenge of War, and even the incoherent mumbling of Commerce were easy to put out of my mind. I could no more ignore Desire than I could shrug off my finger in an outlet. Only the hint of the Maker's cognizance that I retained saved me. Otherwise I'd have dropped everything in favor of standing rapt like the humans, the qephilim, War, Death, and even, if just for a moment, the kray around us.

Of all the Rings that might have answered my call, I hadn't expected Desire. I'd left it behind on Earth. But somehow, it had followed me here. And it was embodied. Only an Earth native could wear a Ring of Incarnation and claim its power. I couldn't imagine who it might be, unless it was that woman Katherine Manners? Had she somehow managed to bridge the divide, and bring the Ring with her? But I sensed no hint of the underlying personality, whether it was Kate or someone else entirely. Only Desire burned, dropping like a bomb.

I pushed Siraja away from ground zero with a violent

shove. The qephilim went skidding at least a dozen feet on the glass, leaving me directly beneath my prodigal Incarnation. I expected to be obliterated in the blast when she hit.

In a way, I suppose I was.

Maybe she hit. Maybe she didn't actually physically touch the hard surface at all. It was irrelevant. Her gathering power, as well as her presence linked with the other three Incarnations, ignited an inferno of incandescent energy. The radiance bloomed like a nuclear sunrise. When that light refracted through the glass, it was bent as if through a prism. Color raced out across the Glass Desert. At the intersection, a door opened. The valves parted, swinging inevitably and unstoppably outward. An even brighter illumination shone out from the interior.

I passed within.

It was like a hand clapping in mine in friendship, laughter from afar, the odor of a pig roasting on spits, lights in the distance and singing, and more – a million sensations and emotions poured through me. It was both too much, and not enough. Too much, because my brain threatened to burst with the unending torrent of knowledge. Not enough, because I knew there was an organizing principle within the Hall that would make sense of it all. I *knew* it. I just had to find it before my brain fried...

And just like that, I had the answer.

I opened myself, and looked out across all Ardeyn, as if viewing it from an infinite height and depth simultaneously. I was in the Maker's Hall. All things were mine to know. It was merely the way things were.

Where I turned my gaze, I saw a bee sipping nectar from one of thousands of daisies growing in a meadow, an eel angling through the waters of Oceanus hungry for its next meal, a magnificently feathered dragon coming in for a landing on a roost set aside in the Citadel of the Harrowing, and a thousand other events both consequential and not.

If I focused on one thing, my view and knowledge of it expanded like a flower blooming with ever deeper fractal petal layers, revealing more and more about what I examined until no secrets remained. Secrets so fundamental that words could not bound or describe them. But a meta-language existed. Using it, the Maker had named things beyond naming.

The battle raging around me decelerated, as time itself seemed to grind to a halt, for all except me. Knowledge of things great and small lapped across my consciousness like an infinite ocean of cognizance. With a start, I realized that, once again, I was the Maker.

When I described darkness, midnight reigned. When I described a mockingbird, the sweetest birdsong that ever was warbled forth. When I described my mind whole and without distortion, so it was.

So I remembered all of it. Even those things I'd hidden from myself in shame.

What I had done before, and what I had allowed to be done. To save Earth in that first flush of Ardeyn's creation, I sealed myself and my friends away beyond time and existence in the real world. To keep Earth safe. There had been no choice. They understood that, didn't they? Was it too much to ask? I simply made their choice for them, a choice all of them would've made, if they'd been given a chance.

Jason complained the most bitterly and vociferously. No one else said a word. Everyone else said they understood. That I'd done the right thing. Who could argue with the logic that the good of many outweigh the good of the few? It was the only choice, they said. But I knew, behind their words, they felt betrayed, to one extent or another, too.

Because I hadn't consulted. I hadn't given anyone any options. Jason called me a selfish bastard and worse, to my face and behind my back. Later, selfish is what he called me when, in his guise as War, he shoved his flaming weapon through my heart.

My guilty heart. Because Jason had been right.

I *was* a selfish bastard. Here, in this place where all things were known, I couldn't evade the truth, or the memory that fell on me like a dead tree, pinning me with regret.

I was a liar. When I'd first taken on the mantle of the Maker, I *could have* returned all my friends back home, translated them into fresh new bodies. Sure, there would have been questions back on Earth regarding the corpses that resembled them found in the computer lab, but they could've at least had a chance to live normal lives.

But to do what I needed to do, to cauterize Ardeyn's intrusion into the Strange, *I* would've had to stay behind. Alone. And I hadn't wanted to be alone, had I?

No. Misery loves company. I'd imprisoned my friends along with myself when I'd cut off the Land of the Curse from its initial connection with Earth. I'd trapped them with me, when I could've let them go free.

Because I'm a fucking coward.

The Maker's Hall provided a godlike perspective to truly see myself as they had seen me. What I saw wasn't pleasant.

Because even though I numbered among the most powerful beings in Ardeyn, save for the kray broodmother that thudded forward, and Lotan who burned under the rocky crust, I had imagined myself a purely moral and unselfish being. The truth was that I had been afraid. In my fear, I'd let logic justify my actions rather than human feeling or true compassion for my friends. I'd thought to conquer my fear through endless plans and contingencies. How much evil would've been avoided if I'd thought of my friends first and acted out of human feeling? Though more by inaction and direct decision, I'd kidnapped my friends and kept them here with me. Jason's betrayal sprang directly from what I'd done.

And what about my other friends I'd trapped here? Had they hated me as fiercely as Jason? Alice, Sanders, and Mel – I couldn't ask them because they were long dead...

Actually, something was odd. For all my transcendence, I couldn't find any histories embedded in the world for Alice and Sanders. Jason and Kate, on the other hand, were close, as was Mel's great-to-the-nth granddaughter, Elandine. Well, War, Desire, and Death were nearby, anyway. The human consciousnesses of the hosts were suppressed, though Elandine seemed to be fighting submergence with a modicum of success.

Wait–

Alarm blazed like an exploding star as I realized War and Desire had rushed into the Hall after me.

Were they... No, they were contained, though it'd had been a close call. If they'd gotten in ahead of me, one of them would've been raised in my place, and taken the Maker's cognizance for themself. The danger of that happening had come and gone. Now they chased down endless corridors of colored light, refracting through an endless maze of prisms. They were caught, until I released them.

The time slow-down was mere illusion, an artifact of my own vastly increased cognizance. In fact, time was slipping by and the planetovore known as the kray broodmother advanced. I had to act soon. Once more, I had to decide.

I focused on the entity that walked in the eye of the storm. She was the same monstrous planetovore that had gazed across the starting grid during our very first trial of the enhanced VR gear. She hadn't forgotten. She'd bided her time, waiting out the years and centuries, sending her kray through the cracks and imperfections of Ardeyn's walls, despite how I'd tried to slow the time so precipitously that no contact could occur.

No plan survives contact with the enemy. And with the Maker's death – *my* death at Jason's hand – the broodmother found more and more weaknesses in Ardeyn's defenses. Exploits mostly in the form of a desperate and reckless Jason Cole, though there'd been others.

I traced every crack, every seam, and every intrusion, from the moment Ardeyn was first dumped into the dark energy network, to now. I held the visualized construct in my mind as a single hyperdimensional object. From that perspective, the entire Land of the Curse was like a fine crystal vase shot through with fractures. One more solid knock, and it would shatter. And the broodmother was a giant fucking hammer.

Repairing the damage would not be easy, given the timeline. If I couldn't eject the broodmother and her armada within the next few minutes, I never would.

Within the manifold space of the Maker's Hall, I had many hands and many mouths to manipulate and name the elements of Ardeyn. Healing the breach in my world would require all that and more. I needed help from the Incarnations. Unfortunately, only Three were manifest. With all Seven, it would have been a tough task, but doable. With only War, Death, and Desire, it would be a gamble.

And sacrifices would have to be made.

"Some Maker you are," muttered one of my mouths. "Not even willing to admit that you're getting ready to do it again. Sacrifice others to save yourself. Making a *logical* plan because you're afraid to do the human thing."

I paused. Was it true?

Yes, there was a chance that by tapping the full efforts of War, Death, and Desire, the underlying human minds and bodies would perish. Jason's mind might be burned out of War, leaving the original entity behind. Or maybe not even that much would remain. Maybe only the Ring would be left behind. I wouldn't feel *that* bad if that happened because Jason, despite that he'd arguably been driven to it, still needed to be put down.

"Katherine Manners and Queen Elandine face the same risks," another me reminded myself. "You'd feel bad about killing them, right? Though if you do nothing, it'll be out of your hands. They're already starting to fade away with the Incarnations riding them so hard. They're giving it their all. And the longer you sit in here dicking around, rationalizing the easy path, the more likely it is they'll never come back. So really, Carter, what do you want?"

"I want to save Ardyen, and Earth with it! Sacrificing a few people to save everyone else shouldn't even be a choice."

It was an agonizing decision. But, yes. Sacrifices had to be made. The good of the many outweighed–

"Don't give me that bullshit, you self-centered fuck! Jason was right! *You* can fix this by yourself. You're just afraid."

Of course I was afraid; it would kill me if I tried it. I'd die. I–

Oh.

The admission shocked me. I hadn't even considered the one other option on the table.

"Because you're a fucking coward." Fear was the antithesis of War, or at least I'd always assumed. But fear was also the antithesis of humanity, of doing the right thing, for me. In a way, I'd been seeing what I hated most in myself when I saw Jason. Jason was kind of like my dark reflection – he was just as afraid as me. We were not so different.

Shame burned through me, all the many instances that multiplied throughout the Hall. Yet *again* I'd considered sacrificing my friends in order to assure success. A tactical impulse designed to hide from myself what I was actually doing.

"Not this time," I promised myself. As I decided to save my friends, even Jason, uncertainty tingled through every micron of my being. Was I brave enough to throw myself in front of the bus to save Jason, Elandine, and Kate? Doubt was a stone in my heart. Trepidation dragged like an anchor.

I feared what I would decide. Even though I was the Maker, I was also Carter. Self-sacrifice wasn't really my thing.

But damn it. For once in my life, I wanted to do the right thing. That wasn't too much to ask of myself. And the fact was, technically I *could* leave everyone else out of the process. Instead, I could meld myself – my *will* – and my existence into the cracks. That would work.

And it would certainly be my end.

The Maker would once more be absent his creation. Without him, the Rings would recede to their earlier, minimum functions. War would go back to being merely the Betrayer. Elandine would have the Ring of "Peace" not of Death. And Desire wouldn't swallow up Katherine Manners whole.

But I was the Maker. In naming my weaknesses and failings, I laid them bare. Seeing them exposed for the mean and pathetic things they were, I cast out doubt and fear.

Warmth like sunlight stroked my face. Light filled my eyes, so that I had to blink back tears. I could do this.

How many people ever get the opportunity to correct their biggest mistakes? If the Maker – if *I* – force someone into a role they don't want and thus stifle their free will, who's to blame if they act out? Me, that's who.

I stretched out my many hands to touch each and every crack and tear in Ardeyn's fabric. I cried out with all my mouths with words that seared like a welder's flame. I did what had to be done. Without doubt or fear.

As before, all things were mine to know, as I turned my multi-faceted gaze across, under, and through Ardeyn. A child lost in the meadows above Ardeyn was shown the way home. The broken leg of an explorer lying alone in a qephilim ruin was mended, a warrior on the Glass Desert succumbing to a kray wound was healed. Minor miracles spread across the Land of the Curse so that for a time it was the Land of the Blessing.

But this was only me stretching my powers, limbering up. To save the world would require more.

So more I gave. Feeling myself fall into smaller and smaller pieces, with godlike cognizance falling away like all the stones in a bridge tumbling into the dark water below at once was both terrifying and exhilarating. The layers of fractal blooms closed, one by one, obscuring their meanings from me, robbing me of the Maker's knowledge of secrets both deep as the true significance of the dark energy network and mundane as the color of a newborn baby's eyes in Mandariel.

Everything was stripped from me, and I poured it all into the fracture Jason had created, welding it shut with my own continuity of being.

In the end, it was easier than I ever expected to lay down the heaviest burden of all: my ego. And so Ardeyn was made whole again.

38: RECOGNITION
Elandine, Queen of Hazurrium

Lantern in hand, Elandine walked the Path of the Dead under the light of the Seven Moons. Their cold radiance splintered on the raised road that wound for miles through the queendom. Crypts honeycombed the rampart beneath their feet. In those metal-clad and lightless cavities, the dead of Hazurrium were interred, from the lowliest beggars to royalty. According to tales told over campfires, the souls of the dead sometimes ventured up from the Night Vault to walk the Path of the Dead, looking for their loved ones to bid them goodbye.

"You won't find her, Your Highness," murmured Navar, who followed a few paces after the queen. Behind the First Protector, what remained of Elandine's forces were arrayed in a line stretching back along the otherworldly route.

"I know," the queen replied, her voice almost too soft to hear.

After a minute of silence, Navar said, "Forgive me for saying this, but... are you all right?"

"You mean, why am I not biting your head off for mentioning my dead sister Flora?"

Navar coughed. "Yes, my queen."

Elandine nodded thoughtfully. It was a good question.

"Being Death meant I had to come to terms with a few things."

"Imagining you giving up your free will, even to an Incarnation, is a difficult task."

Elandine chuckled. "That was the least of what was required of me."

They walked without words for several long minutes. The queen thought she caught a glimpse of two spectral figures gliding along the path in the moonlight, but she wasn't sure. A heartbeat later and they were gone.

Elandine rubbed at her eyes, then sighed. "To summon Death – to *become* an incarnation – I had to stop running from the sorrow, and accept that everyone dies. *Everyone*. Even Flora. Burying my fear of grief under a royal tantrum, or running away across Ardeyn to challenge some *other* threat, wasn't going to work. I had to stamp out the hope that I could avoid that heartache if I just kept ahead of it."

"And so you walked as the Incarnation of Death. Had I not seen it myself, I wouldn't have believed it. As it is, I almost wonder if it wasn't all a dream."

"It was no dream. Death came, and I was Her."

"Will you do so again?"

Elandine cocked her head. Was it possible? "I hope not. I almost lost myself. Drowned in the Incarnation's dominion. The Maker saved me from that. When Carter Strange did whatever he did inside the Maker's Hall, Death blew like a leaf in a gale, lost. And I'm glad. The Ring is back to what it always was. It's mostly powerless once more."

"I'm sorry that your plan to use the Ring to return your sister has failed."

"Seeing Flora alive again was always a fool's hope." The words out of her own mouth sounded strange, not like something she would've ever admitted. But they were true. Flora was gone, and there was nothing she could do about it.

"You have my deepest condolences, Your Majesty."

Sorrow trembled on her cheeks like warm rain. It wasn't

the heart-rending grief she'd always feared to face. Though she felt as if a hollow in her chest filled with cold water, it was bearable. Fresh tears smeared the star and lantern light. She mopped at the moisture with her sleeve.

When was the last time she'd cried?

She remembered Brandalun comforting her when she was ten years old. Her mother had just informed Elandine that her father the Royal Consort had been lost in a border skirmish with Mandariel. Brandalun had been stern and stiff-jawed as she relayed the news, but Elandine was shattered. She wept for five days. She'd been useless. She hadn't taken in any of the instructions provided by her tutors. She could barely mount the will to eat.

When her grief finally broke, Elandine had vowed never to let sadness pull her down again. As she'd grown older, she'd learned that fury was the answer, to many things, but especially whenever anguish threatened. In anger's narrow certainty, there was no room for heartache. Her mother had seemed to approve.

"Where do you think Brandalun *really* is?" Elandine asked.

"If I knew, I'd tell you, Your Majesty," replied the First Protector, her voice not quite hiding a faint defensive tone."

"Of course. I didn't mean to imply otherwise. I just... miss her."

Elandine had been furious with Brandalun for fleeing Flora's death, flying off on another one of her "important quests" rather than face the truth. Yes, Flora had been killed and her mother hadn't been able to bear the pain. But Elandine was her daughter, too.

Brandalun had run away, looking for some mystical mechanism, abandoning the queendom just when everyone needed her most. When *Elandine* needed her most.

Just as Elandine had in turn run away, looking for her mother. Just as Elandine, not even the queen dowager, had *literally* abandoned her rule to a regent after she lost the Ring. She'd had her reasons, but...

She was no better.

She was just like Brandalun.

The truth rolled up over Elandine like a torch flaring to full brightness, or a slowly mounting orchestra reaching its crescendo: she saw everything in herself that she despised in her mother.

They were the same. The same.

"Have I been too severe or unfair when it comes Brandalun?" she asked Navar.

"I'm sure I couldn't say, my queen."

They walked. Flora never appeared. Instead of her sister, Elandine thought of her mother for many miles under the moons and stars.

A glow on the horizon was revealed as a massive walled structure as they drew ever closer. Elandine pointed. "There it is. Citadel Hazurrium. We've got a bitch regent to unseat and a queendom to take back."

39: EVALUATION
Jason Cole, the Betrayer

War was gone. Jason was merely himself. The Betrayer. Again. The Ring was robbed of almost all its power, hardly more than a trinket. Because Carter was dead again. The man's return had empowered the Ring, but his second fatality stripped the power of Incarnation from it once more. Was it ironic, or comedic?

He wasn't laughing.

Instead he smoked, drawing on the stem of an exquisite water pipe one of the Five Princes had shipped down from Mandariel a decade earlier. Which one of those back-biting weasels had sent the gift, he didn't know or care. Jason sucked in a long breath of smooth smoke, then let the smoke curl out of his lungs. His private chamber was already hazed. None of his homunculi had permission to enter, on fear of death. This place was for him alone.

So he sat, burned tobacco, and remembered.

What *is* fucking ironic, he thought, was that *Carter* had been the one who started everything by killing his friends and trapping their minds – betraying them – but somehow Jason was the one saddled with the title of Betrayer! Sure, he and the others had survived in the recursion. But tell that to their parents and friends on Earth. If they had learned the truth, Carter would've gotten the chair.

Jason wondered if he would have done the same as Carter? Would he have sacrificed everyone, including himself, to save Earth? He didn't know, because he'd panicked. He hadn't understood the full picture. But if he'd known, would he have done what Carter had, the first time around? And again, when he'd entered the Maker's Hall and pushed back the kray, sacrificing himself in the process?

No. Never in a thousand years would he do that.

"Carter!" he yelled to no one, "I fucking *hate* you!"

No, you hate yourself, for being such a coward. He always had.

The truth was too uncomfortable to entertain.

His mind skipped away to better times, when he hadn't been alone. Jason missed his friends. He even missed Carter, at least as the man he'd been before everything soured. Jason hadn't really had any friends since coming to Ardeyn, except himselves. And he was sick and tired of himselves.

The question he was actually avoiding came to him again. What the hell was he going to do now?

The peace that the smoke sometimes imparted took hold, and he half-closed his eyes. Things hadn't been a total disaster, after all. Hadn't he reconnected Ardeyn to Earth? Yes, he had. Maybe not in a way that would allow him to return home in the full glory of the Incarnation of War, no. But a bridge had been forged. Now he had time to figure out how to cross it, even if in a lesser guise. This time, he wouldn't have to ask the kray for help. Too much horror and fear lay down that path.

War would've been up to the task of dealing with them! If only–

Stop it, Jason told himself, and inhaled another breath of blue smoke. He'd tried to let it all go, and hand over everything to War. He'd failed. Nothing was going to change that fact.

So he could either give up, hand over the reins to one of lieutenants, and walk away from Megeddon...

Or he could try again.

40: CELEBRATION
Katherine Manners

The bar light shone amber through Kate's martini. Its bittersweet bite was familiar. It soothed her. More than anything else, the unique flavor reassured her that she was home, and safe.

"Then what happened?" asked Liza Banks, leaning avidly across the table. Liza was making short work of her second ruby-colored cocktail. Paldridge nursed a glass of something amber colored. They sat in a bar south of Seattle called Shindig. A little far from Kate's regular city stomping grounds, but not nearly so pretentious, nor crowded, as most places that served specialty drinks to the north. And the martinis were the best.

Kate said, "The next thing I knew, I was standing in the middle of the Glass Desert. The kray were gone, all of them. Even the ichor. It was just me, Queen Elandine and that bastard Jason Cole. We blinked at each other like idiots."

"And Carter? The Maker's Hall?" asked Paldridge.

Kate shook her head. "Gone. Not even a reflection."

Liza shook her head. "That must have been something."

"Everything that happened after Desire went nuclear is hazy. Like I dreamed it. Though I do remember she – *we* – got into the Hall's front door... I wanted in, as badly as Desire did. For Raul's sake. But Carter was ahead of us. He got in front of us, locked us out from accessing the higher functions. It was all so" – she waved her hands – "hard to describe. Metaphysical. Carter said he would take care of the breach. That it was his cost to bear, this time. That he was finally going to be honest about his emotions, and face his fear. Then he melted away."

Liza wrinkled her nose. "Melted?"

"Yeah. Melted, and released whatever Maker's essence he'd collected back into the Hall, and into the Land of the Curse. He... I think he sacrificed himself to save Ardeyn. And somehow, to save me, Elandine, and that dick Jason, too. He saved us from drowning in the Incarnations."

Paldridge coughed and set down his drink with a clink. "So he's dead?"

"I think so."

Liza sighed. "Sad. He would've been such asset for us."

Kate snorted. "Sad because a good man died."

"Of course. Sorry I interrupted," said Liza.

"It's OK."

Liza swirled her drink. "What did you mean by drowning in the Incarnations? I don't understand."

"When Carter did his thing, Desire let go of me. She didn't want to – she just couldn't hold me anymore. She faded away. Same was true of the queen and Death, and Jason and War. Elandine wasn't as excited as I'd have expected, but Jason was furious. He wanted to lose himself in War, in all that game-world-made-real insanity. But without Carter around to energize the Rings, things went back to how they were before. The Rings faded to what they had been. The Incarnations still don't walk Ardeyn. Which seems like a blessing. The whole Age of Myth thing was better as a story than as reality, if Desire was anything to go by."

Paldridge shook his head, tried another mouthful of his

whiskey, then held it up to examine the way the light shone through it.

Kate sipped her martini. The glow from the alcohol in her stomach made it all a little easier to relate. The Ring of Desire yet encircled her right index finger. It no longer possessed any particular ability, especially here on Earth. It was mostly an ordinary ring, despite its striking appearance. Ordinary, except for its ability to translate. Having it with her on Earth seemed safer than leaving it behind in Ardeyn, regardless of how little power remained to it.

"What about Raul?" said Liza. "Did he show up again?"

Kate barely nodded. "He re-materialized, afterward, and kept us from killing that fucker Jason. He reminded Elandine and me that without Jason's help, the kray would've overrun us, and that would have been the beginning of the end of everything, not just Ardeyn. I bet we could've taken him. With all his plans down the toilet, he was a mess. He would've been happy to let us do whatever."

Liza snorted. "I wish Raul hadn't stopped you. Jason might have had second thoughts and threw in with the winning side, but let's not forget he's the reason everything almost went to hell."

"Probably. But I can sort of see how it happened... When Desire and I were in the Hall, Carter implied that Jason's anger wasn't entirely misplaced, and that Carter had done something bad to Jason. I'm not sure what, but Carter felt guilty about something that happened before. Might be why he wanted to do right by his old pal. Give him another chance."

"Stupid," said Liza.

Kate frowned. "Probably, yeah."

"So did you save Raul?" Paldridge asked. "Or is he..."

"I couldn't get into the Hall and reincarnate him, or resurrect him, or whatever."

"Damn," said Paldridge, and awkwardly reached out to pat her shoulder before letting his hand drop again.

"Yeah. I'm *still* mad at him, though. He was a spy from some *other* world in the Strange this whole time, lurking here on Earth. Masquerading as my friend."

"He *was* your friend," Paldridge said. "He pretended to be from Earth, but not how he felt about you. He obviously cared for you."

A crazy thought struck her – had her inevitable fear of disappointment prevented Kate from pursuing a deeper relationship with Raul? Had she just been afraid to take a risk?

She'd wasted so much time being angry at Raul, feeling like he'd betrayed her by keeping his origin secret, when regardless of what logic dictated, he was still her friend. In fact, she missed the hell out of him, despite how much he'd pissed her off by lying for all those years they'd known each other.

That she was mad at him and missed him desperately at the same time – it was crazy.

Maybe she wouldn't even *be* so angry if he didn't mean something to her....

Moisture welled in her eyes, and she scrubbed at them angrily. She and Raul had never been more than friends. But that didn't mean she didn't love him. Even though he was a fucking liar.

"He's still there, in Ardeyn," Kate said. "As a ghost. Waiting for me, until the next time I go back. Which I eventually need to do. I owe him, too. I don't want him to get sucked into Ardeyn's underworld mythology. Something to do with the Night Vault and Umber Judges."

"Sounds medieval," Liza said. "Keeping him safe from that? It sort of makes you a hero."

Kate discovered she couldn't speak any more.

They each sat with their own thoughts for a time.

Paldridge ordered another round. After they came, he said, "So, the other thing to remember is that we're safe. Carter saved us all. Not just you, or even just Ardeyn. It sounds like everyone on Earth owes him."

"Yeah," said Kate, grateful to have something else to think about. "Not sure how we'd pay him back though, since I'm pretty sure he's dead. We should have a wake."

"I know what we should do," said Liza. "We dedicate our new organization in his memory. The man gave his life defending the world from planetovores. It only makes sense that the sole group on Earth that knows about the Strange would honor the person who opened our eyes to the threat."

"So, instead of just the 'Estate,' we call it the 'Carter Morrison Estate?'" asked Paldridge.

"Something like that," said Liza. "We should work out the details. Maybe some kind of Morrison endowment. But we could still call it the Estate for short."

"I like it," said Paldridge.

"Me too," said Kate, raising her glass. "To the Estate!"

"And to Carter Morrison," added Paldridge.

"They called him Carter Strange over there," Kate mused. "In Ardeyn."

"To Carter *Strange*!" said Liza.

Kate clinked her glass against Liza's and Paldridge's. "To Carter Strange. And hey, who knows? Maybe he'll be back. He's come back from the dead before."

ACKNOWLEDGMENTS

Thanks go out to my writing circle for reading and providing feedback on the early chapters of this book – Torah Cottrill, Erin M Evans, Peter Schaeffer, Rob Heinsoo, and Randy Henderson. Thank you Monte Cook and Shanna Germain for suggesting that we write a game based on this then-unfinished novel. Thank you Susan Morris for your always-excellent editorial notes and suggestions for tightening character arcs. Thank you Axel Andrejs for providing coding consultation – all errors that remain are mine. Thank you Phil Jourdan at Angry Robot for your editorial notes on pacing. Thanks to Mel Mickael for one last check. And thanks to Ray Vallese for proofing it, and Dennis Detwiller for pulling everything together.

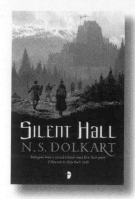
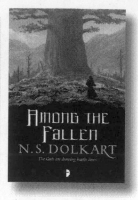

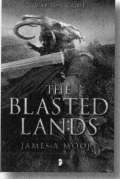
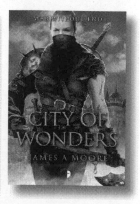

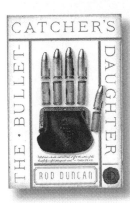

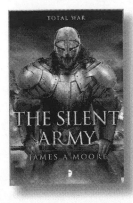
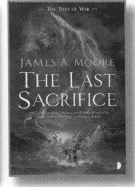

BENEATH THE ORBITS AND SWIRLS

of our natural universe lies a network of dark energy and matter. Those who have learned to access and navigate this chaotic sea have discovered an almost endless set of "recursions" in the shadow of our Earth: Replicant worlds with their own laws of reality, reflected from human experience or imagination, given form in the swirling nothingness of the Strange. Worlds teeming with life, with discovery, with incredible treasures, and with sudden death.

Worlds often jealous of our own.

The secret plunder of these worlds draws the brave, the daring, and the unscrupulous – and it draws dangerous enemies from these recursions back to our Earth.

And slowly but inexorably, it draws the attention of beings from beyond Earth's shoals – beings of unfathomable power and evil from the unknown reaches of...

Explore the Strange and its endless recursions in
THE STRANGE, *the roleplaying game from*
Monte Cook Games

WWW.MONTECOOKGAMES.COM